Prai  W9-CDF-348

"London has its Sherlock Holmes . . . but Wyoming has Joe Pickett." —*New West*

"Outstanding . . . [A] terrible, beautiful tale of courage and compassion and culpability."—*Publishers Weekly* (starred review)

"Box is a skillful writer and plot-spinner with plenty of wily surprises up his . . . sleeve. . . . A thoroughly entertaining mystery." —*Chicago Tribune*

"Ranks with his best . . . Readers should take note of their surroundings before opening this book: once they start reading, they won't know what hit them." —*Booklist* (starred review)

"Intense . . . A perfect choice."
—*Library Journal* (starred review)

"It's great to see the usual Box strengths—exhilarating landscapes, high adventure, thrilling suspense, surprising moral quandaries." —*Kirkus Reviews* (starred review)

"A standout story." —*Billings (MT) Gazette*

"C. J. Box is in top form. . . . It takes a certain kind of crime writer to make a story as psychologically complex as it is nail-biting." —*The Daily Beast*

"Once in a while I'll pick up a book tha leaves me slack-jawed in wonder by the time I put it down." —Bookreporter.com

"High adventure at its finest."
—*Madison (MS) County Herald*

Praise for the Joe Pickett Novels

Endangered

"Is there a crime-fiction family as fully fleshed out as Joe Pickett's? In singing the praises of Box's series, we often praise the plotting, pacing, and the down-to-earth hero's friendship with force-of-nature Nate Romanowski. But Pickett's supporting cast lends a continuity and grounding to this series that sets it apart from all the lone-wolf stuff out there. A carefully constructed plot building to a breathless, thrilling end."—*Booklist*

"Box consistently combines plot and character development with near-poetic setting descriptions to present one of the best ongoing series in any genre." —Bookreporter.com

Stone Cold

"A suspenseful, action-filled ride." —*The Denver Post*

"A superlative outing . . . Box gets everything right: believably real characters, a vivid setting, clear prose, and ratcheting tension. Maintaining those standards over fourteen novels is more than impressive." —Cleveland *Plain Dealer*

"Another dandy tale with an even dandier surprise ending." —*St. Louis Post-Dispatch*

"A blistering page-turner." —*The Arizona Republic*

Breaking Point

"An exceptionally well-told story that will entertain, thrill, and maybe even outrage its readers." —*USA Today*

"Thrilling wilderness chases, chilling stories of the abuse of power, and Pickett's indomitable frontier spirit power this explosive novel." —*Publishers Weekly*

Force of Nature

"An excellent wilderness adventure . . . A violent, bloody, and quite satisfying thriller . . . A rush." —*The New York Times Book Review*

"Proceeds at warp speed." —*The Denver Post*

Cold Wind

"A nonstop thrill ride not to be missed." —*BookPage*

"Keen insight and dark beauty." —*The Washington Post*

Below Zero

"Pickett [is] one of the most appealing men in popular fiction." —*Chicago Tribune*

Blood Trail

"[A] riveting thriller." —*The San Diego Union-Tribune*

Free Fire

"[*Free Fire* is] Yellowstone in all its dangerous glory." —*The Wall Street Journal*

In Plain Sight

"Edge-of-the-chair suspense . . . Heart-stopping action."
—*Library Journal*

Out of Range

"Intelligent [and] compassionate."   —*The New York Times*

Trophy Hunt

"Keep[s] you guessing right to the end—and a little beyond."
—*People*

Winterkill

"Moves smoothly and suspensefully to the showdown."
—*The Washington Post*

Savage Run

"The suspense tears forward like a brush fire."   —*People*

Open Season

"A muscular first novel . . . Box writes as straight as his characters shoot, and he has a stand-up hero to shoulder his passionate concerns about endangered lives and liberties."
—*The New York Times Book Review*

"Superb . . . Without resorting to simplistic blacks and whites, Box fuses ecological themes, vibrant descriptions of Wyoming's wonders and peculiarities, and fully fleshed characters into a debut of riveting tensions. Meet Joe Pickett: He's going to be a mystery star."   —*Publishers Weekly* (starred review)

"Box's book has it all—suspenseful plot, magnificent scenery and a flawed male hero who is tough but truly connected to his family. . . . Profoundly memorable."   —*Boston Herald*

"A high-country *Presumed Innocent* that moves like greased lightning."   —*Kirkus Reviews* (starred review)

"Riveting suspense mingles with flashes of cynical backcountry humor and makes Box an author to watch. I didn't want this book to end."   —Margaret Maron

"A motive for murder that is as unique as any in modern fiction."   —*Los Angeles Times*

NOWHERE TO RUN

C. J. BOX

G. P. PUTNAM'S SONS
NEW YORK

PUTNAM
— EST. 1838 —
G. P. PUTNAM'S SONS
Publishers Since 1838
An imprint of Penguin Random House LLC
penguinrandomhouse.com

Copyright © 2010 by C. J. Box
Excerpt from *Cold Wind* copyright © 2011 by C. J. Box
Penguin supports copyright. Copyright fuels creativity, encourages diverse voices, promotes free speech, and creates a vibrant culture. Thank you for buying an authorized edition of this book and for complying with copyright laws by not reproducing, scanning, or distributing any part of it in any form without permission. You are supporting writers and allowing Penguin to continue to publish books for every reader.

First G. P. Putnam's Sons hardcover edition / April 2010
First Berkley Prime Crime mass-market edition / April 2011
First G. P. Putnam's Sons premium edition / August 2016
G. P. Putnam's Sons premium edition ISBN: 9780735211971

Printed in the United States of America
9   10

This is a work of fiction. Names, characters, places, and incidents either are the product of the author's imagination or are used fictitiously, and any resemblance to actual persons, living or dead, businesses, companies, events, or locales is entirely coincidental.

If you purchased this book without a cover, you should be aware that this book is stolen property. It was reported "unsold and destroyed" to the publisher, and neither the author nor the publisher has received any payment for this "stripped book."

For Mark Nelson
And Laurie, always . . .

PART ONE

THE LAST PATROL

In no other country in the world is the love of property keener or more alert than in the United States, and nowhere else does the majority display less inclination toward doctrines which in any way threaten the way property is owned.

—ALEXIS DE TOCQUEVILLE, *Democracy in America*

TUESDAY, AUGUST 25

1

THREE HOURS AFTER HE'D BROKEN CAMP, RE-packed, and pushed his horses higher into the mountain range, Wyoming game warden Joe Pickett paused on the lip of a wide hollow basin and dug in his saddlebag for his notebook. The bow hunters had described where they'd tracked the wounded elk, and he matched the topography against their description.

He glassed the basin with binoculars and noted the fingers of pine trees reaching down through the grassy swale and the craterlike depressions in the hollow they'd described. This, he determined, was the place.

He'd settled into a familiar routine of riding until his muscles got stiff and his knees hurt. Then he'd climb down and lead his geldings Buddy and Blue Roanie—a packhorse he'd named unimaginatively—until he could loosen up and work the kinks out. He checked his gear and the panniers on Roanie often to make sure the load was well balanced, and he'd stop so he and his horses could rest and get a drink of water. The second day of riding brought back all the old aches, but they seemed closer to the surface now that he was in his mid-forties.

Shifting his weight in the saddle toward the basin, he

clicked his tongue and touched Buddy's sides with his spurs. The horse balked.

"C'mon, Buddy," Joe said. "Let's go now, you knucklehead."

Instead, Buddy turned his head back and seemed to implore Joe not to proceed.

"Don't be ridiculous. *Go*."

Only when he dug his spurs in did Buddy shudder, sigh, and start the descent.

"You act like I'm making you march to your death like a beef cow," Joe said. "Knock it off, now." He turned to check that his packhorse was coming along as well. "You doing okay, Blue Roanie? Don't pay any attention to Buddy. He's a knucklehead."

But on the way down into the basin, Joe instinctively reached back and touched the butt of his shotgun in the saddle scabbard to assure himself it was there. Then he untied the leather thong that held it fast.

IT WAS TO HAVE BEEN a five-day horseback patrol before the summer gave way to fall and the hunting seasons began in earnest—before a new game warden was assigned the district to take over from Joe, who, after a year in exile, was finally going home. He was more than ready.

He'd spent the previous weekend packing up his house and shed and making plans to ride into the mountains on Monday, descend on Friday, and clean out his state-owned home in Baggs for the arrival of the new game warden the first of next week. Baggs ("Home of the Baggs Rattlers!") was a tough, beautiful, raggedy mountain town as old as the state itself. The community sprawled through the Little Snake River Valley on the same unpaved streets Butch Cassidy used to walk. Baggs was so isolated it was known within the department as the "warden's graveyard"—the district where game wardens were sent to quit or die. Governor Spencer Rulon had hidden Joe there for his past transgressions, but after Rulon had won a second term in a landslide, he'd sent word through his people that Joe was no longer a liability. As luck had it, at the same time, Phil Kiner in Saddlestring took a new district in Cody and Joe quickly applied for— and received—his old district north in the Bighorns in Twelve Sleep County, where his family was.

Despite his almost giddy excitement about moving back to his wife, Marybeth, and his daughters, he couldn't in good conscience vacate the area without investigating the complaint about the butchered elk. That wouldn't be fair to the new game warden, whoever he or she would be. He'd leave the other reported crimes to the sheriff.

JOE PICKETT WAS LEAN, of medium height and medium build. His gray Stetson Rancher was stained with sweat and red dirt. A few silver hairs caught the sunlight on his temples and unshaved chin. He wore faded Wranglers, scuffed lace-up outfitter boots with stubby spurs, a red uniform shirt with the pronghorn antelope patch on his shoulder, and a badge over his breast pocket with the designation GF-54. A tooled leather belt that identified him as "JOE" held handcuffs, bear spray, and a service issue .40 Glock semiauto.

With every mile of his last patrol of the Sierra Madre of southern Wyoming, Joe felt as if he were going back in time and to a place of immense and unnatural silence. With each muffled hoofbeat, the sense of foreboding got stronger until it enveloped him in a calm, dark dread that made the hair prick up on the back of his neck and on his forearms and that set his nerves on edge.

The silence was disconcerting. It was late August but the normal alpine soundtrack was switched to mute. There were no insects humming in the grass, no squirrels chattering in the trees to signal his approach, no marmots standing up in the rocks on their hind legs and whistling, no deer or elk rustling in the shadows of the trees rimming the meadows where they fed, no grouse clucking or flushing. Yet he continued on, as if being pulled by a gravitational force. It was as if the front door of a dark and abandoned house slowly opened by itself before he could reach for the handle and the welcome was anything but warm. Despite the brilliant greens of the meadows or the subdued fireworks of alpine flowers, the sun-fused late summer morning seemed ten degrees cooler than it actually was.

"Stop spooking yourself," he said aloud and with authority.

But it wasn't just him. His horses were unusually twitchy and emotional. He could feel Buddy's tension through the saddle. Buddy's muscles were tight and balled, he breathed rapid shallow breaths, and his ears were up and alert. The old game trail he took was untracked and covered with a thin sheet of pine needles but it switchbacked up the mountain, and as they rose, the sky broke through the canopy and sent shafts of light like jail bars to the forest floor. Joe had to keep nudging and kissing at his mount to keep him going up the face of the mountain into the thick forest. Finally deep into the trees, he yearned for open places where he could see.

* * *

JOE WAS STILL UNNERVED by a brief conversation he'd had with a dubious local named Dave Farkus the day before at the trailhead.

Joe was pulling the cinch tight on Buddy when Farkus emerged from the brush with a spinning rod in his hand. Short and wiry, with muttonchop sideburns and a slack expression on his face, Farkus had opened with, "So you're really goin' up there?"

Joe said, "Yup."

The fisherman said, "All I know for sure is I drink beer at the Dixon Club bar with about four old-timers who were here long before the energy workers got here and a hell of a lot longer than you. A couple of these guys are old enough they forgot more about these mountains than either of us will ever know. They ran cattle up there and they hunted up there for years. But you know what?"

Joe felt a clench in his belly the way Farkus had asked. He said, "What?"

"None of them old fellers will go up there anymore. Ever since that runner vanished, they say something just feels wrong."

Joe said, "Feelings aren't a lot to go on."

"That ain't all," said Farkus. "What about all the break-ins at cabins in the area and parked cars getting their windows smashed in at the trailheads? There's been a lot of that lately."

"I heard," Joe said. "Sheriff Baird is looking into that, I believe."

Farkus snorted.

"Is there something you're not telling me?" Joe had asked.

"No. But we all heard some of the rumors. You know, camps being looted. Tents getting slashed. I heard there were a couple of bow hunters who tried to poach an elk before the season opened. They hit one, followed the blood trail for miles to the top, but when they finally found the animal it had already been butchered and the meat all hauled away. Is that true?"

Like most hunters who had broken the law, the bow hunters had come to Joe's office and turned themselves in. Joe had cited them for hunting elk out of season, but had been intrigued by their story. They seemed genuinely creeped out by what had happened. "That's what they said."

Farkus widened his eyes. "So it's true after all. And that's what you're up to, isn't it? You're going up there to find whoever took their elk if you can. Well, I hope you do. Man, nobody likes the idea of somebody stealing another man's meat. That's beyond the pale. And this Wendigo crap—where did that come from? Bunch of Indian mumbo-jumbo. Evil spirits, flesh eaters, I ask you. This ain't Canada, thank God. Wendigos are up there, not here, if they even exist. *Heh-heh.*"

It was not much of a laugh, Joe thought. More like a nervous tic. A way of saying he didn't necessarily believe a word of what he'd just said—unless Joe did.

Joe said, *"Wendigos?"*

THEY BROKE THROUGH THE TREES and emerged onto a treeless meadow walled by dark timber, and he stopped to look and listen. Joe squinted, looking for whatever was spooking his horses and him, hoping reluctantly to see a bear, a mountain lion, a wolverine, even a snake. But what he saw were mountains that tumbled like frozen ocean waves all the way south into Colorado, wispy puffball clouds that scudded over him immodestly showing their vulnerable white bellies, and his own mark left behind in the ankle-deep grass: parallel horse tracks, steaming piles of manure. There were no human structures of any kind in view and hadn't been for a full day. No power lines, microwave stations, or cell phone towers. The only proof that he was not riding across the same wilderness in the 1880s were the jet trails looking like snail tracks high in the sky.

THE RANGE RAN south to north. He planned to summit the Sierra Madre by Wednesday, day three, and cross the 10,000-foot Continental Divide near Battle Pass. This was where the bow hunters said their elk had been cut up. Then he would head down toward No Name Creek on the west side of the divide and arrive at his pickup and horse trailer by midday Friday. If all went well.

THE TERRAIN got rougher the higher he rode, wild and unfamiliar. What he knew of it he'd seen from a helicopter and from aerial survey photos. The mountain range was severe and spectacular, with canyon after canyon, toothy rimrock ridges, and dense old-growth forests that had never been timbered because cutting logging roads into them would have been too technical and expensive to be worth it. The vistas from the summit were like scenery overkill: mountains to the horizon in every direction, veins of aspen in the folds already turning gold, high alpine lakes and cirques like blue poker chips tossed on green felt, hundreds of miles of lodgepole pine trees, many of which were in the throes of dying due to bark beetles and had turned the color of advanced rust.

The cirques—semicircular hollows with steep walls filled with snowmelt and big enough to boat across—

stair-stepped their way up the mountains. Those with out-lets birthed tiny creeks and water sought water and melded into streams. Other cirques were self-contained: bathtubs that would fill, freeze during winter, and never drain out.

PRIOR TO THE FIVE-DAY TREK, Joe had been near the spine of the mountains only once, years before, when he was a participant in the massive search-and-rescue effort for the runner Farkus mentioned, Olympic hopeful Diane Shober, who'd parked her car at the trailhead and van-ished on a long-distance run on the canyon trail. Her body had never been found. Her face was haunting and ubiquitous, though, because it peered out from hundreds of homemade handbills posted by her parents through-out Wyoming and Colorado. Joe kept her disappearance in mind as he rode, always alert for scraps of clothing, bones, or hair.

Since he'd been assigned districts all over the State of Wyoming as both a game warden and Governor Rulon's point man, Joe ascribed certain personality traits to moun-tain ranges. He conceded his impressions were often un-fair and partially based on his mood at the time or things he was going through. Rarely, though, had he changed his mind about a mountain range once he'd established its quirks and rhythms in his mind. The Tetons were flashy, cold, bloodless Eurotrash mountains—too spectacular for their own good. They were the mountain equivalent of supermodels. The Gros Ventres were a rich graveyard of human history—both American Indian and early white—that held their secrets close and refused to ac-commodate the modern era. The Wind River Mountains were what the Tetons wanted to be: towering, incredibly wealthy with scenery and wildlife, vast, and spiritual. The

Bighorns, Joe's mountains in northern Wyoming where his family still was waiting for him, were comfortable, rounded, and wry—a retired All-Pro linebacker who still had it.

But the Sierra Madre was still a mystery. He couldn't yet warm to the mountains, and he fought against being intimidated by their danger, isolation, and heartless beauty. The fruitless search for Diane Shober had planted the seed in his mind. These mountains were like a glimpse of a beautiful and exotic woman in a passing car, a gun on her lap, who refused to make eye contact.

HE DISMOUNTED once he was on the floor of the basin to ease the pain in his knees and let his horses rest. As always, he wondered how horsemen and horsewomen of the past stayed mounted for hours on end and day after day. No wonder they drank so much whiskey, he thought.

Joe led his horses through a stand of widely spaced lodgepole pines that gradually melded into a pocket of rare and twisted knotty pine. Trunks and branches were bizarre in shape and direction, with softball-sized joints like swollen knees. The knotty pine stand covered less than a quarter mile of the forest, just as the elk hunters had described. As he stood on the perimeter of the stand he slowly turned and noted the horizon of the basin that rose like the rim of a bowl in every direction. This was the first cirque. He was struck by how many locations in the mountains looked alike, how without man-made land-marks like power lines or radio towers, wilderness could turn into a maelstrom of green and rocky sameness. He wished the bow hunters had given him precise GPS coor-dinates so he could be sure this was the place, but the hunters were purists and had not carried Garmins. Still, though, they'd accurately described the basin and the cirque, as well as the knotty pine stand in the floor of it.

In the back of his mind, Joe thought that if there really were men hiding out in these mountains stealing elk and vandalizing cabins and cars, they would likely be refugees of the man camps. Over the past few years, as natural-gas fields were drilled north of town, the energy companies had established man camps—clumps of adjoining temporary mobile housing in the middle of sagebrush flats for their employees. The men—and it was only men—lived practically shoulder-to-shoulder. Obviously, it took a certain kind of person to stay there. Most of the temporary residents had traveled hundreds and thousands of miles to the most remote part of the least-populated state to work in the natural-gas fields and live in a man camp. The men were rough, independent, well armed, and flush with cash when they came to town. And when they did, it was the New Wild West. For months at a time, Joe had been called just about every Saturday night to assist the local police and sheriff's deputies with breaking up fights.

When the price of natural gas plummeted and drilling was no longer encouraged, the employees were let go. A half-dozen man camps sat deserted in the sagebrush desert. No one knew where the men went any more than they knew where they'd come from in the first place. That a few of the unemployed refugees of the man camps had stuck around in the game-rich mountains seemed plausible—even likely—to Joe.

He secured his animals and walked the floor of the basin looking for remains of the elk. Although predators would have quickly moved in on the carcass and stripped it of its meat and scattered the bones, there should be unmistakable evidence of hide, hair, and antlers. The bow hunters said the wounded bull had seven-point antlers on each beam, so the antlers should be nearby as well.

As he surveyed the ground for a sign, something in his peripheral vision struck him as discordant. He paused and carefully looked from side to side, visually backtracking. In nature, he thought, nothing is perfect. And something he'd seen—or thought he'd seen—was too vertical or horizontal or straight or unblemished to belong here.

"What was it?" he asked aloud. Through the trees, his horses raised their heads and stared at him, uncomprehending.

After turning back around and retracing his steps, Joe saw it. At first glance, he reprimanded himself. It was just a stick jutting out from a tree trunk twenty feet off his path. But on closer inspection, it wasn't a stick at all, but an arrow stuck in the trunk of a tree. The shaft of the arrow was handcrafted, not from a factory, but it was straight, smooth, shorn of bark, with feather fletching on the end. The only place he'd ever seen a primitive arrow like this was in a museum. He photographed the arrow with his digital camera, then pulled on a pair of latex gloves and grasped it by the shaft and pushed hard up and down while pulling on it. After a moment, the arrow popped free and Joe studied it. The point was obsidian and delicately flaked and attached to the shaft with animal sinew. The fletching was made of wild turkey feathers.

It made no sense. The bow hunters he'd interviewed were serious sportsmen, even if they'd hunted prior to the season opener. But even they didn't make their own arrows from natural materials. No one did. Who had lost this arrow?

He felt a chill roll through him. Slowly, he rotated and looked behind him in the trees. He wouldn't have been surprised to see Cheyenne or Sioux warriors approaching.

* * *

HE FOUND THE REMAINS of the seven-point bull elk ten minutes later. Even though coyotes and ravens had been feeding on the carcass, it was obvious this was the elk the bow hunters had wounded and pursued. The hindquarters were gone and the backstraps had been sliced away. Exactly like the hunters described.

So who had taken the meat?

Joe photographed the carcass from multiple angles.

JOE WALKED back to his horses with the arrow he'd found. He wrapped the point of it in a spare sock and the shaft in a T-shirt and put it in a pannier. He caught Buddy staring at him.

"Evidence," he said. "Something strange is going on up here. We might get some fingerprints off this arrow."

Buddy snorted. Joe was sure it was a coincidence.

AS HE RODE out of the basin, he frequently glanced over his shoulder and couldn't shake a feeling that he was being watched. Once he reached the rim and was back on top, the air was thin and the sun was relentless. Rivulets of sweat snaked down his spine beneath his uniform shirt.

Miles to the southeast, a mottled gray pillow cloud and rain column of a thunderstorm connected the horizon with the sky. It seemed to be coming his way. He welcomed rain that would cool down the afternoon and settle the dust from his horses.

But he couldn't stop thinking about the carcass he'd found. Or the arrow.

*   *   *

THAT NIGHT, he camped on the shoreline of a half-moon-shaped alpine lake and picketed the horses within sight of his tent in lush ankle-high grass. As the sun went down and the temperature dropped into the forties, he caught five trout with his 4-weight fly rod, kept one, and ate it with fried potatoes over a small fire. After dinner he cleaned his dishes by the light of a headlamp and uncased his satellite phone from a pannier. Because of the trouble he'd had communicating several years before while temporarily stationed in Jackson Hole, he'd vowed to call home every night no matter what. Even if there was no news from either side, it was the mundane that mattered, that kept him in touch with his family and Marybeth with him.

The satellite phone was bulky compared to a mobile, and he had to remove his hat to use it because the antenna bumped into the brim. The signal was good, though, and the call went through. Straight to voice mail. He sighed and was slightly annoyed before he remembered Marybeth said she was taking the girls to the last summer concert in the town park. He'd hoped to hear her voice.

When the message prompt beeped, he said, "Hello, ladies. I hope you had a good time tonight. I wish I could have gone with you, even though I don't like concerts. Right now, I'm high in the mountains, and it's a beautiful and lonely place. The moon's so bright I can see fish rising in the lake. A half hour ago, a bull moose walked from the trees into the lake and stood there knee-deep in the water for a while. It's the only animal I've seen, which I find remarkably strange. I watched him take a drink."

He paused, and felt a little silly for the long message.

He rarely talked that much to them in person. He said, "Well, I'm just checking in. Your horses are doing fine and so am I. I miss you all."

HE UNDRESSED AND SLIPPED into his sleeping bag in the tent. He read a few pages of A. B. Guthrie's *The Big Sky*, which had turned into his camping book, then extinguished his headlamp. He lay awake with his hands beneath his head and stared at the inside of the dark tent fabric. His service weapon was rolled up in the holster in a ball near his head. After an hour, he got up and pulled the bag and the Therm-a-Rest pad out through the tent flap. There were still no clouds and the stars and moon were bright and hard. Out in the lake, the moose had returned and stood in silhouette bordered by blue moon splash.

God, he thought, *I love this. I love it so.*

And he felt guilty for loving it so much.

WEDNESDAY, AUGUST 26

2

THE RHAPSODY ENDED AT NOON THE NEXT DAY.
There was a lone fisherman down there in the small
kidney-shaped mountain lake and something about him
was wrong.

Joe reined to a stop on the summit and let Buddy
and Blue Roanie catch their breath from clambering up
the mountainside. The late-summer sun was straight up
in the sky, and insects hummed in the wildflowers. He
shifted in the saddle to get his bearings and searched
the sky for more clouds. The sun had been relentless on
the top of Battle Pass. There was little shade because he
was on the top of the world, with nothing higher. He
longed for an afternoon thunderstorm to cool things
down, but the thunderhead had slowed its sky march
and the rain column now looked like an afterthought.
He hoped for a more serious cloud, and to the south he
could see a bank of thunderheads forming at what
looked from his elevation like eye level.

But first, he'd need to check out the fisherman.

Joe raised his binoculars and focused in, trying to figure out what there was about the man that had struck
him as discordant. Several things popped up. The first
was that although the hundreds of small mountain lakes

in Sierra Madre had fish, the high-country cirques weren't noted for great angling. Big fish were to be had in the low country, in the legendary blue-ribbon trout waters of the Encampment and North Platte rivers of the eastern slope or the Little Snake on the western slope. Up here, with its long violent winters and achingly short summers, the trout were stunted because the ice-off time was brief. Although today it was a beautiful day, the weather could turn within minutes. Snow was likely any month of the summer. While hikers might catch a small trout or two for dinner along the trail, as he had, the area was not a destination fishing location worth two or three days of hard hike to access.

Second, the fisherman wasn't dressed or equipped like a modern angler. The man—who at the distance looked very tall and rangy—was wading in filthy denim jeans, an oversized red plaid shirt with big checks, and a white slouch hat pulled low over his eyes. No waders, no fishing vest, no net. And no horse, tent, or camp, from what Joe could see. In these days of high-tech gear and clothing that wicked away moisture and weighed practically nothing, it was extremely unusual to see such a throwback outfit.

He put away the glasses, clicked his tongue, and started down toward the lake. Leather creaked from his saddles, and horseshoes struck stones. Blue Roanie snorted. He was making plenty of noise, but the fisherman appeared not to have seen or heard him. In a place as big and empty and lonely as this, the fisherman's lack of acknowledgment was all wrong and made a statement in itself.

As he walked his animals down to the lake, Joe untied the leather thong that secured his shotgun in his saddle scabbard.

Joe had often considered the fact that, for Western game wardens, unlike even for urban cops in America's toughest inner cities, nearly every human being he encountered was armed. To make matters even dicier, it was rare when he could call for backup. This appeared to be one of those encounters where he'd be completely on his own, the only things on his side being his wits, his weapons, and the game and fish regulations of the State of Wyoming.

Fat-bodied marmots scattered across the rubble in front of him as he descended toward the lake. They took cover and peeked at him from the gray scree. *What do they know that I don't?* Joe wondered.

"HELLO," JOE CALLED OUT as he approached the cirque lake from the other side of the fisherman. "How's the fishing?"

His voice echoed around in the small basin until it was swallowed up.

"Excuse me, sir. I need to talk to you for a minute and check your fishing license and habitat stamp."

No response.

The fisherman cast, waited a moment for his lure to settle under the surface of the water, then reeled in. The man was a spin-fishing artist, and his lure flicked out like a snake's tongue. *Cast. Pause. Reel. Cast. Pause. Reel.*

Joe thought, *Either he's deaf and blind, or has an inhuman power of concentration, or he's ignoring me, pretending I'll just get spooked and give up and go away.*

As a courtesy and for his own protection, Joe never came at a hunter or fisherman head-on. He had learned to skirt them, to approach from an angle. Which he did now, walking his horses around the shore, keeping the fisherman firmly in his peripheral vision. Out of sight from the fisherman, Joe let his right hand slip down along his thigh until it was inches from his shotgun.

Cast. Pause. Reel. Cast. Pause. Reel.

Interaction with others was different in the mountains than it was in town. Where two people may simply pass each other on the street with no more than a glance and a nod, in the wilderness people drew to each other the same way animals of the same species instinctively sought each other out. Information was exchanged—weather, trail conditions, hazards ahead. In Joe's experience, when a man didn't want to talk, something was up and it was rarely good. Joe was obviously a game warden, but the fisherman didn't acknowledge the fact, which was disconcerting. It was as if the man thought Joe had no right to be there. And Joe knew that with each passing minute the fisherman chose not to acknowledge him, he was delving further and further into unknown and dangerous territory.

As Joe rode closer, he could see the fisherman was armed, as he'd suspected. Tucked into the man's belt was a long-barreled Ruger Mark III .22 semiautomatic pistol. Joe knew it to be an excellent gun, and he'd seen hundreds owned by hunters and ranchers over the years. It was rugged and simple, and it was often used to administer a kill shot to a wounded animal.

The tip of the fisherman's pole jerked down and the man deftly set the hook and reeled in a feisty twelve-inch rainbow trout. The sun danced off the colors of the trout's belly and back as the fisherman raised it from the water, worked the treble-hook lure out of its mouth, and studied it carefully, turning it over in his hands. Then he bent over and released the fish. He cast again, hooked up just as quickly, and reeled in a trout of the same size and color. After inspecting it, he bit it savagely behind its head to kill it. He spat the mouthful of meat into the water near his feet and slipped the fish into the bulging wet fanny pack behind him. Joe looked at the pack—there were *a lot* of dead fish in it.

"Why did you release the first one and keep the second?" Joe asked. "They looked like the same fish."

The man grunted as if insulted, "Not up close, they didn't. The one I kept had a nick on its tailfin. The one I threw back was perfect. The perfect ones go free." He spoke in a hard, flat, nasal tone. The accent was upper Midwest, Joe thought. Maybe even Canadian.

Joe was puzzled. "How many imperfect fish do you have there?" Joe asked. He was now around the lake and behind and to the side of the fisherman. "The legal limit is six. Too many to my mind, but that's the law. It looks like you may have more than that in your possession."

The fisherman paused silently in the lake, his wide back to Joe. He seemed to be thinking, planning a move or a response. Joe felt the now-familiar shiver roll through him despite the heat. It was as if they were the only two humans on earth and something of significance was bound to happen.

Finally, the man said, "I lost count. Maybe ten."

"That's a violation. Tell me, are you a bow hunter?" Joe asked. "I'm wondering about an arrow I found stuck in a tree earlier today."

The fisherman shrugged. Not a yes, not a no. More like, *I'm not sure I want to answer.*

"Do you know anything about an elk that was butchered up in a basin a few miles from here? A seven-point bull? It happened a week ago. The hunters who wounded it tracked it down but someone had harvested all the meat by the time they found the carcass. Would you know anything about that?"

"Why you asking me?"

"Because you're the only living human being I've seen in two days."

The man coughed up phlegm and spat a ball of it over his shoulder. It floated and bobbed on the surface of the water. "I don't know nothing about no elk."

"The elk was imperfect," Joe said. "It was bleeding out and probably limping."

"For the life of me, I don't understand what you're talking about."

"I need to see your license," Joe said.

"Ain't got it on me," the man said, finally, still not turning around. "Might be in my bag."

Joe turned in the saddle and saw a weathered canvas daypack hung from a broken branch on the side of a pine tree. He'd missed it earlier. He looked for a bow and quiver of homemade arrows. Nope.

"Mind if I look in it?"

The fisherman shrugged again.

"Is that a yes?"

"Yes. But while you look, I'm gonna keep fishing."

"Suit yourself," Joe said.

The fisherman mumbled something low and incomprehensible.

Joe said, "Come again?"

The man said, "I'm willing to let this go if you'll just turn your horses around and ride back the way you came. 'Cause if you start messing with me, well . . ."

"What?"

"Well, it may not turn out too good."

Joe said, "Are you threatening me?"

"Nope. Just statin' a fact. Like sayin' the sky is blue. You got a choice, is what I'm sayin'."

Joe said, "I'm choosing to check your license. It's my job."

The fisherman shook his head slowly, as if to say, *What happens now is on you.*

The rod flicked out again, but the lure shot out to the side toward Joe, who saw it flashing through the air. He flinched and closed his eyes and felt the lure smack hard into his shoulder. The treble hooks bit into the loose fabric of his sleeve but somehow missed the skin.

"Damn," the fisherman said.

"Damn is right," Joe said, shaken. "You hooked me."

"I fouled the cast, I guess," the man said.

"Seemed deliberate to me," Joe said, reaching across his body and trying to work the lure free. The barbs were pulled through the fabric and he ended up tearing his sleeve getting the lure out.

"Maybe if you'd stay clear of my casting lane," the fisherman said flatly, reeling in. Not a hint of apology or remorse.

Joe dismounted but never took his eyes off the fisherman in the water. He fought an impulse to charge out into the lake and take the man down. He doubted the miscast was an accident, but there was no way he could prove it, and he swallowed his anger. He led his horse over to the tree, tied him up, and took the bag down. There were very few items in it, and Joe rooted through them looking for a license. In the bag was a knife in a sheath, some string, matches, a box of crackers, a battered journal, a pink elastic iPod holder designed to be worn on an arm but no iPod, an empty water bottle, and half a Bible—Old Testament only. It looked as if the New Testament had been torn away.

"I don't see a license," Joe said, stealing a look at the

journal while the fisherman kept his back to him. There were hundreds of short entries made in a tiny crimped hand. Joe read a few of them and noted the dates went back to March. He felt the hairs rise on the back of his neck. Was it possible this man had been in the mountains for *six* months?

"Don't be reading my work," the fisherman said.

On a smudged card inside the Bible was a note: FOR CALEB ON HIS 14TH BIRTHDAY FROM AUNT ELAINE.

"Are you Caleb?" Joe asked.

Pause. "Yeah."

"Got a last name?"

"Yeah."

Joe waited a beat and the man said nothing. "So, what is it?"

"Grimmengruber."

"What?"

"Grimmengruber. Most people just say 'Grim' cause they can't pronounce it."

"Who is Camish?" Joe asked. "I keep seeing that name in this journal."

"I told you not to read it," Caleb Grimmengruber said, displaying a flash of impatience.

"I was looking for your license," Joe said. "I can't find it. So who is Camish?"

Caleb sighed. "My brother."

"Where is he? Is he up here with you?"

"None of your business."

"You wrote that he was with you yesterday. It says, 'Camish went down and got some supplies. He ran into some trouble along the way.' What trouble?" Joe asked, recalling what Farkus had said at the trailhead.

Caleb Grim lowered his fishing rod and slowly turned around. He had close-set dark eyes, a tiny pinched mouth glistening with fish blood, a stubbled chin sequined with scales, and a long, thin nose sunburned so badly that the skin was mottled gray and had peeled away revealing the place where chalk-white bone joined yellow cartilage. Joe's stomach clenched, and he felt his toes curl in his boots.

"What trouble?" Joe repeated, trying to keep his voice strong.

"You can ask him yourself."

"He's at your camp?"

"I ain't in charge of his movements, but I think so."

"Where's your camp?"

Caleb chinned to the south, but all Joe could see was a wood-studded slope that angled up nearly a thousand feet.

"Up there in the trees?" Joe asked.

"Over the top," the man said. "Down the other side and up and down another mountain."

Joe surveyed the terrain. He estimated the camp to be at least three miles the hard way. *Three miles.*

"Lead on," Joe said.

"What you gonna do if I don't?"

Joe thought, There's not much I *can* do. He said, "We won't even need to worry about that if you cooperate. You can show me your license, I can have a word with Camish, and if everything's on the level, I'll be on my way and I'll leave you with a citation for too many fish in your possession."

Caleb appeared to be thinking it over although his hard dark eyes never blinked. He raised his rod and hooked the lure on an eyelet so it wouldn't swing around. After a moment, Grim waded out of the lake. As he neared, Joe was taken aback at how tall he was, maybe six-foot-five. He was glad he *hadn't* gone into the lake after him. Joe could smell him approaching. Rancid—like rotten animal fat. Without a glance toward Joe, Caleb took the daypack and threw it over his shoulders and started up the mountain. Joe mounted up, breathed in a gulp of clean, thin air, and clucked at Buddy and Blue Roanie to get them moving.

A quarter mile up the mountain, Caleb stopped and turned around. His tiny dark eyes settled on Joe. He said, "You coulda just rode away."

NEARLY TO THE TOP, Joe prodded on his pack animals. They were laboring on the steep mountainside. Caleb Grim wasn't. The man long-strided up the slope at a pace that was as determined as it was unnatural.

Joe said, "The Brothers Grim?"

Caleb, obviously annoyed, said, "We prefer the Grim Brothers."

Later, Joe asked, "Where are you boys from?"

No response.

"How long have you been up here? This is tough country."

Nothing.

"Why just the Old Testament?"

Dismissive grunt.

"What kind of trouble did Camish run into yesterday?"

Silence.

"Some of the old-timers down in Baggs think someone's been up here harassing cattle and spooking them down the mountains. There have even been reports by campers that their camps have been trashed, and there've been some break-ins at cabins and cars parked at the trailheads. You wouldn't know anything about that, would you?"

Caleb grunted. Again not a yes, not a no.

"The elk that was butchered confounds me," Joe said. "Whoever did it worked fast and knew what they were doing. The bow hunters said it must have happened within twenty minutes, maybe less. Like maybe more than one man was cutting up that meat. You wouldn't know who up here could've done that, then?"

"I already told you. I don't know about no elk."

"Have you heard about a missing long-distance runner? She disappeared up here somewhere a couple of years ago. A girl by the name of Diane Shober?"

Another inscrutable grunt.

"The Brothers Grim," Joe said again.

"We prefer the Grim Brothers, damn you," Caleb spat.

Joe eased his shotgun out of the saddle scabbard, glanced down to check the loads, and slid it back in. He'd have to jack a shell into the chamber to arm it. Later, though. When Caleb wasn't looking. No need to provoke the man.

THEY WERE SOON in dense timber. Buddy and Blue Roanie detoured around downed logs while Caleb Grim scrambled over them without a thought. Joe wondered if Caleb was leading him into a trap or trying to lose him, and he spurred Buddy on harder than he wanted to, working him and not letting him rest, noting the lather creaming out from beneath the saddle and blanket. It was dark and featureless in the timber. Every few minutes Joe would twist in the saddle to look back, to try to find and note a landmark so he could find his way back out. But the lodgepole pine trees all looked the same, and the canopy was so thick he couldn't see the sky or the horizon.

"Sorry Buddy," he whispered to his gelding, patting his wet neck, "it can't be much farther."

Caleb's subtle arcs and meandering made Joe suddenly doubt his own sense of direction. He *thought* they were still going north, but he wasn't sure. Out of nowhere, a line came back to him from one of his favorite old movies, one of the rare movies he and his father had both liked, *The Missouri Breaks*:

The closer you get to Canada, the more things'll eat your horse.

Joe could smell the camp before he could see it. It smelled like rotten garbage and burnt flesh.

FOR A MOMENT, Joe thought he was hallucinating. How could Caleb Grim have made it into the camp so much before him that he'd had the time to sit on a log and stretch out his long legs and read the Bible and wait for him to arrive? Then he realized the man on the log was identical to Caleb in every way, including his clothing, slouch hat, and deformed nose, and he was reading the missing half of the book he'd seen in Caleb's daypack earlier—the *New* Testament.

Caleb Grim emerged from a thicket of brush and tossed his daypack aside and sat down next to his brother. Twins. Joe felt his palms go dry and his heart race.

"Why'd you bring *him*?" the brother—Joe assumed it was Camish—asked without looking up.

"I didn't," Caleb said. "He followed me."

"I thought we had an agreement about this sort of thing." His voice was nasal as well, but higher-pitched. "You know what happened the last time you did this."

"That was different, Camish. You know that."

"I didn't know it at the time."

"You should have known. They're all like that—every damned one of them."

"Especially when they got a badge to hide behind," Caleb said.

"*Especially* then," Camish said.

"What happened last time?" Joe asked. He was ignored. They talked to each other as if Joe weren't there. He tried to swallow but his mouth was dry.

The camp was a shambles. Clothing, wrappers, empty cans and food containers, bones, and bits of hide littered the ground. Their tent was a tiny Boy Scout pup tent, and he could see two stained and crumpled sleeping bags extending out past the door flap. He wondered how the two tall men managed to sleep there together—and why they'd want to. The bones meant the brothers were the poachers, because there were no open game seasons in the summer. Joe saw no weapons but assumed they were hidden away. He could arrest them for wanton destruction of game animals, hunting out of season, and multiple other violations on the spot. And then what? he wondered. He couldn't just march them for three days out of the mountains to jail.

Said Caleb to Joe, "You gonna stay up there on that horse?"

"Yup."

"You ain't gonna get down?"

"Nope. I'll just take a look at your fishing license and I'll get going."

The brothers exchanged looks and seemed to be sharing a joke.

"Well, then," Caleb said, long-striding toward the pup tent, "I'll go see if I can find it."

Joe said to Camish, "How long have you been up here?"

Camish looked up and showed a mouthful of stubby yellow teeth that looked like a line of undersized corn kernels. "Is that an official question?"

"An *official* question?"

"Like one I have to answer or you'll give me a dang ticket or something?"

"I'm just wondering," Joe said. "It looks like you boys have been up here for a while living off the land. That's curious. How many deer and elk have you killed and eaten?"

Camish shook his head. "If I don't answer you, it's not because I'm rude, mister. It's because I don't care to incriminate myself in any way. If it ain't an official question and all."

"Okay," Joe said. "It's an official question."

"If I don't agree to see you as an authority, it ain't official. You know, game warden, this place ain't called Rampart Mountain for no reason. You know what a rampart is?"

Joe kept silent, knowing Camish would answer his own question.

"A rampart is a protective barrier," Camish said. "A last stand, kind of."

Camish shook his half of the Bible at Joe. "I been reading this. I'm not all that impressed, to tell you the truth. I can't figure out what all the fuss is about. I find it to be an imperfect book."

Joe didn't know what to say to that.

"At least the first part has lots of action in it. Lots of murder and killings and sleeping around and such. Battles and things like that. Crazy miracles and folk tales—it keeps you entertained. This part, though, it's just too soft, you know? You ever read it?"

Joe said, "Some."

"I'd not recommend it. At least the second half. Instead, I'd read the U.S. Constitution. It's shorter, better, and up until recently it was pretty easy to find."

Caleb crawled backward out of the tent, stood up, said, "Damned if I can't find it, officer. But there's one other place I need to look."

"Where's that?"

Caleb gestured toward the forest behind him. "We got a couple caches back in the trees. I might have put my license in one of 'em."

Joe said, "I'll follow you." Wanting to be rid of Camish and his commentary.

That seemed to surprise Caleb, and again the brothers exchanged a wordless glance that made Joe both scared and angry. They were communicating without words or recognizable cues, leaving Joe in the dark.

"Come on, then," Caleb said. "But you'll have to get down. The trees are too thick to ride through. There's too much downed timber."

Joe studied the trees behind Caleb. They *were* too closely packed to ride through. For a moment, he considered telling Caleb he'd wait where he was. But he wondered if he let Caleb go if he'd ever see him again. And he didn't want to be stuck with Camish, who asked suddenly, "You ever hear of the Wendigo?"

Joe looked over. He'd now heard the word twice—once from Farkus, now from Camish Grim. "What about it?"

Again the stubby teeth, but this time in a sort of painful smile. "Just wonderin'," he said.

Joe waited for more but nothing came.

Then Camish said, "So who owns these fish you're so worked up about?"

"What do you mean, who owns them?"

"Exactly what I asked. These fish are native cutthroats, mainly, and a few rainbows that were planted years ago, right?"

Joe nodded.

"So who owns them? Do you own them? Is that why you're so worked up?"

"I work for the Wyoming Game and Fish Department," Joe said. "Note that word *fish*. We're the state agency in charge of managing our wildlife."

Camish rubbed his chin. "So *you* own the fish."

"Technically . . . no. But we're charged with managing the resource. Everybody knows this."

"Maybe," Camish said. "But I like to get things clear in my mind. What you're saying is that American citizens and citizens of this state have to go out and buy a piece of paper from the state in order to catch native fish in wild country. So you're sort of a tax collector for the government, then?"

Joe shook his head, lost in the logic.

"So if you don't own the fish and you didn't put them here, what gives you the right to collect a tax on folks like us? Don't we have any say in this?"

"I guess you can complain to the judge," Joe said.

"Does the judge get his paycheck from the same place you do? Sounds like a racket to me. You've got me wondering who the criminal is here and who isn't."

Joe climbed down quickly and tied Buddy to a tree. He said to Caleb, "Let's go."

Caleb grinned. Same teeth as Camish. "Pissed you off, didn't he?"

Joe set his jaw and made a wide arc around Camish, who looked amused.

JOE FOLLOWED CALEB GRIM on a nearly imperceptible trail through the pine trees. The trees were so thick that several times Joe had to turn his shoulders and sidle through the trunks to get through. The footing was rough because of the roots that broke the surface. Not that Caleb was slowed down, though. Joe found it remarkable how a man of his size could glide through the forest as if on a cushion of air.

"So," Joe said to Caleb's back, "where are you boys from?"

"More questions," Caleb grunted.

"Just being friendly."

"I don't need no friends."

"Everybody needs friends."

"Not me. Not Camish."

"Because you've got each other."

"I don't think I appreciate that remark."

"Sorry," Joe said. "So where do you guys hail from?"

"You ever heard of the UP?"

Joe said, "The Union Pacific?"

Caleb spat. His voice was laced with contempt. "Yeah, game warden, the Union Pacific. Okay, here we are."

The trail had descended and on the right side of it was a flat granite wall with large vertical cracks. Caleb removed a gnarled piece of pitchwood from one of the cracks and reached inside to his armpit. He came out with a handful of crumpled papers.

Joe tried to see what they were. They looked like unopened mail that had been wadded up and stuffed in the crack. He saw a canceled stamp on the edge of an envelope. When Caleb caught Joe looking, he quickly stuffed the wad back into the rock.

"Nope," he said. "No license here."

"Is this a joke?" Joe asked. "You didn't even look."

"The hell I didn't."

Joe shook his head. "If you've got a valid license, I can look it up when I can get to a computer. In the meanwhile, though, I'm giving you another citation. The law is you've got to have your license in your possession. Not in some rock hidden away."

Caleb said, "You're giving me another ticket?"

"Yup."

He laughed and shook his head from side to side.

"There'll be a court date," Joe said, unnerved from Caleb's casual contempt. "If you want to protest, you can show up with your license and make your case."

"Okay," Caleb said, as if placating Joe.

"And I'm going to write up both of you for wanton destruction of game animals. I saw all the bones back there. You've been poaching game all summer."

Caleb said, "Okay."

"So why don't we get back," Joe said.

Caleb nodded, shouldered around Joe, and strode back up the trail.

As Joe followed, he wondered if he'd been suckered, and why.

CAMISH WAS STILL ON HIS seat on the log and he watched with no expression on his face as Joe emerged from the woods. A cloud had finally passed in front of the sun and further muted the light. While they were gone, Camish had started a small fire in a fire pit near his feet and had cleaned and laid out the trout Caleb had brought back.

"Guess what," Caleb said to Camish, "he's going to give us *tickets*."

"Tickets?" Camish said, placing his big hand over his heart as if pretending to ward off a stroke.

Joe felt his ears get hot from the humiliation, but said, "Wanton destruction of game animals, for starters. But we've also got hunting and fishing without licenses, and exceeding the legal limit of fish."

Again, Joe caught the brothers exchanging information through their eyes.

Joe wrote out the citations while the Grim Brothers watched him and smirked.

Caleb said to his brother, "You're gonna get mad, but I told him we were from the UP. And you know what he said? He said, *'Union Pacific?'"*

Camish laughed out loud and slapped his thigh.

"Oh, and earlier, you know what he asked me?"

"What?"

"He asked if we'd ever run across any remains of that girl runner. You know, the one who took off running and never came back?"

"What did you tell him?"

"I said sure, we raped and killed her."

Camish laughed again, and Caleb joined him, and Joe looked up from the last citation he was scribbling and wondered when he'd left Planet Earth for Planet Grim.

HE HANDED THE CITATIONS to the brothers, who took them without protest.

"I'd suggest you boys get out of the mountains and straighten up and fly right," Joe said. "You're gonna have big fines to pay, and maybe even jail time if the judge comes down hard."

"Straighten up and fly right," Camish repeated in a soft, mocking tone.

"What's the reason you're up here, anyway?" Joe asked. "I find people all the time looking for something they can't get at home. What's the story with you two?"

The brothers looked at each other.

"You wanna tell him?" Caleb said.

Camish said, "Sure." He turned to Joe. "Let's just say this is the best place for us. I really don't want to go into detail."

Joe waited for more that didn't come. Finally, he reverted to training and said, "If you want to contest the citations, I'll guess I'll see you boys in court."

"Gee," Camish said. "Do we have to wear ties?"

Caleb snorted a laugh at that.

"You can wear what you want," Joe said, feeling ridiculous for responding.

Caleb said to Camish, "But we got folks to look after."

Camish shot Caleb a vicious glance, which shut his brother up.

"What folks?" Joe asked.

"Never mind my brother," Camish said. "He knows not what he says sometimes."

Caleb nodded, said, "I just babble sometimes."

"Is there someone else up here?" Joe asked.

"Ain't nobody," Camish said.

"Ain't nobody," Caleb repeated.

JOE MOUNTED BUDDY, clucked his tongue to get him moving, and started back up the hill. He was never so grateful to ride away. He tried not to look over his shoulder as he put distance between himself and the camp, but he found he had to if for no other reason than to make sure they weren't aiming a rifle at him.

They weren't. Instead, the Brothers Grim were laughing and feeding the citations into the fire, which flared as they dropped the tickets in.

*　　　*　　　*

THAT NIGHT HE DISCOVERED his satellite phone was missing. He remembered powering it down and putting it away into its case the night before, after leaving the message for Marybeth. He emptied the contents of both panniers and checked his daypack and saddlebags looking for it. He thought: They took it. He re-created the encounter with the brothers step-by-step and pinpointed when it likely happened. When he'd followed Caleb to the cache.

"The arrow," he said aloud and rooted through all of his gear again. It was gone as well.

His anger turned to thoughts of revenge. If the brothers used the phone—and why else would they have taken it?—their exact location could be determined. It was how the feds tracked down drug dealers in South America and terrorists in the Middle East. Joe could bring a team back up into the mountains and nail those guys.

Being out of radio contact was not unusual in itself, and often he didn't mind it one bit. This time he did. Marybeth would worry about him. In fact, he was worried himself. And what if the brothers hadn't taken his phone for their own use? What if they'd taken it to isolate him, to cut off his communication with the outside world?

LATER, AS GRAY WISPS of clouds passed over the moon and the wash of stars were so close together they looked like swirls of cream, he lay outside his tent again in his sleeping bag, with the shotgun across his chest, and he thought how different things could have turned out if he'd taken Caleb's advice and simply ridden away when he had the chance.

*   *   *

EVERY YEAR at the Wyoming Game Wardens Association meeting, after a few drinks, wardens would stand up and recount the strangest incident or most bizarre encounter they'd had the previous year. There was a sameness to many of the stories: poor hunters mistaking deer for elk or does for bucks, the comic and ridiculous excuses poachers came up with when caught in the act, out-of-state hunters who got no farther into Wyoming than the strip club in Green River, and run-ins with hermits, derelicts, and the unbalanced. It was always amazing to Joe how more often than not those who sought solace in nature were the least prepared to enter it. But it was exactly the opposite with those brothers. He felt he was the one who was encroaching, as if he'd barged unasked and unwanted into their living room.

They were the reason he'd lain awake all night with his hand on his shotgun as if it were his lover.

Joe thought bitterly, This isn't fair. This was not how it was supposed to be on his last patrol.

It was like walking into a convenience store for a quart of milk and realizing there was an armed robbery in progress. He didn't feel prepared for what he'd stumbled into. And unlike other situations he'd encountered over the years—and there were countless times he'd entered hunting and fishing camps outnumbered, outgunned, and without backup—he'd never felt as vulnerable and out of his depth.

HE THOUGHT HOW STRANGE it was that no one—hunters, ranchers, hikers, fishers—had ever reported seeing the Grim Brothers. How was it possible these two had lived and roamed in these mountains and not been seen and remarked upon? Two six-and-a-half-foot identical twins in identical clothing? That was the kind of legend that swept through the rural populace and took on a life of its own. It was exactly the kind of tale repeated by men like Farkus at the Dixon Club bar.

So how could these brothers have stayed out of sight?

Then Joe thought, *Maybe they hadn't.* They'd certainly been seen before.

But whoever had seen them felt compelled to keep their mouths shut. Or maybe they never lived to tell.

AFTER SEVERAL HOURS, Joe dragged his bag a hundred yards from the camp into a copse of thick mountain juniper on a rise that overlooked the tent and his horses. If they came for him, he figured, he'd see them first on the approach. He sat with his back against a rock and both the shotgun and the .308 M-14 carbine with peep sights within reach. Finally, deep into the night, he drifted into an exhausted sleep.

He didn't know how long he'd been out when his eyes shot open. It was still dark, but the eastern sky had lightened slightly. A dream had terrified him, and he found he'd cut into the palm of his hand with his fingernails and drawn blood.

In the dream, Caleb sneaked into his camp, rolled him over in his sleeping bag, and took a vicious bite out of the back of his neck. The pain was horrific, worse than anything he'd experienced.

To assure himself it had been his imagination, he glided the tips of his fingers along his nape to make sure the skin wasn't broken.

THURSDAY, AUGUST 27

3

THE ONLY SOUNDS JOE COULD HEAR AS HE RODE
from the trees into a sun-splashed meadow were a breeze
that tickled the long hairs of Buddy's black mane and
made far-off watery music in the tops of the lodgepole
pines, the huffing of his horses, and the squeaks and mews
from his leather saddle.

That was until he heard the hollow *thwap* somewhere
in the dark trees to his right, the sizzle of a projectile
arcing through the air like a shooting spark.

And the *thunk* of the arrow through the fleshy top of
his thigh that pinned him to the saddle and the horse.
The pain was searing, and he fumbled and dropped the
reins. Instinctively, he gripped the rough wooden shaft of
the arrow with his right hand. Buddy screamed and crow-
hopped, and Joe would have fallen if the arrow hadn't
been pinning him on the saddle. He felt Buddy's back
haunches dip and dig in, and suddenly the gelding was
bolting across the meadow with his eyes showing white
and his ears pinned back.

Horses, after all, were prey animals. Their only defense
was flight. Joe let go of the arrow shaft and held on to the
saddle horn with both hands. The underbrim of his
weathered Stetson caught wind and came off. He got a

flash vision of how he must look from a distance, like those poor monkeys that used to "ride" greyhounds and "race" at tracks and arenas, the monkeys jerking and flopping with every stride because they were tied on.

Buddy tore across the meadow. Blue Roanie followed, hooves thundering, gear—Joe's tent, sleeping bag, food, clothing, grain—shaking loose as the canvas panniers caught air and crashed back and emptied against the ribs of Blue Roanie.

Both animals were panicked and thundering toward the dark wall of trees to the left. Joe threw himself forward until his cheek was hard against Buddy's neck and he reached out for a fallen strap of leather in order to try for a one-rein stop. He knew the only way to slow the gelding down was to jerk his head around hard until his nose was pointing back at Joe.

He reached for the rein and the world shot by and in his peripheral vision he saw Blue Roanie suddenly sport an arrow in his throat and go down in a massive dusty tumble of spurting blood, flashing hooves, and flying panniers.

Joe thought, *This is it. They never had any intention of letting me get away after I met them and saw their camp.*

And: *This is not where I want to die.*

JOE MANAGED TO SLOW BUDDY to a lope just before the horse entered the wall of trees on the edge of the meadow and he welcomed the plunge into shadowed darkness because he was no longer in the open. Buddy seemed to read his mind or more likely think the same thought and he continued jogging his way through the thick lodgepole pine forest, entering a stand where the trunks seemed only a few feet apart. The canopy of the trees was so thick and interlaced overhead that direct sunlight barely dappled the forest floor, which was dry and without foliage and carpeted with inches of dead orange pine needles. It smelled dank and musty inside the stand, and Buddy's hoofprints released ripe soil odor through the crust of needles.

The shaft of the arrow jerked back on a skeletal branch that seemed to reach out and grasp it. Joe gasped from the electric jolt of pain and bangles of brilliant red and gold shimmered before his eyes. Buddy cried out and shinnied to the left and thumped hard into the trunk of a lodgepole, crushing Joe's left leg as well. The impact sent a shower of dried pine needles that covered Joe's bare head and shoulders.

Finally, Buddy stopped and breathed hard from exertion and pain.

"It's okay, Buddy," Joe whispered, reaching forward and stroking Buddy's mane. "It's okay."

But it wasn't.

"Let's turn around, okay, Buddy?" Joe asked. "So we can see if anyone's following us."

Joe pulled steadily on the right rein—the only one he'd managed to recover—until Buddy grunted and swung his big buttocks to the left and pivoted. There was barely enough room in the trees to turn.

Joe looked back at where they'd come from. He could see no pursuers. Buddy huffed mightily, and eventually his breathing slowed and became shallow.

Then, in the distance, back in the open meadow, Joe heard a whoop. They were still out there. Which meant they had no intention of retreating into the forest after the attack, which Joe had hoped.

Joe opened his eyes wide and tried to clear his head, to think. Buddy's labored breathing calmed, but the forward angle of his ears indicated he was still on alert. Joe was thankful his horse would be able to see, hear, or smell danger before he could.

Grasping the rough shaft of the arrow in order to steady it, Joe leaned painfully forward in the saddle. His Wranglers were black with blood that filled his boot and coursed through Buddy's coat and down his front leg to the hoof. The air smelled of it. He couldn't tell if it was all his blood or mixed with his horse's blood. The arrow was a replica of the one he'd found in the tree trunk the day before, a smooth unpainted length of mountain ash, fletched with wild turkey feathers. Taking a big gulp of air, Joe pulled cautiously on the arrow and was rewarded with another bolt of pain that made him instantly light-headed. Buddy crow-hopped and made an ungodly sound like the scream of a rabbit being crushed. The arrowhead was buried in the leather of saddle and Buddy's side, and there was no give. The barbs held. Joe let go and eased back, grimacing. He hoped the brothers hadn't heard Buddy.

He couldn't gauge how far the arrow had penetrated Buddy's side because he didn't know how long it was in the first place. It was possible the point was barely under the skin. If it was buried several inches, though, there would be organ damage and internal bleeding. Buddy could die.

Joe did a quick inventory of what gear was still with him. His yellow slicker was still tied behind the saddle and his saddlebags were filled with gloves, binoculars, his Filson vest, candy bars, a packet of Flex-Cuffs, his patrol journal, a citation book. His .40 Glock semiauto was on his belt. He cursed when he reached back for the butt of his shotgun and found an empty saddle scabbard. He'd lost his weapon of choice either on the wild ride across the meadow or in the trees, where Buddy had banged through them like a pinball. He wished he hadn't un- lashed it. And if only Blue Roanie had been able to fol- low, he thought. His first-aid kit was in the panniers. So was his .308.

He had to get out of the saddle to assess the wounds to his horse and to his leg. The arrow wouldn't come out as is. So he took another gulp of air, leaned forward, grasped the shaft with both hands, broke the back end off, and tossed the piece with the fletching behind him. Then grasping his own leg like he would heave a sandbag, he slid it up and off the broken shaft. The movement and the pain convulsed him when his leg came free and he tumbled off the left side of the horse onto the forest floor, out.

WHEN HE AWOKE, he was surprised it wasn't raining because he thought he'd heard the soft patter of rain in his subconscious. But the pine needles were dry. Joe had no idea how long he'd been out, but he guessed it had been just a few minutes. The dappling of sunlight through the branches, like spots on the haunch of a fawn, were still at the same angle. He was on his side with his left arm pinned under him and his cheek on the ground. His right leg with the holes in it was now largely numb except for dull pulses of pain that came with each heartbeat. His left leg throbbed from being crushed against the tree trunks.

It came back to him: Where he was and how he had got there.

Joe groaned and propped himself up on an elbow. Buddy stood directly over him. That's when Joe realized it wasn't rain he'd heard, but drops of blood from his horse striking the dry forest floor.

He rose by grasping a stirrup and pulled himself up the side of his horse. He paused with both arms across the saddle as he studied the dark and silent tangle of trees they'd come through. He saw no one. Yet.

The saddle was loose due to Buddy's exertion and it was easy to release the cinch. He stood on his horse's right side where the arrow was and gripped the saddle horn on the front and the cantle on the back and set his feet. "I'll make this as painless as I can, Buddy," he said, then grunted and swung the saddle off, careful to pull it straight away from the arrow so the hole in the leather slid up the shaft and didn't do any more side-to-side damage. Buddy didn't scream again or rear up, and Joe was grateful.

He examined the wound and could see the back end of the flint point just below a flap of horsehide. The point wasn't embedded deeply after all. Apparently, the leather—and Joe's leg—had blunted the penetration. So why all the blood? Then he saw it: another arrow was deep into Buddy's neck on the other side. So both brothers had been firing arrows at him from opposite sides of the meadow. The neck wound was severe.

The first-aid kit was in the panniers. In the kit, there was hydrogen peroxide to clean out the wounds and compresses to bind them and stop the bleeding.

He had to stop the flow. But how?

JOE SAT IN THE GRASS with his pants pulled down to his knees. His left leg was bruised and turning purple. There were two holes three inches apart in the top of his right thigh. The holes were rimmed with red and oozing dark blood. They were the diameter of a pencil and Joe was fascinated by the fact that he could move the skin and view the red muscle fiber of his right quadriceps. He'd need to bathe the wounds, kill the growing infection, and close or bind the holes. Quickly. The excruciating pain had receded into the numb solace of shock and the blood had the viscosity of motor oil. He clumsily wrapped his bandana over the holes and made a knot. He stood with the aid of a tree trunk and pulled his pants back up. Buddy watched with his head down and his eyes going gauzy as his blood dripped out.

"I'll take care of you first, Buddy," Joe said in a whisper, "then I'll take care of me."

Before limping back through the timber toward the meadow and Blue Roanie's body, Joe emptied most of his canteen over the wound in Buddy's neck until the water ran clear. He drank the last of the water and tossed the canteen aside, then tied Buddy's reins to a tree trunk.

"Hang in there and don't move."

He was encouraged by the fact that Buddy's head was down and his ears weren't as rigid. It might mean the brothers had left the area. Or it might mean his horse was dying.

JOE MOVED SLOWLY. His legs wouldn't allow him to go any faster. He lurched from tree to tree, holding himself upright by grabbing trunks and branches, anything that would help him take the weight and pressure off his leg wound. He made a point not to look down at his injury for fear he'd pass out again.

It took twenty minutes before he neared the meadow where he'd been bushwhacked. If the brothers had come into the trees after him, he would have run into them by now. He had no doubt they'd have finished him off. Maybe with arrows, maybe with knives, maybe with his own guns. He found his hat and fitted it back on his head.

Joe hated the fact that his only available weapon was his .40 Glock service piece. He was a poor pistol shot. Although his scores on the range for his annual recertification had risen a few points in the past two years, he still barely qualified. He knew if it weren't for the sympathy of the range officer who'd followed his exploits over the years and graded him on a curve, he could have been working a desk at game and fish headquarters in Cheyenne. Joe's proficiency was with a shotgun. He could wing-shoot with the best of them. His accuracy and reaction time were excellent as long as he shot instinctively. It was the slow, deliberate aiming he had trouble with.

As he staggered from tree to tree toward the meadow, he vowed that if he got off the mountain alive he'd finally take the time to learn how to hit something with his service weapon.

He felt oddly disengaged, like he was watching a movie of a guy who looked a lot like him, but slower. It was as if it weren't really him limping through the trees with holes in his leg and his best horse bleeding to death on the side of an unfamiliar mountain. Joe seemed to be floating above the treetops, between the crown of the pines and the sky, looking down at the man in the red shirt moving toward what any rational observer would view as certain death. But he kept going, hoping the numb otherworldliness would continue to cushion him and act as a narcotic, hoping the pain would stay just beyond the unbearable threshold so he could revel in the insentient comfort of shock. And he hoped the combination of both would keep at bay the terror that was rising within him.

Now, though, there were four things of primal importance.

Find Blue Roanie's body and the panniers. Recover his shotgun. Return to Buddy with the first-aid kit. Get the hell off the mountain.

THE PINE TREES THINNED and melded into a stand of aspen. He couldn't remember riding Buddy into aspen at all, but at the time he'd been addled and in furious pain. He recalled gold spangles in his eyes and realized now that they'd been leaves that slapped against his face as Buddy shot through the trees.

Aspen trees shared a single interconnected root system that produced saplings straight from their ball of roots through the soil. They weren't a grove of individual trees like pines or cottonwoods, but a single organism relentlessly launching shooters up through the soil to gain territory and acquire domination, to starve out any other trees or brush that dared try to live in the same immediate neighborhood. A mountainside of aspen was enjoyed by tourists for the colors and tone, but it was actually one huge voracious organism as opposed to hundreds or thousands of individual trees. Joe had always been suspicious of aspens for that reason. Additionally, the problem with aspen for a hunter or stalker or a crippled game warden was their leaves, which dried like brittle parchment commas and dropped to the ground. Walking on aspen leaves was akin to walking on kettle-fried potato chips: *noisy*. Joe crunched along, left hand on a tree trunk or branch and right hand on the polymer grip of his Glock, when he realized how loud he was, how obvious. And how silent it was, which meant the brothers were still there.

*　　*　　*

ON HIS HANDS AND KNEES, Joe shinnied over downed logs to the meadow. With each yard, the lighting got brighter. His wounded leg alternated between heat and cold, pain and deadness. When his leg was hot, he knew he was bleeding. He could smell the metallic odor. When it was cold, his leg felt better. But it scared him, because dragging his leg felt like pulling thirty pounds of cold meat through the leaves. If it was cold, it was gone. So in a way, he welcomed the waves of heat.

Trees thinned. The meadow pulsed green and bright in the sunlight. Joe heard one of the brothers laugh like a hyena: *Cack-cack-cack-cack-cack*. The sound made the hairs on the back of Joe's neck prick up, as if he were a dog.

And he thought: *This is as basic as it can be. I'm a dog. They're animals as well. Or something like animals.*

What he saw through the tumbled pick-up sticks of untrammeled timber made his skin crawl.

The brothers were on either side of Blue Roanie. They were laughing in the way they laughed, which was blunt and brutal, the laugh of men who were comfortable with themselves and had no desire to please anyone else.

Cack-cack-cack-cack-cack.

One of them held his bow with one hand and a bundle of arrows in the other.

The other brother dropped a knotty pine war club so he could admire Joe's shotgun. The .308 carbine was in the grass near his feet.

Blue Roanie didn't move. He was dead. The arrow that had pierced his neck had severed an artery and he'd bled out, and the black blood formed a large pool like liquid tar in the grass. Joe was grateful his end had come quickly.

The Grim Brothers stripped the body of Blue Roanie,

taking his saddle and bridle and tossing them to the side. Caleb ducked under his front leg and lifted it on his shoulder with a grunt. Camish produced his bowie knife and used it to pry Roanie's horseshoe off. When he was through, he moved on to the other three. As the horseshoes came off, they were tossed into a pile near the saddle. They landed with a metallic *clink*.

The dead horse was now scavenged of anything valuable, he thought. But they weren't done. With brutal efficiency, they skinned the horse and pulled the hide away from the carcass as if it were a new living room rug. Then, with the skill of a butcher, Camish severed the front quarter, barely touching a bone or joint with his blade.

Caleb struggled under the weight of the severed front quarter but still managed to carry it away. Joe had never contemplated what the front leg of a horse weighed, but he guessed one-eighty to two hundred pounds. More than *he* weighed. He thought, *They're strong, too.* Inhumanly strong.

Joe knew he was up against a force he'd never faced but somehow he'd always imagined was out there. He didn't like his chances.

He briefly closed his eyes and thought of Marybeth, how she'd miss him. Worse, he thought of his daughters, who simply assumed he'd always prevail and come home and be Dad. If only they knew this situation. But the last thing he'd want them to see was a man named Grim carry away the front quarter of a horse they'd loved. Blue Roanie was in the second generation of Pickett Family horses, and like his predecessor, he'd been killed in action.

They'd be righteously angry, Joe thought. And Marybeth. How to explain that her horse Buddy had bled out in the middle of nowhere because Joe couldn't recover the first-aid kit? She'd understand, of course. So would the girls. But he didn't want them simply to understand. He wanted them to think of him as their hero and their bulwark against everybody and everything out there. He didn't want them to think of him as the man who failed. As the dad who failed and let himself die.

He thought: *I'm in trouble, but I've got more to live for than just me.*

He had a sidearm he was no good at shooting and the Brothers Grim had his shotgun, carbine, gear, first-aid kit, intimate knowledge of the mountains, and a violent sense of purpose. All he had was his determination to help his horse, fix his leg, and get home to his family.

He was outgunned, outnumbered, and outmatched.

Still disembodied, still watching himself from above, still not able to really believe what was happening before him and his sudden unwelcome descent into brutality, he observed with clinical detachment as the Brothers Grim disemboweled Blue Roanie with a knife and slid her bundled entrails out onto the grass like a mass of steaming ropy snakes. Caleb reached down into the gut pile and came out with the huge dark liver. It was shaped like a butterfly with black fleshy wings. Caleb raised it to his mouth and took a ferocious bite. With rivulets of black blood streaming down his mouth, he offered it to Camish, who took a bite as well. The pagan hunting tradition complete, the brothers set about further dismembering Blue Roanie.

He could tell by the way they shot wary glances at the trees for him that when they were done, he'd be next on their schedule.

4

AT THE SAME TIME, IN SADDLESTRING, WYO-
ming, Marybeth Pickett saw the last thing she wanted to
see through the living room window: her mother's full-
sized black Hummer as it roared into the driveway. The
grille, a mouthful of chrome canine teeth, stopped inches
from the back of Marybeth's parked minivan.

"Crap," Marybeth said.

"Excuse me?"

Marybeth turned quickly from the window and felt
her face flush. "I'm sorry," she said into the telephone to
Elizabeth Harris, the vice principal of Saddlestring High,
"I didn't mean you. I just saw something outside that . . .
alarmed me."

"Goodness, what?"

"A predator," Marybeth said, immediately sorry she
had voiced it.

Harris said, "I read in the paper where people in town
have been seeing a mountain lion. Did you see it?"

"No, I was mistaken," Marybeth said, and quickly
moved on. "But you were saying?"

What Harris was saying was that April Keeley, their
fifteen-year-old foster daughter, was absent again for her
math tutor. It was the third time she hadn't shown up

since summer makeup courses had begun the week before, she said.

"This is news to me," Marybeth said acidly. "I should have been informed before this."

"It sort of fell through the cracks," Harris said. "We're short-staffed in the summer and we thought you'd been called."

"I haven't been."

"Obviously, we know she has plenty of making up to do," the vice principal said, lowering her voice to sharing-a-conspiracy level. "We're fully aware of her . . . *difficulties*. But if we want April to be able to be competent with her classmates at the ninth-grade level—and we do—she needs to be there on time and prepared to complete the remedial coursework before the school year begins."

"I'm sorry," Marybeth said. "I had no idea. I mean, she left for school on time after breakfast. . . ." She recalled two of April's friends, Anne Kimbol and Michelle McNamara, standing shoulder-to-shoulder together on the front porch waiting for April and clutching their math textbooks. Those girls were trouble.

She looked up to see Sheridan, eighteen, standing in the threshold of the hallway in her maroon polyester Burg-O-Pardner smock, about to go to work for the afternoon. The logo for the restaurant—a hamburger wearing a cowboy hat and boots with spurs, and holding a carton of their special Rocky Mountain oysters—was on a patch above her breast pocket. Sheridan, like Marybeth, was blonde and green-eyed and serious.

Sheridan wanted to save some money for her senior year in high school, and she'd discovered to her surprise she was a pretty good waitress. She was juggling her part-time job with "optional" summer basketball practice.

Sheridan played forward for the Saddlestring Lady Wranglers. Although she had her mother's concentration and determination to make it all work, her basketball coach—a venal, sideline-strutting peacock of a man who interpreted Sheridan's job and other interests as a personal affront to *him* and his potential success—had threatened to take her out of the starting lineup if she missed another practice. The coach, she thought, would make her senior year in high school miserable.

Sheridan had overheard her mother and mouthed, *"April, again?"*

Marybeth nodded to her daughter and said to the vice principal, "I'll make sure it doesn't happen again. I'll drive her there myself if I need to and watch her go inside. I'll deliver her to the classroom if necessary. And the good news is my husband will be back next week for good. If I can't bring April in, I'll ask Joe to do it. He's used to shuttling kids." And thought, Wherever *he* is. That he hadn't called the night before still bothered her. There were so many things she needed to tell him, so many things they needed to talk about, starting with the fact their foster daughter's behavior was spinning out of control.

Mrs. Harris thanked Marybeth and said something about the unseasonably warm weather, and Marybeth nodded with distraction as if the vice principal could see her, said "Bye," and disconnected the call.

She placed the phone in the charger and asked Sheridan, "What is she doing, that girl? Where is she going and who is she with?" Putting Sheridan into the tough decision of ratting out her foster sister or maintaining the shared silence of the sisterhood.

"Do you know what's going on?" Marybeth asked. "It's for her own good. . . ."

Sheridan took a deep breath and prepared to say something when Missy knocked sharply on the front door.

"Later," Sheridan said.

Marybeth thought she knew what was going on: Sheridan and April were battling. And it was going beyond normal sibling rivalry into full-fledged war. In the past year, Sheridan had assumed the old pecking order—with her in the top spot because she was the oldest and most responsible for April's return—would resume. But April had come back with a trunk full of adult trauma and experience with which she challenged Sheridan. And everyone else. It was not the idyllic situation Marybeth had assumed it would be. And, Marybeth thought, as April herself thought it would be.

"For now," Marybeth said dourly. "Later, we talk." She gestured to the front door. "Would you please let her in?"

Sheridan welcomed the reprieve and shouted over her shoulder to her thirteen-year-old sister, "Lucy, there's somebody here for you!" and ducked back down the hallway with a satisfied smirk.

"I WAS SURPRISED TO SEE your car home on a Wednesday," Missy said, sweeping into the house with a kind of full-sized presence that belied her sixty-four years and petite figure. She wore a black silk pantsuit embroidered with the silhouettes of dragons, a purchase from China when she'd attended the 2008 Summer Olympics with her fifth husband, Earl Alden, known as the "Earl of Lexington," who was a multimillionaire media mogul with a ranch outside of town and homes all over the world. With each husband, Missy had traded up. Her last husband, Bud Longbrake, had lost his ranch to her in the divorce when he'd discovered the handover was in small print in the prenuptial agreement he'd signed when he and Missy got married.

"I took the day off," Marybeth said, looking around for either of her daughters for help or support. But Sheridan had slipped out the back to go to work and Lucy was hiding behind the door she'd been tricked to open to let her grandmother in. "Joe will be back the first of next week, as you know. I've been putting boxes of the girls' things in his office and I needed to clean it all up."

"Oh," Missy said, "Joe. I'd *so* forgotten about him. I've gotten used to just you and the girls."

"I'll bet," Marybeth said.

"There you are!" Missy said, turning and seeing Lucy behind her before her granddaughter could slither across the wall and dart up the stairs undetected.

"Hi, Grandma Missy," Lucy said.

Missy enveloped Lucy in her arms, but turned her head slightly so her makeup wouldn't smear on her granddaughter's shoulder. Marybeth was startled to see Lucy was nearly the same height and build as her mother after a summer of fierce growth. Missy said to Lucy, "How's my favorite granddaughter?"

"I'm fine," Lucy said, forcing a girlish smile she reserved for photographs and her grandmother.

"Please, Mom . . ." Marybeth said.

"You know what I mean," Missy said, dismissing her.

The animosity between Sheridan and her grandmother had almost reached the level of acrimony as that between Joe and Missy. So Missy no longer made an effort to pretend that she didn't prefer Lucy. Like Missy, Lucy went for fine clothing and fine things. Missy disapproved of Sheridan's nascent interest in falconry and science and her lack of interest in all things Missy.

To Lucy, Missy said, "And are you wearing that silk dress I brought you from Paris? The electric blue one?"

"School hasn't started yet," Lucy said. "But I will."

Missy nodded with satisfaction.

Marybeth knew Lucy was fibbing. Lucy'd told her she was embarrassed by the dress. That it might as well have had MY GRANDMOTHER IS RICH embroidered on the back of it. That she'd *never* wear something like that to a seventh-grade dance. She'd also confessed she was getting more and more embarrassed in general by her grandmother, who sometimes acted as if they were contemporaries as well as allies. Marybeth still bristled at the memory of Lucy telling her Missy had said one of the bonds between them included the fact they "shared common enemies." Meaning Marybeth and Joe.

Marybeth thought, *Not now . . . I don't have time for this.*

MARYBETH'S business management company, MBP, had recently been purchased by a local accounting firm looking to widen its base. They'd retained her to run the company for a year while they incorporated her employees and contracts into the firm. Now that Joe was being sent home, it should have been the best of all worlds. But it wasn't.

Managing the sale of her business, the transition into a larger and entrenched company, the running of the household with three teenage girls, and Joe's yearlong absence had become almost unbearable. It was as if she were overseeing three full-time operations at once, she thought, and no one seemed to realize or appreciate the pace and scope of her responsibilities. Even Joe, who at least tried. The last time they'd talked, two nights ago over a scratchy satellite phone, Marybeth had declared that she was considering taking up heavy drinking. Joe had said, "You're kidding, right?"

They sat on opposite sides of the dining room table. Her mother reached across and grasped her hand and said, "You haven't heard a word I've been saying, have you?"

"I thought you were talking to Lucy," Marybeth said.

"No, Lucy managed to slip away," Missy said, through a pearly-cold smile. "She's never going to wear that blue dress, is she?"

"Mom, I don't *know*," Marybeth said with a sigh.

"It's not a trivial matter. I can sense her slipping away from me. Perhaps due to the influence of her older sister and her father."

"Please, not now."

Missy pulled her hand away and sat back in her chair. Missy had always won battles by withdrawing her affection. It worked almost every time. She knew her beauty—and now her wealth—gave her power over others. Missy dramatically studied Marybeth over the rim of her coffee cup.

Marybeth anticipated what was coming.

"You're killing yourself," her mother said, putting the cup down. "I hate seeing what I'm seeing. You have weary eyes, and I can see wrinkles where I've never seen them before. There, on the corners of your mouth from fretting. Now I hear through the grapevine you're thinking of buying a new house."

"What grapevine?" Marybeth said, not answering the question. The down payment the accounting firm had paid for MBP was enough for them to look seriously for a new home outside of town, where Joe wanted to live. He'd never liked their house in town even though he refused to admit it. Marybeth wanted to have her horses accessible again, and to wake up with the possibility of seeing wildlife. Removing April from easy contact with whatever kids she was hanging around with would be a plus as well, she thought. Lucy would miss suburban living and access to her friends and social whirl, and Marybeth hadn't told her about a possible move.

"No one buys property in this county without The Earl or me hearing about it," Missy said. "You should know that by now."

Missy and Earl Alden had combined their ranches and were now the largest landowners in Twelve Sleep and Big Horn counties. Joe had recently speculated Missy would likely be looking to add to her holdings now that she had access to Alden's millions, and would likely soon acquire a Third World country.

Missy said, "It just saddens me that . . ."

"You don't have to finish," Marybeth said sharply and showed her palm as if saying *Stop*. "I know what you're going to say."

Said Missy, "I'm sure you do. It's just that you had—and have—such promise. And here you are . . ."

Marybeth set her cup down with enough force that both women looked to see if she'd cracked it.

"If you want to continue down this road with me right now, I'll have to ask you to leave," Marybeth said, keeping her voice even. "I'm not kidding."

Missy appraised her coolly. "I know you're not."

"So what do you need, Mom? I mean, it's nice you dropped by and all, but I took the day off of work so I could get some things done around here. I'm on edge waiting for Joe to call. And I know you well enough to guess that you didn't just drop by to have my cheap coffee."

Missy nodded. "I do wish you would serve that coffee I brought you from Africa."

"Okay, that's it," Marybeth said angrily, pushing away from the table.

"Please, sit down," Missy said. "I'm sorry I said that. Everything I say seems to come out as an insult, even when I don't intend it to come out that way. Please sit down."

Marybeth glared at her mother, pointedly looked at the clock above the stove, then back. Meaning, *You've got five minutes.*

Missy said, "I'll get to the point. You know that friend of yours—Nate? The falconer who got in so much trouble a while back? I need to talk with him."

"Why do you want to talk to Nate Romanowski?" Marybeth said, surprised.

Missy didn't break her gaze. She *never* broke her gaze. "Do I really have to spell it out?"

"Yes, you do."

"Well, actually, The Earl thought of him," Missy said, sipping and trying to conceal the displeasure she got from the last swallow of her daughter's coffee. "I was thinking I'd take care of the problem myself."

"What problem?"

"Bud."

"What about Bud? He's a ruined man. You ruined him. Why pick on Bud Longbrake?"

Missy said, "He can't let go. He can't move on. He just stays in Saddlestring and drinks the Stockman's Bar dry every night. He tells anyone who will listen his pathetic story and he says terrible things about The Earl and especially me. He's like a cancer."

"A cancer you caused," Marybeth said. "Mom, you broke his heart and *stole* his ranch."

Missy made a tut-tut sound with her tongue. "The transfer was perfectly legal, sweetie. Men are so emotional these days. I long for the time when men were tough and stoic. Now all they do is cry and whine and vomit out their *feelings*. What happened to our warriors? Where have all the cowboys gone, Marybeth?"

Marybeth was speechless.

"Anyway," Missy said, changing tack, "lately, Bud's been calling the ranch and my cell phone. He's threatening me. I want to hire Nate Romanowski to scare him off."

"Nate doesn't do things like that," Marybeth said, alarmed.

Missy smiled. "Then there are obviously things about your friend that you don't know all that well. You see, The Earl had some research done."

Marybeth looked at the clock above the stove. "I've got to get some work done now. You've got to go home."

"I'm not asking you to do anything to Bud," Missy said. "All I'm asking is for you to pass along a message to Mr. Romanowski that I'd like to speak with him."

"I don't see Nate anymore," Marybeth said. "He's in hiding. There are federal warrants out on him, Mom," she said, practically pleading.

Missy was undeterred. "Your husband talks to him. And Sheridan still does, doesn't she?"

"I don't know," Marybeth lied.

Missy lowered her head slightly and smiled woman-to-woman. "Marybeth, if anyone can get Mr. Romanowski's attention, it's you. Do you forget what you told me a few years ago?"

Marybeth sighed and shook her head. "You never fail to disappoint. That's why I don't confide in you anymore,

Mom. It's like handing you bullets to use on me at a later date."

"That's a cruel thing to say. By the way, did Joe ever know?"

Marybeth's voice got hard. "*Nothing happened.* Besides, Joe and I don't keep secrets from each other."

Missy chuckled and shook her head. "Oh, dear, you still have so much to learn."

"I have to get to work," Marybeth said, pushing away from the table. "Besides, Nate's in love these days. He's different. He'd never consider your proposition."

"Honey," Missy said, "how do you think he makes a living? Haven't you ever wondered about that?"

Marybeth had. But like Joe, she never wanted to find out.

"Let Nate make up his own mind," Missy said. "He's got a mind of his own, doesn't he?"

Marybeth refused to respond.

"Just pass along the word," Missy said, standing up. "That's all we ask. Tell him we'll make it more than worthwhile for him. You know The Earl. He's fed up with Bud, and money's no object. As for Nate, my understanding is his lady love has a toddler she's raising on a teacher's salary. I'm sure she could use some support."

Marybeth snatched both cups from the table and took them to the sink so she could keep her back to her mother.

"You owe me this one," Missy said quietly. "Don't forget what we've done for Vicki, the girl you pawned off on us last year. Vicki is getting the very best of care, thanks to us."

Marybeth closed her eyes and bit her bottom lip. Vicki was a foster child who'd entered their lives and needed extensive mental and physical treatment. Marybeth had only one place to turn: Missy. Since then, a pair of grandparents had shown up and offered to take Vicki in when she completed treatment, but Missy still paid the bills. Marybeth knew at the time she was handing her mother more bullets.

"Thank you for the coffee," Missy said. "Have Nate call me on my cell."

Marybeth didn't turn around. She heard her mother call good-bye to Lucy down the hallway and go outside. In a moment, the motor on the black Hummer roared to life.

WHEN THE PHONE RANG she snatched it off the cradle, expecting Joe's voice.

Instead, a man said, "May I please speak to Mr. Joseph Pickett?"

"This is Marybeth Pickett. Who may I ask is calling?"

The man identified himself as Dr. Vincent DeGrasso of the Rimrock Extended Care Facility in Billings, Montana. Marybeth felt a chill sweep through her.

"Joseph's father is George Pickett, correct?"

"Yes."

DeGrasso obviously made these kinds of calls often. "I hate to call with bad news, Mrs. Pickett, but Joseph's father has taken a serious turn. Somehow, he convinced a friend to smuggle in a half gallon of vodka last Sunday, and from what we can tell he drank it all in one sitting. The alcohol reacted with his medication and he went into toxic shock. Right now he's in the ICU and his organs are shutting down."

Marybeth closed her eyes. "How long?"

"We doubt he'll last the week. Even if we can keep him

alive, he's not ever going to be lucid or functional again. A decision needs to be made."

"My God."

"There was a moment of consciousness this morning," DeGrasso said. "George asked for his son. He seemed to realize it was his last request."

5

A BREEZE CAME UP AND CARRIED THE SMELL OF blood, entrails, and tallow from Blue Roanie's body to Joe, who watched the brothers at work from the aspen grove. They'd draped the hide over a log, then efficiently dismembered the horse. They didn't speak or gesture but worked in a quiet rhythm of flashing knives and strong bloody hands, with no pauses or wasted movement. Within ten minutes, they'd dismembered it.

All his gear had been gathered and was piled a few yards from the carcass of Blue Roanie. He could see everything he needed but couldn't get close enough to get it. A hundred yards was too far for an accurate shot with his handgun. If he missed, which he surely would, he would reveal his position and the brothers could make short work of him with the .308 or his shotgun or possibly finish him off with arrows. His Glock had fourteen rounds in the magazine. He wished he had his spare magazines, but they, like the first-aid kit, were in the panniers. Still, though, if he could lure the brothers in close enough and somehow keep them together, he'd have a decent chance of taking them down with the sheer volume of his firepower.

But how to get them close and unaware?

He thought again, *I'm in trouble*.

And he recalled the day before, when he'd first encountered the brothers. When he'd inadvertently set this ghost train in motion . . .

HE WISHED NOW he had ridden away when he had the chance so he could return with a small army to arrest the Brothers Grim. Because now the wind had reversed—as had his opportunity to get away intact—and Camish stepped away from the carcass of Blue Roanie and sniffed at the air like a wolf. They were trying to *smell* him. And then Camish suddenly pointed in Joe's direction in the aspen grove.

Oh, no, Joe mouthed. He wouldn't have thought it possible.

Caleb and Camish wordlessly retrieved their weapons and ran across the meadow in opposite directions. Caleb left with Joe's carbine, Camish right with his shotgun. *They were going to kill him with his own guns*. Both brothers were much too far away for Joe to take an accurate shot.

Instinctively, he scrambled back on his haunches. A hammer blow of pain from his right thigh sat him back down, and he gulped air to recover.

He glanced up to see Caleb dart into the left wall of trees. Camish was already gone. They obviously knew he'd been hit and they assumed—correctly—he couldn't run.

Joe thought they were going to flank him, come at him in a pincer through the trees.

Gritting his teeth from the sting of his wounds, Joe rose to his knees. The position wasn't as painful as before. He raised the Glock with both hands, and swung it left, then right, looking over the sights toward the trees, hoping to catch one of them in the open, get a clean shot.

His training trumped the urge to try to kill them without warning. He shouted, "Both of you freeze where you are and toss your weapons out into the open. This is OVER. Don't take it any further."

He paused, eyes shooting back and forth for movement of any kind, ears straining for sound.

He continued, "Now step out into the open where I can see you. Keep your hands up and visible at all times."

No response, until Camish, a full minute later, said from where he was hidden to the right: "Naw, that isn't how it's going to work. Right, brother?"

Joe was shocked how close the voice was. Just beyond the thick red buckbrush, the voice was so intimate it was as if Camish were whispering into his ear.

"Fuckin' A," said Caleb from the dense juniper and pine on his left.

Said Camish, "I thought we weren't gonna use that kind of language anymore."

"Yeah—sorry. I forgot. I just got so caught up in the situation . . ."

Joe was taken aback how once again they were talking above him, as if he weren't there or he didn't matter and they didn't care if he heard them. This scared him as much as anything, how they minimized his presence, depersonalized his being. And he thought how much easier it was to be cruel and ruthless when you didn't consider your adversary an equal.

So he cut in to remind them he was there. He did it with a lie.

"I hate to break it to you boys," he said, "but you think because you stole my satellite phone it means no one knows where I am. That's not the case at all. You need to listen to me. Twice a day I call in my coordinates. I called 'em in just before I rode up on Caleb. I haven't talked to dispatch since then, but they know exactly where I was and which way I was headed. They'll be able to pinpoint this location within a mile or two, and they'll be worried. Help is on the way, boys. It could be here anytime."

Joe glanced up into the sky as if looking for the helicopter he'd just made up. But all he could see were dark afternoon thunderheads tumbling slow motion across the blue sky. There wasn't even a distant jet trail.

"So let's end the game," Joe said, taking their silence as possible evidence of their contemplation.

Camish said to Caleb, "You believe that, brother?"

Caleb snorted, "Fuck no."

Camish said, "Language."

"Sorry."

"I don't believe him either. He's a liar."

"Another damned liar," Caleb said with contempt. "After a while, a man starts to wonder if there's a single damned one of 'em who doesn't lie."

And the afternoon exploded. Joe threw himself to his belly and covered his head with his hands as his shotgun boomed from the left. From the right, Camish fired the .308, squeezing off rounds as quickly as he could pull the trigger. The thin tree trunks around him quivered with the impact of double-ought pellets and .308 slugs. Chunks of bark and dead branches fell around him and the last dry leaves in the aspen grove shimmied to the ground. The air smelled sharply of gunfire.

The shots stopped. Joe did a mental inventory. He wasn't hit, which was a small miracle. But the proximity of the brothers, and the metal-on-metal sounds of them furiously reloading, convinced him he likely wouldn't survive another volley. An infusion of fear and adrenaline combined to propel him back to his knees, gun up.

A pine bough shuddered to his left, and Joe fired.

Pop-pop-pop-pop.

Through the ringing in his ears, he thought he heard someone cry out.

"Caleb," Camish cried, "you hit?"

Caleb's response was an inhuman moan ending in a roar, the sound of someone trying to shout through a mouthful of liquid.

Then Joe swung the Glock a hundred and eighty degrees to his right. The forest was silent, but he anticipated Camish to be at roughly the same angle and distance as his brother, since they'd entered the trees at the same time and with the same determination.

Pop-pop-pop-pop-pop.

No cries, no sounds. And it was silent again to the left.

Maybe he'd backed them off. Caleb was wounded, maybe fatally. Camish? Who knew?

A dry branch snapped to the left, and Joe wheeled and fired off three wild shots. Another snapped to the right and he pointed and started to pull the trigger out of malevolence and fear when he quickly lowered the Glock and cursed himself.

"Not many shots left, by my count," Camish said clearly from the shadows. "Since your spare magazines were in those panniers, you may be out of luck."

The slide on the Glock hadn't kicked fully back, which meant he had at least one round left. He tried to count back, to figure out how many live rounds he still had, but he couldn't concentrate. At least two rounds left, he hoped. He'd need that many . . . His heartbeat pounded in his ears, making it hard to hear or think. He thought,

The brothers were formidable before. Now that at least one of them was wounded . . .

LURCHING FROM TREE TO TREE, blood flowing freely again from the wounds in his right thigh, Joe crashed through the timber back toward where he'd left Buddy.

The Grim Brothers couldn't be far behind.

He'd find his horse, apologize, and spur him on. Push the horse down the mountain. Eventually, he'd hit water. He'd follow the stream to something, or somebody.

Buddy weighed a thousand pounds and had nine gallons of blood. Joe weighed 175 pounds and had six quarts of blood. He didn't know how much he or his horse had left.

6

AN HOUR PAST SUNDOWN, BUDDY COLLAPSED onto his front knees with his back legs locked and his butt still in the air. Joe slid off, and as soon as his boots hit the ground he was reminded sharply of the pain in his own legs, because they couldn't hold him up. He reached out for a tree trunk to steady himself, missed, and fell in a heap next to his horse.

Buddy sighed and settled gently over to his side, and all four of his hooves windmilled for a moment before he relaxed and settled down to the occasional muscle twitch, as if he were bothered by flies.

Joe was heartbroken, but he did his best not to cry out. He crawled over to Buddy and stroked the neck of his gelding and cursed the Grim Brothers because they'd made it impossible for him to tend to his horse, to stop the bleeding. Now it was too late. And he knew that possibly, *possibly*, he could have saved his horse by leading him and not mounting up, that without Joe's weight and direction Buddy could have walked slowly and cautiously and maybe the blood would have stopped flowing out.

Buddy blinked at Joe and worked his mouth like a camel. He needed water, or thought he needed water. But it wouldn't help.

"I'm sorry," Joe said, reaching back for his weapon. "I'm sorry for being selfish."

Two rounds left. Buddy deserved to go quickly. Joe pressed the muzzle against Buddy's head, said a prayer, and started to squeeze the trigger.

He thought better of it and holstered the Glock. The shot could be heard and give away his location. Plus, he might need both bullets. So he unsheathed his Buck knife.

He said another prayer. Asked both God and Marybeth to forgive him for what he was about to do.

USING A STIFF BROKEN BRANCH with a Y in the top of it as a crutch, Joe continued down the mountain in the dark. A spring burbled out from a pile of flat rocks, and the water flowed freely and seemed to pick up volume. He kept the little creek to his right. The stream tinkled at times like wind chimes, he thought. It was a nice sound, and reassuring to know there was fresh water to drink, but he had to keep reminding himself not to get too close because the rush of water could drown out the sound of anyone coming up behind him. He followed the spring creek until it joined a larger stream, which he guessed was No Name Creek.

The moon was up and full, as were the bold white paintbrush strokes of the stars, and there was enough light on the forest floor to see because the pine needles soaked up the light and held it like powder-blue carpet. The stillness of the night, the constant pain of his legs, the awkward rhythm of his descent, and the soft backbeat percussion of his own breath was an all-encompassing world of its own and nearly made him forget about the danger he was in. It lulled him. He was jolted back into the present when a covey of blue grouse flushed from tall brush, and the heavy beating of their wings lifting off through the boughs nearly made his heart stop.

For the next hour, his life became as simple as it had ever been because it was reduced to absolute essentials: *Place one foot before the other, keep weight off that right leg, keep going, keep senses dialed to high.*

He thought about home, and his vision was vivid. It was as if his brain and soul had left the damaged container and floated up through the trees, raced three hundred and eighteen miles to Saddlestring, and entered his house by slipping under the front door, where he floated to the ceiling and hovered there.

SHERIDAN WAS AT the kitchen table filling out application forms for college. Lucy was in the living room watching television, painting her nails, and glancing down periodically to check for text messages on the new cell phone on her lap. Their dog Tube, a Lab-and-corgi cross, slept curled at her feet. Marybeth put dirty dinner dishes into the dishwasher and scraped what remained of the spaghetti into a plastic container for the refrigerator.

Sheridan was speaking to Marybeth, but Joe couldn't actually hear the words, even though he knew what they were. He felt privileged to eavesdrop.

But what if they accept me? It could happen, you know.

It's not that, honey. I know it's possible because of your grades. But unless financial aid comes with it, there's no way we can send you there. It's completely on the other side of the country!

I could handle it. I'm tougher than you think.

It's not that. You're the toughest kid I know. I'm not sure I'm tough enough to have you gone that far away. What's wrong with a community college at first? The first two years are the same no matter where you go.

Didn't you go East?

That was different. Your grandmother insisted and I needed to get away. I came back for grad school, though. That's where I met your dad.

So it was okay for you, but it isn't for me? Thanks for the ego boost, Mom. I really appreciate it.

It's not that. It's the money. We've had this discussion before. Your dad and I . . .

I might get a scholarship, you know.

And if you do, we can discuss it. But a scholarship doesn't cover travel, and housing, and all the other things.

I'll work. I can work. I work now. I'm a great waitress, you know.

I know.

LUCY IN THE FRONT ROOM *called out.*

I just hope you go somewhere cool so I can visit. Are there colleges in New York City?

Of course. Are you an idiot?

Mom, can I have her room when she leaves?

Please, girls. Not now.

AND JOE WISHED *he was there but he didn't know what he could add to the conversation.*

Where was April? he wondered. Why wasn't she in the room?

The woodstove was lit, the smell comforting. There was no better smell than wood smoke on a cold fall night. He'd still need to get wood for the winter once he got home. The two cords he'd cut the year before had to be just about gone by now. He needed to keep his family warm.

Joe was abruptly jerked back to the present. The smoke he'd smelled wasn't in his imagination.

IN THE DAYLIGHT, he might not have found it. If it weren't for the smoke that hung like a nighttime shadow in the trees, he would have limped right past. But he stopped and turned slowly to the right and slightly in back of him. There was a cut in the hillside on the other side of the little stream where another tiny spring creek fed into the flow. The cut went fifty yards back into the slope and doglegged to the right. The smoke came from where the dogleg ended.

Joe winced and nearly blacked out as he crossed the stream from rock to rock, unable to use his crutch to keep his weight off his injured legs. He paused on the other side and heard moaning and realized it was his own. He closed his eyes tightly and was entertained by fireworks on the inside of his eyelids. When he opened them, there was a cabin ahead. A faint yellow square of light seeped through a small curtained window from an inside lantern.

The cabin, he knew, shouldn't exist. There was no private land within this part of the Medicine Bow National Forest, just like there were no roads. He thought, *Hunters? Poachers? Forest rangers? Loggers?* Then: *Outlaws?*

The curtain on the single small window quivered as he made a fist to knock on the rough pine door. Whoever was inside knew he was there. And if they were armed?

Then a wild thought: What if the Grims lived here?

He collapsed as the door opened and fell inside. A woman said, "Oh my God, no . . ."

Then: "Who *are* you? Why did you come here? Oh no, you'll be the *death* of me."

FRIDAY, AUGUST 28

7

WHEN JOE AWOKE, HE WAS ON HIS BACK ON THE floor of the cabin in a nest of thick quilts. He reached up and rubbed the right side of his face, which was warm from the heat of an iron woodstove. A curl of steam rose from the snout of a kettle on the surface of the stove, and inside a small fire crackled.

He could remember things: vivid nightmares reliving the attack, throwing off the quilts as he fought off demons, awaking with a fever and drinking water and broth, rolling to his side to urinate into a plastic jar, the touch of her fingers on his bare thigh as she bandaged it, her frequent prognostications of doom.

The cabin was small, old, and close. He guessed it had been built in the 1950s or 1960s, to judge from the gray color of the logs and the age cracks in the pine plank ceiling. Although it was only one room inside and was packed with possessions in the corners and on the shelves, it seemed clean and organized. Red curtains were drawn over small framed windows on each wall.

She was sitting at a small table wearing thick trousers, heavy shoes, a too-large man's shirt, and a fleece vest. It was hard to tell her age. Her long brown hair fell to her shoulders and her forehead was hidden behind thick bangs.

Her clothes were so large and loose he couldn't discern her shape or weight. He couldn't even see the rise of her breasts. Her eyes were blue and cool and fixed on him. Her mouth was pursed with anticipation and concern.

"How long have I been out?" he asked.

"Eighteen hours," she said. "More or less."

He let that sink in. "So it's Friday night?"

Her face was blank. She shrugged, "I think that would be correct. I don't think in terms of days of the week anymore."

He nodded as if he understood and tried not to stare at her and unnerve her more than she already was. There was something pensive and off-putting about her, as if she would melt away if he asked too many questions.

Joe folded the quilt back. His pants were off, but she hadn't removed his boxers. He looked at the bandage on his right leg. It was tightly wrapped and neat. There were two small spots of dried blood, looking like the eyes of an owl, where the holes in his thigh were. His other leg was purple and green with bruises.

"Thank you," he said. "You saved my life."

She nodded quickly. "I know." She said it with a hint of regret. "I really don't want you here one minute past when you can leave. Do you understand me?"

Joe nodded. "Do you have a phone here? Any way I can make a call?"

"No, I don't have a phone."

"A radio?"

"No."

"Any way to communicate with the outside world?"

"This is my world," she said, twirling a finger to indicate the inside of her cabin. "What you see is my world. It's very small, and that's the way I like it. It's the way I want to keep it."

He took in the contents of the cabin but tried not to let his eyes linger too long on any one item. There were burlap sacks in one corner: beans, coffee, flour, sugar. Canned goods were stacked near the sacks. A five-gallon plastic container was elevated on a stout shelf with a gravity-feed water filter tube dripping pure water into a galvanized bucket. The drops of water from the tube into the bucket had punctuated his dreams.

Dented but clean pots and pans hung from hooks above the stove. Several dozen worn hardback books stood like soldiers on a shelf above a single bed covered with homemade quilts. Another shelf had small framed photos, but he couldn't see who was in the photographs. There was a heavy trunk under the bed and a battered armoire with brass closures next to the bed, which made up the north wall.

The kitchen counter, as such, was a four-poster butcher block near the corner of the stove. From his angle on the floor, he could see knife handles lined up neatly on the side of it.

"This is it," she said. "You're seeing it all. And me, that's all there is here."

"So you live alone?"

"Alone with my thoughts. I'm rarely lonely."

"Have you lived here very long?" he asked, wondering why he'd never heard of a lone woman in a cabin in the mountains.

"Long enough," she said. "Really, I don't want to get into a discussion with you."

Joe sat up painfully. His head swooned and it took a moment to make it stop spinning. He assessed his condition and said again, "You saved my life."

She nodded curtly.

"I'm a Wyoming game warden. My name is Joe Pickett. I was attacked by two brothers up on top of the mountain. I wouldn't be surprised if they were still after me."

She grimaced, but he could tell it wasn't news to her.

Of course, he thought, she'd seen his badge and credentials. Which made him quickly start patting the folds of the quilts.

"I had a weapon," he said.

"It's in a safe place."

"I need it back," he said. "And my wallet and pants . . ."

She put her hands palm-down on the table and fixed her eyes on something over Joe's head.

She said, "Your wedding band, I saw it when you fell into my cabin. It got to me, I'm afraid. Otherwise I might have pushed you back outside and locked the door and waited for them to show up. I'm amazed they aren't here by now."

He was taken aback by the casual way she said it.

Finally, he said, "I think I hit one of them. Maybe I hit them both."

Her eyes widened in fear and she raised a balled fist to her mouth.

"What?" he asked.

She said, "This isn't good."

"That I may have hit them?"

"That you may have wounded them."

Joe felt his scalp twitch. "So why did you help me?"

"I told you. The wedding band. I assume you have a wife."

"Yes."

"Do you love her?"

"With all my heart.'

"Kids?"

"Three daughters."

She pursed her mouth again and shook her head. "I'm a sucker for wedding bands. And it may turn out to be the death of me."

"That's why you helped me?"

A quick, regretful nod.

"Are those pictures of your family?" Joe asked, gesturing up to the shelf behind her bed.

Her eyes flared, and she rose to her feet so quickly her chair shot back. She strode across the floor and turned each frame facedown. When she was done, she returned to the chair and sat back down and glared at the spot on the wall above his head. She'd yet to make direct eye contact, which didn't bode well, he thought. Like she didn't want to empathize with him. Like she thought he might not be around much longer. Or . . .

"Are you blind?" Joe asked.

She did a quick snort and her mouth clenched. "Of course not."

"I'm sorry," he said quickly, "Since you wouldn't look at me, I thought . . ."

"I saw you earlier. I know what you look like. I know what you stand for. You work for the government."

"*State* government," Joe said.

"Still."

"It's different from the federal government."

"So you say."

"Really."

She swiveled in her chair and wrapped her arms around herself. "Hmmmph." As if it were final.

"I didn't mean to upset you," he said. "So you know them—the Grim Brothers."

"Of course."

There was something about her face, Joe thought. Something familiar about her. He knew he didn't know her personally and hadn't met her before. But he'd seen her face. Or a photo of her. He wished his head were more clear.

"Have we ever met?" he asked.

"I sincerely doubt it."

"Are you from around here originally?"

"No."

"So how long have you lived here?"

She was obviously annoyed by his questions. "I told you—long enough."

"How do you know the brothers?"

Her eyes finally settled on him. He felt it was a small victory.

"They come by. They bring me firewood and meat. They look out for me. All they ask from me is my silence and my loyalty. You're making me betray them."

Joe said nothing. How much further should he push? he wondered.

"Did they bring you elk meat recently? Like a week ago?"

"I don't recall," she said icily.

He said, "If you'll give me my gun, I'll leave."

"They're not all bad," she said, once again looking away. "They provide me protection. They understand why I'm here and they're quite sympathetic."

"Why *are* you—"

"They don't ask for much," she continued, cutting him off. "They could demand so much more, but they don't. They respect my need for privacy."

"Tell me your name," Joe said.

She hesitated, started to speak, then clamped her mouth shut.

"I told you mine," he said.

"Terri," she said finally. "My name is Terri Wade. But you don't know me, and it doesn't matter."

The name was unfamiliar to Joe. "Look," he said. "I know this cabin shouldn't be here. This is national forest, and there shouldn't be any private dwellings. The private land is all in the valleys. Aren't you worried forest rangers will find you and make you leave?"

She stared at a spot near Joe's head, as close as she would get to eye contact.

Terri said, "I told you—the brothers protect me. They wouldn't let that happen. This is *my* cabin. These are *my* things." As her voice rose, she gestured by jabbing her right index finger into the palm of her left hand on the word *my*. "No one has the right to make me leave if I don't want to leave."

Said Joe, "So why are you here?"

"I'm here to wait out the storm. I'll go back when it finally passes. And that's all I'm going to say about it."

"What storm?"

"That's all I'm going to say."

"About this storm . . ."

"You keep asking me questions. Look, I'm here to try to reassemble my life," she said. "I don't put my nose into anyone's business, and I expect the same from others. Including you," she said, again jabbing her finger into her palm. "*Especially* you."

"I understand," Joe said.

Wade suddenly sat up straight and lifted her chin to the ceiling. "Hear that?" she whispered.

Joe shook his head.

"There's someone on the roof," she said softly.

8

HE LOOKED UP WHEN HE HEARD THE SOUND. THE ceiling was constructed of adjacent rough-cut pine planks. The wood looked green and soft and showed evidence of recent repair work on the structure. As he stared, one of the planks bowed slightly inward, then another did the same about a foot away. Fine dust from between the planks floated down and sparked in the light of the lantern. There was someone heavy up there. A board creaked loudly enough that whoever was on the roof froze for a moment. More dust filtered down through the light.

Joe rocked forward, his leg screamed silently, and he reached out and touched her hand. He mouthed, "Where's my gun?"

Her eyes glistened with tears, and she shook her head as if she didn't want to be involved.

"My gun," he whispered.

Again, she bit her lip and shook her head, but when she did so she inadvertently revealed a tell with an unconscious glance toward the trunk under her bed.

He raised one finger to his mouth to urge her to stay quiet and scuttled across the rough floor and his makeshift bed to the trunk. He slid it out and unbuckled the hasps with his back to her so she couldn't protest. When he raised the lid, he found the Glock and his belt on top of folded piles of worn clothes. Despite the situation in front of him, Joe felt a twang of deep sadness for whatever situation had brought her here to live like this.

He worked the slide of his handgun and ejected a live cartridge. Another was in the magazine. So he still had two rounds. When he looked up at her she seemed distressed, as if she wished she had taken the bullets. He nodded to thank her for not taking them and let the magazine drop and loaded the loose cartridges again and jacked one of them into the chamber. Two shots, he thought. Just two shots.

They both jumped when there was deep voice outside the door. "Terri, do you have company in there?"

Joe recognized the voice as Camish. The smart one. Which meant Caleb was on the roof. Which also meant that he wasn't dead and certainly wasn't wounded badly enough to take him out of production. Unless, Joe wondered, there were somehow more of them. The idea of more than two Grim Brothers gave him a sudden spasm in his belly.

He caught Wade's eye, asked in a whisper, "Is it possible there's more than the two brothers?"

She shook her head. He thanked her with his eyes for the answer, and she looked away as if feeling guilty for a new betrayal.

"Terri?" Camish repeated. "I know you heard me." His tone wasn't unkind. In fact, Joe thought, it was resigned, like a father's voice when he had to reluctantly reprimand a child.

"Not now," Terri said loudly toward the door. "Leave me alone."

"Oh, Terri, it doesn't work like that. We know he's in there." Again the sad, reprimanding tone.

"Please," she said. "Come back later. Come back tomorrow."

"You mean after he's gone?" Camish asked, and Joe detected a slight chuckle. "You want us to come back when he's gone? That's a crazy notion, Terri. He really hurt my brother. And you know the situation. We can't let him go. You *know* that."

"I don't want any violence," Terri said toward the door. "I told you before I don't want violence. You promised. You *promised* me."

Camish said, "Yes, we did. We promised you. And there's no need for any violence at all. We just want that government man inside your place."

Joe thought, *Government man?*

Then he looked at her and saw nothing other than torment. Her hands were knotted into white-knuckled fists and her shoulders were bunched and her mouth was pursed into a shape that reminded him of a dried red rose. She was in agony, and it was because of him. He felt sorry for her, grateful she'd displayed kindness and humanity toward him, and he wanted to save her.

He wanted to save himself as well.

Camish said, "Then we have no choice, do we?"

She asked, "No choice to do what?"

Joe thought, *They're going to burn us out.*

Then Camish said, "Let the fumigation begin!"

Fumigation?

Suddenly, the cabin filled with acrid, horrible steam. Joe looked at the door at first for the origin, then realized it was coming from the wood stove. Terri sat back in her chair and buried her face in a napkin to try to avoid the foul-smelling steam that reeked of meat and animal fat and sulfur.

Joe recognized the odor from his youth, shook his

head, and whispered, "Caleb is urinating down the chimney pipe."

She looked at him with undisguised alarm.

He motioned for her to get down on the floor by motioning with his open hand.

"I can't . . ." she said, glancing toward the closed door and Camish outside.

"Get down," Joe hissed. "I don't want you hurt."

He didn't want to threaten her with the gun to make her respond. Not after what she'd done for him. But she seemed frozen, conflicted. He said, "GET DOWN."

Too loudly, he thought. Caleb no doubt heard him on the roof. Which resulted in a strong stream coursing down the red-hot chimney, a giggle from Camish outside, and a thick plume of horrible steam inside the cabin.

Joe angrily ignored it all and thought of Blue Roanie and Buddy and noted two particular ceiling planks bending downward from Caleb's boots and visualized him up there, legs spread on either side of the chimney, aiming down the hot pipe, smiling at his brother outside and letting loose.

Joe raised the weapon, calculated the height and stance of his target on the roof, acknowledged that the last time he'd shouted a warning it had resulted in an attack on *him*, aimed the muzzle at what he guessed would be Caleb's chest, and squeezed the trigger. . . .

The .40 Glock barked, but not where he'd aimed, because Wade screamed "No violence!" and launched up at him from the floor and hit him clumsily with her shoulder in his wounded thigh. The impact threw him back and the slug thudded into a log chest-high inside the cabin.

It was as if her action had somehow downshifted the pace of the confrontation into slow motion, as if time had slowed down for Joe Pickett. Not that it aided him necessarily, but he suddenly felt like the almost incapacitating terror of the situation had been stripped away as well as the fog of uncertainty, and he could see things clearly as they happened, even if he could do nothing to prevent them.

Joe fell back into the woodstove from the tackle and the back of his thighs were singed on contact with the woodstove and the pain was startling. He fell forward to his knees with both hands still around his gun, fully cognizant he had a single bullet left for the Grim Brothers and, God help him, for Terri Wade if she came at him again. He could smell the acrid odor of burnt hair from the back of his legs, but he was pretty sure the burns were superficial.

He raised his weapon and peered down the length of it toward Wade's forehead. She was crying, and tears streamed down her cheeks and pooled under her chin. Her mouth sagged open as she cried and he thought it was horrible, that he'd rarely seen a human in so much pain before, and he thought he'd be damned if he felt it necessary to hurt her to save himself. And he lowered the gun and wondered what Marybeth would counsel.

Camish shouted: "Terri, get down!"

She dropped to her knees with her eyes locked in sympathy with Joe, then stretched out on the floor and covered her head with her hands.

Joe looked up.

The thick cabin door rocked with the force of a shotgun blast. A softball-sized hole at eye level was suddenly there, as was gun smoke inside the cabin and half-inch splinters of wood on every flat surface. Joe flung himself backward, away from Terri Wade, away from the stove. He remembered the small curtained window over her bed in the back of the cabin. He wondered if the window was wide enough for his shoulders to fit through since there was no back door. With Caleb on the roof and Camish in front of the cabin, it was his only escape route. Unless, of course, there was someone else with them.

Another blast punched a second hole through the front door. Wade screamed, begging them to stop, telling them they could come in and get the government man. The pellet load dislodged the shelf in the back of the cabin and the picture frames were scattered across the floor. One of them settled between Joe's hands and he caught a glimpse of it. The photo was of a family—not including Terri Wade—enjoying themselves on a beach. It was obviously staged and generic-looking. The price of the frame—$9.99—was printed within the photo. He didn't have time to figure out why she'd never put her own choice of picture in the frame, but left it as-is from the store where she'd purchased it.

And Joe thought, once again, *Government man?* He didn't like to be thought of that way. He wasn't a government man—he was a *wildlife* man.

The front door blew open. Caleb had come off the roof and broken it in with his shoulder. The hinges burst before the knob and dead bolt, which made Wade say, "Oh!"

And Caleb stood in the threshold for a moment, eyes wide and mean, a blood-sodden bandage around the lower part of his face, and Joe realized he'd clipped the end of Caleb's chin off the day before and he thought, *Good for me!*

Except he hadn't finished the job, which put him in a much worse situation now.

Joe raised his Glock, centered the front and back sight on Caleb's chest, and fired.

Caleb winced and took a step back, but didn't drop.

He held the .308 at parade rest and seemed momentarily incapable of raising it and aiming at Joe. Joe thought, *Why didn't he go down?*

Camish blew through the front door, and when Terri Wade rose and threw herself at him, he greeted her with a stiff-arm that quickly got her out of the line of fire without flinging her to the floor.

Joe reared back and pitched his weapon through the glass of the back window and followed it.

Camish yelled, "Hey, stop!" and raised his shotgun.

Joe glanced over his shoulder as he stepped on the bed and saw the O of the muzzle and steeled himself for the force of a shotgun blast in his back. A double-aught shell contained nine lead pellets over a third of an inch in diameter. At this range, it would be over quickly: a full load of it could practically cut him in half. But again, Terri Wade rammed Camish the way she'd thrown herself at him. The shotgun exploded, but the load smashed into the wall near Joe's left shoulder.

"Damn you, Terri," Camish yelled as he shoved her aside again. He could have clubbed her with the butt of the shotgun and Joe expected it, but he didn't.

Joe covered his face with his arms and dived toward the broken window. The remaining glass gave way and he was outside, his arms and neck wrapped in the curtain, rolling in pine needles. He tossed the curtain aside, and as he did he thought he saw the shadow of a figure near the corner of the cabin. The figure was tall and slight, and he instinctively dropped to a shooter's stance and rose to a knee. Although he didn't have his pistol, he acted as if he did and thrust both hands forward, his left cupping his right, yelled, "*Freeze!*" and the figure ducked silently around the corner out of view to avoid being harmed. He scrambled to his feet and his right boot tip accidentally thudded against something heavy on the ground—his empty gun. He recovered it and staggered downhill toward the creek he'd followed earlier. Behind him, he heard Camish rack the pump again and yell for Joe to stop. There was a high-pierced wail from Caleb in the background, as if he'd just realized he'd been shot again.

Joe figured Camish must be at the cabin window because he could hear glass breaking, and that he was probably using the barrel to knock down the remaining shards of glass so he could aim unimpeded. Joe stepped behind a tall pine tree as the blast stripped the bark off the other side of the trunk. The tree shook from the impact and sent a cascade of pine needles to the forest floor.

Before Camish could rack in another shell, Joe flung himself away, trying to keep the tree between the cabin and himself, trying to get his legs to respond. Electric bolts of pain shot up into his groin from the wounds. Each tree and bush he passed provided more cover and protection, and he hoped he could vanish into the darkness before Camish could aim well and fire again. His shotgun with the double-aught buckshot was an extremely lethal short-range weapon, but it lost its punch with every step Joe made into the woods. The pattern of shot would widen as the velocity of the pellets dispersed.

There was another shot, and double-aught pellets smacked trees and ripped through brush on both sides of him. He felt two sudden hot spots—one in his right shoulder and another that burned under the scalp near his right ear. He tripped and pitched forward, falling hard.

On the ground, he distinctly heard Camish say, "Got him." And a female voice say, "Are you sure?"

Joe didn't pause to assess the new wounds, and he didn't stand up in case Camish could still see him. Instead, he crawled through the dirt on his hands and knees, putting as much distance as possible between himself and his attacker, plunging himself deeper into darkness. After ten minutes of crawling, he used a fallen tree to steady himself and rise to his feet. As he ran, he swiped at the burn in his scalp and felt hot blood on his fingertips. His shoulder was numb except for what he imagined as a single burning ember buried deep into the muscle.

He was splashing through the creek before he realized it was there. The icy water shocked him but felt good at the same time. There was shouting back at the cabin, and another inhuman wail.

Joe paused and tried to catch his breath. He listened for the sound of footfalls but didn't hear them. Yet. Squatting on his haunches, he cupped his hands and filled them with icy water, which he drank and used to douse his neck wound.

Terri Wade had saved his life twice, yet he'd left her back there with them. He rose and turned in the creek, looking back in the direction of the cabin. What would they do to her? Could he possibly stop it?

He hoped they'd spare her. After all, it was him they were after and Camish seemed to have chosen not to hurt her when he easily could have. But Camish was distracted at the time and Caleb was injured. Now that Joe was gone and they had her to themselves?

Joe had an empty weapon and again he was losing blood. His strength was fueled by pure adrenaline and anger and nothing more. But he couldn't just leave her. Could he?

He waited fifteen minutes hidden in streamside buckbrush, absently fingering the shotgun pellet that was lodged under his scalp. They weren't coming. Which meant they'd stayed in the cabin with her. Doing what?

Joe stood uneasily. His only advantage was they no doubt thought he was down for good after the shotgun blast. They wouldn't expect him to come back from the dead.

It puzzled him that they hadn't pursued him or searched the brush for his body to administer a kill shot, if necessary. The brothers had pursued him for miles over rough terrain to find him at the cabin. Why would they simply assume he was dead? And if they did, why would they leave a body to be found?

As he trudged back up the mountainside toward the cabin, he put his questions aside and made a plan.

LIKE TWO NIGHTS BEFORE, he smelled wood smoke before he could find the cabin. The smoke was strong and hung in the trees. Which meant they were still there. Joe was puzzled as to the reason, unless Caleb had finally collapsed and Camish was tending to him. That Caleb had taken a .40 round and barely reacted still bothered Joe.

He wanted to believe Terri Wade was still alive and unhurt.

He kept his eyes open wide. He'd adjusted to the darkness and could see much better than when he'd run. If Camish or Caleb were searching for his body where Camish had fired and seen him go down, Joe was confident he'd see them first. His shoulder was numb from the pellets and his right arm hung uselessly at his side.

His plan, such as it was, depended entirely on surprise. He'd quickly enter the open front door and wrench his .308 from Caleb and shoot Camish first. Then Caleb. And keep Terri Wade at bay so she couldn't stop the carnage.

It almost didn't register that the forest was getting lighter until he realized why: the cabin was burning.

"No," he said aloud, and began to lope through the trees. His head swooned from the pain.

He stopped at the edge of the clearing. Tongues of flame licked out through the windows and illuminated the dark wall of trees that hid the cabin. The fire crackled angrily, and there were soft *POOM* sounds of the canned food exploding inside.

Had they left her to burn to death?

Rather than rush the cabin, he skirted it in the tree line until he could see the front. Fire filled the open front door. If she was in there, he'd have to run through it. He tried to see inside, tried to get a glimpse of her on the floor or the bed.

A spout of orange flame shot out of the roof, and the fire started to consume the wooden shingles where Caleb had stood.

Joe took a deep breath and prepared to run toward the cabin when he suddenly froze to his spot. He'd seen something in his peripheral vision, three faces like faint orange moons, hanging low in the dark trees to his left.

He stayed behind a tree trunk and turned away from the bright flames, trying to make his eyes adjust again. Trying to find what he thought he'd seen in the darkness.

Then he saw them: Caleb, Camish, and Terri Wade a hundred feet away. Watching the cabin burn. Their disembodied faces reflected the fire like orange orbs. Tears streamed down Wade's face and glistened in the firelight. She looked upset but unhurt. Most disturbingly, she appeared to be with them willingly, standing by their side. Caleb was stoic, likely in shock from his bullet wound. Camish looked demonic, his eyes reflecting the fire. They obviously hadn't seen him, probably because they didn't expect to.

Wade turned away into the darkness, dousing her face.

Then a moment later, to Caleb's left, a fourth face appeared. She must have been looking away before, he thought, toward where they were headed as opposed to where they'd left. The sight jarred him and he waited for another look, which didn't come. All had turned and were walking away and could no longer be seen.

He closed his eyes tightly, trying to visualize who he'd glimpsed.

Thinking: *No. You've seen her face so many times the past two years on fliers put up by her parents. Her face has been burned into your subconscious. You're seeing things. It couldn't have been* her.

LATER, BEHIND HIM, he heard the cabin collapse in on itself with the rough crackling of timber.

The stream to his left, trees and boulders to his right, the sky filled with pulsing stars and a moon bright enough to see by, the injured game warden started walking slowly out of the Sierra Madre.

The stream would lead somewhere; a ranch house, a road, a natural-gas field serviced by energy workers.

He had no answers, only questions.

He hoped his questions could somehow keep him occupied and alive long enough to get off the mountain.

SATURDAY, AUGUST 29

9

NATE ROMANOWSKI TRAMPED UP THE SWITCH-
back canyon trail with a fifteen-pound mature bald eagle
perched on a thick welder's glove. As he hiked, the eagle
maintained its balance by clamping its talons on the glove
and shifting its weight with subtle extensions of its seven-
foot wingspan, often hitting Nate in the face.

"Stop that," he said, flinching.

The bird ignored him.

A satellite phone hung from a leather strap around
Nate's neck, and his Freedom Arms .454 Casull, the second most powerful handgun in the world, was in a shoulder holster beneath his left armpit. It was a warm
late-summer day, in the high eighties, and as he approached the rim of the canyon, it got warmer and a
slight breeze blew hot and dry.

Exactly two cotton-candy cumulus clouds paraded
across an endless light blue palette of sky that opened up
as he rose out of Hole in the Wall Canyon, where he lived
in a cave once occupied by infamous Old West outlaws.
He'd chosen the location a year and a half before, when
the FBI office in Cheyenne had declared him a high-
profile felon and a first-priority suspect in crimes he'd
committed and some he hadn't. Hole in the Wall was

perfect for him to hide out in due to its remote location on private land in north-central Wyoming and the fact that no one could descend into it unseen. He'd booby-trapped the trail with snares and wires tied to alarms and explosives, which he'd carefully stepped over on the way up, and only three people knew of his existence: his love Alisha Whiteplume, his friend Joe Pickett, and Sheridan Pickett, his apprentice in falconry.

Nate was a master falconer: tall, lean, with broad shoulders, long legs, and a footlong blond ponytail that hung down his back. He had a hawk nose and icy blue eyes, and he went weeks without talking except to himself and his birds of prey. In a clapboard mews he'd constructed of weathered barn wood he'd raided from outlaw cabins and corrals, he boarded a redtail hawk, a prairie, a massive gyrfalcon, a wicked little merlin, and his prized peregrine that would pursue and kill anything that flew or ran. Plus the bald eagle he carried. The eagle had been shot with an arrow the year before and was seriously damaged and ineffectual. Joe Pickett had delivered the wounded eagle to him, hoping Nate could rehabilitate it. So far, despite hundreds of hours of care, the eagle was still dependent on him and useless for any purpose other than show-horsery. It had no desire to fly, to hunt, or to become independent and eagle-like. He was beginning to seriously dislike the bird and suspected it was an incorrigible head case.

If it weren't for the fact that Sheridan was his apprentice and Joe had once gone to the mat for him and earned his undying loyalty and his vow of protection for the Pickett Family, Nate would have long before snapped the neck of the national symbol and buried her at the bottom of the canyon. Some creatures, he'd decided years before when he was overseas with Special Forces, were better off dead. That included many, many human beings. This eagle, who would no longer fly or hunt, was on borrowed time. The predator had inadvertently become prey.

"You need to be an eagle," he said to her as he climbed.

Again, as always, she ignored him and righted herself by spreading her wings and hitting him in the face.

He paused at the rim of the canyon. The terrain in front of him was flat and without features. He could see for miles all the way to the foothills of the Bighorn Mountains and the one two-track road that led to Hole in the Wall. The late-summer grass was yellow like straw, interspersed with sagebrush clawing up toward the sky. There were no vehicles on the road or parked on the side of it.

Behind him, the other rim of the deep canyon was less than a quarter mile away. It was clear as well.

He emerged from the canyon and sat down in the grass, sweating from his exertion from the climb out. He put the bald eagle next to him and let her step off of his gloved hand where she stood next to him, inert and majestic. No bird, he thought, looked better on principle than a bald eagle. No bird was more complicated, either, with its seven thousand feathers perfectly engineered to withstand extreme weather and conditions. But if the eagle wouldn't fly or hunt or protect herself, what could he do?

THERE WAS A SINGLE MESSAGE on his satellite phone from Marybeth Pickett and it was less than an hour old. He dialed her cell phone number in Saddlestring.

"Nate?" she answered.

"You sound agitated. Is everything all right?"

A short pause. Then: "You know I've never called you before."

"No, you haven't."

"I'm worried about Joe. I think something's happened to him."

"Down in Baggs? What's wrong?"

"I don't know. He went on a horseback patrol Monday and I haven't heard from him in four days. He left a message saying everything was okay Tuesday night, and then nothing. I haven't heard from him since."

Nate said, "Maybe his phone went out or something. You know things like that happen."

"Yes, I know. But I just have a feeling something's terribly wrong. I can't shake it. I'm really worried about him. We've been married a long time and sometimes you just know things. I can't explain it."

Nate said, "Where did you hear from him last?"

"Some lake in the Sierra Madre. He left a message. It's killing me I didn't talk to him personally. I keep listening to that message over and over again. He says everything's fine, but I get a bad vibe. Like he didn't even know things were going to go bad for him. He's got Buddy and Blue Roanie with him, but I've got a really bad feeling."

Nate scrunched his face although he knew she couldn't see it. This was unusual. She was a tough, attractive woman, pragmatic and not prone to panic. He had a soft spot for her.

He said, "Have you talked to anyone else?"

"Everyone I can think of. I called Game and Fish dispatch in Cheyenne and they hadn't heard from him either. I talked to the director of the agency, and he didn't even know Joe was gone. And I left a message for Governor Rulon, who is at some national conference in Washington, I guess."

"You did?"

"I'm desperate," she said. "He expects Joe to be on call for him whenever *he* needs something. I told him he needs to be on call for *us*."

"So Joe's by himself as far as you know?"

"Yes, damn it. He told me before he went there was some kind of incident down there. Some hunters said they shot an elk and somebody butchered it before they could tag it. He was going up into the mountains to find whoever might have done it."

"No backup?" Nate said.

Marybeth groaned. "He never has backup. That's the way game wardens work, Nate. It drives me crazy."

"What else have you done?"

"I called the sheriff down in Baggs. He didn't help my state of mind, because he said there were all sorts of rumors about weird things happening in the mountains down there. He said ranchers had pulled their cattle from leases in the mountains because they thought there was something strange going on. And there'd been break-ins at cabins and trailheads."

"The Sierra Madre," Nate said. "Isn't that where that runner vanished a while back?"

"Yes!"

"So the sheriff didn't give you any help?"

"It's not that he refused," she said. "He just wasn't sure what to do. Joe didn't exactly file a flight plan, which sounds like Joe. The sheriff called me today and said he'd talked to some ranch hand who'd shuttled Joe's pickup and horse trailer around the mountains. The truck is sitting there, I guess. But Joe hasn't shown up. Nobody knows where he is."

Nate said, "Fly, damn you. Kill something."

"What?"

"I was talking to a bird. Never mind." Then: "When is he supposed to be down?"

"Today. This morning. He said before he left that he'd call as soon as he got to his truck."

Nate said, "I don't want you to take this the wrong way, but shouldn't you give him the chance to call before you conclude something's wrong? Maybe his phone went bad up in the mountains and he just hasn't been able to reach you."

Silence.

Nate said, "Marybeth, are you there?"

She said, "Yes. Are you suggesting I'm hysterical? That I'd call you with no good reason?"

He thought about it. "No."

"I told you, I have a bad feeling. Something's happened."

"Okay," he said. "Call me again if you hear anything at all."

"I will. And there's something else. I know the situation you're in. I'd never compromise you unless I thought we needed help. You know that, don't you?"

"Yes."

"I've got to go now."

He punched Disconnect.

ALISHA WHITEPLUME, the reason he'd climbed out of the canyon, arrived within the hour, as planned. He saw her pickup a mile away through heat waves. He stood and walked down the two-track to meet her.

The truck stopped, and she leaped out. She was luminescent, he thought. Long dark hair with highlights that shined blue in the sun, smooth cappuccino complexion, sparkling dark eyes, rosebud mouth. She wore a starched white sleeveless shirt, tight Lady Wranglers, Ariat lace-up boots, her prized Idaho Falls Rodeo barrel-racing championship buckle. God, he loved her.

Alisha worked as a teacher on the Wind River Indian Reservation near Saddlestring. She'd traded her corporate career to come home.

She wrapped her arms around his neck and kissed him. He kissed her back.

He said, "Where's Megan Yellowcalf?"

"With my mom," she said. Her two-year-old daughter was adopted from Alisha's best friend, who'd died. "We've got the entire weekend before school starts."

Nate said, "There's been a development."

She stepped back, eyeing him.

"We need to go to Saddlestring. And I may need to be gone."

"Joe?" she said.

"Yes."

"Not Marybeth?"

"Her, too. Joe may be in trouble."

"Your thing," she said.

"My thing."

She put her hands on her hips and stepped back. "I'll never understand this hold he has over you."

Nate shrugged.

She noted the eagle that waddled toward Nate and stood a foot behind him. "What about the bird?" she asked.

"It's not going anywhere," he said.

"Kind of like our relationship." She laughed. "What's wrong with him?"

"Her," he corrected. "She won't fly. Her spirit is broken. I can't get into her head and figure out what it is."

"Maybe," she said, "you have trouble with the female mind."

Nate said, "Maybe."

10

"MARYBETH-SHERIDAN-LUCY-APRIL, MARYBETH-
Sheridan-Lucy-April, Marybeth-Sheridan-Lucy-April, Marybeth-Sheridan-Lucy-April . . ." Joe muttered in a kind of
hypnotic cadence as he walked, saying the names over
and over again like a mantra, saying the names with his
breath when his voice seemed too loud, "Marybeth-
Sheridan-Lucy-April, Marybeth-Sheridan-Lucy-April . . ."

The mantra gave him comfort and strength and a reason to keep going.

It was approaching dusk. He'd walked through the
night and for the entire day, scared to stop and rest for
more than a few minutes. Although it seemed vague and
faraway now, he recalled dropping to his knees the night
before alongside the creek to drink. After filling his belly
with icy cold mountain water that tasted of pine needles,
he'd rolled to his side and closed his eyes, thinking he
could take a short nap, that he needed some sleep. But as
his eyes closed—oh, it felt so good to close his eyes—a
voice deep inside his brain shouted an alarm, saying, *If
you close your eyes, you'll never open them again in this
world.* The voice was loud enough to resonate and stir
him, and he'd painfully rolled over to his knees, gasped at
the pain in his thigh, shoulder, and scalp, and rose again

to his feet. He hadn't stopped since because he'd become convinced that to stop was to die.

As he walked and chanted, he'd turn periodically, searching behind him for followers who weren't there or so stealthy he couldn't see them. He doubted he'd been followed because the Grim Brothers didn't know he'd survived the shotgun blast. Still, though, he couldn't be certain.

Tube, Joe's dog, bounded through the buckbrush on the other side of the creek, just out of clear view. Tube was a strange dog, a Lab-corgi mix, with the head and stout body of a bird dog and the stunted drumstick legs of a corgi. That it was able to move so fluidly through the shadows of the brush seemed curious to Joe, and he was getting angry that his dog wouldn't come closer even when he called to him. More curious was that Tube seemed to have picked up several friends, maybe half a dozen other dogs, and they paralleled Joe's advance down the mountain but kept out of plain sight.

"Tube, darn you," Joe shouted, his voice cracking. "Get over here."

But Tube stayed with his friends in the shadows. Joe could hear them panting from time to time, as well as an occasional growl, snarl, or yip as one of them warned off another for some transgression. The dogs had been with him for at least an hour, maybe more. Joe vowed to sell Tube when he could find someone who wanted to buy an odd-looking dog who wouldn't behave.

He tried not to pay attention to his injuries or to dwell on them. Despite his intention, he found his wounds strangely fascinating as well as alarming. He had no idea how much blood he'd lost, but he knew it was too much. He was light-headed and weak. His body was broken yet still functional, as if his muscles had a will of their own, and his skin was perforated in four places. That he might be able to heal from his wounds seemed like a miracle of the highest order. In the meantime, he kept his eyes on the game trail ahead of him and repeated his mantra.

Because the creek was the only source of fresh water in the area, animals congregated near it. That morning, he'd spooked a huge four-point mule deer buck who'd been drinking in the creek. At mid-morning, a beaver slapped its tail on the surface of a pond in warning and scared him nearly to death. The beaver dived with a *ploop* sound, leaving ringlets on the surface of the pond he'd created by damming the stream. Joe had seen badgers, porcupines, rabbits, and a flock of mallards that, for a while, kept rising and flying a few hundred feet ahead of him to land again and again. They seemed put out that Joe kept coming. He felt sorry for ducks in Wyoming since there was so little water to be had.

But he was getting pretty fed up with that pack of dogs. Especially Tube.

AS HE TRUDGED AND CHANTED in a pain-dulled daze, he thought of the legend of Hugh Glass for inspiration.

Hugh Glass was a mountain man in these same Rocky Mountains who, in 1823, was looking for berries to eat when he encountered a grizzly bear. The bear mauled Glass almost beyond recognition, chewing most of Glass's scalp and face off, creating massive wounds all over him with its teeth and three-inch claws, including an exposed rib cage, and leaving him for dead. So did Glass's companions, who, after five days of waiting in the middle of hostile Arikara Indian country for the comatose man to finally die, took his rifle and knife and left him.

But Hugh Glass didn't die. And when he woke up and

realized he'd been abandoned without food, water, or weapons, he had the determination to roll over and start to *crawl* south toward Fort Kiowa, nearly two hundred miles away. What kept him going was his will to live and his fantasies of bloody revenge on the men who'd left him to perish.

He couldn't walk for weeks, and he lived off roots, grubs, and berries he found along the way. He managed to set his broken leg, and when his open wounds began to rot from gangrene, he opened a decomposing downed log and scooped the maggots he found inside into his wound to eat away the infected flesh.

The berries and roots kept him going until he happened on a freshly killed buffalo calf and the wolves who took it down. Using a heavy stick to scare the wolves away, he fell upon the calf and ate raw meat by the handfuls for days until the carcass began to purple and rot. But the meat strengthened him, his broken bones knitted, and he was finally able to stand. And he began his six-month trek to Fort Kiowa. . . .

Compared to what Hugh Glass had gone through, Joe thought, this was a happy little picnic in the woods.

"Marybeth-Sheridan-Lucy-April, Marybeth-Sheridan-Lucy-April, Marybeth-Sheridan-Lucy-April . . ."

"WOLVES," JOE SAID ALOUD, startled by the realization that had come to him because of his recounting of the Hugh Glass story. "Those are *wolves* following me."

Not Tube. Not dogs. Not his fevered imagination. *Wolves.* Six to eight of them, keeping just out of his vision on the other side of the creek but staying abreast of him.

But there weren't supposed to be wolves in the Sierra Madre. The wolf packs were in the northwest section of

the state, centered around Yellowstone where, years before, the federal government had introduced Canadian
gray wolves into a region they may not have ever roamed.
Joe had agreed with the idea initially, even though it was
a controversial program much loved by most observers
but despised by ranchers and hunters. The unintended
consequences, though, were significant. Although the
wolves were supposed to cull the expanding elk herds,
domestic cattle were killed and moose numbers had been
decimated. The wolf population had exploded into Montana, Idaho, and Wyoming, although measures were in
place—supposedly—to keep the numbers down and the
wolf packs localized. Sure, there had been reports of
wolves in the area in the past and even alleged sightings
south into Colorado. But the federal wildlife agencies dis-
counted the reports, insisting that citizens had seen coyotes, or large domestic dogs gone feral.

In a break in the buckbrush, he saw two of them. They
saw him as well and stopped as if frozen in mid-stride. A
large silver-and-white wolf, shadowed by a bigger one
that was jet black. The silver wolf weighed maybe eighty
pounds, and the black wolf was easily a hundred and
twenty. Their round piercing amoral eyes cut holes
through him.

"Go away," he croaked, raising his left arm and waving it.

The sound startled them, and they flinched. The silver
wolf backpedaled, turned on her haunches, and vanished
into the brush. But the black wolf stood his ground, lowered his head, and arched his shoulders. For a terrifying
moment, Joe braced for an attack.

"Get out of here!" he bellowed, and flung a pair of
handcuffs from his belt. The cuffs arced through the air
and landed with a jangle five feet in front of the wolf, and

the animal turned with a lazy shrug and followed the silver wolf back into the shadows.

Joe stood for a moment, breathing hard, trying to hear where they'd gone, if anywhere. It was extremely rare for a wolf to attack a human in the wild. There were very few instances of its happening. But they'd certainly shadowed him for a mile or so, and he thought how appealing he must look to them: obviously wounded, caked with dried and fresh blood, without a serious weapon. He could imagine one of them darting across the creek and hamstringing him like wolves hamstrung elk and moose. Once their prey was incapacitated, the rest of the pack could move in.

He found a stout branch that was still heavy and green, that looked like it had been blasted from a tree by a lightning strike. The branch was nearly three feet long, bulbous on the butt end, and tapered like a baseball bat. His right shoulder was worthless, but he took a few practice swings with his left and the branch whistled cleanly through the air. He smacked the trunk of a pine tree with a reassuring *thunk*, which sent a shower of pine needles to the forest floor.

"Hear that?" he shouted into the air, hoping the wolves were listening. "That'll be your head if you try to take a bite out of me!"

He could neither see nor hear where the wolves had gone, but despite his shouts and his club he didn't think they'd gone far.

"Wolves this far south," he thought, as he continued down the creek. "Wait until they hear about *this* in Cheyenne."

Farther down the creek, Joe stumbled on a massive five-point elk antler that had been shed earlier that summer. He tossed the branch aside and picked up the antler, turning it and admiring the thick beam. One tine was sixteen inches long and an inch thick at the base. Forked tines on the end were six inches each and sharp as spear points. The antler was heavy but a hell of a weapon, he thought. Much better than a club.

If the wolves attacked he could really do some damage, he thought.

HIS MANTRA EVOLVED from a country-and-western rhythm into reggae and then into blues. Joe kept thinking about what had happened, what he'd seen, what he didn't know.

Why was Terri Wade in an isolated cabin? What was her relationship with the Grim Brothers? What was with the store-bought picture frames containing promotional shots? And could that have possibly been who he thought it was with them? The girl? He shook his head, not able to wrap his mind around the prospect. Again, he thought he'd seen her visage too many times on fliers and in the newspapers. He'd imagined her, he was sure. But there had been four faces. That, he was convinced of.

And what about the brothers themselves? Why were they up there and what were they doing? What caused them to hide in one of the roughest and most remote sections of the least populated state in the union?

IT WAS ALMOST IMPERCEPTIBLE how the terrain changed, how cottonwoods took over from the pine trees, how bunches of cheater grass replaced the pine needle floor. Without actually realizing it, Joe knew he'd descended from the mountains into a valley. He veered right away from the creek and the trees, and as the sun set he was on the edge of a hay meadow. Instead of the smell of pine and the dank vegetation of the creek, he smelled the sweet smell of cut hay and thought he caught a whiff of gasoline.

Joe turned and looked behind him. The mountains went up and back, peak after peak, until the range melded with the sky countless miles away. He was struck by how big the mountains were, how hulking, imposing, and still. And he was awed by the fact that he'd actually walked out of them.

At the edge of the timber, in the shadows, he saw the lone black wolf. He stood broadside, big and dark, his eyes seeing Joe much more clearly than Joe could see him. The wolf stood as if he were prevented from coming any closer, as if he'd hit his boundary line and could proceed no farther.

Joe nodded toward the wolf, whom he respected for tenacity, and said, "See you later."

AS HE BROKE OVER A RISE, the hay meadow was spread out before him as far as he could see. Cut hay, smelling even sharper now, lay thick in long straight channels. After days of mountain randomness, he was impressed by the symmetry of the rows.

A half mile away, a green John Deere hay baler crawled across the field, its motor humming and grunting as it turned rows of cut hay into fifty-pound bales that it left behind like tractor scat. It was dark enough the rancher had his headlights on, and the twin pools of yellow made the hay look golden and the cut field an electric green carpet.

As Joe walked toward the baler with the antler in his hand, something in his brain released and his wounds exploded in sudden pain. It was as if now that his rescue was at hand, the mental dam holding everything back for three days suddenly burst from the strain.

His legs gave way and he fell to his knees and pitched forward into the cut hay.

The mantra slowed to a dirge. *"Marybeth-Sheridan-Lucy-April, Marybeth-Sheridan-Lucy-April, Marybeth-Sheridan-Lucy-April . . ."*

IN THE DARK, what seemed like hours later, he heard a boy say, "Hey, Dad, look over here. It's that damned game warden everyone's looking for."

PART TWO

RELOADING WITHOUT BULLETS

He is mad past recovery, but yet he has lucid intervals.

—MIGUEL DE CERVANTES, *Don Quixote*

TUESDAY, SEPTEMBER 1

11

ON THE THIRD DAY OF HIS STAY IN THE BILLINGS hospital, after he'd been moved out of the intensive care unit, Joe awoke to find a tall, thin man in ill-fitting clothes—white dress shirt, open collar, loose tie, overlarge sports jacket—hovering near the foot of his bed. The man had world-weary brown eyes and a thin neck rising like a cornstalk out of the gaping collar of his shirt. His hair was light brown, peppered with silver. A pair of smudged reading glasses hung from a cord around his neck. Joe got the immediate impression the man was or had been in law enforcement. His aura of legal bureaucracy was palpable. He said, "Joe Pickett? I'm Bobby Mc-Cue, DCI."

Wyoming Department of Criminal Investigation.

McCue reached into his jacket with long spidery fingers and came out with a shiny black wallet, which he flipped open to reveal a badge. Just as quickly, and before Joe could focus on the shield or credential card, he snapped it shut and slid it back inside his coat.

"I read the statement you gave the sheriff down in Carbon County," McCue said. "I was hoping I could ask you a few more questions just to clarify some things. We're trying to fill in some of the gaps."

"What gaps?" Joe raised his eyebrows, which elicited a sharp pain where they'd removed the shotgun pellet behind his ear and stitched it closed. The skin on his face seemed pulled tight from scalp to chin and ear to ear, and it hurt to do much more than blink his eyes.

"Nothing major," McCue said. "You know how this works."

"I should by now, yes."

Joe had already given statements to Carbon County Sheriff Ron Baird, Baggs Police Department Chief Brian Lally, his departmental supervisor, and the Game and Fish Department investigator assigned to the case. Although Joe had absolutely no reason to lie about anything, he was concerned there could be contradictions or problems if all the statements were compared. Each investigator had asked basically the same questions but in different ways, and Joe had no control or approval over what they wrote down when he answered. Even though what had happened in the mountains was clear in his mind, it was possible that his statements, when laid side-by-side, might not completely jibe. It was the nature of the game, and one played—sometimes unfairly—by investigators, prosecutors, and defense attorneys. Joe had played it himself. So he knew to be alert and careful each time he was questioned. He couldn't afford to be sloppy or off-hand. He wished he could recall more of the interrogation by Baird immediately after he'd been rescued, when his head was still cloudy with exhaustion and his wounds were fresh. He hoped he hadn't said something he'd come to regret.

"Mind if I borrow this?" McCue said, gesturing toward Joe's tray table.

"Fine."

McCue nodded man-to-man to Joe, slid the tray table

toward himself, and opened a manila folder on top of it. He fitted the glasses to his eyes, then slid them as far down his nose as they would go before they fell off. Joe was distracted by how cloudy the lenses were.

"Just a couple of questions," McCue said, peeling back single pages within the file. Joe recognized them as copies of the original sheriff's department statement given to Ron Baird.

"About the Brothers Grim . . ."

"They prefer 'the Grim Brothers,'" Joe said.

McCue looked over his lenses at Joe appraisingly. "They do, do they?"

"Yup."

"Okay, then. Caleb, the first one you encountered at that lake. It says here he gave you permission to look through his possessions."

Said Joe, "Yes, and when I think back on it, I don't know why he did. He must have known he didn't have a fishing license, which is all I wanted to check on. But, yes, he let me look through his bag."

McCue placed a bony finger on a dense paragraph of text. "It says here he had a variety of items in the pack."

"Yes."

"Can you be more specific?"

"I thought I had."

McCue nodded and read from the statement, "'The subject's daypack contained several items, including a water container, a knife, a diary, half of a Bible, and an iPod and holder.'" He looked up expectantly.

"I think that was pretty much it," Joe said, trying to recall all the contents. "There were some matches and some string I think, also. Oh, and there wasn't the iPod itself, just the holder. I'm pretty sure I made that clear to the sheriff, but he must have misunderstood me."

McCue nodded quickly, and Joe noticed the agent seemed to be tamping down his reaction to avoid revealing anything.

"Is there a problem?" Joe asked.

McCue ignored the question. "Can you describe the iPod holder to me?"

Joe searched his memory. "It was one of those things that strap to the upper part of your arm. My wife Marybeth has one for workouts at the gym."

"What color was it, can you recall?"

"Pink."

"You're sure?"

Joe nodded.

"You're positive?"

"Why is that important?" Joe asked.

"It may not be at all. I'm just covering all the bases. You know how this works," McCue said, then quickly flipped over the page to another. Joe saw something in ink written in the margin, and McCue stabbed his fingertip on the passage.

"You say Caleb claimed he was from the UP."

"Yes."

"And you thought, being from the Rocky Mountain West, that UP meant 'Union Pacific.'"

Joe didn't say anything.

"Did you know it could have meant Upper Peninsula, as in the Upper Peninsula of Michigan? That's what they call it there, the 'UP.'"

"I know that now," Joe said. "One of the sheriff's deputies down in Baggs was from Michigan and told me. I feel kind of stupid, now, not knowing it."

McCue nodded, apparently agreeing with Joe's assessment of himself.

"Hey . . ." Joe said, but McCue flipped another page and stabbed another note.

"You say there were four people besides you at the cabin that burned down. Caleb and Camish Grim, Terri Wade, and one other. You suggest that when you saw the profile of the fourth person you thought of Diane Shober. Is that correct?"

Joe felt his face get hot. He realized how ridiculous it sounded when McCue said it.

"She came to mind," Joe said. "But nowhere in that report did I claim it was her. As I said to the sheriff down there, and my own people in Cheyenne, her name came to mind probably because I'd seen her photo on so many fliers in that part of the state. Plus, I knew that's where she went missing because I was part of the search team. So when I caught a glimpse of a youngish female in the dark down there, I think I naturally thought of her. I've never *said* it was her."

McCue bored in. "Do you stand by your impression, though?"

Joe shook his head. "I stand by the fact that I thought of her at the time. I don't know how I can stand by an impression. And the more I think about it now, the more I think my mind might have jumped to conclusions." Joe smiled, which pulled at his scalp. "I've been accused of that before. Sometimes I'm right. Usually, I'm not."

"So I hear," McCue said without irony. "Can you describe her?"

"I already did," Joe said. "I didn't get a clear look at all. In my mind, I can recall I thought she was blonde, female, and younger than Caleb and Camish and Terri Wade."

"How tall was she?"

Joe shrugged, which hurt. "I don't know. She stood away from the others, so I've got no perspective."

"How old?"

"Like I said, my impression was she was younger. But I'm not sure why I say that."

"What was she wearing?"

"I have no idea."

"Her build?"

"Thin," Joe said. "Like you."

McCue nodded to himself, as if Joe had confirmed something.

"Are you going to tell me what this is all about?" Joe asked.

McCue looked up. "Eventually."

"I'm done answering questions until you let me know why you're asking them."

"Fine," McCue said, closing the folder. "I've got what I need for now."

"That's *it*?"

McCue unhooked his reading glasses from his ears and let them drop on the cord. "That's it."

"Where can I contact you?" Joe asked, "Cheyenne? One of the other offices? Where are you out of? I've never seen you around."

McCue simply nodded.

"Was that a yes or a no?"

"Thanks for your time," McCue said. "I'm sure we'll be seeing each other again."

"Leave me your card," Joe said. "I may think of something later."

McCue said over his shoulder, "I'll leave one for you at the nurses' station."

And he was gone.

Ten minutes later, Joe pressed his nurse call button and asked for Agent McCue's DCI business card.

"What?" she said. Then: "There's no card here I can see. I'll check with the other nurses, but I didn't see him stop by on his way out."

"Is there another nurse station?"

"There are several on each floor."

"Would you mind checking with them?"

The pause was no doubt accompanied by rolling eyes, Joe thought. She said, "I'll ask around and let you know."

LATER THAT AFTERNOON, Joe opened his eyes and saw something he didn't want to see, so he closed them again, hoping it would go away.

"I know you're awake," his mother-in-law, Missy, said from the foot of his bed.

"I'm sleeping," Joe said.

"You most certainly are not."

"I'm sleeping and having a real bad dream."

"Open your eyes. I need to talk to you."

Joe sighed and cracked his right eye. He knew he was wincing because it hurt when he winced. "Where's Marybeth?"

"She's getting some lunch down in the cafeteria with the girls. She should be back in a half hour or so."

"I wish she'd hurry," Joe said.

Missy narrowed her eyes and leaned forward, her small manicured hands gripping the footrest. "You could be a little more grateful," she said. "Earl and I sent one of his jets to bring you up here from that little Podunk clinic near Baggs so you could have the finest medical care available in the region. Where was it?" she asked, then answered her own question. "Craig, Colorado, or some-place vile like that."

Joe vaguely remembered the flight. He nodded his appreciation, but he knew strings would be attached. As far as Joe knew, Missy had yet to perform a stringless act in her adult life.

"So the least you can do is hear me out," she said.

"I don't like the doctor," he said. "He's arrogant." Joe based his appraisal on an exchange he'd had with Dr. Nadir two days before, when Nadir had shaken his head at Joe and said, "An arrow and buckshot wounds? What is this, the Wild West again? The OK Corral?"

"All good doctors are arrogant," she said. "Especially the Indian ones. That's because they're good. The only ones better are Japanese or Chinese, you know. Unfortunately, it's a little too cold for Asians out here. They like warm weather, I understand."

"I was fine in the clinic," Joe said, ignoring her comments.

"That clinic is for oilfield workers who get hit on the head with a wrench. It isn't for the husband of my daughter or the father of my grandchildren."

Joe shrugged, which hurt his right shoulder where they'd removed the double-aught shot pellet.

"Listen," Missy said, "I want to know where Nate Romanowski is hiding."

"Lots of people want to know that," Joe said.

"I need to ask him for a favor."

Joe nodded. Marybeth had filled him in on her mother's plan to hire Nate to intimidate her ex-husband. "So that's why you're here?" Joe said. "The reason why you flew me up to Billings? So you could be here if and when Nate shows up?"

Her eyes sparkled, revealing her answer.

"And here I was thinking you cared about my health and welfare," Joe said.

"Someone has to care about it," she said. "You certainly don't. Don't you think you're getting a little old for this sort of thing? Don't you think maybe it's time to grow up and settle down and get a real job that provides for your family? A job where you can come home at night and be there for your wife and daughters?"

Joe said, "Don't beat around the bush, Missy. Tell me what you really think."

"It needs to be said."

"Not all of us can be media moguls. Or married to one."

Her eyes flashed. "Earl Alden turned a million-dollar inheritance into a seven-hundred-million-dollar empire."

"That first million probably helped," Joe said.

"You're over forty years old," she said, "and your life consists of running around through the woods like a schoolboy—or a kid playing cowboys and Indians."

She leaned forward and her eyes became slits. She said, "For the sake of my daughter, maybe it's time to put away childish things."

Joe didn't have a comeback and he couldn't say what he was thinking, which was, *Maybe you're right.*

TALKING WITH THE GIRLS was awkward, he thought. He got the feeling they agreed with that sentiment because they seemed to look at everything in the room besides him. They didn't like seeing him sick or injured in a hospital bed any more than he liked being seen by them in one.

"You look like you're doing better," Sheridan said.

"I am."

"We're all ready to go home."

"Me, too," Joe said.

"Did Mom tell you about basketball? Coach is mad at me already, and he said if I missed practice so I could come see you, I wouldn't play anymore."

"I'm sorry," Joe said.

"I'd rather be here," she said, and smiled sadly. Joe reached out and squeezed her hand.

"Billings sucks," April said. "Billings is nearly as boring as Saddlestring."

"Our little ray of sunshine," Joe commented. April scowled at him.

Sheridan said to April, "Maybe you should have stayed in Chicago."

"Maybe I should have," April shot back.

"Girls, please," Marybeth said, sadness in her eyes.

Sheridan huffed and crossed her arms and looked away. April narrowed her eyes and glared at her, reminding Joe of a rattler coiling to strike.

April looked older than she was, he thought, which was perfectly understandable given the life she'd led. Her Wyoming reentry had not gone smoothly. She was sullen, sarcastic, and passive-aggressive toward her foster parents. When Marybeth complained to Joe about her, Joe responded by reminding Marybeth that April was fifteen and her behavior was fairly normal for her age. When Joe complained to Marybeth about April's sullen attitude, Marybeth defended her foster daughter with the same reasoning. Both wondered if they'd be able to wait her out, all the while hoping she'd become sunny and productive and not wreck the dynamics of the family in the meantime. Meanwhile, the process for adoption had begun but stalled due to the complexity of April's legal status. According to their lawyer, the problems weren't insurmountable, but they'd take time to sort through. It would be costly, and Joe and Marybeth had asked him to set the case aside until Joe returned permanently to Saddlestring and could help oversee the progress. Since then, April hadn't asked about how the adoption was going, and Marybeth hadn't brought it up. The silent impasse, Joe knew, would have to be broken soon.

"There's a nice mall," Lucy said about Billings, ignoring April. "Mom said she'd take us there this afternoon."

"Good," Joe said, winking at Marybeth.

"Wow," April said, rolling her eyes, "A *mall*. These people in Montana have thought of everything."

"April," Sheridan moaned.

April gestured toward the television set mounted on the ceiling that Joe had yet to turn on. "They've even got television, but probably, like, one channel."

Joe searched in vain for the remote control to prove to her Montana had cable, but he couldn't locate it.

"I just want everyone to be happy," Lucy said, grinning. "Starting with me."

"It always starts with you," April said.

"It's got to start somewhere." Lucy grinned, but her eyes showed a glint of triumph for the comeback.

"Nice one," Sheridan said.

"Get me out of here," April said to no one in particular.

Marybeth took them to the Rimrock Mall.

12

TWELVE SLEEP COUNTY SHERIFF MCLANAHAN said, "Knock-knock" but didn't actually knock when he entered Joe's hospital room with a deputy trailing. McLanahan was Joe's age and the two had known each other for ten years, since Joe had moved to Saddlestring and McLanahan was a nascent deputy under the legendary Sheriff O. R. "Bud" Barnum. Barnum had vanished off the face of the earth five years before, and there had always been whispers that Nate Romanowski had had something to do with it. Unfortunately, McLanahan had run for sheriff and won as a protégé of Barnum. He'd adopted the same ham-fisted, authoritarian approach to the job that Barnum had perfected. Nothing happened in the county that McLanahan wasn't aware of or involved in, but at the same time he managed to keep an arm's-length distance from the machinations, using intermediaries—often his team of four dull-witted cookie-cutter deputies—so if the situation went sour he could claim no knowledge of it.

Joe knew McLanahan disliked him and resented his presence, and he was aware that behind the scenes the sheriff had tried to get him reassigned or fired outright. The sheriff saw Joe as unwanted competition, and their clashes over the years had got more bitter, again a continuation of Barnum's reign. Joe hadn't seen McLanahan in the year he'd been in Baggs, but their relationship resumed where it had left off, when the sheriff said, "I'm startin' to wonder if they've got you in the right kind of hospital here, Joe. I'm startin' to think maybe it might be best to put you in one of those facilities with the rubber walls and elevator music because there's a bunch of us fellers startin' to believe you've gone *crazy as a damned tick*."

He ended the sentence with a tinny uplift and a rural flourish, and the deputy behind him snorted a laugh of pure obligation.

Joe winced and fished for the control that powered his hospital bed so he could raise the head of it. He didn't like the sheriff seeing him prone or in his stupid cotton gown. The fabric, he'd discovered to his horror, was decorated with a pattern of tiny yellow ducks. As the motor whirred and the head of the bed raised, Joe said, "I could have gone the rest of my life without seeing you again, sheriff."

McLanahan clucked his tongue as if to say, *Too bad for you*, then settled heavily in a straight-backed chair to Joe's right where Marybeth had been for two days. She'd left her sweater over the back, but McLanahan either didn't notice or didn't care.

McLanahan, originally from Virginia, had long ago completed a physical and mental transformation from a hotheaded deputy who spoke in a rapid-fire cadence to a slow-talking Western character who collected and used frontier folkisms that often made absolutely no sense to Joe. He wore a scuffed brown leather vest with a five-star sheriff's badge, a big silver buckle, jeans, and crepe-soled cowboy boots. He owned three horses he'd never ridden that served as props for campaign posters and a twenty-acre parcel he referred to as his "ranch." His huge mustache now stretched from his upper lip to his lower jaw and obscured his mouth, although his eyes were still sharp, small, and devious and gave him away as someone more into calculation and mythmaking than cow's punching, Joe thought. The sheriff cocked a heel over the lower railing of Joe's bed and removed his brown sweat-stained hat and fitted it on his raised knee. McLanahan was losing his hair, Joe noted, and he'd gained thirty pounds since he'd last seen him. The deputy, whose nametag read SOL-LIS, was dressed in a crisp department uniform shirt and dark black jeans. He had a military buzz cut and dull, hooded eyes. McLanahan had long ago established a policy that the only Western character in the sheriff's department would be the sheriff.

"Two hours ago, I got off the phone with the state DCI boys and Sheriff Baird down in Carbon County," McLanahan said. "They're coming down the mountain as we speak. What they told me made me climb in my rig and drive two hours north across the state line so I could tell you in person."

Joe nodded. After Joe gave his version of events to the sheriff, Baird had quickly requested a team of investigators from the state to ride with him and his deputies into the mountains after the Grim Brothers.

"Does this have to do with some kind of inconsistency in my statements?" Joe asked. "An agent named McCue from DCI was asking me more questions earlier today."

"I don't know him," McLanahan said. "And no, it has nothing to do with him, whoever the hell he is. Naw, what I heard I found out from the search team themselves."

Indeed, Joe thought.

"Unlike a certain game warden," McLanahan said, "the search team didn't misplace their communications gear, so I've been getting updates every few hours for the past three days. There's eleven men on horseback been all over those mountains. They been everywhere you described. Guess what they've found?"

Joe felt his mouth go dry.

"Nothin'," McLanahan said. "Not a single goddamn thing to corroborate your tall tale."

Joe shook his head. He remembered describing the saddle slope where he'd found the arrow, his ride with Caleb to their camp, and the location of Terri Wade's cabin. Although it had been dark when he found the cabin and escaped from it, he vividly recalled the cutback where it was and the distance from the creek.

"That's impossible," Joe said. "They couldn't locate *anything*?"

McLanahan said, "Nope."

"My horses and my tack?"

"Nope. Oh," McLanahan said, raising a knobby finger, "let me take that back. They did find your campsite by some lake on the way up. All that proves is that you did go up there into those mountains, but as far as I know, that hasn't been in dispute."

Joe shook his head. "I don't understand."

"Neither do they, except maybe you're completely full of shit on this whole deal." He lowered his eyelids. "I always say if you find yourself in a hole, the first thing to do is stop digging."

Joe looked away. "It makes no sense. I mean, I can see how it might be hard to find that little pup-tent camp of the brothers. It was deep in the timber and there wasn't a good trail to it. I might not be able to find it myself right away. But on top they should have found the remains of my horses, and where that cabin was burned down."

"Provided those things exist somewhere other than your imagination," McLanahan said. He raised a large hand with his fingers out and used his other index finger to count out and bend the fingers down one by one. "No brothers. No burned-down cabin. No crazy woman. No long-lost girl runner. No damned wolves. No . . ." McLanahan stared at his fist in mock puzzlement, then said, "I plumb ran out of fingers. We got more lies here than I got fingers to count on."

Sollis stifled a smile.

Said McLanahan, twisting the knife, "And no one can find your missing person named Terri Wade. As you can imagine, there are three or four women with that name around the country, but all of them are accounted for. But your gal—she doesn't exist. And you know in this day and age, people can't simply disappear without leaving a record."

Joe said, "That's the name she gave me. It's not like I saw any ID. She could have been lying."

"A lot of that going around," McLanahan said, and Sollis chuckled.

"They must be in the wrong drainage," Joe said, ignoring them both. "It's easy to get lost up there. I couldn't give coordinates because they took my GPS. . . ."

"No GPS!" McLanahan said. "I forgot about that. And no satellite phone, either. No nothing."

"I'm not lying," Joe said.

"I'm sure you're convinced of that. Fabulists become convinced of their own stories."

"Why would I make up a story?" Joe said. "Look

around you, McLanahan. We're in a hospital. These injuries are real. Do you think I wanted to be here?"

"It ain't so bad," he said. "I seen some of the nurses."

"I need to talk to Sheriff Baird," Joe said. "I need to hear this from him myself."

"Feel free. He should be down into town tomorrow or the next day. I'm sure he'd love to talk with you, too. This search they just been on wiped out most of his discretionary budget for the rest of the year, payin' all those men to go up that mountain to find a whole lot of nothing. Yes, Baird is a pretty crabby man right now."

Joe wasn't sure what to say. The news had taken the wind out of him.

"Well," McLanahan said as *way-all*, sitting up in his chair and slapping his thighs, "I best be getting back to the office. I just wanted to make sure you heard the happy news straight from the horse's mouth. In case the governor called or some reporter. If I was you, I'd claim chemical dependence and say you were checking into rehab. That seems to work pretty well for celebrity types such as yourself."

McLanahan stood and clamped on his hat. His eyes sparkled. Joe realized how much McLanahan hated him for closing cases in the sheriff's jurisdiction without involving his department. He remembered how angry the sheriff had been when Governor Rulon asked him to get out of the way two years before. He'd harbored his bitterness and could now unleash it.

"Look," Joe said, "I'll talk with Baird and the DCI when I can and try to figure out where they went wrong up there. It doesn't make any sense, unless the Grim Brothers were able to wipe out all the evidence. I wouldn't put it past them."

"Yeah," McLanahan said, smiling contemptuously beneath his mustache, "according to your statement they seem larger than life itself! Like supermen of the mountains. You shoot 'em in the face and in the chest and they still keep coming, like . . . *mountain zombies!*"

Which made Sollis laugh out loud.

"What are you saying?" Joe asked. "That I put myself in here for some reason and made it all up?"

McLanahan raised his hand and formed a pistol with his fist and fired it at Joe. "Bingo," he said.

Joe shook his head, stunned.

"Do you remember a deputy I had once named Hayder?" the sheriff asked. At the sound of the name, Sollis rolled his eyes. Joe said nothing.

"Well, Ol' Hayder was in his cruiser one night up on Bighorn Road. Somebody had reported high school kids drag racing up and down that road, so dispatch sent him up there to find out what was going on. He hid his unit in a bunch of trees and waited, hour after hour, for some of them speed demons to show up so he could make an arrest and get out of my doghouse. But he got real bored, because there was nothin' happening, so he started fiddling around with his Taser. I don't know what the hell he was thinkin', but somehow he shot himself with it. Right in the neck!"

Sollis went, "Ha-ha-ha," and wiped at the nonexistent tears in his eyes, even though he'd likely heard the story a dozen times.

McLanahan continued, "Well, if you've ever been hit by a Taser, you know what it can do to your bodily functions when that current goes through you, and Ol' Hayder soiled his pants. He threw the door open and rolled around on the ground outside the car with muscle spasms. When he finally recovered, he was too damned embarrassed to tell anyone at the department what had happened, so he made up a crazy story about being jumped by three bikers who he claimed ambushed him and got his Taser out of his belt and used it on him while he bravely fought them off. He even named a couple of lowlifes in town we'd been after for a while as the assailants, and we had them arrested. Hayder almost got away with it, too, except one of those drag-racing kids had seen the whole thing and videoed it with his cell phone camera. It seems the speed demons knew all about Hayder in those trees, so they were gonna sneak up on him and slash his tires or some other kind of damned kid prank. The kid who took the video got picked up for careless driving a few days later and told Sollis here he'd show him something if we'd throw away the ticket. He got his phone out and we watched it and busted a gut. Ol' Hayder didn't show up for work the next day, and we ain't seen him since."

Joe said nothing.

"So what I'm sayin'," McLanahan finished as he paused at the door, "is I can see a scenario where maybe you was intoxicated on liquor or your own ego and you dropped your shotgun. It went off, peppering your shoulder and neck. Your horses reared and dumped you and you injured your leg. I'm thinkin' maybe you landed on a downed log and a sharp branch stuck through your thigh. Then the horses ran off and left you there with nothin' at all. So being the big-shot celebrity you are in the middle of nowhere, you didn't want to tell the governor what happened, so you made up one hell of a good story."

"Get out," Joe said. "You're a damned idiot and an embarrassment."

McLanahan's eyes flashed and he started to come out

of his chair. Joe didn't back down. McLanahan apparently thought better of getting into a fistfight with a man in a hospital bed and said, "The easiest way to eat crow is while it's warm. The colder it gets, the harder it is to swaller."

Joe said, "It's hard to believe the West was won with stupid sayings like that."

"The only thing I don't like about this whole deal," McLanahan said, ignoring Joe, "is that I understand you're coming back to Saddlestring. Everything else, though, just tickles me to no end."

"Let me give you some of your own cornpone advice," Joe said. "Never miss a chance to shut up. Now get out."

"And give my best to the lovely Mrs. Pickett."

As a result of McLanahan's visit, Joe gripped the railings of his bed with both hands and stared at the blank screen of the television. There, he saw a distorted reflection of himself at what looked like the edge of an abyss.

How was it possible a team of eleven men couldn't confirm his story? Where had the Grim Brothers gone? Was it possible they'd never been there at all? That everything Joe recalled was some kind of a fever dream?

A phone burred on a stand next to his bed. Until it rang, he hadn't known there was a telephone there.

A crisp female voice said, "Hold for Governor Rulon."

Joe closed his eyes. How much worse could this day get? he wondered.

"Joe! How in the hell are you?"

The governor's voice was deep and raspy. There was heavy background noise, overlapping conversations, the bark of a laugh.

"Hello, sir. I'm fine."

"Good, good. Can you hear me okay? I'm in Washington giving hell to these bastards, and I've got a few minutes between meetings. I don't have long, so we need to get to the point."

"Okay."

"First, how is Marybeth? How are the girls?"

"Good all around. They're here with me. . . ."

"Tell me straight: are you nuts? Did you go goofy down there in exile?"

Joe swallowed. "No."

"I got part of the story from my chief of staff, who's in touch with DCI. I've been anxiously awaiting news of a bloody shootout where two brothers are killed and two women are rescued in the mountains. Instead, I hear they can't find anything or anybody."

"I just heard from Sheriff McLanahan," Joe said. "They must have been searching in the wrong places."

"Hmmm."

Joe asked, "Do you know a DCI investigator named Bobby McCue? He was in here earlier today asking me a bunch more questions about what I saw up there. Do you know why DCI is questioning my story?"

"What did you say his name was?"

"McCue."

"The name is familiar somehow, but I can't say I place him. You say he was with the state?"

"That's what he claimed."

"We have too many goddamned employees," Rulon huffed. "I can't know every one of 'em."

Strike two, Joe thought.

Rulon said suddenly, *"The Brothers Grimm?"*

"They prefer the Grim Brothers."

"Diane Shober?"

"I don't swear it was her. I made that clear to the DCI. I said outright I may have been mistaken."

"Wolves?"

"Yes, sir."

"We don't have wolves in southern Wyoming."

"You do, sir. C'mon, governor. How can you doubt me? Have I ever lied to you? Or anybody?"

"Well, no," Rulon said. "You haven't. Sometimes I wish you would. An honest man can be a big pain in the butt to a politician, you know."

Joe smiled.

"Have you been contacted by the press yet?" Rulon asked. "They're going to eat this story up."

"No."

"Especially the Diane Shober angle. I know how those bastards think. They won't care about Terri Wade or you. But they'll be on the missing-runner thing like fat kids on a pie.

"Do not under any circumstances talk to them," Rulon said. "Say 'no comment' and direct any inquiries to my office. We won't talk to them either, but they don't know that yet."

"Okay," Joe said.

"It's gonna be damage-control mode. Luckily, we've had a little experience with that lately," he said, almost wistfully. "How this plays out will be a reflection on me and my administration, since I hired you and tried to squirrel you away where you wouldn't do any more damage. If this story gets out . . ."

"It's not a story," Joe said, gritting his teeth. "It's the truth. It's what happened. I'm in a hospital bed because of those brothers."

"That sheriff of yours calls you a fabulist," Rulon said. "We won't be able to keep him quiet."

"No," Joe agreed.

Rulon paused. "Okay, then. I've got two calls I need to return. They both have to do with you. The first is from Chuck Coon at the FBI. He says he wants to be briefed, but I think he may know something about those brothers that he doesn't want to reveal. As you know, the feds always have something going on behind the scenes."

Joe grunted. Governor Rulon was getting more and more disparaging of the federal government all the time. Joe used to think he did it to gain popularity with his constituents. In a state where more than 50 percent of the land was owned and managed by federal bureaucracies, the battles between locals and Washington were fierce. Rulon had recently been quoted in national newsmagazines calling the government "thieving, blood-dripping vampire jackals" and "jackbooted fascist thugs." Joe was beginning to think Rulon believed every word he said.

"I'll have my staff talk to Coon," Rulon said. "We may find out something that way that could benefit us. I'm curious he called, to be honest. I'm guessing he did it on behest of his apparatchik superiors."

Joe found it interesting that Coon had called as well.

Rulon said, "And then I have a harder call to return. It's the kind of call I hate to make because it makes my stomach churn. Maybe I should have you do it."

Joe said, "Who, sir?"

"Diane Shober's parents. Somehow, they found out about your story. They want to find their daughter and bring her home."

Joe felt his stomach clench.

"Look," Rulon said. "I'm officially placing you on administrative leave until we can get a handle on all of this. So go home and close the curtains and don't answer the door or the phone. The media can be tricky bastards and blunt objects, and I don't want you talking to them. That's an order. Stay inside and don't come out until you hear from me or my chief of staff. Got that?"

"Yes, sir." Joe swallowed. "But . . ."

"No buts except that one you've got in a sling. I'm not hanging you out to dry because you've never lied to me, even when I wanted you to. Right now, though, we've got to go to ground until we can figure out the best course of action."

Joe said, "I never got to thank you for letting me go home."

"Oh, this is thanks enough." The governor snorted, and laughed bitterly at his own joke. "And welcome home. It looks like you're going to be seeing plenty of it in the next few days."

Rulon punched off, and Joe lowered the phone to his lap, looked back up at the blank television screen, and clearly saw the abyss this time.

13

ON THE EASTERN SIDE OF THE SIERRA MADRE, ON the opposite side of the range where Joe Pickett had ascended days before, Dave Farkus crept his pickup along an overgrown two-track through the timber toward his fall elk camp. The afternoon was warm and still, the last gasp of summer, and the insects in the tall grass hummed and jumped with the manic passion of the soon-to-die. Farkus ran his windows up to prevent grasshoppers from jumping inside. Grasshoppers bugged him.

He'd had a bad day so far, but there were signs of improvement. Being in the mountains on a nice summer day was always an improvement over just about anything.

He'd spent most of the day in Encampment, where he'd had a miserable lunch with his soon-to-be-ex-wife, Ardith. Ardith had fled Baggs two months before and driven over the top of the mountains to Encampment, population 443 before she arrived to make it 444, where she worked as a bartender at the Rustic Pine Saloon, serving beers and microwave popcorn and pizzas to loggers, tourists, and fishermen. He'd been disappointed to find her not despondent. Farkus had never really liked her, but it disturbed him mightily that she didn't like *him*. He wasn't even sure he wanted her back. But if she did, he could leave. At least then the fellows would think it was his idea, not hers.

And even though he'd taken the day off, driven all the way over the top, delivered a stack of mail as well as her Book-of-the-Month and Fabric-Swatch-of-the-Month packages, she said she had no intention of ever coming back. The divorce paperwork was filed and wouldn't be recalled. It was a matter of days before it was official and she'd be free, she said.

He'd even presented her with a Styrofoam cooler filled with packages of deer, antelope, and elk steaks as well as a pair of goose breasts, several mourning doves, and a young sage grouse he'd poached. Her so-called appreciation still rang in his ears.

"How romantic," she'd said. "The gift of meat. It's just so . . . *you*."

He'd wanted to tell her about his role in the big doings on the mountain, how he'd been the last man to see and talk to the game warden before he rode his horses up there. And he wanted to tell her his theory about what had happened. He was proud of his theory. But she said her shift started at one P.M. and she had to go.

"Don't forget the cooler," he'd said as she gathered herself up. As she did, he looked at her closely and determined she'd lost a few pounds and the blouse she wore was new and fairly tight across her breasts, meaning she probably had a boyfriend. The poor sap, he thought. He wondered if she did things with him she'd refused to do with Farkus.

"I don't really need all this meat," she said. She made an *"Ooof"* sound as she grasped the handle of the cooler and hefted it from the tabletop. "It's a lot of heavy meat, all right."

He said, "Heavy like my heart."

She looked back at him, smiled crookedly, said, "And just as frozen."

SO HE BOUGHT A TWELVE-PACK of Keystone Light at the Mangy Moose because Ardith didn't work there, and he'd drunk six of them on the way up. In the bed of his Dodge pickup were canvas Cabela's outfitter tents to be unfolded and put up, cooking stoves to be assembled, an eating table to be unfolded, and grates for the fire pit.

Fall couldn't come soon enough, he thought. Fall was his favorite season. Fall meant elk hunting, and elk camp, and the camaraderie of the boys. He could do what he excelled at—hunting, cooking over a fire, resuming his only true love affair with the outdoors—and discard the things he hated or was poor at, like being married to Ardith, working for the energy company, or running his household.

Farkus's objective was to "claim" the camp by establishing it before other elk hunters could do the same thing. It wasn't a problem with the locals. They all knew where Dave Farkus and his party camped. But every year there were more and more hunters from places like Cheyenne and Casper, and more out-of-staters who didn't know or appreciate a damned thing about tradition or heritage. Officially, he and his buddies had no real ownership of their camp. The site was a nice opening in a stand of aspen with enough room to park 4 x 4s and ATVs. It had flat spots for the tents and a couple of old-growth pines within walking distance for hanging a meat pole. The forest was public land, and reservations weren't taken by the U.S. Forest Service—nor permits issued. But elk hunters didn't like setting up camp next to other hunters, and no one had ever moved into the area once the season started and the camp had been established. So the idea was to get up into the mountains before any other party could get there and stake out their traditional site. This year, it was Farkus's turn to be the scout.

The last week had been interesting, even though Ardith didn't want to hear about it. He'd been somewhat of a celebrity because he'd been the last person to talk to the game warden before all hell broke loose in the mountains. He'd been interviewed by the sheriff, state boys from DCI, including a lone investigator named Bobby McCue, and the local newspaper. It was the only time he could remember seeing his name in the local paper for a reason other than his DUI arrest last winter.

Like everyone else, he'd waited anxiously to find out what Sheriff Baird and the search team found. Speculation at the Dixon Club bar had been intense. When the search team returned and said they'd found nothing—*nothing*— to corroborate Joe Pickett's story, it was like the air went out of the balloon. Farkus himself felt oddly let down. He wanted to hear tales of a wild and bloody shoot-out, or at least a good chase. Secretly, he'd hoped they would find some mutilated or cannibalized bodies, which would bolster his theory. Despite the fact they hadn't, he still floated his speculation of the Wendigo. In fact, he'd told the fellows at the bar the fact the search team hadn't found anything supported his theory even more. Wendigos, he explained, weren't human. They could vanish and reappear. What Pickett had encountered were two Wendigos up there. They came out when they could do harm and they had the advantage on their side. But when they saw the size of the search team and the amount of weaponry, they'd vanished. The Wendigos would be back, eventually.

Which made Farkus grateful that his elk camp was on the *other* side of the mountain.

*   *   *

WHEN HE STOPPED THE PICKUP and got out to release a quart or so of the processed Keystone Light, he
noted the tread marks in the two-track road. After zipping up, he squatted and looked at them more closely.
The tracks were fresh, and there were dual sets of them,
one on top of another. Like a vehicle pulling a trailer.

"Damn it," he said aloud. "If some bastard got up here
before me to claim that campsite, there's gonna be a rodeo."

Farkus climbed back into his pickup and cracked another bottle of beer. He drank the foam top off so it
wouldn't slosh on his lap from bouncing down the rough
road as he drove. He pushed forward, steaming, but lik-
ing how the beers took the edge off his annoyance at
Ardith's behavior for him and always had.

HE CURSED WHEN, through the trees, he saw a late-
model pickup and an eight-horse trailer parked right in
the middle of his elk camp. No tents yet, though. He
hoped whoever had stumbled into the site had it just for
day use and had no plans to set up camp. If so, Farkus
could at least dump the tents and stoves there for the
time being and come back in a day or two. He hit the
buttons for his power windows to lower the driver and
passenger windows so he could yell a greeting.

He could see the rear ends of at least six horses tied up
to the trailer. Four of the horses had saddles, the other
two were equipped with sawbuck pack frames awaiting
panniers, and one stood in reserve.

But the men who turned as he approached in his
pickup looked like neither fishermen nor hunters. There

were four of them at least. The men were young, fit, and hard-looking. Two wore black; two wore camo. The men in black had buzz cuts and chiseled, lean features. One was tall and lanky with red hair and the other was dark and built like a linebacker. Both men had holsters strapped to tactical vests. The men in camo were not as threatening looking, but certainly seemed fit and serious. One was blond with aviator sunglasses and a trim pale mustache. The other had a long sharp nose, black hawk eyes, and a thick black mustache that looked to Farkus like a work of art. Farkus noted the man's face was daubed green and black with greasepaint.

"Jesus," Farkus whispered, slowing his pickup to a stop twenty yards from the site.

Rifle barrels poked out from piles of gear on the forest floor. A quick glance at the rifles revealed them to be automatic assault-type weapons with long magazines, the kind known to Farkus as "black rifles." Cases of electronic equipment were stacked, along with duffel bags. Farkus never spent much time on horseback but he knew a major expedition when he saw it. He craned his head out the window to try to catch a glimpse of the license plates on either the pickup or trailer, but because of the angle of the vehicle and the trees in the way, he couldn't see either.

He didn't like the looks of what he'd stumbled upon. These men didn't belong, and Farkus didn't want to find out why they were there. The presence of these men in the trees was jarring and unnatural. Cowboys, fishermen, campers, hikers, even bow hunters—sure. But these men didn't jibe with a bucolic late-summer afternoon.

The tall red-haired man in black approached Farkus with his hand on the grip of his pistol, like a cop. The others fell in behind him at first, but fanned out, taking a step to the side with every two or three steps toward

Farkus. Spreading out, making it impossible for him to keep track of them all at once.

"Can I help you with something?" the redhead asked in a way that belied the actual words.

"I was about to ask you the same thing," Farkus said, voice cracking. "You fellas seem to be in my elk camp." Then he quickly added, "Not that there's any problem with that."

"Your elk camp?" the man said, not really asking like he wanted to know more but instead to buy time while his compatriots took positions on all sides of the pickup.

Said Farkus, "Never mind. I'm sure you'll be gone by the season opener. So I'll just be going now."

Before he could jam his truck into reverse and hightail it out of there, his rearview mirror filled with the chrome grille of a black SUV with smoked windows.

"Hey," Farkus said, to nobody who cared.

The SUV eased up so closely behind him that he felt the bumpers make contact.

Farkus saw the red-haired man turn to whoever was driving the black SUV and arch his eyebrows. Like awaiting the word. In the rearview, Farkus could see a single occupant in the SUV, but he couldn't make him out too well. He saw the driver nod once.

Instantly, the red-haired man in the dark uniform mouthed, "Get him."

The driver stayed behind the wheel while the men in position broke and streaked directly at him from all four directions. The lead one, the redhead, had drawn his pistol and held it flat along his thigh as he ran.

Suddenly, the open driver's window was blocked by the body of the linebacker. He'd leaped on the running board and was reaching through the open window into the cab for the wheel. Farkus got a close-up view of a veiny bare hand as it shot across his body and grasped the steering wheel. The man's other hand grasped the shifter and shoved it into park.

Farkus said, "Jesus, you guys!"

The passenger door flew open and the redhead launched himself inside the cab, scattering empty beer bottles across the bench seat and to the floor. Farkus felt a sharp pain as a high-topped fatigue boot kicked his leg away from the accelerator and brake pedals. The man plucked the keys out of the ignition and palmed them.

Farkus felt the springs of his truck rock. He looked up. In his rearview mirror, the mustached man in camo climbed into the bed of his pickup directly behind him with *his* pistol drawn.

A cold O from the muzzle of a pistol pressed into his temple from the linebacker on the left. He squirmed as the redhead in the cab jacked a cartridge into his handgun and shoved it into Farkus's rib cage. The pale man in camo now stood directly in front of his pickup, aiming a scoped AR-15 at his face.

Farkus thought, *No one is ever going to believe this in the Dixon Club bar.*

FARKUS GOT OUT of his pickup at gunpoint. The red-haired man told him to put both hands on the hood of his truck and spread his legs. He was patted down by the black-clad linebacker, who found and pocketed his Leatherman tool and Buck knife. The sharp-featured camo man rooted through the cab of his pickup and found his Charter Arms 9mm in the glove box.

The man who'd been driving the SUV left it parked behind the pickup, and Farkus realized with a start that he knew him. It was that state guy, McCue. What was he doing here? He stood back with his hands in his pockets, watching silently. He wore a rumpled and ill-fitting suit, a pair of reading glasses dangled from a chain around his neck, and he looked tired.

"What's this?" the camo asked, holding the gun up.

"My handgun. You know, for snakes."

"Snakes?" The man laughed.

"I always have it with me. Everyone is armed around here. This is Wyoming, boys."

The red-haired man in black said, "We're going to cuff you to your vehicle until we get back."

Farkus said, "How about you guys just let me go about my business and I swear I won't say a word? I don't know who you are or why you're up here in the first place. I can keep a secret. Ask my wife if you don't believe me," he said, hoping like hell they'd never take him up on that offer.

The red-haired man said, "What makes you think you've got a choice in the matter?" He turned and said, "Got a second, Mr. McCue?" To Farkus, "Don't move a muscle."

"Okay," Farkus said. Then pleading to McCue: "Aren't you supposed to be with the state cops? Shouldn't you be helping me here?"

McCue rolled his eyes, dismissing the notion. Farkus felt the floor he thought he was standing on drop away and, with it, his stomach.

But as the two men walked out of earshot, Farkus rotated his head slightly so he could see them out of the corner of his eye. He didn't have to hear them to get the gist of what they were discussing: *him*. The "cuffing him to his vehicle" statement was a feint. It didn't pass the smell test. He'd obviously stumbled onto something he wasn't supposed to see. Farkus felt a shiver form in his belly and roll through him. McCue gestured toward the trees beyond the camp. The red-haired man shook his head and squinted, looking off into the woods as if they'd provide the answer.

Farkus knew his life rested on the decision McCue would make. He wondered how—and if—he could influence that decision. While he searched for an angle— Farkus's life was an endless procession of angle location—he craned his neck around farther and sneaked a look at the back of their vehicle and the horse trailer. Michigan plates. Vehicles and visitors from that state weren't unusual in the mountains during hunting season. But this wasn't hunting season.

"Damn," he said. "You boys came a long way. Where you from in Michigan?"

They didn't answer him.

But he had his angle. He said, "Boys, I don't know what you're doing here, but it's obvious you're about to head off into the mountains to find something or somebody. I know these mountains. I grew up here and I've guided hunters in this area every fall for twenty-five years, and let me tell you something: it's easy to get lost up here."

Farkus felt like whooping when McCue turned to him, actually listening and not looking at him as if measuring his body for a coffin.

Farkus said, "These mountains are a series of drainages. The canyons look amazingly similar to each other when you're in them. People get lost all the time because they think they're walking along Cottonwood Creek when it's actually Bandit Creek or Elkhair Creek or No Name Creek."

He nodded toward the piles of equipment in the camp, and the red-haired man followed his gaze. Farkus said, "Even with a GPS it's easy to get rimrocked or turned around. You know what I'm saying here. I can help you find what it is you're looking for. Trust me on this."

McCue said, "He's got a point."

The red-haired man disagreed, said, "Mr. McCue, we have all the men and equipment we need. Taking along another guy will slow us down."

McCue waved him off. "That sheriff over in Baggs had more men and more equipment, and they didn't find them. Maybe having someone along who knows the mountains will help. Equipment fails sometimes."

The red-haired man was obviously in no position to argue with McCue. But he was unhappy. He pointed to Farkus. "You can come along as long as you're actually useful. But you need to keep your mouth shut otherwise. And when you turn into dead weight . . ."

"I'm dead meat," Farkus finished his sentence for him. "I understand." He took his hands off the hood.

Farkus had no idea what was going on or what these men were after. But that didn't matter now. What mattered was getting through the next ten minutes before McCue changed his mind.

He pointed toward a fat sorrel without a saddle. He said, "So, is that my horse?"

14

JOE SAID TO MARYBETH, "I CHANTED YOUR NAME for two straight days. It helped me to keep going."

It was nearly midnight. Sheridan, Lucy, and April were back in the motel. Marybeth had come to say goodnight before she left to join them. She looked at Joe with sympathy and curiosity.

"And I'm so sorry about your horses," he said.

"After the girls are gone, all I'll have are my horses," she said. "But you seem determined to kill them all off."

He winced.

"I'm sort of kidding," she said.

He squeezed her hand. "We'll get more horses. I know you're always on the lookout for good ones."

"In fact," she said with a sly smile, "there are a couple of fine little quarter horses down on this ranch in Colorado between Boulder and Longmont. . . ."

He asked, "How is my dad? Have you heard?"

"He's failing fast."

"Have you talked to his doctors?"

She nodded.

"Any hope?"

She shook her head.

After years of estrangement, Joe had become reacquainted with his father, George, on a case three years before, when he'd been assigned to Yellowstone Park by Governor Rulon. Days after they'd made contact, George had been severely beaten, because he'd made the mistake of holing up in Joe's room and men who'd come after Joe had found George instead. He'd never fully recovered and had been in a senior care facility in Billings since. Joe and Marybeth had paid for George's care with money they didn't have. In addition to the injuries he'd sustained, George had dementia and his body was rotted by alcoholism.

"Maybe I can see him," Joe said. "He's here somewhere in this hospital, right?"

"Yes. But I don't know if that's a great idea right now in your condition—or his," she said.

"Still," he said.

"You chanted my name?" she said, changing the subject.

"It was my mantra. You and the girls. I said your names over and over again to myself. Like this: '*Marybeth-Sheridan-Lucy-April.*'"

"I'm touched," she said, but he knew from her furrowed brow she was holding something back.

"What?" he asked.

"Joe, I've got to ask you, is something wrong? You seem different somehow. I'm more than a little worried about you."

"In what way?"

She rose, took his right hand, and squeezed it with both of hers. "This thing you went through with those brothers. It seems to have affected you very deeply. Are you sure you're okay?"

"I'm fine."

She breathed deeply and looked longingly into his eyes. "Not really," she said.

"I'm fine."

Said Marybeth, "The girls noticed it. They asked me if you were going to be all right. Sheridan especially said she thought there was something different about you."

He waved it off. "Look, I'm hurting. I have holes all over me. I've been through quite an experience and I'm trying to sort it all out. I hate it that my daughters—and you—are saying these things."

"Is it because they hurt you, those brothers?"

"I've been hurt before."

"Then what?" Marybeth kneaded his hand and pursed her lips.

Finally, he said, "I guess I feel like I left a piece of me up there on that mountain. I don't feel completely whole."

"You'll heal up."

"It's not that."

"Then what?"

Joe shook his head. "I'm still sorting it out. I feel like I missed something obvious. Something right in front of my eyes. But for the life of me, I can't figure out what it was. I feel like I asked them all the wrong questions, and I couldn't see what was in front of my eyes. Not that I can see it now, either. But those brothers—they beat me at every turn. They were faster, smarter, and meaner. I was outgunned and outmuscled."

Marybeth frowned at him. "Don't say that."

"It's true. Plus it doesn't help that McLanahan and the sheriff in Baggs think I made it all up."

"McLanahan's an idiot."

"There was a DCI agent here today," Joe said. "Or someone claiming to be a DCI agent. He asked some pretty strange questions, and I felt he was trying to trip me up for some reason. And no one seems to have ever heard of this guy before."

"That's odd," she said.

"To be honest, I heard some doubt in the governor's voice, too."

"Joe," she said, "Rulon's a lot of things, but he's still a politician."

He shrugged and winced.

"What did my mother say to you today? When the two of you were alone?"

Joe sighed. "She said it was time I put away childish things. Like my job."

Marybeth's eyes flared. "I knew it. I just knew she'd use this opportunity to try and get under your skin."

Joe said, "I'm wondering if she wasn't right."

"That's ridiculous. Why do you listen to her? I don't."

He tried to shrug, but his right shoulder screamed at him. "Ow," he moaned.

"Don't do that. Are you in pain? Do you want me to call a nurse?"

He shook his head no.

"Joe," she said. "You're tired. You need some sleep. We can talk about all of this tomorrow."

He said, "How are we affording the motel? How much are you paying per night?"

"Don't worry about that. We can afford it."

"But . . ."

"I said not to worry about it, Joe," she said with authority. "You need to rest and not worry about things. You'll be back at home in no time, rested and healed."

He nodded. "Yup." He told her about being placed on administrative leave.

"And pay no attention to my mother. I can guess what she said because I know her. Joe—" Marybeth released his hand and brushed her fingers across his lips. "You are the man I married. I knew what I was signing on for. I've never been resentful or angry with what you do for a living, and I know you're not the kind of man who could give that up. You do what you do because you're hard-wired for it. You get yourself into situations because you have a certain set of standards that are simply beyond her. So pay no attention to her. She's crazy and without scruples. She doesn't understand me, or us. So just put her out of your mind. I thought you'd done that years ago."

"I thought I had, too," he said. "But she got to me because I was thinking along the same lines."

"Only because you're in a hospital bed and you're confused by what McLanahan told you," Marybeth said. "You'll think differently when you're recovered."

"I hope so."

She paused. Then: "I hope you don't think you need to go back up there after them. The sheriff down in Baggs will catch them. They'll eventually find them and bring them to justice. You don't have to make this a personal quest."

He nodded, but he didn't mean it.

She kissed him goodnight and ignored the nurse filling the doorway and looking at her watch as a means of advising them visiting hours were over.

Before she left the room, he said, "Thank you for what you said."

She smiled painfully and said she'd be back in the morning.

AT 3:15 A.M., JOE SLID his legs out from under the blankets and eased out of the bed. His leg wounds were tightly bound, but the movement caused sharp needle-like pains that zapped up into his abdomen and belly. He paused at the doorway to get his breath back and pulled on a pair of boxers so his buttocks weren't bare out of the back of the duck-covered cotton gown.

The hallway was quiet and dimly lit. The nurse station was to his right, so he padded left in his open-backed hospital slippers. Hugging the wall so he couldn't be seen by the night nurse, he slid along the slick block wall to the end of the hallway and the elevators. Two floors up was ICU.

George Pickett was in room 621. Joe paused before going in and tried to gather strength and resolve. He had no idea what he would find inside.

He eased into the room and stood with his back to the wall near the door, out of sight in case a nurse or aide walked by and glanced in.

Dim blue-white neon lights lit George on his bed. Dozens of tubes curled up and away from his body into the gloom. Bags of clear liquid hung over him. It was as if his father were a long-forgotten potato gone to root in a dark pantry.

Joe shuffled closer. His father looked like a skeleton wrapped in loose latex, as if his yellow skin could slough off of the bones into a pile on the linoleum if he were jostled. Joe froze in mid-breath when George's eyes shot open and his father's head turned on his pillow toward him.

"Dad?"

George said, "What I could really use right now, son, is a drink." His voice was reedy and dry.

"Hello, Dad. How are you doing?"

"Give me a drink."

Joe reached out for the water bottle on the tray table and his father's face folded in on itself in a grotesque scowl. "Not that! I said I wanted a drink!"

"Ah," Joe said.

His father's rheumy eyes looked at something above and to the left of Joe, but the scowl remained.

"I can't," Joe said.

"Who the hell are you, anyway?"

"Joe."

"Joe? I had a son named Joe."

"That's me," he said, feeling his heart break.

"You're my son, but you won't give me a drink?" George rasped. "Then what the hell good are you?"

And with that, he died.

Joe heard an alarm burr at the nurse station, and he stepped back and aside as an emergency team rushed into the room and surrounded George's body, which seemed to have deflated even more. Despite the chatter of the attendants, he could hear the pneumatic *cack-cack-cack* of his father's death rattle, and he couldn't shake the thought that his dad was getting in one last laugh.

15

DAVE FARKUS HAD SPENT MOST OF HIS ADULT LIFE working hard to avoid hard work. His philosophy was to save himself for pursuits he favored—hunting, fishing, poker, snowmobiling, mountain man rendezvous reenactments, and blasting through the mountains on his 4 x 4 ATV.

Avoiding hard work required discipline and a complete awareness of his surroundings, as well as an intuitive sense of when to be in the wrong place when extra time or effort was demanded. Like golf or fly-fishing, it was a lifelong pursuit that he knew he might never perfect but he could certainly continue to improve. When his soon-to-be-ex-wife, Ardith, suggested bitterly he consider writing a pamphlet on the techniques he employed to maintain his lifestyle, Farkus told her it would be too much work.

Before everyone had been laid off from the natural-gas pipeline company, he'd been supremely skillful at the art of slipping into the men's room or taking a break moments before the shift supervisor entered the shop to outline new assignments or ask for volunteers for a big new job. When dirty and grueling tasks were demanded, like sandblasting old valves or replacing blown motors in pump units, Farkus expertly anticipated when the jobs would have to take place, due to his intimate knowledge of the industry and workplace, and would schedule a dentist appointment or mandatory drug test for that day.

It was easier to game the system in his new job working for the county. Bureaucracy was made for shirking, and he felt kind of stupid it had taken so many years to settle into his true calling. Today, for example, he'd gotten a tip that all the bus drivers would have to go into the garage and assist a contract cleaning crew on a top-to-bottom scrubbing of the vehicles. Which is why he'd taken a personal day to go over the mountains to try to spot-weld his marriage back together instead.

Dave Farkus always figured there would be high-intensity brownnoses who would take on the tough jobs and want to be heroes. He let them. Part of his philosophy was that it was as important to have slackers as to have go-getters within every work crew. For balance.

Additionally, in the thirty years since he'd graduated from high school (barely), he'd made it a point to avoid anything to do with horses, like ranch work. Horses were unpredictable, prone to break down, and involved after-hours maintenance. So after three hours of riding up into the timber nose-to-tail with the four men and their horses, he said, "So, if we find whatever it is you're looking for, will you let me go home?"

Which made the red-haired rider in black, named M. Whitney Parnell, according to the nametag on his rifle scabbard, snort and exchange looks with Smith. Farkus gathered from observation that Parnell was in charge of the whole operation. Smith and the two camo-clad men, the tall thin one with the nose named Campbell and the blond man named Capellen, were subservient to Parnell.

Parnell rode out ahead, followed by Smith. It was necessary to ride single-file because the trail was narrow and trees hemmed in both sides. Farkus rode a fat sorrel horse in the middle. Behind him were Campbell, Capellen, and the two packhorses.

"You see," Farkus explained, "I'm just thinking my role here is to help you out because I know these mountains and you don't, but if in the end you're not going to let me go, well, you know what I'm saying. Where's my motivation, you know?"

This time, Smith snorted derisively and touched the butt of his rifle. *"Here's your motivation."*

Farkus craned around in his saddle to see if the riders behind him were more sympathetic. Campbell simply glared at him, his face a mask of contempt. Capellen, though, looked miserable. His face was bone-china white and his eyes were rimmed with red. He clutched the saddle horn with both hands as if to remain mounted.

"Capellen looks bad," Farkus said.

"He's just fine," Campbell said through gritted teeth. "Turn around."

"He looks sick or injured to me," Farkus said. It was obvious Campbell and Capellen stuck together, just as Parnell and Smith were a team. What had brought them all together besides McCue? he wondered.

"Besides," Farkus said, turning back around, "shouldn't you let me know what we're after? I can't help guide if I don't know what we're hunting for."

What Farkus didn't tell them was that he had no idea where they were.

Parnell said, "We'll tell you what you need to know when you need to know it and not before. I should have been more explicit and said if you came with us that you'd need to keep your mouth shut and stay out of the way. I didn't figure it was necessary at the time because we have the guns and gear and all you've got is that stupid expression on your face. I guess I thought the additional conditions would be obvious and implied."

Farkus grunted. Said, "You can't blame a guy for wondering about his fate."

"Dave," Parnell said, not even turning in the saddle, "you're a loser from Bumfuck, Wyoming. You have no fate. So shut up."

"Yeah," Smith echoed. "Shut up, Dave."

From behind him, Campbell said, "If you keep yapping, I'm going to put a bullet into your head."

Farkus looked over his shoulder, grinning uncomfortably, hoping for a hint that Campbell was kidding, that he was chiding him with insults the way men do with each other.

Instead, Campbell reached down and patted the butt of his AR-15 and mouthed, *"Bang."*

THEY CONTINUED CLIMBING. Farkus recognized a couple of the mountain parks from previous elk hunts, but he knew if they kept riding west, he'd soon run out of country with which he was familiar. The fact was that Farkus had always hunted with the same philosophy he used at work. He was happy to let his buddies pore over maps and determine where they'd hunt and develop the strategy for the day. Farkus would just go along. He'd never actually guided hunters in these mountains, as he'd let on earlier. Rather, he'd always volunteered to be the man behind the log looking out on a meadow while his buddies walked the timber to spook out the animals. Just as he'd always take on the role of holding the leg of the elk that was being field-dressed so he wouldn't have to get down into the gore.

He didn't dare let on that while he'd found Cotton-wood Creek once, he'd thought it was Elkhair Creek and his buddies had come and found him before he spent the night lost. Or that the location of Bandit Creek was a complete mystery to him.

And at the clipped pace they were riding, they'd be near the summit by nightfall. He'd never been to the summit of the mountains before. His butt hurt and his knees ached from bending them unnaturally around the belly of his sorrel so his boots would fit into the stirrups. He was hungry and the beer buzz he had going earlier was being replaced by a dull headache. The fat sorrel labored more than the other horses, probably the reason they'd held her in reserve.

The slow realization came over him that he'd likely not see his pickup or Ardith or the Dixon Club or another twelve-pack of Keystone Light ever again. This foray into the Sierra Madre might cost him everything.

Farkus looked furtively over his shoulder, making it a point not to establish eye contact with Campbell. Capellen was still with them, but had drifted farther back. Capellen was leaning forward in his saddle with his head down and looked to be in great pain. As Farkus watched, Capellen listed to the side and vomited up a thin yellow-green stream into the high grass.

"Excuse me," Farkus said, trying to get Parnell's attention.

"Shut up, Dave," Smith and Capellen said in unison from in front of him and in back of him.

THE MEN DIDN'T TALK, except to make random observations that were answered by grunts from the others.

"It's cooling down a little," said Capellen.

Campbell said, "This is a live-game trail, judging by the fresh deer scat."

"That's elk," Farkus corrected, surprised the man hadn't ever seen elk shit before. "The pellets are twice the size of deer."

"Oh."

Smith walked his horse out of the line and let everyone pass him. "Gotta piss," he said. "Go ahead. I'll catch up."

Farkus used the opportunity of the temporary opening ahead of him to nudge his horse and catch up with Parnell and get the man's attention without including any of the others.

"Let me get this straight," Farkus said. "You guys aren't with the sheriff's team that came up here from the other side a few days ago and you're not with the state cops."

"Correct."

"Feds?"

"Not hardly."

"You're operating on your own, then?"

"Correct."

"So who are you with?" Farkus asked. "Who is Mc-Cue? Does this have to do with what that game warden said happened to him? I was the last one to see him before he went up. Did you know that? I was fishing down on the creek way over on the other side when I seen the game warden saddling up. I told him my theory. Do you want to hear it?"

Parnell said, "You're talking too much."

"Ever hear of a Wendigo?"

"Of course," Parnell said. "I'm from the UP."

"The Union Pacific?"

From behind him, Campbell drew his handgun and jacked a cartridge into the chamber and barked, "*Shut the fuck up*, Dave."

Farkus shut up. Pork-bellied cumulus clouds floated across the sky like foam bobbing on the surface of a river. When they crossed the sun and doused it, the temperature cooled instantaneously and he shivered. The air and atmosphere were both thin at this altitude, and temperature fluctuations were almost comically extreme.

Then he realized what was wrong with Capellen. "He's got altitude sickness. I recognize it. It always happens above eight thousand feet. I helped guide a couple of hunters from Florida a few years back and one of them got it bad and spent the entire week in his tent. It hits guys from flatland states like Michigan."

"What can be done for it?" Smith asked Farkus.

"Keep him drinking water, for one thing. But really the only thing that will cure him is to get off the mountain. I'd be happy to ride with him back to camp—"

"Nice try."

Parnell said, "We aren't leaving him, and we aren't going back."

So Capellen rode in agony, moaning, complaining that he had the worst headache he'd ever had in his life and that he was so dizzy they might have to tie him to his saddle to keep him from falling off.

Farkus said, "I'm not gonna ask whether you're after the woman that game warden described or the girl runner if that's really her, or the Grim Brothers themselves. I'm not gonna ask that."

Parnell nodded. *Good.*

"And I'm not gonna ask who you work for or why you aren't in contact with the locals in this area. I'm not going to ask you where you're from in Michigan or why you came this far."

"Shut the fuck up, Dave," Campbell growled from behind him. He sounded *very* annoyed again, Farkus thought.

"All I'm gonna ask," Farkus said, pushing, "is if you're gonna let me go after all of this is over."

Parnell shrugged, said, "Probably not."

Farkus felt the blood drain out of his head and pool like dirty sludge in his gut.

From what Farkus could observe without asking, the expedition was heavily armed and expensively geared up. He counted three AR-15 Winchesters and a heavy sniper's rifle and scope probably chambered in .308 Magnum. All of the riders packed at least one semiauto in a holster, and judging by the bulges at their ankles above their boot tops, they likely had additional pistols. And that's just what he could see.

He had no idea how much additional weaponry they had in the heavy panniers carried by the packhorses. He'd seen plenty of electronic equipment when he'd stumbled into the camp, but it had all been packed away out of his sight. What he'd recognized, though, were radios, GPS devices, sat phones, range finders. Other pieces were unfamiliar to him, but they looked like tracking devices of some sort.

Tracking what? he wondered.

They rode through a gnarled stand of knotty pine. The trees were twisted and beautifully grotesque with football-sized growth tumors bulging out from the trunks and branches. It was as if they'd left the forest and entered some kind of primeval funhouse, and Farkus said, "Do you realize what this wood is worth if we took it back and sold it? I know furniture makers who'd pay a fortune for this stuff." Then, remembering that he'd claimed knowledge of the area, he said, "Every time I come here, I try to figure out how to get a vehicle into the area to gather up some of this knotty pine. But as you can see, there aren't any roads."

He got silence in response, except for the now-inevitable, *Shut up, Dave.* He was grateful no one challenged him.

They cleared the knotty pine stand and rode into a mountain park where the trees opened up to the now-leaden sky. Farkus noted how overcast it had become, like the clouds that were previously bouncing across the sky had hit a barrier and gathered up, blocking out the blue, like tumbleweeds stacked against a barbed wire fence.

Parnell pulled up and climbed down from his horse, looking up at the sky as if it were sending him a message. Smith said to Parnell, "Think we'll get a reading yet?"

"That's what I want to find out."

Parnell let his reins drop and his horse stepped to the side of the trail and began grazing, clipping long bunches of tall grass with its sharp yellow teeth and munching loudly enough to cue Farkus's horse to do the same. When the fat horse bent her head down, she nearly pulled Farkus out of his saddle because he'd been holding the reins too tightly.

Recovering his balance, he said to Parnell as the man walked past, "I think I'll stretch my legs, too."

"Stay mounted," Parnell said, flicking his sharp, dark eyes at Farkus.

Farkus sighed and stayed in the saddle. He took his boots out of the stirrups, though, and flexed his legs. God, his knees hurt.

Parnell walked back to his horse after digging through the panniers in back. He carried an electronic instrument of some kind about the size and thickness of a hardback book. Farkus could see several lit-up digital windows on the instrument as well as a screen that glowed like a GPS display. Good, he thought. Parnell knows *exactly* where they were.

Parnell mounted up, holding the panel between his arm and his tactical vest. He unfolded a stubby antenna from the unit and adjusted a dial. To Smith and the others, he said, "I've got a faint signal. We're headed the right direction."

From in back of Farkus, Campbell said, "Any idea how far?"

Parnell adjusted the metal knob. "Nearly ten miles. Over the top and down the other side of the mountain."

"Where we thought they'd be," Smith said, nodding.

Farkus moaned. "Ten more *miles*? On horseback?"

"Shut up, Dave," Smith said casually.

Even with the overcast, Farkus could tell there was only an hour of daylight left, at most. He said, "Don't tell me we're gonna keep riding in the dark? I'm tired, hungry, and I've got a little hangover. I could use a rest."

It happened quickly behind Farkus, the sound of a swift boot kick into the flanks of a horse and the squeak of leather and thumping of hooves. Suddenly, Campbell was right beside him, their outside legs touching. Campbell had his sidearm out, a deadly-looking two-tone semi-auto with a gaping muzzle that he pressed against Farkus's cheekbone.

"Do you know what this is?" Campbell hissed. Farkus didn't move his head—he couldn't—but he swung his eyes over. Campbell was squinting and the skin on his face was pulled tight. "This is a Sig Sauer P239 SAS Gen 2 chambered in .357SIG. I've been wondering what it would do to a man's head from an inch away. Do you want me to find out?"

Farkus knew he shouldn't say anything, but he couldn't help himself. "No, please."

Smith had turned in his saddle and was watching them now with a smirk on his face. "I was kind of wondering that myself."

"Please, no," Farkus said, his voice cracking. "Put the gun away. You see, I've always been a talker. I'm sorry. I'll shut up. I'll start now." To himself, Farkus said, *"Shut up, Dave."*

Campbell's face twitched. "What's that smell?"

Farkus felt hot tears in his eyes from fear and shame. He said, "I've ruined the saddle."

Campbell leaned away and lowered the pistol. Farkus looked down as well. A wet stain blotted through the denim of his crotch. Dry leather on the pommel soaked it in, turning it dark.

To Parnell, Campbell said, "This guy is becoming a liability."

Parnell's dead-eye silence didn't reveal a thing about what he was thinking. But what he didn't do, Farkus noted, was disagree with Campbell.

Campbell said, "Dave, I'm starting to think you're just a bullshitter, because all I've heard out of your pie-hole is bullshit. And don't think I didn't notice how you caught yourself back there when we rode through that knotty pine. You'd never been there in your life, have you? I'm thinking you don't know where the hell you are right now and I don't see how the hell you're going to help us."

A minute went by. Toward the end of it, Campbell raised the Sig Sauer to eye level.

Despite the cold feeling of dread that coursed through him, Farkus said, "That's where you're wrong. Hell, I've not only hunted up here, I used to move cows from the mountains down to pasture on the other side."

Campbell shook his head, not buying. Then he gestured to the horizon, toward the highest point. "What's the name of that peak?"

To Parnell, Campbell said, "Check his answer against your map, and we'll see if he's lying."

Farkus pointed, stalling for time, "That one? That one there?" He searched his memory, trying to recall conversations from his buddies around the campfire talking about where they'd been that day. Years of conversations to sort through. He wished he'd paid more attention.

His mouth was dry. He could recall his friend Jay telling a story about wounding a young bull elk and tracking it in the snow all the way to . . .

"Fletcher Peak," he said.

Parnell studied his map. While he did, Farkus tried to think of how he could talk his way out of this. Could he say, *Well, that's what we always called it.* . . .

But Parnell said, "Fletcher Peak. Ten thousand, eight hundred feet."

Farkus tried not to close his eyes as joy replaced dread.

Campbell lowered the weapon.

And Farkus thought, *I wish I knew where the hell we are.*

WEDNESDAY, SEPTEMBER 2

16

WITH MARYBETH AT WORK AND THE GIRLS AT school, Joe had the revelation that he'd never been alone in his own house before. It was remarkably quiet. He felt like both a voyeur and a trespasser as he limped through the rooms carrying a plastic five-gallon bucket filled with tools and equipment. His only company was Tube, who, since they'd returned two days before, had not let Joe out of his sight. In fact, Tube trailed him so tightly that the dog would bump into the back of his legs if Joe stopped.

At dinner the previous night, Joe had queried Marybeth and his daughters for their wish lists of repairs, maintenance, and projects. He listed the chores on a legal pad and finally begged them to stop after he filled the first page and after April requested he build "a wall of separation" between her bed and Lucy's in the room they shared so she "wouldn't have to look at her face, like, *ever*." He was embarrassed there was so much to get done, which was a testament to his long absences over the past two years. In addition to his own list—painting the house, fixing a leak in the garage roof, cleaning the gutters, shoring up his leaning slat-board fence, sorting out his long-neglected Game and Fish office—Joe figured he had at least a week's worth of projects ahead of him. By then, he hoped, his in-house sentence would be over and Governor Rulon would lift his order of administrative leave.

Certainly Marybeth had welcomed him home and was pleased he was getting to all of the neglected projects, but Joe could feel tension building between them. Marybeth ran the house and family, and she did a good job of both. She had become used to him not being around. Joe's presence, especially since he was at home during the day, disrupted her management and routine. He sympathized with her and found himself feeling sorry for himself as well. Joe didn't like being inside so much.

Although the home they owned on the quiet residential street in Saddlestring was much more conventional and convenient for Marybeth's business and the girls' school and activities, Joe still pined for past houses in the country. He'd even mentioned to Marybeth when they pulled into the driveway from Billings that it seemed the neighboring houses on each side had somehow encroached a few feet closer to theirs. This was not the first time he'd had this impression, and it made him doubt his sanity.

After he turned off the water to the toilet so he could reset the float to make it stop trickling constantly, Joe parted the curtain and checked to see if his neighbor, Ed Nedney, was still out in his yard. He was. He was out there reseeding a one-foot patch of slightly bare earth in his backyard with a rake so it would grow to be as perfect as the rest of his yard. Nedney was a former town administrator who'd retired solely, Joe believed, to keep his lawn and home immaculate and because it gave him more time to disapprove of Joe's home maintenance regimen.

Joe had watched Nedney through the window all morning while he himself was on the phone making arrangements for his father's body with a Billings funeral home. He didn't look forward to discussing the costs with Marybeth later that night. Marybeth's business transition was facing hurdles now that the downturn in the economy had finally reached Wyoming. The buyers were slowing down the process and making noises about pulling out of the sale. Since the sale had been negotiated, half of her retail clients had either closed shop or taken their financial management in-house to save money. Marybeth had laid off two of her four employees and was in the process of prospecting for more clients while running her office on a day-to-day basis. Because the state had frozen salaries, including Joe's, money was tight.

In a calming and well-practiced baritone, the funeral home director had explained the costs and options for cremation and urns.

The cremation alone would cost $1,835. Joe contained his alarm.

He told Joe, "Our charge for a direct cremation (without ceremony) includes basic services of funeral director and staff, a proportionate share of overhead costs, removal of remains, necessary authorizations, minimum container, minimum urn, and cremation. Another option that has proven very meaningful to families is to have a traditional service followed by cremation. The cost for this type of service is three thousand nine hundred fifty dollars."

Joe wondered if it would be bad form to ask how the cost compared with that of a burial, but assumed a burial would cost more. Plus, he couldn't ask his girls and wife to attend the funeral for a man they'd never met. Meaning it would be a burial with one mourner—him. Cremation was the only option.

"That's kind of expensive," Joe said. "We can do the cremation, but it's more than I thought it would be."

"The process must be thorough to maintain dignity,"

the funeral director said in a well-practiced response. "Now we should talk about an urn."

"Okay."

Joe thought of his father's last laugh. Now he thought he knew what it was about.

"If an individual weighs one hundred eighty pounds at the time of cremation, they will require an urn one hundred eighty cubic inches or larger," the man said. "Do you know the weight of your loved one?"

Joe said, "I'd guess one-sixty."

He could hear the funeral director tapping on computer keys. "You have many, many choices of urns," he said. "Many people these days like to purchase an urn that would mean something to the departed. We have urns available from forty-five dollars to five thousand, so it would help if you could give me the parameters of your budget."

Joe hadn't thought about budgeting the funeral. He thought, *How much is he worth to me, this man who walked out on our family so many years ago and never even bothered to make contact with his wife or sons?* Then, ashamed of his conclusion, he said, "We don't want to make a big deal of it. Simple is best." By simple, he meant cheap.

"Very well," the man said. "Maybe I can help you make a decision. As I mentioned, the trend is toward themed urns. Did your father like to golf? We have golf urns ranging from fifty dollars to two thousand dollars. Fishing? Fishing urns are very popular here in Billings, as you might guess. We have fishing urns in metal, ceramic, glass, and biodegradable. Did your father like to fish?"

"No."

"And we have cowboy boot urns, another popular choice in Montana and Wyoming. Hunting urns as well. Did your father like to hunt?"

Said Joe, "My father liked to drink. Do you have urns

resembling a bottle of gin or Old Grand-Dad bourbon? Or maybe one shaped like a suitcase? He was fond of packing up and leaving."

The funeral director paused for a few beats before he said, "You are kidding, aren't you?"

"Sort of."

With excess pomposity, the funeral director said, "We laugh so that we will not cry."

"Yup, we do," Joe said, and ordered a simple ceramic urn for $100 and the funeral director promised to FedEx the remains to Saddlestring within a day.

WHEN THE TOILET WAS FIXED, Joe called Sheriff Baird in Carbon County. He wasn't in his office, but the dispatcher said, "Oh, it's you" and patched Joe through to Baird's county pickup. From the first word, Joe knew McLanahan's version of events was accurate.

"It's the fabulist," Baird said.

"I'm not sure what to say to that, sheriff."

"Don't say anything. When you start talking, it costs me too much damned money and time."

"The Grim Brothers must have covered their tracks," Joe said. "They knew you'd be looking for them, I guess."

"Then they did a hell of a good job, because my team couldn't confirm a single thing you said. Do you know how much it costs to mount an eleven-person search-and-rescue team and outfit them for the mountains? Do you have any idea?"

Joe looked out the window. Ed Nedney was standing on the dividing line between his perfect lawn and Joe's matted and leaf-strewn grass. Nedney was shaking his head and puffing on his pipe.

"I'd guess quite a bit," Joe said.

"Damn straight. Plus, I had to personally call the parents of Diane Shober and tell them their daughter wasn't found. That was not a pleasant experience."

Joe felt his neck get hot. "I never claimed I saw her. You must have put that out."

"Yeah, stupid me," Baird said. "I believed what you told me. I'm spending way too much time trying to defend your story. The state even sent a man to interview me this morning."

Joe felt a twinge in his belly. "What do you mean, the state?"

"DCI. They sent an agent over here to ask me questions about your statement, even though he had a copy of it with him."

"What was his name?"

"I don't know, McQueen or something. He didn't give me a card."

"Was it McCue?" Joe asked, leaning into the phone. "Bobby McCue?"

"Yeah, that's him. An odd duck. I don't like the state looking over my shoulder."

Joe shook his head. "He came to talk to me in the hospital. Same guy. I can't figure out what his game is or who he's really with."

Baird snorted. "That's all I need is some damned rogue investigator running around down here. Maybe I'll have to sic the FBI on him."

"The FBI?"

"Let me find that message," Baird said. "I grabbed it at the office before I left." Joe could hear paper being unfolded. "Special Agent Chuck Coon called. He wants me to call him back regarding what we found or didn't find in the mountains."

"I know Coon," Joe said, remembering that the governor had also mentioned federal interest. "He's a good enough guy, but I don't know why they're interested."

Said Baird, "DCI, FBI, the *National Enquirer*. You sure as hell know how to stir up a hornet's nest. For nothing, I might add."

"They're up there," Joe said. "The Grim Brothers, Terri Wade, and the mystery woman. You just didn't manage to find them. They know those mountains better than anyone alive, and they probably watched you the whole time. Luckily, you had numbers and firepower on your side so they left you alone."

Said Baird, "They sure as hell did."

"Come on, sheriff. You're well aware of all the break-ins and vandalism over the last couple of years. You've heard from ranchers who've pulled their cattle from leases. You *know* they're up there."

Baird was silent.

"Look," Joe said, "I'm sorry you couldn't find them. And I'm sorry about your budget. But those brothers will stay up there and something else will happen unless they're located. We both know that."

Baird said, "I don't know a damned thing, Joe, other than I'm pulling into the parking lot of the county building right now where I've got to go inside and tell the county commissioners that I've blown the entire annual discretionary budget of the sheriff's department and it's just September. You want to drive down here and explain it to them with me?"

Joe said, "I can't leave my house right now."

"Thought so."

"But I wish I could," Joe said. He sounded lame even to himself.

"I need to hang up now. I've gotta go let the commissioners peel the bark off me."

"I'm sorry."

"You sure are." With that, Baird punched off.

THE WOMAN WHO ANSWERED the phone in the state Department of Administration and Information Human Resources office in Cheyenne said, "I've got three minutes to help you or you'll need to call back."

Joe glanced at the digital clock on his desk. It was 11:57 A.M.

"You go to lunch in three minutes?" Joe asked.

"Two minutes now," she said.

Joe closed his eyes briefly, took a breath, and asked her to confirm that either Bobby McCue or Robert McCue was employed by the State of Wyoming. Joe knew that although additional information couldn't be given out regarding personnel information, the state was obligated to provide the names of employees because it was public record.

"Spell it," she said. Joe tried M-C-C-U-E to no avail. He suggested M-C-C-E-W, then M-C-H-U-G-H. No hits on her computer system. "You'll have to try back later," she said.

Said Joe, "I realize it's noon and noon is your lunch break. But can you please give me five more minutes? I promise I'll buy you lunch next time I'm in Cheyenne."

Through gritted teeth, she said she had to go and she did.

At 12:01, Joe called the Department of Criminal Investigation and asked for Bobby McCue's voice mail.

"We don't have an employee with that name," the receptionist said.

"Thank you." Joe slammed down the phone and moaned. Tube raised his head and cocked it inquisitively.

Joe threw back the curtains and shoved the window open. Nedney looked up, surprised.

"Hey, Ed," Joe said. "Get off of my lawn."

Nedney looked down at his feet. The tips of his shoes had crossed the property line.

"Hey, you're trampling my grass," Joe said.

"Is that what it is?" Nedney said, slowly removing the pipe from his mouth, a self-satisfied smile on his lips.

"Good one," Joe conceded and closed the window and put the drapes back in place, already sorry he'd taken his frustration out on his neighbor.

As he limped through the kitchen with his bucket of tools, bound for the mudroom to fix the door that wouldn't shut properly, he felt he was being watched. Joe paused and slowly turned around. Tube was right with him, as always, but the sensation hadn't come from his dog.

Had Nedney entered his backyard?

Slowly, Joe raised his eyes to the window over the sink that overlooked his back lawn.

Nate cocked his eyebrows at him from outside. Through the glass, Nate mouthed, "Hey."

Joe grinned. It had been a long time.

17

JOE AND NATE WORKED TOGETHER ON DINNER. Joe had pronghorn antelope backstraps in the freezer from the previous fall, and Nate rubbed the meat with sage, garlic, salt, and pepper and prepared it for the grill. Joe roasted green beans in the oven and boiled potatoes on the stove for mashing later. Nate said, "This is uncomfortably domestic."

Said Joe, "This is the least I can do since I'm rattling around the house all day. At some point in the very near future, though, I may need to learn how to do something besides grill red meat every night."

Nate cocked his head to the side the way a puzzled falcon did. *"Why?"*

Joe chinned toward the kitchen window where Nate had stood earlier and said, "Why'd you scare me like that?"

"I couldn't let anyone see me come in the front door," Nate said, shaping a long sheet of foil to wrap around the meat to catch the drippings. "I'm still a wanted man, remember? I saw your neighbor out front, and by the look of him he seems like the type of guy who would call the cops on me because I look suspicious."

"You're right about that," Joe conceded. "But haven't

things cooled down now since Coon took over the FBI field office?" Joe asked. Coon had replaced Special Agent Tony Portenson, who'd finally gotten his wish and had been reassigned to the East Coast as a reward for breaking the Stenko case the fall before. Although Nate was officially still a fugitive, Coon had told Joe that he planned to redirect the agents previously assigned to capturing Nate to other cases. The same way prosecutors had discretion, bureau chiefs had some leeway on the priorities of their offices, Coon had explained with a slight wink.

"Let's just say I haven't heard of any intense efforts to find me lately," Nate said. "I've got a friend or two in the federal building who keep me informed on things like that."

Joe said, "I don't want to hear any more."

Nate smiled and winked. Nate had connections everywhere, and Joe didn't want to know who they were or how they knew Nate. The less he knew about Nate's background, means of support, or day-to-day life, the better, he thought. As it was, he knew he could be brought up on charges for harboring a fugitive.

While Joe plucked the potatoes out of the pot to cool, he told Nate the story of what had happened in the Sierra Madre. Nate was intensely interested, but listened in silence while nodding his head. Finally, he said, "I've got a couple of questions."

"I'm sick of answering questions about it," Joe said. "Nobody seems to believe me, anyway."

"I can see why," Nate said, raising his eyebrows. "So I'll boil them all down to one."

Joe nodded.

"When are we going up there to find those bastards?"

Before Joe could answer, the front door opened and

Marybeth stepped in, trailed by April and Lucy. All three froze when they saw Joe and Nate in the kitchen.

"Oh, my," Marybeth said, her eyes wide.

"Who is *that*?" April asked Lucy, taking in Nate from his ponytail to his scuffed boots. Joe saw Marybeth grimace involuntarily at April's reaction. And he saw April's face harden into a mask when Sheridan ran across the room and hugged her master falconer.

AT THE TABLE LATER, Joe listened as Nate and Sheridan, who'd arrived late due to basketball practice, debated what kind of falcon should be her first to fly. Although she'd lost her passion in the sport for a while because she was angry with Nate, his presence seemed to have rekindled her interest. Sheridan thought she should start out with a prairie falcon, while Nate suggested she get and fly a merlin.

He said, "Merlins are pretty little falcons, and they don't get enough credit. They're small but fast and surprisingly strong."

Sheridan shook off the idea. "Merlins are birds for beginners. They have short wings and they just kill small things."

"You *are* a beginner. Besides, Merlins can be trained quickly and flown within a few weeks. They're more loyal than long-winged falcons."

Sheridan made a face. "You told me once loyalty had nothing to do with it. You said it was about creating a special partnership between falconer and falcon. You said if one needs the other one too much, the special partnership is ruined and the falconer might as well get a dog."

Nate looked to Joe for help. Joe shrugged. It was usually him on the receiving end of Sheridan's arguments, and he enjoyed seeing Nate become prey to his own words.

"Well, I've got a dog," Sheridan said, gesturing at Tube. "Now I want a falcon. A real falcon. You said yourself a prairie is second only to a peregrine as far as you were concerned."

Nate said, "But a merlin . . ."

"Forget merlins," Sheridan said. "Can you help me get a prairie falcon?"

Nate sighed.

"I thought so," Sheridan said.

Joe noticed the amused look on Lucy's face. Lucy had been following the exchange, as well as carefully observing April stare at Nate the whole time. Lucy said to April, "Be careful your eyes don't pop out and fall on your plate. You wouldn't want to accidentally eat them."

April, the spell momentarily broken, flushed red and hissed, *"Shut up, Lucy."*

"Girls," Marybeth said, and smiled a quick smile at Nate and Joe.

Joe thought, *There is a LOT going on here.*

AFTER THE DISHES WERE CLEARED and cleaned—it was the first time Joe could remember all three girls helping without being asked, apparently to impress their guest—Joe went out on the front porch. The sun had slipped behind the Bighorns an hour before, and because of the elevation, the temperature had already dropped twenty degrees. Although it was barely September, there was already a fall-like snap to the air. He'd noticed earlier that fingers of color were probing down through the folds of the foothills, and the leaves on the cottonwoods of the valley floor were starting to cup. V's of high-altitude geese soared south along the underbelly of a moon-fused cloud. All were signs of an early winter. Nevertheless, he thought he'd suggest to Nate and Marybeth that they sit outside in the back. He knew Nate had more questions and he wanted to answer them out of earshot of the girls. Marybeth should be there because she so often provided insight he never considered, plus she said she'd spent a few hours earlier that day doing Internet searches trying to locate what she could online about Terri Wade, Diane Shober, and the Grim Brothers.

Joe went back inside the house to check the humidor in his office, hoping he still had some smokable cigars. But because he hadn't filled the humidor well with water for months, the two cigars that remained crackled drily between his palms and were irredeemable.

He nearly ran into Lucy in the hallway when he came out. She was in her nightgown, and he anticipated a complaint about April when she said, "I think I saw someone in the backyard."

"Was it Nate?"

"No, Nate's in the kitchen talking with Mom."

As she said it, there was a heavy thump against the siding outside, as if someone had tripped in the dark and reached out to prevent a fall. Joe continued down the hall with Lucy padding in bare feet behind him. Sheridan stuck her head out of her bedroom doorway and said, "What was *that*?"

"I'm not sure, but I'm going to find out."

There were a number of possibilities. Maybe Nedney had seen Nate and called the feds or the sheriff; one of Nate's friends or enemies had followed him here; a reporter from the *National Enquirer* investigating the Terri Wade story had located the witness; Camish and Caleb had tracked him down to finish the job. Or maybe something more innocent: high-school boys trying to spy on his daughters. The last possibility made Joe angrier than any of the previous theories.

He looked up to see Marybeth rising from the table and Nate striding across the living room. He'd hidden his .454 on the top shelf of the coat closet.

Joe bypassed the .40 Glock in his office drawer and snatched a 12-gauge Mossberg pump from his gun rack. He used the piece for goose hunting since it took 3-inch Magnum shells, and he jammed three into the magazine and worked the slide to put one in the chamber. His six-battery steel Maglite slipped into his belt.

Joe turned to Marybeth, who hovered in the hallway as if positioning herself between her daughters and any outside threat. He said, "Make sure the curtains are closed in the back bedrooms and the girls are in our room in the front of the house."

He waited while Marybeth shooed Sheridan, April, and Lucy across the hall in their nightgowns into the master bedroom. April sulked, Lucy went willingly—practically skipping—and Sheridan shot a look at Joe and Nate as if she wished she were with them instead of with her sisters and mom. When the girls were across the hall-way, Marybeth leaned out and silently mouthed, *"Okay."*

Although the operation had gone quickly and smoothly, Joe thought again of what his mother-in-law had said to him. How his job endangered his family. Here it was again. His girls were *used* to this sort of thing, and that wasn't normal or right, was it?

Nate said, "Let's go out the front and come around to the back on both sides."

Joe nodded, said, "I'll take the left side."

As they slipped out the front door into the dark, Joe whispered over his shoulder, "Take it real easy, Nate. I

live in this place. No shooting or pulling off ears if it can
be avoided."

Nate grunted his understanding. Then: "When we get
in position, I'll make a noise to get their attention. You
be ready on the back side and come up behind them."

"Okay."

"Let's take this slow."

"Of course."

JOE KEPT LOW TO AVOID being illuminated by the
house windows and the lone streetlamp on the corner of
the block. He went left, reminded painfully of the injuries
in his legs. Once he was on the side of the house, he'd be
in shadow. He avoided the concrete path and kept to the
grass to avoid making noise. There was a narrow strip of
grass between his house and Ed Nedney's, and he'd turn
at a ninety-degree angle at the corner and follow it to a
six-foot wooden gate that led to his backyard. There, he'd
wait for Nate's distraction before opening the gate.

He turned the corner. Ed Nedney's front porch light
clicked on and Nedney stepped out on his landing, apparently to light his pipe. A match flared and lit up Nedney's
face, and he turned his head and saw Joe with the shotgun. Nedney froze, the match paused a few inches from
the bowl of tobacco. He started to speak, but Joe held his
index finger to his lips and hissed, *"Shhhhh."*

Nedney's eyes were wide. Joe thought, he has a decision to make: obey Joe's command or say what he was
going to say. The match burned down in Nedney's fingers. Another time, two years ago, his neighbor had come
outside to find Joe marching another man across his yard
at gunpoint. Nedney hadn't liked the experience one bit.

His neighbor inhaled to speak, but Joe shot his arm out and pointed his finger at him, gesturing for him to go back inside. Although he was clearly angry, Nedney tossed the match aside, turned on his heel, and scuttled into his house. Probably to call the police or start drafting covenants for the neighborhood forbidding residents from lurking around in the dark with shotguns, Joe thought. Joe hoped Nate was in position so whatever was going to happen would happen quickly and he could warn Nate to keep out of sight in case the police were coming.

He paused at the back gate and tried to see into the backyard through gaps in the wood slats. He got a glimpse of the two large cottonwood trunks, Lucy's bike propped up against a planter, and a small swatch of the cracked concrete porch. He couldn't see who had made the noise, but the hairs on the back of his neck were up and he was sure someone or something was back there.

Of course, he thought, it could be innocent. Possibly neighborhood kids playing around. Or an animal—a stray dog, a coyote down from the foothills, a badger looking for dog food to eat, even a deer or bear. A few years before, Joe had been called out to shoot tranquilizer darts at a mountain lion perched in the fork of a mountain ash tree. And there was the occasional moose, elk, antelope, wolverine . . .

Behind the fence in the backyard was an empty field dotted with sagebrush that smelled sweet in the late summer and perfumed the dry air. That was the way Nate had approached their house earlier and Joe peered through the gap in the fence to see if the back gate was open. It was. He knew Nate had closed it earlier, which eliminated the animal options and indicated someone was back there. Whether the intruder had slipped out while he and Nate armed up and sneaked around or was still there was yet to be determined.

Then Joe heard it, a rhythmic wheezing sound. Somebody breathing, but not easily. Whoever it was remained in the backyard, but Joe couldn't get an angle through the fence to see him.

From the other side of the house came an eerie high-pitched call mimicking the sound of an angry hawk: *skree-skree-skree-skree*.

Joe quickly pushed through the gate and was startled when the hinges moaned angrily from lack of oil. He dashed through the opening into the backyard, putting distance between the open gate and himself in case whoever was back there had been as surprised by the rusty hinges as he'd been. There was only one human form he could see, and the man was standing in the muted light beneath the kitchen window with his back to Joe, looking in the direction of the hawk sound. The man was big and blocky, wearing a cowboy hat, an oversized canvas Carhartt ranch coat, and jeans. The left cuff was carelessly pulled outside a cowboy boot and bunched on the top of the boot. What looked like an M1911 .45 ACP semiautomatic pistol was hanging down in his right hand along the hem of the ranch jacket.

Joe said, "Freeze where you stand or I'll cut you in half with this shotgun."

Joe recognized the hat, boots, and pistol. He raised his Maglite alongside the barrel of his shotgun after twisting it on so he could see clearly down the sights while aiming. The beam was choked down to the minimum size, and he trained it on the man's head and shoulders.

He said, "Bud, is that *you*?"

Bud Longbrake, Missy's ex-husband and Joe's ex-father-in-law, stood like a bronze statue of a washed-up cowboy caught in a spotlight. Slowly, Bud turned his head a little so he could talk to Joe over his shoulder. "Hey, Joe. I didn't know you were home."

His voice was bass and resigned, and his words were slurred.

"I live here, Bud," Joe said. "You know that. So what are you doing sneaking around in my backyard? Oh, and drop the Colt."

Bud said, "If I drop it on the concrete, it might go off."

"Then bend over and put it at your feet and kick it away, Bud."

"Oh, all right." It took him a moment to bend all the way over, and he grunted while he did it. He gave the weapon a kick with his boot. Joe thought Bud had gained quite a bit of weight since he'd last seen him, and his movements were stiff as if his joints hurt.

"Okay, turn around slowly," Joe said. "Keep the palms of your hands up so I can see them."

Bud did, and Joe put the beam of his flashlight on Bud's face. He was shocked by what he saw. Bud's eyes were rimmed with red and his cheeks were puffy and pale and spiderwebbed with thin blue veins. His nose was bulbous and looked as if it had been rubbed gray with woodstove ash. A three-day growth of beard sparkled like silver sequins in the beam of the flashlight.

"You look like hell, Bud," Joe said, lowering the shotgun but keeping the flashlight on the old rancher.

Bud said, "You know, I feel like hell, too." He swayed while he said it, as if he'd been hit with an ocean wave at knee level or he was doing some kind of lounge dance very poorly. His arms circled stiffly in their sockets, and he took a step forward to regain his balance. "Whoa," he said.

"Sit down," Joe said, propping his shotgun against Lucy's bike. "Grab one of those lawn chairs."

"I'll do that," Bud said, pulling a chair over and collapsing into it. The *whoosh* of his exhale floated in Joe's direction, and the alcohol content was so high Joe was grateful he didn't have a lighted cigarette. He hoped the chair wouldn't collapse under the ex-rancher's weight.

Nate remained hidden, and Joe purposefully didn't look in his direction. Although Bud seemed completely harmless now, it was good to have Nate there monitoring the situation. It was preferable Bud didn't know it.

Said Bud, "I heard this damned poem in the bar the other night I can't get out of my head. It's a Dr. Seuss poem. It goes:

"I cannot see, I cannot pee

"I cannot chew, I cannot screw

"Oh my God, what can I do?

"Dr. Seuss, you say," Joe said. "I doubt *that*."

Bud continued, *". . . My body's drooping, have trouble pooping*

"The Golden Years have come at last

"The Golden Years can kiss my ass."

With that, Bud paused and grinned a new jack-o'-lantern smile that was the result of missing teeth. One gone on top, two on the bottom.

"Are you through?"

"Yup," Bud said. "There's more, but I can't remember the lines. So yeah, I'm through." He said it while digging into his ranch coat and coming out with a tin of Copenhagen. Joe watched as he formed a huge wad with his thumb and two fingers and crammed the snuff into the right side of his lower lip in front of his teeth. The wad was so big it distorted his lower face.

"So what are you doing here?" Joe asked. "I don't appreciate you sneaking around my house at night."

"I'm sorry," Bud said, shaking his head. "I really am."

Joe couldn't believe how this man had changed in just two years. Bud had been one of the best-liked and most influential ranch owners in Twelve Sleep County. He was generous and avuncular, served on boards and commissions, donated thousands to Saddlestring charities, and almost single-handedly kept the 4-H Club and rodeo arena afloat. He'd been a kind step-grandfather to Sheridan and Lucy, and he'd briefly employed Joe as foreman of the Longbrake Ranch when Joe had been fired from the Game and Fish Department. But here he was, broken and embarrassing. And armed.

He looked up, trying to focus. "Missy told me," he said.

"Told you what?"

"Missy told me she'd hired that Nate Romanowski to put the hurt on me. To knock hell out of me and send me down the river in a pine box. I know what that character can do with that big cannon of his he carries around."

Joe moaned.

"She said he was coming here, to this house, and he was going to kick the living crap out of me in front of my friends and buddies."

"She said that, did she?"

Bud nodded. "She called me yesterday and told me that. She said she was giving me fair warning to get the hell out of town and stop bothering her. I thought about it some, I'll admit. I couldn't sleep at all last night, and I had a beer for breakfast to help me decide what to do. I been on a tear ever since," he said, tipping an imaginary glass of bourbon into his mouth. "Then I said to myself, the hell with it. I ain't scared of no Nate Romanowski. I came here to get the drop on him and maybe bring this thing to a head."

Joe sighed. He was as angry at Missy for inadvertently revealing Nate's whereabouts as he was disappointed in what Bud had become. "It's probably hard to sneak up on guys when you can hardly stand up."

Bud nodded. "You're telling me?"

"She's a cancer," Joe said. "Why do you still listen to her?"

"A cancer?" Bud said, sitting back and slapping his thighs with his big hands, "Cancer can be cured most of the time. No, she's a damned witch! She's an in-the-flesh witch! She put her spell on me for a while and she took everything I owned, and now she's working on that guy, the Earl of Lexington. She'll have everything he's got soon, I'll bet you money. I mean, if I still had some."

Joe said, "I won't take that bet."

Bud laughed drily. "The only revenge I got is that the way things are going, I'm not sure I could have afforded to pay the taxes or comply with all the new regulations they're putting on us out here. I'm glad somebody else has to deal with that shit. But I don't like the idea of your friend coming after me, either."

Joe said, "Bud, Nate's not after you. That's all in Missy's imagination. Not that she hasn't tried to hire him to intimidate you, but that's not what Nate does."

Bud said, "What does he do?"

Which momentarily left Joe at a loss for words.

The kitchen drapes parted, and Joe saw Marybeth look out. Her face fell when she saw Bud Longbrake and how he looked. Joe nodded to her and indicated that everything was fine. Before she let the curtains fall back into place, he could see her purse her lips and shake her head sadly.

"I asked what he did," Bud repeated.

"I take drunk old ranchers home," Nate said, stepping out from the shadows where he'd been hiding. His .454 was low at his side but not in the holster.

At the sound of Nate's voice, Bud's arm rose stiffly and he fluttered his hands and his boots kicked out in alarm.

"Calm down," Nate said to Bud, putting a hand on his shoulder. "If I was going to kill you, you'd already be dead."

Joe shrugged to Bud, as if to say, *You know he's right*.

"Where's your pickup, Bud?" Nate asked.

Bud gestured vaguely toward the sagebrush field in back of the house. "Out there somewhere," he said.

"Why don't we go find it?"

"Then what?" Bud asked.

"Then I'll take you home. Are you still living in that apartment over the Western wear store on Main?"

Bud nodded.

"Then let's go."

Bud didn't move.

Nate reached out and grasped Bud's ear and twisted it. "I said, let's go."

Joe had seen Nate twist off enough ears. He said, "Nate . . ."

But the pressure caused Bud to rise clumsily and stand up. Nate let go of Bud's ear and Bud pawed at it with his free hand like a bear cub.

"Can I at least see the girls?" Bud asked Joe. "I miss them girls."

"They're in bed," Joe fibbed. "It's a school night, Bud."

"I do miss them girls."

"They miss you, too," Joe said. "You were a good grandpa to them."

"Until that witch screwed it all up."

Joe nodded.

"You know the worse thing about her?" Bud said suddenly.

Joe braced himself.

"I still love her. I still goddamn love her, even after all she did to me."

Joe said, "That is the worst thing, all right."

"What about my Army Colt?" Bud asked Joe. "I like to have it within reach."

"Go home, Bud. I'll drop it by later."

"Come on," Nate said. "Can you find your keys?"

Bud clumsily started patting himself. In addition to his pickup keys, he located his can of Copenhagen and a warm bottle of beer. Bud twisted the cap off and took a long drink, and offered it to Joe and then Nate.

"No thanks, Bud," Joe said.

As Nate guided Bud out the backyard toward the distant truck, Joe heard Bud say, "If you really want to kill me, I probably wouldn't put up too much of a fight."

"Shut up," Nate responded.

LATER, AS JOE CRAWLED into bed, Marybeth said, "It's so sad what's happened to Bud. I don't know what's going to become of him."

He moved close to her and she turned away to her side. Their bodies fit so well together, he thought.

She said, "I keep expecting to get a call from the sheriff's office asking us to come down and bail him out of jail. Or identify a body." She didn't sound sleepy.

He said, "Your mother's body count is getting pretty high. How did you manage to turn out so well?"

"I guess I'm the black sheep of the family."

Joe chuckled. "Yup. No one can accuse you of trading up."

"Do you think he'll come back? Bud, I mean?"

Joe pulled her closer. Her body felt warm and soft. He buried his face into her hair. "I doubt it. He knows now Nate's not after him. And deep down, Bud's a good man. He'll wake up and be ashamed of himself for showing up here, I think."

"Mmmm."

"Marybeth," he whispered into her ear, "I was wondering . . ."

"Joe," she said, cutting him off. "First, we need to talk."

"About what?"

She took a deep soft breath and paused. "I can see the direction this is all headed. I could see it tonight when you and Nate got your guns and went outside. It was like your sails were full. I know it was me who called Nate for help, but at the time I wasn't sure when I'd see you again, if at all.

"You're thinking of going back up into those mountains, aren't you? You want to find those brothers," she said.

He closed his eyes, even though she wasn't looking at his face. "No one believes me, honey."

"I do."

"I keep thinking about everything that happened— how they whipped me. I keep thinking about Terri Wade and . . . that other woman. Something was going on up there and I couldn't see it at the time. I still can't. But whatever it is, it's still there. That the sheriff in Carbon

County and all those DCI boys couldn't find the Grim Brothers at all puzzles the heck out of me. That the FBI seems to be monitoring the situation makes no logical sense. And who is this Bobby McCue representing? There are a load of unanswered questions, starting with why the Grim Brothers are up there in the first place. Plus, there are lives at stake. Even though Terri Wade and the mystery woman seemed to be there willingly, I just don't buy it. No woman would choose to be alone in the wilderness like that with those two brothers around. I think they're being held, even if they didn't act like it. Just walking away doesn't feel right."

She turned to face him. He could see the side of her face in the soft light of the moon outside. She still looked youthful, attractive, strong. He wanted her.

She said, "Be thankful you were able to walk away, Joe."

"Yeah, I know."

"Maybe it was a blessing," she said. "You may not be so lucky the next time."

He said nothing for a long time. Then: "I'll tell you something I have trouble putting into words. I'm *scared* to go back up there. I've been scared a lot in the past. But this one is different somehow. I don't think I can beat them."

She reached out and touched his cheek. She spoke softly, "Eventually, those brothers will get caught or turn themselves in. And who knows—maybe those women are up there on their own accord. Not all women have brains in their heads, Joe. Some are actually attracted by men like that, which sickens me. But for once, why not let the system work? You don't need to be the one driving it this time."

She said, "For God's sake, they aren't even in your district anymore. You've been reassigned, so they're someone else's problem now. We both know the governor wants you to stay out of it. And the sheriff down there probably never wants to see you again. If you went after them, it would be purely personal, and that's not good."

"Still," he said.

"Look," she said, propping herself up on an elbow. His arm that had been draped over her fell away from her movement. "You've been gone a long time. You see the situation here. April is like a stick of dynamite walking around in a room filled with candles. She's just going to go off if we aren't there to help and guide her. Sheridan's got a year left before she goes to college, Joe. To *college*! She's in a situation right now where she goes to practice every night and that hysterical coach of hers mistreats her because she won't suck up to him. She doesn't say much about it. She's miserable—but she won't quit. Who does that remind you of?"

Joe grunted.

She said, "I don't sleep well when any of my children are unhappy, even if I can't do anything about it. And there's Lucy. I don't want her to think she's been forgotten amidst all this drama."

He reached out and stroked her naked shoulder.

"I've never asked this before," she said, "But I'm asking now: *promise me you won't go after them.*"

Joe sighed and rubbed his eyes hard.

"I know it's against your nature," she said. "I know you think your advantage is your inability to simply let things go. But something happened up there. They got into your head and under your skin and they stole a part of you. You can't get it back, Joe. You've just got to heal. And you've got to be home to heal. Where I need you right now. *I need some help here, Joe.*"

He said, "You're serious, aren't you?"

"Yes."

"Okay," he said. "I promise."

He was shocked how relieved he was when he said it, how a tremendous downward pressure on him seemed to release and dissipate. He felt lighter and slightly ashamed of himself.

The truth was, he needed her permission *not* to go after the Grim Brothers. Because from what he'd experienced, they'd likely beat him again. And this time, he doubted they'd let the job go unfinished.

"Come here," he said, pulling her to him.

She came.

18

DAVE FARKUS RODE IN THE DARK WITH HIS LEFT arm up in front of his face in case the fat horse walked under a branch. He couldn't see a thing, and he was terrified. He was also severely chilled, because the temperature had dropped once the sun went down behind the clouds.

"I'm freezing," Farkus said.

Ahead of him, Smith turned and said, "Shut up, Dave."

Smith, like the other three, had put on night vision goggles to ride by. Where Smith's eyes should have been, there were dark holes. Only when one of the other riders looked directly at him could Farkus see a dull ball of red deep inside the lenses, which unnerved him. It was as if the twin eyepieces were drilled into their brains. Occasionally, if the riders adjusted their goggles or briefly removed them, he could see their faces bathed in an eerie green.

Farkus said, "I feel like I'm in a goddamned zombie movie."

EARLIER, PARNELL HAD ORDERED them all to put on body armor and night-vision goggles—except for Farkus, of course. Smith and Campbell had dismounted and dug in the panniers and handed out the bulletproof vests. Farkus could hear the soft clink of ceramic plating as the vests were strapped on. Then, in the last few minutes of dusk, he watched them check lithium batteries and adjust the straps of the goggles in a well-practiced way. Campbell and Smith debated the merits of their goggles, and Farkus listened carefully.

"I was hoping for generation fours instead of these ATN gen threes," Campbell told Smith. "There's hardly any moon at all and the gen fours will reach out a thousand yards in these conditions."

Smith said, "But we're still talking one hundred fifty to four hundred yards with these babies at two grand a pop. Not too bad."

Farkus said to them both, "Obviously, this ain't your first rodeo."

Campbell began to say more—he was obviously a gear geek—but after Farkus spoke he caught himself.

But Farkus learned plenty from the short exchange, if little to do with night vision goggles. The expedition was well financed by a third party, and the men were well trained even if they were seeing some of the equipment for the first time. Which meant, as he'd suspected, that the men were mercenaries—hired hands. So it wasn't personal with either them or their target. That could work in his favor, he thought. He'd have to play it cool, but he was used to that. Avoiding hard work meant learning the motivation and proclivities of those around you. It's what he did.

OCCASIONALLY, FARKUS was brushed by a pine bough on his head or leg and he cursed his fat horse. But she could see better than he and there was no choice but to simply hold on and hope she didn't walk under an overhanging branch that would knock him out of his saddle or poke his eye out.

The arrangement of the goggle-eyes behind him was interesting. Campbell rode erect and invisible in his saddle, and his eyes were level with Farkus. Capellen, though, slumped forward, head down and moaning, goggles askew and leaking green ambient light.

AS THEY RODE, FARKUS COULD see Parnell consulting his equipment. Based on the reading of his electronics, Parnell would subtly shift direction. The others would adjust as well. Farkus simply trusted his horse to want to stay with the others. He was grateful horses were such needy and social creatures, and glad he wasn't riding a cat.

Parnell said, "They're on the move."

"Which way?" Smith asked.

"Away from us. And they're moving at a pretty good clip."

Said Smith, "I'm surprised they're moving at night. Do you think they know we're coming?"

"Who knows what they're doing or why?"

"Those guys have always been unpredictable," Campbell said from behind Farkus. "They've adapted well."

Okay, something new, Farkus thought. *They know their targets pretty well.*

Parnell said, "Not well enough to turn off the sat phone they took off that game warden."

Ah, Farkus thought, *that's what he's tracking.*

"Is the signal still strong?" Smith asked.

"Strong enough. We've closed within three miles and

we seem to be holding at that distance as they move. Those guys can cover a lot of ground, as we know."

So, Farkus thought, *we're after the Brothers Grim after all. But why?*

"Hold it," Farkus said. "If it's just a matter of tracking these guys down through their sat phone, why couldn't the sheriff and his boys find 'em?"

Said Parnell, "Because the brothers didn't turn it on until just a day or so ago. They're smart, those bastards."

FARKUS HAD GOT USED TO his own odor when a stronger and more pungent smell wafted through the trees. Parnell and Smith pulled their horses up short and the fat horse followed suit.

"What *is* that?" Smith asked.

"Something dead," Parnell said.

"This way," Campbell said, peeling off from the line of horses and riding into the trees to his right. "Stay here, Mike," he said to his sick companion. "No reason to get any sicker smelling this than you already are."

"I'll stay with him," Farkus volunteered.

"Nice try," Smith sighed, and reached out and slapped the back of Farkus's head as he rode by. Farkus was heartened by the gesture. The slap wasn't hard or mean-spirited. It's what males did to each other to acknowledge that the other guy was sort of okay after all.

Stifling a smile in the dark and complimenting himself on his reliable charm, Farkus spurred the fat horse into the trees with the others.

The smell got stronger. Farkus winced and pulled his T-shirt collar up out of his shirt and tried to breathe through the fabric. It didn't help.

Back on the trail, he heard Capellen cry out with a short, sharp yelp.

"Probably getting sick again," Campbell said. "Poor guy."

"HERE THEY ARE," Smith said up ahead. "The game warden's story checks out so far."

"Here what is?" Farkus asked. "I can't see anything, remember?"

"At least two dead horses," Parnell said. "Maybe more. I can see skulls and ribs and leg bones, but it looks like the carcasses are cut up. Some of the bones are stripped clean of meat. They must have had to cut up the bodies to move them in here so the sheriff's team wouldn't find them. Since these guys were butchers, it probably wasn't a big deal to cut the horses apart."

Farkus could detect the smell of fresh soil mixed into the stench of decomposition. *"Butchers?"* he said. No one replied.

"And they buried them," Smith said. "So they probably didn't stink at the time those other guys were up here. But something's been digging them up."

Campbell said, "Probably a bear. They've got bears here—black and grizzly. Mountain lions, too. They've got lots of critters that like horsemeat."

Farkus said, "Or wolves. The game warden said he saw wolves. Look around you, guys, do you see any wolves?" His voice was tight. He had a pathological fear of wolves that came from a dream he'd had when he was a small boy. In the dream, a pack of wolves dragged him down as he ran toward school and ate him. He'd never seen a live wolf before, and he didn't want to see one now. Or, worse, to not see a wolf sneaking up on him in the dark. He tried to make his eyes bigger so he could see into the trees around him. He wished they had an extra set of night vision goggles, and he vowed to take Capellen's if the sick man wouldn't use them properly.

"Don't panic," Parnell said to Farkus. "I'd see 'em if they were here."

"Whatever it was eating on this horse, it hasn't gone far," Smith said, shifting in his saddle. "The damage looks fresh." Farkus saw the dull red orbs of Smith's goggles sweep past him as the man looked around.

"Let's get back," Parnell said. "And see how Capellen is doing."

"That's a good idea," Farkus said.

"DAMN," CAMPBELL SAID as they walked their horses through the trees back to the trail, "Capellen fell out of the damned saddle. We should have tied him in it, like he asked."

Smith said, "There's something sticking out of him."

The way he said it made Farkus hold his breath.

"It's an arrow," Parnell whispered. "Those fucking brothers found *us*."

Farkus couldn't see Parnell, Smith, or Campbell, but he could sense from the leather-on-leather creaking that all three men were turning in their saddles trying to get a panoramic view of what might be out there in the trees.

"This is when we could have used those gen fours," Campbell muttered.

CAPELLEN WAS ALIVE, but the arrow was buried deeply into his chest. His breathing was harsh, wet, and heavy.

The shot had been perfectly placed in the two-inch gap between the ceramic shoulder pad and the armored strap. Farkus stayed on his horse while the others tried to lift the wounded man back onto his mount. As they pushed him up, his arm flopped back and knocked Smith's goggles off his face. In the sudden pool of bouncing green light from the eyecups, Farkus watched as they shoved Capellen onto the saddle like a sack of rocks. Capellen simply fell off the other side of the horse into the dirt, snapping off the shaft of the arrow in the fall and possibly driving the projectile farther into his chest. In the glow of Smith's goggles, Capellen's bloody clothing under his armpit looked like it was soaked in black motor oil and his open eyes showed white from rolling back in his head.

"Oh, shit!" Campbell cried, and reached up to readjust his goggles. As he did so, the light blinked out and doused the macabre scene.

Farkus said, "Put him behind me. This old horse is stout enough to carry us both. I'm sure he can hold on."

The men didn't pause or talk it over. They gathered Capellen up, and Farkus felt the weight and heat of the man behind him. Capellen leaned into Farkus with his arms around his ribs and dropped his face into his back.

"Get his gun," Parnell said. Smith pulled Capellen's weapon out of his holster, and Farkus fought an urge to mouth, *"Damn."*

There was a wet *cack-cack-cack* liquid sound when Capellen inhaled. Farkus recognized the sound from hunting. The arrow had pierced a lung, and probably collapsed it. Capellen's chest cavity was filling up with blood. He would drown from the inside, like an elk hit in the same place. It was a miserable and drawn-out way to die, Farkus guessed. If Capellen was a game animal, there would be no question but to stop the suffering with a bullet to the head or a slit across his throat.

Farkus thought: *This is just like hunting and these men are just meat and organs, sacks of bones, like elk. It's time to quit being scared of them.*

But he didn't feel the same way about whoever had shot the arrow and had taken them all by surprise.

"Let's move back to where we've got an advantage," Parnell said, turning his horse around and riding past Farkus and Capellen, back down the trail they'd come on.

"Are we headed back to the rock face?" Smith asked, turning his mount.

"Absolutely," Parnell said.

Farkus remembered it well, and it made sense. Just below the summit, the trail had switchbacked through a massive rock slide where it looked like an entire wedge of the mountainside had given way and fallen like a calf from an iceberg, leaving a long treeless chute of rubble and scree. And a few room-sized boulders. It would be a perfect place for them to go: treeless so they could see for half a mile with their night vision goggles. And well beyond arrow range from an archer in the trees.

Parnell had kicked his horse into a canter, and they retreated quickly.

Farkus had his reasons to take Capellen. The first was his hope they'd forget about the handgun, which they didn't. But Capellen still wore his night vision goggles, and Farkus reached over his shoulder and snatched them off. After fumbling with the straps, he managed to pull them on. The pitch-black night turned ghostly green and he could see everything! The clarity was astonishing, even though the color scheme was largely green and gray. When he glanced up at the sky, the few stars that peeked down between the clouds looked like Hollywood spot-lights. He was shocked how dense the forest was as the trees shot by on both sides. Up ahead, he could see Par-nell and Smith pushing their horses, and he could see the big butt muscles of their mounts contracting and expand-ing with their new gait. When he saw how tight the trees were that he'd come through earlier, he wondered how it was he hadn't been knocked off.

"When we get to the rocks," Farkus said to Capellen, whose head bounced on Farkus's back as they rode, "we're trading pants. You look like my size, and why should you care if your pants are clean or dirty?"

The fourth reason he'd volunteered to take Capellen was still forming in his mind, Farkus thought. But by taking their buddy, they might decide he, Dave Farkus, was all right after all. He was on their side. And they might forget about him and quit telling him to shut up every time he spoke.

And he could work the new angle and get the hell away from them before the Grim Brothers killed them all.

"THEY MUST HAVE SPLIT UP," Parnell said, a note of puzzlement in his voice. He adjusted the dial on his equipment. "One of them has the sat phone and has fi-nally stopped moving. The other one is down there somewhere." He motioned toward the dark wall of trees. "They split up so we'd march right toward the guy with the sat phone while the other one waited for us here."

"Do you think he's still there?" Campbell asked.

"I doubt it," Parnell said. "He knows we have the high ground and a clear field of fire. He's not stupid enough to try to take us on up here in these rocks."

Smith nodded. "He waited until we left Capellen alone before he attacked him. That way, he had the odds on his side as well as the element of surprise. I wonder how long he's been tracking us?"

Parnell shrugged.

"Maybe all night," Smith said.

Campbell turned. "Farkus, what the hell are you doing back there?"

Farkus said, "Trying to make Capellen more comfortable. I took his vest off so he could breathe easier. I'm sure he won't mind if I wear it for a while."

"What are you doing with his pants?"

"WHAT IS IT with those guys?" Smith asked no one in particular. "We couldn't see a damned thing without our night vision equipment, but whoever went after Capellen didn't seem to have that problem. And I seriously doubt those guys have any real technology to use."

"They're not human," Farkus said.

"Bullshit," Parnell spat.

They'd made it to the rock slide without being attacked. The horses were picketed on a grassy shelf above them, and Capellen lay dying in Farkus's jeans with his back to a slick rock. There had been no movement on the scree beneath them or in the wall of trees below since they'd arrived an hour before.

Smith said to Farkus, "If they aren't human, then what the hell are they?"

"They're Wendigos," Farkus said, pleased to finally be able to introduce his theory.

Smith said, "Jesus. But that doesn't work because these guys used to be human."

"That's exactly how it works," Farkus said. "They start out human, but something goes wrong. It's usually related to terrible hunger, but sometimes it's like a demon enters into them and turns them into monsters.

"I know it sounds crazy, but things have been happening up here in these mountains for the last year that don't make sense. It's common knowledge in town that something's going on up here."

Hearing no objection, Farkus forged on, keeping his voice low. "One night, in the Dixon Club, I asked an old Indian I know. He's a Blackfoot from Montana by the name of Rodney Old Man. That's the first time I heard about Wendigos. Then I did some research on the Internet and checked out a couple of books from the library. It's scary stuff, man. These people who turn into Wendigos look like walking skeletons with their flesh hanging off of their bones. They stink like death—like those horses we found back there. And they feed on dead animals and living people. They're cannibals, too, but they're really weird cannibals because the more human flesh they eat, the bigger they get and the hungrier they are. And they can *see in the dark*."

Farkus said, "You guys are from Michigan, which is close to Canada, where most of the Wendigos come from. Do you know the story of an Indian named Swift Runner?" Farkus asked. No one spoke. "Now there was a man filled up with the spirit of the Wendigo. Killed, butchered, and ate his wife and six children.

"You hear of a guy named Li just a couple of years ago? Up in Canada? He cut the head off a fellow bus passenger he'd never met before and started eating him right there on the bus."

Parnell hissed, "Shut up, *now*," and put the muzzle of

his weapon against Farkus's forehead. Parnell's face was flushed red with anger. The soundtrack for his rage was Capellen's wet breathing, which had got worse.

"Gotcha," Farkus said.

AS THE EASTERN SKY LIGHTENED enough for Farkus to shed his night vision goggles, Capellen died with a sigh and a shudder.

"Poor bastard," Parnell said. "There was nothing we could do to save him."

Farkus didn't say, *Except maybe take him to a hospital.*

Parnell stood up and peeled his goggles off, said, "We'll pick up his body on the way out. He's not going anywhere."

Then: "Let's get this thing over with so we can go home."

THURSDAY, SEPTEMBER 3

19

IT HAD BEEN A LONG TIME SINCE JOE HAD GOT UP earlier than the rest of his family and made them breakfast. He cooked what he always cooked, what he knew how to make, what he thought they should want even though he wasn't sure anymore that they did: pancakes, scrambled eggs, and bacon. He'd drunk half a pot of coffee and his nerves were jangling by the time Marybeth came down the hall in her robe.

"Smells good," she said.

He poured her a mug of coffee.

"Thank you," she said. "I hope you don't take it personally if the girls don't dive into that big ranch breakfast you just created. Don't forget—they're getting older and more health and weight conscious all the time. It's a struggle to get them to eat a banana or cereal in the morning before school. Most of the time I'm giving them something as they dash out the door."

"That's because you don't tempt them with bacon," Joe said. "Bacon is magic."

She let that pass. "Any sign of Nate?"

"Nope. My guess is he's out at his old place on the river or staying with Alisha."

"I'd guess Alisha."

"I'm sure you're right."

She said, "I'm glad we talked last night."

"For starters," he said.

She smiled and looked away. He watched as she peered through the front room toward the picture window, squinted, and turned to him. "Who is parked in front of our house?"

"What?" There hadn't been any vehicles in front when he'd gone out earlier to collect the weekly Saddlestring *Roundup*. Now, though, there was a massive red Ford Expedition with Colorado plates blocking Marybeth's van in the driveway.

Joe walked to the front window in his apron with a spatula in his hand, just in time to see the passenger door open and Bobby McCue swing out. McCue was talking with someone inside. Although the windows were darkened, Joe could see at least two other heads besides the driver.

Marybeth joined him at the window, and they both watched as a man and a woman got out of the Expedition. The man was tall and red-faced, and his movements were swift and purposeful. He slammed the door shut and strode around the front of the vehicle. He wore an open safari jacket, jeans, and heavy boots, as if he planned to traverse the Outback later in the day. The woman, in a knee-length navy blue jacket, wrapped her arms around herself as if trying to make herself smaller. She was short, thin, dark, and furtive. She appeared uncomfortable or nervous, and she looked to the red-faced man for their next move. He gestured toward the house with a brusque nod and walked right by her, swinging his arms. She followed him up the concrete walkway in front of Bobby McCue.

"Do you know them?" Marybeth asked.

"I know the guy in the back. He's the one who came to see me in the hospital and lied about being from DCI."

"What do you suppose they want?"

"I don't know," Joe said, "but if they want to talk, I'll steer them into my office. Do you mind feeding the girls?"

Marybeth said, "That's what I do every day, Joe. I think I can handle it."

THE RED-FACED MAN SAID, "Brent Shober" and stuck out his hand.

Joe reached out and shook it. "I was wondering when I might hear from you."

"This is my wife, Jenna."

"Hello, Jenna. I'm Joe Pickett."

She smiled tightly and looked away from him.

"And our investigator, Bobby McCue."

"We've met," Joe said, nodding toward McCue. McCue shrugged and winked, as if he and Joe were brothers in arms in law enforcement subterfuge. Joe shook his head, denying the bond.

Joe had to clear papers from his two office chairs and fetch a folding chair from a hall closet so all three could sit down in his cramped home office. They filled the room. He closed the door and sidled past them and around his desk and sat in his office chair. Joe didn't want any of them seeing his girls as they went about their morning routine getting ready for breakfast and school.

"You gonna wear *that*?" Brent Shober asked, indicating Joe's apron. Joe flushed. He'd forgotten about it. But he didn't feel like taking it off, either. He put the spatula on his desk next to his pen and pencil set.

"What can I do for you?" he said.

Brent snorted and sat forward, putting his elbows on Joe's desk. He glanced quickly toward McCue and Jenna before forging ahead. "We're here because Bobby got ahold of the statement you made to the sheriff in Carbon County, right?"

Joe said, "Now before you jump to conclusions, I never said I positively identified your daughter. I'm sorry to say that, but . . ."

"Look, Pickett," Brent said, cutting Joe off. "I'm not one to beat around the bush. We're here because we need you to help us locate Diane."

"Didn't you just hear what I said?"

Brent shook his head as if it didn't matter. "We've spent the last week in agony while that search team went up into the mountains to check out your story. We waited for any kind of word from them. When they found nothing—nothing at all—it was like another twist of the knife in my back, right? And I'm getting sick and tired of having my hopes raised up and smashed back down. You're the only one, apparently, who knows where to find her. We need you to do just that. If necessary, I'll hire you. Just name your price."

"It isn't about money," Joe said.

"Everything's about money, right?" Brent said. "I can see how you live here," he said, gesturing vaguely around Joe's cluttered office. "I also know your personal situation from Bobby here. You've been put on the shelf. You've got nothing to do and who knows if you'll even get your job back. Right?"

Joe didn't like talking to people who ended statements with the word "Right?" for the reason of preempting any possible disagreement. But before he could speak, Brent said, "For two long, hard years, Jenna and I have done everything we could to get the word out that our daughter was missing and doing everything we could do to find her. I personally spent two weeks this summer talking to law enforcement to *remind* them she hadn't been found and putting fliers in every public place I could in northern Colorado and southern Wyoming. Finding her is my obsession, Pickett. I know she's alive and well. I just know it, right? And up until Bobby got ahold of that statement of yours, I was starting to think about giving up hope. Not that I did give up, but I was considering the possibility, if you know what I mean, right?"

Joe had learned not to even try to talk to Brent Shober, so he didn't.

Brent stood up. He clearly wanted to pace, but there was no room. So he bent over Joe's desk so his face was even closer.

"My little girl was on a schedule to go to the Olympics, something her old man barely missed out on. I was a one-thousand-meter man. I don't know if you've ever heard of me or not, but no matter. A month before the trials, I screwed up my knees. Still, I missed qualifying by only six seconds. Diane, though, she was on track. She was getting stronger by the month. That's why we moved part of our company from Michigan to the mountains out here, so she could train at high elevation and gain endurance and strength. She was on track, right?"

"Right," Joe said.

"Then she goes for a long run and never comes back. We haven't seen her or talked with her in *two* years. Think about that. It's been eating us up, Jenna and me. I nearly lost my company—I build super-high-end office parks— because I spent so much time talking to local yokels and listening to every crackpot who said they might have seen her. That's because I put out that half-million-dollar reward, right?"

Even though Brent's eyes burned into him, Joe let his return gaze slip away. McCue sat in his chair like a good hired soldier, betraying nothing. There was a slight smile on his face, as if he enjoyed seeing someone else on the other end of Brent Shober for a change. He'd likely heard the story twenty times, but he didn't betray his boredom or familiarity. Jenna, on the other hand, made a point not to look at Joe or her husband, even when he referred to her. No doubt she shared his pain, Joe thought, but she didn't share his bombast.

"So," Brent continued, "for two years this has been our quest—to find our Diane. We've hired private investigators, I've gone personally to meet with the FBI in D.C., Denver, and Cheyenne, and we've even listened to hack psychics tell us she is definitely alive, and definitely waiting for us to rescue her. Her no-good fiancé used to work with us, but he's given up the fight. That little rat bastard picked up and moved to Baja and we haven't heard from him in months. But I'm not giving up, Pickett. I know she's still up there somewhere, that somebody's got her, right?"

Joe felt pummeled and somehow at fault. "Mr. Shober, I can't even imagine what it would be like to lose your only daughter."

Brent stuck out his palm to stop Joe from talking. "No, Pickett, you can't imagine what hell feels like."

Joe wanted to say, *But I have a pretty good idea . . .* when Jenna Shober spoke for the first time. She said, "Diane is our youngest. We have an older daughter and an older son. But they aren't . . ."

Brent cut her off, said to Joe, "So we need you to go back up there. Take as many men as you need. Hire experts, if you have to, and send me the bill. But you are the only soul alive who has seen her in the past two years, and you are the only one who has a chance of finding her again, right?"

"Wrong." Joe felt as if he were being screwed into the floor with guilt. He wished he'd never have mentioned her name.

Brent Shober sputtered, "What did you say?"

"I said 'wrong,'" Joe repeated. He pointed at McCue. "I told your guy and every investigator since I made the initial statement that I didn't get a good look at the fourth person up there. It was dark, I was hurt, and I was influenced by all those fliers you put up. Her name popped into my mind, is all. I wish I could tell you different, but I have no idea at all who that woman was."

Brent shook his head. "You're backing out on me."

Joe said, "I was never *in*. Look, at least let me ask you a couple of questions before we end here." He was fully aware of his promise to Marybeth and he was honorbound to keep it, even though the circumstances may have changed. But his curiosity was up.

Brent turned to Jenna, incredulity on his face, as if he were being confronted by madness.

Joe forged on. "Did you or Diane ever know a couple of brothers named Grim? Or Grimmengruber? Is there any reason to believe if this person I saw was your daughter that she'd be with them?"

Brent screwed up his face with utter contempt. "That's the most fucking ridiculous question anybody has ever asked me. Of course we don't know anybody like that."

"What about Diane?"

"Jesus, are you deaf? We don't know anybody like that. We'd never know white trash like that, right?"

Joe paused. He looked at McCue, then back to Brent Shober. "How do you know what they're like?" Joe asked. "I never said a word about them. I never used the term 'white trash.' So how would you not ever know any-one like that if you don't know a thing about them?"

Brent's face got redder, and Joe could see the cords in his neck pull taut from his clavicle to his jawline.

McCue said, "He knows what's in your statement and the report. I told him all that."

Joe wasn't sure. He looked to Brent's face for clues but read only fury. Jenna wouldn't meet his eyes.

Brent closed his eyes and took several deep breaths, obviously to calm himself. A full minute passed. Joe started wondering where his pepper spray was amidst the clutter. Just in case.

Finally, Brent said, "To accuse me of anything is be-yond ridiculous. I love my Diane more than life itself."

Joe felt ashamed. "Really, Mr. Shober, I didn't mean to imply you were guilty of anything."

Brent waved him off and continued. "Do you realize, Pickett, what a special girl she is? That she has the capa-bility of representing her family and her country in the Olympics? Do you know how rare that is? Do you realize that in the life of a long-distance runner, you get maybe—*maybe*—two shots at the Games? That's how short the window is. And if you miss your chance, you never get it back for the rest of your life. You grow old knowing you had your shot and you didn't take it."

Joe said, "Are we talking about Diane here?"

McCue was faster than he looked, and was able to throw himself in front of Brent Shober before the man could leap over the desk and throttle Joe.

McCue and Jenna managed to get Brent turned around, and McCue wrapped him up and guided him out the door. Brent yelled over his shoulder, "YOU'VE GOT TO HELP ME! *YOU'VE GOT TO HELP ME!*" even as

McCue pushed him across Joe's lawn toward the Expedition. Jenna followed, her head down.

As they reached the SUV, he turned and looked back at the house, as if sizing it up for demolition.

AFTER THEY DROVE AWAY, JOE moaned, collapsed on the couch, and put his head in his hands. He ached for Brent and Jenna Shober. What torment they'd gone through. Torment like that would likely turn him into someone like Brent, or worse. He didn't have to like the man to feel sorry for him.

He closed his eyes and tried to recall the fourth person on the mountains, but her face became no clearer.

AFTER CLEARING AWAY the breakfast dishes and noting that the girls *had* eaten the magic bacon but little else, Joe called the FBI field office in Cheyenne and asked for Special Agent Chuck Coon.

When the receptionist asked who was calling, Joe gave his name. When she came back, she said Agent Coon was in a meeting and would have to get back to him. So Joe called Coon's private cell phone number.

"Hello?" Coon said.

"It's me, Joe."

"Damn, I didn't recognize the number. If I knew it was you, I would have let it go to voice mail."

"You gave me this number last year, remember?" Joe said. "You said to use it if I couldn't get through to you."

"That was last year," Coon said.

When they were both working on the Stenko case, Coon wanted Joe to be in contact. Joe pictured the agent on the other end of the conversation. He had close-cropped brown hair, small features, and a boyish, alert face that didn't jibe with his tightly wound manner. He had a young son and another child on the way. He'd worked for several years under Tony Portenson before Portenson got his wish and got reassigned. Joe assumed Coon and the entire FBI office had sighed a collective sigh of relief when Portenson walked out the door.

Joe asked about the baby on the way (she was due in a month) and Coon's son (four and starting preschool), and he briefed the agent on his family and how things were going now that April was back with them. It all took two minutes. Then: silence.

Which said to Joe that Coon was being very cautious.

"You know why I'm calling," Joe said.

After another pause, Coon said, "Why don't you tell me just so, you know, I don't start giving national counterterrorism secrets away or something like that?"

"The Grim Brothers," Joe said.

"I was afraid that was what you'd say."

"Tell me about them."

"There's nothing to be said."

"Which means exactly what?"

"Joe," Coon said with some finality, "the Grim Brothers don't exist as such."

Joe's stomach hurt. "Please translate? As such?"

"Exactly that. They don't exist."

"Are you saying I made them up?"

"Not exactly. But I can't go much further than what I already said. Let's just leave it at this: it's a matter we're keeping our eye on. The bureau doesn't comment on ongoing investigations. You, of all people, should know that."

"Man, I'm confused."

"So," Coon said, "how is that dog of yours? Tube, wasn't it?"

"Not so fast," Joe said. "I need to get something straight. Are you saying they don't exist because you can't find them in your database? Or that you think I made them up?"

Coon sighed. "They're not in the database, Joe. Caleb, Camish Grim, or G-R-I-M-M, or Grimmengruber, or any combination thereof. They gave you a false name, Joe."

"Why would they do *that*?"

Coon exhaled, as if he were going to answer Joe, but he caught himself. "I've already said enough, I think."

"But I'm investigating them, too. So's the governor and DCI. I thought we shared information these days?"

Coon laughed, "When did you come up with that one? Nice try, though. Besides, at some point in this conversation, were you going to let me know you're on administrative leave? Did you think I wouldn't know that?"

Said Joe, "Chuck, what is going on here? Why are you guys so interested in what happened up there? From what I know, it's purely a local or state matter on the surface unless you got asked to assist. I know the state didn't ask you to come in on this, and I doubt Sheriff Baird would. So that means there's some other reason. I don't buy it you have nothing else to do and you're bored."

"As I said, the FBI doesn't comment on ongoing . . ."

"Sheesh, I know, I know. But why is there federal interest?"

"I'm sorry, Joe. That's the best I can do."

Joe said, "You've done *nothing*."

"I'm sorry you feel that way, Joe. My best to Marybeth and the girls. And don't call me on my cell again." With that, he punched off.

Joe closed his phone and stared out the window. Ed Nedney was back outside putting fertilizer on his lawn.

Despite what Coon withheld, he'd inadvertently confirmed a couple of things. There *was* an investigation going on, and it was obviously big enough he'd felt the need to play it coy. That the bureau hadn't tipped off DCI or the governor of their investigation was suspicious. Even so, Joe was heartened they believed him and his story after all.

JOE SPENT THE AFTERNOON walking aimlessly though the house with his bucket of tools, but his mind was back up in the Sierra Madre. He tried scenario after scenario and came up with nothing plausible. When he tried to link up the Grim Brothers, the FBI, Terri Wade, the mystery woman, the UP . . . he got nowhere.

He realized he'd forgotten about dinner, and he looked at his watch. There was an hour before Marybeth and the girls got home. He'd told Marybeth he'd cook burgers on the grill, but he'd forgotten to get the meat out of the freezer and he hadn't been to the store to buy buns or the other things on the list she'd left him. On the way to the kitchen to see what he could scramble up, the doorbell rang.

It was Jenna Shober. She was alone and crying.

20

"HOW MANY MORE OF THESE ARE THERE?" SMITH asked, gesturing toward the perfectly round lake in the bottom of the alpine cirque. Vertical rock walls rose sharply on three sides of the water, and the fourth side was sloped and grassy. A trout nosed the surface and concentric rings rippled out across the still water until it finally flattened again.

"There's at least two more cirques," Farkus said. "They kind of stair-step their way down the mountain. The cirques trap the snowmelt so it can't flow anywhere. We used to fish these lakes."

The sky had cleared and morning was warming up. They'd been riding for five hours on the western side of the mountains, rimming the series of spectacular cirques Farkus had surprised himself by knowing about. He'd fudged his knowledge a little, because he hadn't visited the area since way back in high school with some friends who'd backpacked up from the valley floor to fish the mountain lakes. He'd been drunk approximately the whole time, so his recollections were vague and imprecise. He remembered falling off a rock into one of the lakes while drinking a half a bottle of sloe gin. The water was bone-chilling. His lone trip up here was years before the Forest Service had shut down access roads into the area, but at last he had an idea where he was. He knew that if they kept traveling in a westerly direction, they'd eventually hit the creek and trailhead where he'd originally met Joe Pickett.

Farkus had actually become useful to Parnell, Smith, and Campbell. Plus, his tales of the Wendigo had helped distract Smith and Campbell, he could tell. Of course, he'd just made up the part about Wendigos being able to see in the dark, but they'd never know that. Smith and Campbell now seemed jumpy. Farkus could tell Parnell had picked up on that, too, and he no doubt feared a loss of control over his team.

For the first time since they'd stopped him and forced him out of his truck two days before, Farkus felt he might just have a chance after all. Since he knew vaguely where he was now and his companions were becoming less vigilant by the hour, he might be able to escape.

Problem was, it was this area where the game warden was headed to investigate the stolen elk. Which meant this is where Joe Pickett had encountered the Grim Brothers.

Parnell's tracking device chirped. He read the display and announced they were practically on top of their target.

"How close?" Smith asked.

"Half a mile, maybe. Over the next ridge, I'd guess. We've been closing the gap all morning."

"Are they still going the other way?"

"No," Parnell said. "He's coming at us right now."

Smith drew his AR-15 rifle out of his saddle scabbard and laid it across the pommel of his saddle. Campbell checked the loads of his rifle, even though Farkus had seen him do it at least twice before.

"So," Farkus said to Parnell, "are you gonna finally tell me what this is all about?"

"No."

FARKUS FELT A KNOT BUILD in his stomach as they got close to the ridge. Whoever they were after, if Parnell's equipment was reliable, was just over the other side. Parnell had veered from the established trail into a thick stand of gnarled pine trees. When they were in the cover, Parnell dismounted, and Smith and Campbell did the same. For a brief moment, Farkus considered kicking the horse and riding away while the three of them were down. But which direction? If he went back the way they'd come, he'd be in the open for a hundred yards and a well-placed shot could pick him off, borrowed body armor or not. And if he thundered over the rim, he might ride straight into the Grim Brothers.

He sighed and dismounted with the rest of them.

Parnell motioned for them to come close and listen. He whispered, "Let's get our weapons ready and tie up the horses here so they can't see them. When we're locked and loaded, we'll crawl through the trees to the edge of the ridge and scope it down. Remember, those boys have body armor, too. So go for headshots."

Farkus said, "They do?"

"At least that's what we were told."

Then: "Smith, you ready?"

Smith nodded once.

"Campbell?"

"Yes, sir."

He turned to Farkus. "You stay here and don't even think of trying to get away like you were a minute ago. If you try to run, I'll shoot you so fast you'll be dead before you hit the ground."

Farkus swallowed and looked away.

"So," Smith said to Parnell, "you're thinking they're down in this cirque?"

"That's what I think," Parnell whispered.

"Let's not miss," Smith said to the others. "The last thing we need is a wounded Cline brother coming after us."

Farkus said, "Cline? I thought their name was Grim?"

"Shut up, Dave," Parnell said, shooting Smith a punishing look.

FARKUS STOOD OFF to the side with the horses, thinking *Cline*? Where had he heard that name? Something about Michigan . . .

When Parnell's tracker chirped again, he read it and appeared startled. His scalp twitched above his forehead even though his face was a mask.

"What?" Smith asked.

"He's on top of us," Parnell whispered. "He's coming up the rim right at us. He's *running* up the side of the cirque."

Farkus quickly dropped down to his hands and knees, wishing he could make himself even less of a target.

Parnell and Smith raised the barrels of their AR-15s, pointing them through the trees toward the lip of the rim. Campbell quickly slung his scoped rifle over his shoulder, because his scoped weapon wasn't useful at close range, pulled his Sig Sauer, and steadied it out in front of him with two hands.

Farkus heard the rapid thumping of footfalls and saw a flash of spindly movement from the other side of the rim and then a full set of antlers. The big five-point buck mule deer with a satellite phone wired to its antlers came lurching up over the side in a dead run.

Parnell and Smith turned it into hamburger.

21

"WE DIDN'T KNOW DIANE WAS MISSING UNTIL she'd been gone for four days," Jenna Shober said in a low, soft voice rubbed raw with sandpaper from two years of crying. "Can you imagine that?"

"No," Joe said.

They were in the living room. He assumed she'd head back to his office but she only made it as far as the couch. She'd folded into the far corner of it with her back against the armrest and her hands clamped tightly between her legs. Her head was tilted slightly forward, so when she talked to Joe she had to look up. But she spent most of the time staring at her knees, recalling what happened from a script so obviously seared into her being that at times she seemed to be reading from it.

"If we'd known right away—even a day after—we could have done something," she said. "Brent would have done everything in the world to find her. She couldn't have been that far from the trailhead in just one day—only as far as she could run. So at least we would have had a known radius where to look. She usually ran four miles in and four miles out—eight total. Sometimes when she was in hard training, she'd double that. But because the trials were just a month away, her training schedule was pretty regular and eight miles total would have been about right. She loved to run in the mountains. She'd rather run in the mountains than in the best facilities in the world.

"She started her last run on a Tuesday. We didn't find out she was missing until Friday night, when her fiancé finally called."

"Tell me about him," Joe said.

She looked up. "His name is Justin LeForge. He's a triathlete, one of the best. I don't know if you've heard of him or not. He's placed in the top three at the Hawaiian Ironman, and he won a big race in Nice, France, and the Wildflower in California."

Joe shook his head. "I'm not familiar with triathlons, sorry."

She continued, "Anyway, Justin and Diane seemed like the perfect couple. They were beautiful—thin, fit, athletic, attractive. Ken and Barbie in track clothes, one of my friends said. A little odd when it came to politics and worldview, but young people can be like that. They met down in Colorado Springs at the Olympic Training Center. Brent thought Justin was the greatest, and he bragged constantly about his future son-in-law. But everything wasn't as it seemed."

Joe said, "What do you mean when you say they had odd political beliefs?"

She laughed a dry laugh. "They were certainly counter to her father's, for one. Brent has always been very involved politically. We give a lot of money to candidates, and as a big developer he is used to being, um, close with them. There's a lot of federal money these days, you know. It has to go to somebody, is the way Brent puts it, so it might as well be him. Anyway, Justin was a big fan of that writer Ayn Rand. You know her?"

Joe said, "I read *Atlas Shrugged* in college. It was pretty good until that last speech. I never could finish it because of that ninety-page speech at the end."

"Justin said he was an Objectivist, like Ayn Rand. You know, staunch capitalism, anti–big government. Lots of kids go through that."

Joe nodded, urging her on.

"Justin and Brent butted heads a few times, and Diane was right there in the thick of it. I always wondered how much of her new philosophy she truly held and how much was because of Justin. And how much of it was simple rebellion, mainly against her dad. They're both strong-willed people, Brent and Diane. The funny thing is Justin is just as bullheaded as Brent, but Diane never seemed to see the similarity.

"They were selfish, both of them. Part of it came from Objectivism, I guess. I've never been around two people more self-absorbed than my daughter and her fiancé. They lived in the same house but they never really *lived* together, if you know what I mean. She did her thing and he did his. It was all about running, working out, eating food as fuel. It was all about their bodies—how they looked, how they could trim a second off their best time. They looked at their friends, relatives, families—and the rest of the world—as their support team. I used to complain about it, how Diane would only talk about herself when she called and never ask about her brother or sister or me, but Brent just sloughed it off and said that's how athletes had to be when they reached a certain level. And as you could see, Brent is a little like that."

Joe said, "Back to the four days between her disappearance and you finding out about it."

"Oh," she said, squirming farther back into the couch, making herself smaller. "I'm sorry. I went on a tangent."

"It's okay," he said, stealing a look at his wristwatch and deciding: *Pizza tonight.* Delivered.

"Well, as I said, we didn't hear from Justin until Friday night. It was a maddening conversation. He said he didn't have much time to talk because he had to catch a flight for a race in Hawaii. It was like, 'By the way, I'm not sure where Diane is. I haven't seen her since Tuesday. Gotta go, wish me luck.'"

"Man," Joe said, sitting back.

"That's how he was. That's how he still is. Cold as a fish."

"How did he explain it?"

"He didn't, really. He said she'd left him a note Tuesday morning saying she was going to drive north of Steamboat Springs and go for a run in the mountains. This in itself wasn't unusual. Her car was gone, of course. Later, much later, he said he figured she decided to get a room in Steamboat and use it as her base to train from for a few days. He said they'd been fighting and she probably needed a little time away, that it had happened before and it was no big deal. Can you imagine that?"

"No," Joe said, deciding if he ever met Justin LeForge he'd smack him in the mouth.

"That's when Brent contacted the authorities. We didn't have much to go on, and you can imagine how angry and scared we were. At the time, we didn't even know which mountains or in which *state*. On Monday, the sheriff in Walden, Colorado, got a report that her Subaru was reported at a trailhead across the border in Wyoming. That's when things finally started to happen. Search-and-rescue teams, helicopters, news alerts, all of it."

Joe nodded. "I was on the search team."

"Thank you," she said sincerely. "A lot of good men

and women spent days trying to find her. But by that time, she'd been gone over a week. All I could think about was that she'd fallen and broken her leg and was waiting for help that never came. I was terrified she was suffering up there somewhere. I was horrified that she wouldn't be found at all or that her body would be found. I can't even tell you how awful that week was. Or how everything is coming back now."

Joe said, "About Justin . . ."

She waved her hand. "I know what you're probably thinking—that maybe he had something to do with it. We did, too, eventually. Especially when he just stopped caring and calling. But according to the police, his alibi was airtight. He was training all Tuesday and Wednesday with his coaches. The note she left him was in her handwriting. When my husband hired Bobby to investigate, the first thing we asked him to do was to check out Justin's alibi. But Bobby said there was no doubt Justin's story held. In fact, Justin found a girl—another runner—who testified Justin was with her from Tuesday through Thursday. He was cheating on my daughter, Mr. Pickett."

She looked at her hands. "I no longer suspect Justin, even though I despise him. He just didn't care. And as tough as it was for me to accept, I realized he didn't care enough about Diane to hurt her. She really meant nothing to him. He's got a new girlfriend now, and he's moved from Colorado. We haven't heard anything from him in months, although I still follow his races on the Internet. When Bobby told us about your statement, Brent called him on his cell phone and left a message that there might be some new information. Justin hasn't returned the call."

Joe sighed. Her pain gave him a knot in his stomach. That his report had given her a glimmer of hope made his palms cold.

She looked up. "I hope you can forgive my husband for the way he acted earlier. If there is such a thing as being obsessed to the point of insanity, that pretty much describes Brent now. I'm watching him fall apart in front of my eyes. Sometimes, I think it would be better if some hunter found her bones. At least then it would be over. If the news didn't kill him, he might finally be able to recover. But this not knowing . . ." She let the sentence trail off.

"It's been *so* hard on Brent," she said suddenly. "He worshipped his daughter, even though she distanced herself from him in the end."

Joe thought about that.

Suddenly, the front door burst open and Sheridan flew inside the house, running straight for her bedroom. Joe looked outside and saw her pickup truck in the driveway with the door open and the motor running.

"Crap!" Sheridan said, seeing Joe and Jenna Shober. "I'm sorry. I didn't realize you were there."

"What's up?" Joe asked.

"I forgot my basketball shoes," she said. "I've got to get them and go. Practice starts in ten minutes. Sorry."

With that, she ran into her room and ran out with the shoes. "Sorry to interrupt," she called out over her shoulder. "See you later, Dad."

"See you later," Joe said, even though Sheridan had shut the door and jumped back into her truck.

"She's pretty," Jenna said.

"Thank you," Joe said, distracted.

Jenna reached out and squeezed Joe's hand. "Hold on to her tight," she said. "Don't let her go."

Joe knew what she was thinking. The same thing *he* was thinking.

*   *   *

SHE TOOK OUT a large envelope from her purse. "We meant to show you these things earlier," she said. "But things got heated and Brent forgot. These days, he gets so wrapped up in the *how* that he forgets about the *why*. He just assumed you'd jump up and go find our daughter. When you didn't, he lost it and forgot about the envelope. When we got to the motel, I slipped it into my purse and lied about going shopping. Brent would never have approved of me coming here myself to talk with you."

Joe nodded, still dumbstruck from seeing Sheridan and imagining what it would be like if she left one day and never came back. He paid polite attention to a postcard she handed to him.

"This was sent to our Michigan address a year ago," she said.

The card was a generic COLORFUL COLORADO postcard with faded images of Pikes Peak, the Maroon Bells, a skier turning down a slope, and the Denver skyline. He flipped it over. It was postmarked from Walden, Colorado, but over the border.

The handwriting was crimped and severe, as if the author had struggled with the words. He guessed the sender was male.

Jenna:

I'm sending this to you on behalf of your daughter Diane. I saw her and she is fine. She says not to worry about her. She asks that you not share this message with her Dad.

It was signed, *A Friend*.

Joe handed the card back. "Any idea who sent it?"

"No. But it gives me hope."

He kept his voice soft. "Her disappearance wasn't a secret. I mean, anyone could have sent this to you. It could be a cruel hoax, or it could be someone well-meaning trying to ease your pain."

She looked down. "I know that. But I want to think it's real."

A moment went by as Joe tried to form his question as diplomatically as possible. "So, did you show it to Brent?"

She shook her head quickly but didn't look up.

He sat back. "Why not?"

She looked away. He could see moisture in her eyes.

"You didn't want him to know," Joe said.

She whispered, "It's tough."

Joe was confused. He knew he was on thin ice. Finally, he said, "Jenna, is it possible the relationship between your husband and your daughter was, you know, a little too close when she was growing up?"

Jenna refused to answer, which was an answer in itself, Joe thought.

Minutes passed. Joe didn't press. And he tried not to stare at her while she sat silently, looking away.

At last, she said, "Would you like to look at some photos?"

"Sure," he said. Anything to move past his last question, he thought.

He'd seen most of them before in the initial briefing before he'd struck out with the search-and-rescue team, and others on fliers the Shobers had posted, but he didn't want to hurt her feelings by not looking at them. He did look at them to try to find what it was about the unknown woman he'd seen that made him think of Diane Shober. Maybe a profile or an expression? But thus far, none of the photos made a direct connection.

Most of the shots were of Diane running in competitions. She had a determined set to her face, and her blonde hair flew back like frozen flames. Her fists were clenched, her arms pumping, the muscles in her arms, thighs, and calves taut as ropes.

"Here," Jenna said, "this is the one we wanted you to see."

Joe took it. The photo was not from a track meet, but from training. In it, Diane wore tight running clothes but she looked happy and relaxed and she had a nice open-faced smile. The right front fender of her Subaru poked out from the bottom left corner of the photo, and behind her were lodgepole pine trees and a glimpse of a cobalt blue sky between openings in the branches. Joe wondered if the shot had been taken at the same trailhead where her car had been found.

"Justin sent us that picture," Jenna said. "He said he took it a week or so before she disappeared but he'd forgotten it was in his camera. He sent it to us almost a year after she'd been gone."

Joe nodded. As he studied the photo, it hit him. He jabbed at the shot with his index finger. "Oh, man," he said.

On Diane's left arm was an iPod in a pink case.

"This looks *exactly* like the case Caleb had in his daypack," Joe said softly.

"Bobby made the connection," she said. "He said he asked you about it when you were in the hospital."

"Yes, he did."

"Brent was supposed to show that to you today, but he was so upset he forgot. That's why I came back."

Joe shook his head. What was the possibility the case he'd seen in Caleb's daypack was similar but different?

Given the remoteness of the tableau, the odds were tremendous they were the same item.

He looked up. How to say it without upsetting her? "Mrs. Shober, they look the same. Yup, they do. But that doesn't mean she's up there with them. I told you I was probably mistaken. And there's the possibility they found this case on a trail or even stole it from a car or something." *Or found it on her body and took it*, he thought but didn't say.

He started to hand the photos back, but one of them nagged at him. He flipped through the stack again to a shot of Diane in a heated discussion with two other women runners in what was obviously a track meet at a stadium. All three wore uniforms that looked the same. Joe looked up for an explanation.

"Oh, that one," Jenna said. "It's from college. I have that one in there because I think it shows Diane's passion. Those other two girls are on her team, and one of them had lost a race because a competitor tripped her deliberately. Diane was *so* angry. . . ."

But what Joe was struck by was the gesture Diane was making: stabbing her right index finger into the palm of her left hand to make a point.

"Your daughter," he said, "has she always been blonde?"

Jenna laughed. "Since high school, anyway. She dyes it religiously."

Joe took his index finger and placed it along the brow of Diane's face in the photo, creating bangs. "So if she doesn't color her hair, it turns back to the original dark brown," he said.

"Yes."

Joe looked up. "Do you know the name Terri Wade?"

Jenna looked back quizzically. "Of course I do. She

was our housekeeper when Diane was growing up. Diane loved her, we all did. But she left us years ago. She and Brent had a disagreement. . . ."

Joe's jaw and shoulders dropped. He flashed back to that moment when he saw the faces reflected in flame.

Jenna saw his reaction, said, *"What?"*

"Mrs. Shober—I saw Diane. She's using the name of your old housekeeper," he said. "A name she's comfortable with. She let her hair go brown and she dressed frumpy so I wouldn't recognize her. But at one point outside that burning cabin, she turned away and then turned back. The angle of her face or the way the fire made her hair look lighter and her face look younger and resembled the photo on all the flyers. It made me think there were two women when there was only one." He thought back again to that scene in the woods, that one quick glimpse of the "fourth face." Wade turning away into the darkness, then the flash of one he'd thought was a different woman. Except it hadn't been. It had been Diane all along. He shook his head in amazement. "And she's got the brothers thinking her name is Terri Wade because they used it when they talked to her. I told you earlier I was probably mistaken but I don't think so now. She was alive when I saw her last. So you need to know that. But . . ."

Her expression didn't change but her eyes glistened with tears. "So you won't help us?"

He couldn't look into her eyes any longer. He handed the photo back and said, "I'm sorry."

She started to say something, but her throat caught with a sob and she snatched the photo back and turned angrily away.

As she shoved the photos back into the envelope, Joe stared at the ceiling, the window, the floor. Anywhere but at her.

"Joe?" It was Marybeth, from behind him. He hadn't heard her come into the house from the garage and place her briefcase on the kitchen table. And he didn't know how long she'd been there in the doorway to the kitchen, or how much she'd heard.

He turned.

"Go," she said. "Go find her."

A MINUTE AFTER a sobbing and grateful Jenna Shober left their house, Joe said to Marybeth, "But I promised you."

"You promised me when we didn't know it was really Diane up there," she said. "And when I put myself in Mrs. Shober's shoes, if Sheridan or April or Lucy were missing . . ."

Joe nodded. "If you're sure . . ."

"Take Nate," she said.

"Of course."

WHEN THE DOORBELL RANG, Joe expected either Brent or Jenna Shober, not the FedEx driver. He signed for a medium-sized box that wasn't as heavy as it looked.

From the kitchen, Marybeth said, "What is it, Joe?"

"Dad," he said.

22

THEY WERE RIDING BLIND, STILL BEARING WEST toward the high rim of the last cirque, Parnell in the lead, when Farkus said, "So all this time we were tracking a deer?"

Parnell didn't answer. He glowered, though. Farkus thought the man was humiliated but didn't want to show it.

Farkus said, "What I gather is these guys are *the* Cline Brothers? Of the Cline Family? What was their mother's name? The one in the news?" It came to him and he answered his own question: "Caryl Cline. I remember seeing her on TV. She had a following out here, you know. But why did the game warden say their name was Grim?"

"Because I'm sure that's what they told him."

"Why would they do that?"

Parnell started to answer as he approached the edge of the rim, but he suddenly reined his horse to stop with a violent pull. "My God! There's someone down there."

"Is it one of the Clines?" Smith asked. "Did you see him? Did he see you?"

Parnell shook his head slowly, "It isn't one of them. You are *not* going to believe the scene down there."

Intrigued, Farkus, Campbell, and Smith nudged their horses forward. As the horse walked, Farkus stood in his stirrups and strained to see over the rim. With each step of the horse, he could see a little more terrain below as it opened up to him. He was careful not to expose any more of himself than he had to. He was certain that the rim dropped away into a sheer rock wall. On the other side of the cirque, the wall wasn't as steep. There was a trail through scree on the other side of a pure blue mountain lake. And then he saw her.

"It looks like a naked woman," he said, a smile stretching across his face. "Finally, something good has happened."

IT TOOK HALF AN HOUR for the four horsemen to circumnavigate the last cirque to the trail down to the lake. Occasionally, as they rode near the rim, Farkus would rise up and catch a glimpse of the woman. It was too far to see her clearly, but what he could see was as interesting as it was baffling. She was swimming. He wondered if the water was as cold as he remembered. He caught flashes of pale white skin, long dark hair fanning in the fantastically clear water, a glimpse of bare shoulders and small breasts and long limbs. There was a pile of clothing in the rocks near the shore of the alpine lake.

"I feel like I died and went to heaven," Farkus said. "I been hunting up here all my life just hoping to see something like this. D'you suppose she's alone?"

"Don't let her see you," Parnell said. "There's something oddly sirenlike about this situation."

"Sirenlike?" Farkus said. "You talk in code, Parnell."

"Shut up, Dave," Smith said. "You obviously don't know your classics."

Parnell ignored them both, said, "We're staying just long enough to find out if she knows anything about the Clines."

*　　*　　*

THE TRAIL DOWN to the lake was wide enough at first that the horsemen could ride two abreast. Parnell and Smith led; Farkus rode with Campbell. The trail narrowed about twenty yards from the lake and slivered between two large boulders. As they descended, Farkus could catch glimpses of the surface of the water on the far side of the lake and the high rock face that led up to the rim where they'd first seen the woman. But because of the size of the boulders on either side of the trail, they couldn't see her yet.

The steel shoes of the horses clicked on the crushed rock of the scree. Farkus could feel his heart beat faster. He reluctantly held back on the reins so Parnell and Smith could squeeze through the opening in the boulders first. He wondered if she would scream when she looked up and saw four men coming toward her on horseback. He kind of hoped so. He also hoped he could get to the pile of clothing before she did.

But the whistling sound he heard was not a scream, and he looked up to see a thick green branch slice through the air on the other side of the boulders at chest height. On the end of the branch was a two-foot pointed stake. Farkus caught a flash of it in the air streaking toward Parnell and it thumped into the man with a hollow sound. While the fire-hardened stake didn't penetrate Parnell's body armor, the velocity of the impact threw him backward off his horse and he hit hard on the rocks in front of Farkus.

"Ambush!" Smith hollered ahead of him a half second before a shotgun blast blew him out of the saddle.

Farkus's horse reared and bellowed and he flew backward out of his saddle, hands windmilling through the air as if to find a hold. He landed hard and facedown in the loose shale, and grit was jammed into his nose and mouth. Inches from his face, a horse's hoof slammed into the rocks, and another right behind his head.

Two heavy *booms* came from behind a man-sized slab of rock to the right of the boulders, and he was crushed under Campbell's dead body as it fell on him, pinning him to the ground under the man's weight.

The last thing he saw before his eyes closed was the figure of a very tall man rise out of the rocks. There was something wrong with the man's face, like there was a dried red rose on the tip of his chin. The man was thin and gaunt. His face was pale and sunken and flesh peeled away from his nose. He wore a red plaid shirt with big checks, and a white slouch hat pulled low over his eyes. Farkus watched him limp over from where he'd hidden in the rocks to where Parnell was writhing on the ground, trying to get breath. He shot Parnell point-blank in the head. Parnell's body thrashed with the muscle spasms of the dead.

Then he heard, "You all right, Caleb?"

The response was a cross between a goose honking and a calf bawling.

Farkus turned his head toward the voice and saw the same man who'd spoken first. He thought he was seeing double.

And from the lake he heard a scream. Or was it a shriek of joy?

He thought: *Wendigo. And there's more than one of 'em.*

"OPEN YOUR DAMNED EYES," a voice growled. "I know you ain't dead."

Farkus felt a pure terror course through him like a cold electric shock. He hoped his facial muscles didn't twitch, didn't betray him. But he was afraid they had.

For the past hour, he'd lain still on his back. Campbell's heavy dead body crushed him, and as the time went by it seemed to get heavier. Campbell's body lay crossways across Farkus, facedown. Beneath him, several sharp stones poked into his lower abdomen and thighs and the nose of a boulder pressed against the left side of his skull. His arm—which was trapped behind his back under Campbell's body—was numb from lack of circulation.

He'd spent the time since the ambush trying to play dead. He kept his eyes closed and tried to keep his breathing relaxed while his other senses roared with fear.

He'd heard a few voices. One of them, female, asked, "Who are they? Are they the ones from Michigan?"

And Caleb or Camish say, "Yup, I recognize two of 'em. The other two I don't know. That one doesn't look like he should be with them."

There were other conversations, but the roaring of blood through his ears blocked them out. He tried to stay calm, play dead. Tried to recall stories he'd read of victims of mass firing squads or massacres who survived by pretending they were killed. Wondering how in the hell they were able to pull it off when he felt like screaming.

Then the voice telling him to open his eyes. He was *caught*.

Something sharp tugged at the skin on his cheek and he flinched. There was no way of pretending anymore.

He opened his eyes as the brother with the dirty compress on his chin—it wasn't a red rose after all—withdrew the point of a knife. Both brothers hovered over him, looking down. Their faces were in shadow because the sun was directly over their heads and beating down. Farkus squinted, trying to see them. They were mirror images of each other, except for the bandage on the face of one of the brothers.

"This probably isn't going to be your best day ever," one of them said in a flat midwestern accent.

PART THREE

OUTLIERS
AMONG US

I must lose myself in action, lest I wither in despair.

—Alfred, Lord Tennyson

FRIDAY, SEPTEMBER 4

23

JOE DROVE HIS PICKUP AND EMPTY HORSE TRAILER past the sign on the highway that read ENTERING WIND RIVER INDIAN RESERVATION. Nate sat in the passenger seat, running a BoreSnake cleaning cable through the barrel and five cylinders of his .454 Casull. The pickup reeked of cleaning solvent and gun oil, and Joe lowered his window to flood the cab with fresh air. The FedEx box from Billings was lashed to the sidewall of the pickup bed with bungee cords.

As they rolled down a battered two-lane toward Alisha Whiteplume's uncle's ranch, Nate said, "Is the governor aware of what we're doing?"

"I thought it best not to tell him," Joe said.

"Is that wise?"

Joe said, "Probably not, but I can live with it and this way he has deniability."

"What about your director? What does he know?"

Said Joe, "Nothing. As far as he's concerned, I'm on administrative leave."

"Marybeth's okay with it, though?"

"She's the one who said go," Joe said.

Nate grinned. "Let's go with the higher authority, then."

"That's what I always do," Joe said.

Nate said, "Something I learned years before in special operations when dealing within the bureaucracy was, *'It's always better to apologize than to ask permission.'*"

"Exactly."

Joe said, "I'll call Sheriff Baird as we start up into the mountains, but not before. He needs to know we're in his county even if the news makes him blow a gasket. I can't see him coming after us, having spent his budget and all, and he really can't prevent us from going back up there."

Nate loaded the cylinder with cartridges the size of cigar stubs and snapped it closed and holstered the revolver. "Okay, I'm ready," he said. "What are you packing?"

Joe said, "I picked up a new twelve-gauge at the pawnshop."

Nate dropped his head. "The pawnshop?"

"It's a good pawnshop. Besides, not everyone spends their conscious hours thinking about their immediate weaponry and how they'd react if attacked. Believe it or not, Nate, but there are even people who don't own guns."

"I know that," Nate said. "Don't assume I disapprove. The more who don't own guns, the greater my advantage. Even so, back to you. Another Remington Wingmaster?"

"Yup. I lucked out. There aren't as many guns available these days as there used to be. Folks are hoarding them. Oh," Joe said, reaching down and patting the .40 Glock on his hip. "And my service weapon."

Nate narrowed his eyes. "Are you *ever* going to take the time to learn how to hit something with that? You drive me crazy."

Joe shrugged. "I've done some damage with it."

"From an inch away and by spraying the landscape with slugs." Nate snorted. "A *monkey* could do that."

Joe smiled. "Every time I pull this gun, I think it's the

last time I'll ever do it. Not because I think there will be world peace—I just never think trouble will come my way again."

Nate shook his head in disgust. "But it always does," he said.

Joe curled his mouth on the sides and nodded. "Yup, it seems to."

"That doesn't just happen," Nate said.

"Oh, maybe it does," Joe said.

Nate shook his head and looked away. They eventually settled into a comfortable and familiar silence.

JOE'S PHONE BURRED and he plucked it from his breast pocket and looked at the display. "Uh-oh," he said.

Nate said, "Who is it?"

"It's a 777 number I don't recognize. But 777 is the state phone prefix. It's probably the governor or one of his staff calling."

The phone continued to ring.

"Are you going to answer it?" Nate asked.

Joe dropped the phone back into his pocket, then bent forward and clicked off his radio under the dashboard as well.

"Radio silence," Nate said. "I like radio silence."

"Unless, of course, Marybeth calls," Joe said.

"Obviously," Nate said.

"THIS ONE'S GOT a lot of moving parts, doesn't it?" Nate said after fifteen minutes. Joe knew he was referring to the situation in general.

"Yup."

"And a bunch of parts we don't even know yet."

"That's the feeling I get."

"Are the feds with us or against us on this one?"

Joe shrugged. "That's something I can't quite figure out yet. The FBI seems very interested in it, but from the outside. Usually, they move in and try to take over. This time, it's like they're trying to stay out of it but control things at the same time."

"Have you talked to that agent you know, Coon?"

"Yup, I called him but he didn't tell me much. He said he couldn't comment on ongoing investigations, as if I were a reporter or something."

"Ongoing investigations? And he hasn't tried to get in touch with you since?"

"Nope," Joe said.

"That tells me something right there," Nate said.

"Me, too."

"He should have contacted you again by now, if for no reason other than to see how you're doing. There's a reason he's stayed away, and that's probably because he doesn't want to communicate with you and maybe let something slip out."

Joe nodded. "The governor said there were some indirect federal contacts. Plus, Coon was adamant that the Grims, or Grimmengrubers, didn't exist. At the time, I thought he was telling me I was nuts. In retrospect, I think he was telling me the names didn't jibe with his investigation. In other words, he knows these brothers exist, but not under those names."

"I wonder what he's hiding," Nate said. "And I wonder how far it goes up the chain."

Joe's phone rang again. He said, "Another 777 number."

Nate said, *"It's always better to apologize than to ask permission."*

Joe breathed deeply and dropped the phone back into his pocket without answering.

ALISHA'S UNCLE, WILLIE SHOYO, had herded a dozen of his horses into a temporary corral made of twelve-foot rail panels in the sagebrush well out of sight of his home and barn. Beyond the corral were undulating grasslands that rose in elevation and melded with the dark brush marching downward from the mountains. The horses in the corral obviously didn't like being penned up together, and they were restless and jockeying for preeminence in the nascent herd. In the distance, horses that hadn't been selected by Shoyo grazed on yellowing grass and pretended they weren't paying attention to the arrival of the pickup and horse trailer.

As Joe parked and swung out of his truck, he heard the solid thump of a kick and the squeal of the kicked in the pen. It didn't take long for horses to start establishing the pecking order.

Willie Shoyo wore a King Ropes cap, a green snap-button cowboy shirt, a big buckle with an engraving of a Shoshone rose, and crisp Wranglers tucked into the tops of scuffed Ariat boots. He stood near the corral with his boot on the bottom rail and crossed arms on the top. His hands seemed darker and older than the rest of him, the skin on the back of his hands like coffee-stained leather. Joe thought he had a pleasant face—smooth and round, with sharp dark eyes. Willie's horses were prized as great cow ponies, and a few had won money in team penning competitions.

Willie said to Nate, "Alisha told me you'd like to rent a few horses."

Nate said, "Three or four, we haven't decided."

"Three," Joe said. "Geldings. Two for riding and one

for packing. I haven't had much luck with mares in the mountains."

Willie sized up Joe for the first time and nodded. "I've got plenty of geldings to choose from."

Alisha Whiteplume drove up as Joe looked over the horses in the pen. She got out of her car and stood still appraising Nate with her hands on her hips. Nate ambled over to her, and she didn't change her expression or posture.

Shoyo had watched the interaction as well. He said, "I understand what you're saying, Mr. Pickett. Mares can be too emotional at times, even though most of them want to please you. But you can never make them completely happy, in my experience."

Nate looked over from where he stood with Alisha to Joe and Shoyo and said, "Are we talking about horses here?"

THEY WERE ALL STOUT quarter horses, sorrels and paints with white socks and all of stolid disposition. Joe wished he'd brought Marybeth because she knew horses better than he. All of the geldings looked good to him.

"How about those three?" he said to Willie, gesturing toward a Tobiano paint, a sorrel, and a red roan.

Willie nodded his head. "Those are good ones," he said. "Calm and a little dumb. Bombproof."

"Good."

Nate hadn't paid any attention to the transaction, but stood outside the pen nuzzling Alisha. Joe helped Willie cut the three from the herd and shoo the unpicked horses out of the pen through the gate. The released horses ran hard to join the others out in the grass, raising plumes of dust behind them like the tails of comets. The three remaining snorted and paced and looked offended not to be allowed to go with the rest of the herd.

Willie told Joe, "The three horses you picked are named Washakie One, Washakie Two, and Washakie Three."

"You're kidding," Joe said.

Willie shook his head. "I'm not." He pointed out toward the foothills. "Washakie Four through One Hundred Forty-two are out there grazing."

Joe smiled, "Got it. It's easier to remember their names when they're all named Washakie."

Shoyo said, "I know each one by color and personality, but they come and go so often I quit giving them individual names."

Said Joe, "Will you take a government voucher for the cost?"

A frown passed over Willie's face.

"It's a state voucher," Joe said quickly, realizing what the deal was, "not a federal one."

"So I can't charge you three times the going rate, then?" Shoyo lamented. He looked as offended as Washakie One, Two, and Three.

"Sorry."

The cloud passed, and Willie said, "Okay, then."

From near the pickup, Alisha said, "Uncle Willie, are you sure you want to do this? You've heard what happens to Joe Pickett's horses, haven't you? They meet the same fate as his vehicles."

"Thanks, Alisha," Joe said, his face flushing. He wanted to argue, but he had no argument.

"I've heard," Willie said. "We can hope these horses bring you more luck."

"I'll need it," Joe said.

Willie said, "I understand you need a couple of saddles and a pack saddle outfit, too, because you lost yours with your horses. I can lend you those."

"Thank you," Joe said.

"I'm doing this as a favor to my favorite mare," Willie said, glancing toward Alisha and talking loud enough so she could hear. "I mean my favorite *niece*."

"What's he talking about?" Alisha asked Nate suspiciously.

Nate shrugged and said to her, "I don't understand all this horse talk. You know that."

AS JOE AND NATE APPROACHED Muddy Gap, towing the horses in the horse trailer, and took the highway toward Rawlins, the Green Mountains loomed like sleeping lions on the horizon. Nate said, "I don't see where the woman fits. Do you think she's up there with those brothers voluntarily, or is it some kind of Stockholm-syndrome type of deal? Is she a hostage, a kidnap victim, or a willing accomplice?"

Joe shook his head. "First, we don't know if it's Shober or if she's still okay. She could be anybody."

"Yeah, yeah," Nate said dismissively.

Said Joe, "If you saw those brothers in person like I did, there's no way you'd think anyone in their right mind would stay with them willingly. They creeped *me* out."

"Maybe you didn't meet them in the best circumstances," Nate said.

Joe shrugged. "Diane is a puzzle. I don't see how those guys could have taken her up into the mountains if she didn't want to go. She didn't seem to fear them nearly as much as she regretted letting them down by taking me in. Are you thinking she's the key to all of this?"

Nate sat back and sighed. "No. I can't figure out how she fits. Or why, of all the places on earth, she'd end up there."

Joe grunted.

Nate said, "Well, she *had* to know people were looking

for her a couple of years ago, right? So even if those Grim Brothers grabbed her and kept her captive at the time, from what you said she was moving around of her own free will. If nothing else, she could just up and *outrun* those knuckleheads."

"If it was even her," Joe said wearily.

"And if it isn't," Nate asked, "then who is it?"

"Don't know."

"If it isn't, how are you going to tell Mrs. Shober?"

Joe cringed.

After a few more miles, Joe said, "Nate, I want to thank you for coming along. I couldn't do it without you."

Nate said, "We haven't done anything yet except rent some horses."

Joe didn't say anything.

"This thing spooked you, didn't it?"

No response.

"You don't have to be ashamed," Nate said. "You got your butt kicked over and over. These guys ran circles around you up there and took everything you had, including your confidence. I can tell. You don't want to go up there for revenge as much as to see if you can get your courage back, isn't that it?"

"I'd rather not talk about it," Joe said, swerving to avoid hitting a jackrabbit that darted out onto the blacktop. There were so many dead, flat rabbits on this stretch of road that the asphalt looked cottony in places, as if the rabbits had been violently hurled down to the pavement from the sky in a fit of pique.

"Like I said, they kicked your butt up one side of the mountain and down the other," Nate said.

"You're really irritating sometimes," Joe mumbled.

"But what I can't figure out is why they didn't finish the job," Nate said, looking over and locking his eyes on the side of Joe's face. "They had you down from that shotgun blast, but they didn't follow up. Guys like that, who hunt for a living, would know to find you in the grass and cut your throat or put one or two into your head. Why didn't they do that?"

Joe shrugged. "I've been wondering that since I woke up in the hospital."

Said Nate, "I guess maybe Camish was worried about Caleb since you shot him, or they were both tending to 'Terri Wade' or Diane Shober or whoever the hell she is. But it doesn't jibe. They should have hunted you down and finished the job. Then they should have burned your body and buried the remains so deep no one would ever find you. That's what *I* would have done."

Joe said, "Not that you have experience in that sort of thing."

"I do, though."

"Nate, I was being sarcastic."

"Sarcasm doesn't become you," Nate said. "Back to my point. Why didn't they finish you off?"

Joe looked over. "I have no idea."

"Maybe they aren't as bad as you think?" Nate said.

"Not a chance," Joe said. "They're *worse*. They've got a woman up there against her will. And who knows what else we'll find?"

Nate rubbed his chin. "Maybe we'll find that lady wants to stay."

"No way," Joe said again.

"Another thing," Nate said. "They called you a government man. I find that interesting. Not a game warden or a fish cop or whatever. But a *government man*."

Joe said, "I've been called everything else, but I've never been called that before."

"But that's what you are."

"I guess I never thought of myself that way," Joe said. "I'm surprised they used that choice of words."

Nate smiled slyly. "That says something about their worldview, doesn't it?"

Before Joe could answer, his phone rang again. He expected a 777 number but saw on the display it was from MBP Management. Joe opened the phone, said, "Yes?"

She said, "Has the governor found you yet?"

"No."

"He called here a few minutes ago. When I told him you weren't here, he didn't sound very happy."

"I can imagine," Joe said.

"He said he's been trying to reach you all day."

"Yeah, well . . ."

"When he asked me where you were, I couldn't lie to him," Marybeth said. "I mean, he's your boss. And he is the governor."

Joe considered telling her it was better to apologize, but thought better of it and said, "I understand."

"He asked what you were driving and which route you were taking."

Joe frowned. "He did?"

"That's not all," she said. "He told me this thing is blowing up all of a sudden and he needed to find you. Then he hung up. You know how he is."

The cutoff toward Rawlins was ahead, and Joe tapped the brake to release the cruise control so he could swing into the turn. "Yup," Joe said, "I know how he is."

He closed his phone and dropped it to the seat. They topped a rise before dropping down into Rawlins. When they crested the hill, Joe saw the blue and red wigwag lights, the phalanx of state trooper vehicles, and the long row of eighteen-wheelers directly ahead, all waiting to pass through the roadblock.

"Oh, no," Nate said, sitting up straight.

Joe looked over and saw his friend strip off his shoulder holster and cram it beneath the bench seat like a high-schooler hiding his open container.

"I'm not going back to Cheyenne," Nate said softly.

Joe considered braking and turning around, but he was on a one-way exit and the ditches on either side of the road were too steep for him to pull the horse trailer through without high-centering the rig.

"I've got to keep going," Joe said, "unless you have any ideas."

"You could let me out here," Nate said. "Let me run for it."

Joe looked ahead. He counted four highway patrol cars and a Carbon County sheriff SUV.

"They'll run you down in two minutes," Joe said.

"Not if I take them out," Nate said. Joe knew the .454 rounds were capable of penetrating the engine block of a vehicle, and he'd seen Nate do exactly that.

"If you take them out, we're both going to prison," Joe said, easing on his brakes so he wouldn't rear-end a Walmart eighteen-wheeler. At that moment, both of his side mirrors filled up with the grinning chrome grille of another semitruck.

"We're hemmed in," Joe said.

Ahead of them, uniformed troopers walked along the shoulder of the road from car to car.

Nate sat back, his eyes glassy. He read aloud the words painted on the back of the rig ahead of them.

He sneered. *"Always Low Prices. Always."*

24

Two state troopers approached Joe's pickup, one on each side of the road. The trooper on the left was tall and stoop-shouldered and had a brushy mustache and hangdog jowls. The trooper on the right was short and wide and his hard, round belly strained at the buttons on his uniform shirt. When he looked up and saw Joe, his eyes narrowed and he put his right hand on the grip of his weapon. Joe couldn't hear him speak to the other trooper, but he read his lips: *It's him.*

The tall trooper put his hand on his gun as well, and as they walked up Joe lowered the driver's and passenger-side windows.

"You Joe Pickett?" the tall trooper asked. His name badge read BOB GARRARD.

"Yes, sir."

The other trooper couldn't take his eyes off Nate, looking at him with practiced and wary cop eyes that came from approaching hundreds of pulled-over vehicles on the highway. He stayed a few feet away from the vehicle so, if necessary, he could draw cleanly and fire.

"I wouldn't do that," Nate said to him. Even though his gun was under the seat, Nate sounded as deadly as he looked, Joe thought.

"Governor Rulon is looking for you," Garrard said to Joe. "Our orders are to take you to him."

"To Cheyenne?" Joe said. "That's three hours away."

"What, are you on a schedule?" Garrard asked, with a hint of a sneer.

"Sort of," Joe said.

"Naw, not to Cheyenne," the trooper said. "He's at the airport. He flew in about an hour ago and he's waiting for you."

Garrard looked in the back of Joe's pickup. "What's in the box?"

"My dad," Joe said. "I don't know where to spread his ashes."

Garrard did a double take. "So you're just driving him around the state? Like taking him on a vacation?"

Joe nodded.

The squat trooper on the other side of the truck said to Nate, "We were supposed to be looking for one guy. Pickett. Who might you be? Do you have some ID on you?"

"No." Nate's voice was soft but firm. Joe knew it was the way he spoke just before he tore someone's ear off.

Joe said with false but distracting cheer, "Lead the way, men, and I'll follow. The governor's waiting, remember?"

He was grateful that both troopers decided to drop their line of inquiry and depart with both ears attached.

TWO HIGHWAY PATROL CARS led the way to the small airport, and another trooper car followed Joe's truck and horse trailer. The patrolmen kept their wigwag lights flashing, and citizens on the road pulled to the side to let the caravan pass.

"This is ridiculous," Nate grumbled. "I didn't realize he had his own private police force."

"Well," Joe said, "he does."

Harvey Field had several prop Cessna aircraft belonging to France Flying Service. A small Cessna jet was parked on the runway near a cinderblock building that served as the private terminal. On the tail of the airplane was a Wyoming bucking horse silhouette.

"There's Rulon One," Joe said. "He's here, all right."

RULON WAS A BIG MAN, with a round face and silver-flecked brown hair that always looked barely combed. He had a ruddy complexion that could quickly turn fire-engine red, and the movements of his arms and hands were dartlike. He stood at the head of a small table in the conference room of the terminal wearing an open-collared shirt and a dark blue windbreaker with the name GOV SPENCE embroidered over the breast. Jeans and lizard-skin cowboy boots completed the picture. Special Agent Chuck Coon of the FBI sat slumped at the table to Rulon's right and the governor's new chief of staff, a trim retired military man named Carson, sat at Rulon's left. Both looked uncomfortable.

"You," Rulon said, pointing at Joe, "need to answer your damned phone."

"I get that," Joe said, looking from the governor to Coon, who recognized Nate with palpable alarm.

"And look who's with him," Coon said. "The infamous Nate Romanowski."

Nate kept quiet.

"None of that here," Rulon said to Coon.

"But he's a fugitive," Coon said to Rulon. "For crying out loud, I can't just look the other way."

"Yes, you can, for now," Rulon said. "Or I'll have *you* arrested. Don't forget, I've got my troopers outside."

"On what charge?" Coon said.

Rulon shrugged. "I don't know. Interfering with the governor, maybe."

"That's not a law," Coon said, a little unsure of himself.

"Sure it is," Rulon said. "Right, Carson? And if it isn't a law, it should be. Write that down, Carson. We need a new law next session about gubernatorial interference."

Carson blanched and looked away.

"Anyway," Rulon said, slapping the top of the table, "that's not why we're here."

Joe said, "Why are we here?"

Rulon paused and his face reddened. Joe awaited an explosion, but Rulon pointed his finger at Coon and said, "Because the feds are dumping murderous miscreants into my state and not telling me about it."

"It's not like that," Coon said heatedly.

Joe shook his head, confused.

"Got a minute?" Rulon said to him, then answered his own question: "Why, of *course* you do. Have a seat, both of you."

"Joe," Governor Rulon said, "I'm not one to believe in government conspiracies, and the longer I'm in the government the more I'm convinced they cannot exist. Do you know why?"

Joe knew that just as before, Rulon wasn't really asking him, so he said nothing.

Said Rulon, "It's because government, by nature, is damned sloppy and incompetent. And the bigger it gets, the worse it becomes in those subject areas. There's just too many people involved with too many agendas for a secret—any secret—to be kept very long. Someone always leaks, or gets drunk and brags, or tries to impress someone else by telling what they know. That's why I don't do secrets. Not because I wouldn't like to, right, Carson?"

Carson didn't answer, either.

Rulon continued, "It's because secrets can't be kept. I'm not being noble. Secrets just won't work in government, and they shouldn't. And when you get to the federal level," again, he pointed at Coon, "it gets even harder. There are hundreds of thousands of employees with hundreds of thousands of partisan and personal agendas. The only conspiracy that exists is the conspiracy of incompetence."

Rulon paused, pleased with his phrasing. He said, "Conspiracy of incompetence—I like that. Write that down, Carson. I can use it in a speech."

This time, Carson dutifully wrote it down on a yellow legal pad, obviously grateful for something to do.

"So," Rulon said, "conspiracies don't exist in government for long. But a couple of things are timeless, especially in Washington: greed and corruption. Especially with the very long-term political class. And by that, I mean certain senators and congressmen of both political parties, the ones who've been there so long they've forgotten what it's like back here in the real world. It gets to the point where it's all about *them*. These are the power brokers, the old lions who traffic in influence, favors, and pork. The ones surrounded by staff and sycophants telling them day after day how great and powerful and eloquent and statesmanlike they are."

Joe sat down, but Nate remained standing. Joe looked out the window at the runway. Beyond the governor's plane several tumbleweeds rolled across the pavement. In between the two runways, pronghorn antelope grazed.

"Am I boring you, Joe?" Rulon asked suddenly.

Joe looked up. "With all due respect, governor, I was hoping you would get to the point."

Rulon froze, his face turning crimson. Instead of yelling or firing Joe on the spot, a slow grin formed. He held his hands out, palms up.

"Why can't I be surrounded by sycophants who tell me how great I am?" Rulon said. "Instead, I get guys like you, Joe."

Joe shrugged. "Sorry, sir."

"Maybe I should run for Senate. Carson, write that down."

"Please, sir," Carson said, his voice begging.

"Okay," Rulon said, winking at Joe, "I'll cut to the chase. Have you ever heard of Senator Carl McKinty of Michigan? Thirty-year senator, he is. Democrat, of course—he's from Michigan—but that hardly matters since I am, too, and we couldn't be farther apart on just about everything. He's chairman of the Natural Resources Committee. That's where I've tangled with him. He's on the Homeland Security Committee as well."

Joe said, "I've heard his name."

"Have you heard of a woman named Caryl Cline?"

Joe rubbed his jaw. "The name is familiar, but I'm not sure why."

"Five years ago," Rulon said, "she was all over television. She was a self-proclaimed activist for private property rights. She got that way because her Senator McKinty worked a sweetheart deal in the Upper Peninsula in Michigan for a huge tract of land she owned. He convinced the local government to condemn the land her family had owned for a hundred and fifty years in order to give it to a hotshot developer. The local government did it because the developer promised a higher tax base than from the little meat-processing company run by the family. And it was perfectly legal, because our brilliant Supreme Court in the *Kelo versus City of New London* decision said it was just fine for governments to do that."

"Hold it," Joe said. "Didn't most of the states pass laws prohibiting local governments from doing that?"

Coon said, "Yes. But up until 2005 there were no laws to stop it in Michigan. So when it happened, it was okay all around. At the time in Michigan—and we're seeing it more and more all over the country—the only way to stop it was civil disobedience with the hope that the local or state government would be ashamed and give up."

"And that's what she did," Rulon said, taking over again. "She took her fight public. She did all she could to call out the senator and the local county commissioners who condemned her land. She and her three sons got their guns and said they'd fight for their property—that no government had the right to take private land or shut down a legitimate small business just so the tax revenue would be higher with the new owners."

Joe said, "Okay, I remember her now. The media kind of made fun of her."

"That's right," Rulon said. "Because she looked and talked like what she was—a rural midwestern white woman. She had crooked teeth, glasses that were taped together in the middle, bad hair, and she wore these big print dresses. She looked like a stereotypical hillbilly. They called her 'Ma Cline.' They did their best to make her unsympathetic, but she became a symbol with a few political commentators and just plain folks and she struck fear into the hearts of certain politicians."

Joe remembered the I'M WITH MA CLINE bumper

stickers that were popular at the time. He still saw some around.

Rulon said, "Do you remember what happened to her?"

Before Joe could speak, Nate said, "She was murdered."

For the first time, Rulon turned his full attention to Nate. The governor studied Nate as if sizing him up. Joe knew Rulon considered himself an excellent judge of character. He wondered what Rulon's judgment was of his friend.

"'Murder' is not the right word," Coon interjected. "She was killed, yes. But it happened in a firefight at the Cline compound in the UP. There is some dispute whether she was killed by law enforcement or by her own family."

Nate said, "No, there isn't." He shook his head, said, "It always amuses me how a family home or small business suddenly becomes a 'compound' when you folks decide to attack it."

Coon said, "Owning the language and getting it out there first is a way to assure the public will be with us. Cynical, but true."

The news story came back to Joe. He remembered how it had been reported; the Cline Family was armed to the teeth and refused to leave their land. The local sheriff as well as federal law enforcement ATFE—and FBI— moved in on the Clines after arrest warrants had been issued for firearms violations, refusal to comply with the condemnation order, and dozens of other charges. Gunfire greeted them, and two members of the strike force were wounded before the tactical units unleashed holy hell on the "compound." In the end, Caryl Cline, her husband, Darrell, and one of three sons were killed. Joe recalled the news reports showing unpainted bullet-riddled shacks deep in a shadowed forest. He also recalled the outrage of the more extreme elements and accusations of government malfeasance. But because the violence took place off-camera, the location was remote, and several other similar incidents happened around the same time, the particular story faded quickly. In fact, when he thought about it, he hadn't heard anything about follow-up investigations, or reports suggesting that the situation was any different than originally portrayed: the inbred white trash family paid the price for firing on federal law enforcement officers doing their duty.

"I'm confused," Joe said. "What does this have to do with us?"

Rulon said, "Up until yesterday, I would have asked the same thing. But at this point, I'll ask Special Agent Chuck Coon to pick up the story."

25

JOE THOUGHT COON LOOKED AS IF HE WERE racked with turmoil, as if it would physically hurt him to talk. The FBI agent reached back and rubbed his own neck and seemed to be staring at something on the table-top he found fascinating.

Rulon lowered his voice and looked kindly toward Coon. "Mr. Coon is one of the good guys in this whole situation. He came to me yesterday afternoon because his conscience was bothering him. I know how far out on a limb he is now, and how much courage it's taken when he could have easily said nothing at all."

Coon thanked the governor with his eyes, then turned to Joe and Nate.

"What the governor said about greed and corruption is all too true," Coon said. "Especially these days. There's just so much money sloshing around in the government that anything is possible. They can't hire federal employ-ees fast enough or throw billions at projects fast enough. They spend money like a pimp with a week to live. The only growth industry is us—the government. Luckily, we're somewhat insulated from it out here in the field, but in D.C.—*man*."

Joe shook his head and slipped a glance toward Nate

to gauge his reaction. Nate looked back and waggled his eyebrows, as if to say nothing he would hear could surprise him. Joe was constantly amazed at the network of contacts Nate seemed to have across the country. He'd purposefully never asked Nate about the company he kept because he didn't want to know.

Coon leveled his gaze at Joe, pointedly ignoring Nate. He said, "Some background is necessary. Senator McKinty is on the Homeland Security Committee, as mentioned. He knew the government was looking for land for a new counterterrorism effort, a training facility far removed from any population centers. He knew because his staff knows the federal budget inside out and they're under orders to be on the lookout for opportunities to preempt senators with less seniority and stature to deliver the pork back home. As you know, Michigan has been in a one-state depression for years, so anything he can deliver keeps him popular and gets him reelected time after time. The Upper Peninsula is pretty hard hit, so he wanted to locate the facility there, but there wasn't a big enough piece of state land that would meet all the specs. So he worked with the locals to identify several huge private holdings that provided the geographical diversity necessary for the facility. He worked with the developer to target the land. What no one knew was that he'd arranged for his son to be a major shareholder in the development as well. You see, McKinty's largest campaign contributor is himself. This was a way of creating a permanent major donor. There are no laws preventing a senator from contributing to his own campaign."

Nate said, "Bastards."

Joe looked over to try and shush him. Nate glared back.

Coon said, "So he delivered an eight-hundred-fifty-million-dollar defense facility to his constituents. Few knew he was personally going to benefit, and those who knew didn't care because that's how things are done. All you have to ask yourself is: How many of our representatives enter office as fairly well-off financially, but on a salary of a hundred seventy-five thousand dollars per year retire as millionaires? That's one way how it's done."

"The Clines were a major problem, though," Coon said, "because they became grassroots heroes for refusing to relocate their business or leave their land. Even though the media didn't much cover the showdown, it was all over the Internet and talk radio. That put pressure on Senator McKinty and he wanted them gone, and used his pull with federal agencies to put the pressure on them. The Clines were well known as independent backwoods renegade types, and it didn't take long for legitimate charges to be brought against them."

"Still," Joe said, "it was their land. How can the government just take it?"

Coon shrugged. "We can. We do."

Nate spat, "Bastards."

"Anyway," Coon said, "not every member of the Cline family died that day. Two of them survived."

Joe felt his scalp twitch and his stomach clench. Coon read Joe's face.

"That's right," Coon said. "The two surviving sons were arrested. They were belligerent and claimed they were political prisoners and they wouldn't spend one minute in jail. It was shaping up to be a major federal trial, but Senator McKinty again got involved. He didn't want a trial that could blow open the whole controversy again, and he didn't want his personal connection to the facility widely known. So he sent his staff to the Justice Department, and a deal was cut. If the two surviving

Cline sons would drop their claim to the land and agree not to pursue any civil legal action against law enforcement, they wouldn't be prosecuted. Instead, they'd be given new identities and be placed in the Federal Witness Protection Program and allowed to go away. Otherwise, federal prosecutors would go after them with both barrels and send them to prison for the rest of their lives. Needless to say, their court-appointed public defenders urged them to take the deal."

"Hold it," Joe said, shaking his head. "Prosecutors wouldn't cut those brothers a deal based on what you've said, would they? If they really fired on federal officers? What did the brothers have to bargain with?"

"Not much," Coon said. "But there were people in the administration who didn't want any undue attention on the land seizure, either. They had enough on their plates at the time with accusations about creeping socialism and such. The last thing they wanted was more controversy about government takings. And don't forget, federal prosecutors are political appointees. They know where their bread is buttered."

"This stinks," Joe said.

Coon nodded. "Welcome to the big time, Joe."

"And I bet I can guess the names of the brothers," Joe said. "Camish and Caleb. Grimmengruber was the name they were given for the witness protection program."

Joe continued, "They told me they were from the UP, but it didn't click at the time. And the fact they ran a meat-processing company explains how professionally they were able to butcher the elk and my horses."

Coon nodded. "They were supposed to go to Nevada. There were sweet auto mechanic jobs all lined up for them. But en route, just about a hundred miles from here in Wyoming, they overpowered their federal escort and took off. Needless to say, they never showed up in Nevada. We lost track of them completely, but our agency was told to keep an eye out for them. Until you gave your statement, we had no idea where they ended up."

Rulon said, "And I would have never put this all together except for Senator McKinty himself. As I said, I've been tangling with him for a couple of years, because he's the chairman of the Natural Resources Committee and he refused to release mineral severance payments to the State of Wyoming that are owed to us. We're talking hundreds of millions. He wants all that money to stay in Washington so he can siphon it off, the prick. He wouldn't answer my letters or take my calls until this week. Now, all of a sudden, his staff said he's rethinking his opposition to releasing the funds. But there's a condition. He wants the Clines—or the Grim Brothers—to be left alone up there in the mountains. They made up this goofy story of wanting to look out for their former constituents, but I saw right through that. He doesn't want them to resurface and start talking."

Joe said to Coon, "So why'd you talk to the governor?"

Coon shook his head. "There's only so much I can take. I just want to do my job out here and solve crimes and put bad guys in prison. I don't want any part of deals cut in D.C. between senators and attorneys general. I've got a son. I want to be able to look him in the eye. And I want to be able to look at myself in the mirror."

Joe said, "You are a good man."

Coon smiled. "I'm a bad bureaucrat, though."

"That makes two of us."

Nate said to the governor, "Hold it. McKinty just wants the Clines, or the Grim Brothers, *left alone?*"

Rulon said, "He didn't say it in so many words, but yes, that's what his staff is asking."

Nate shook his head. "That doesn't make sense. He doesn't want them left alone. He wants them silenced. That's the only way he can skate on this."

Rulon said, "He's a U.S. senator. He's not a killer, for Christ sake. Man, I thought *I* was cynical."

Nate said, "When did he approach you about the deal?"

The governor said, "Last week. Why?"

Nate said, "Because I think he wanted you to not put any more effort into finding those brothers right away until he could take care of it himself. I wouldn't be surprised if he, or his son, or the developer, or the facility general manager—whoever could do it at arm's length and not directly involve McKinty in any way—sent a team up there to solve the problem once and for all. And it wouldn't surprise me if he reneged on his offer once he got confirmation that the Clines were no more."

Rulon turned to Carson while pointing his finger at Nate. "This son of a bitch should be our point man in Washington. He's got a vicious and devious mind."

"No, thanks," Nate said. "I used to work for them. I know how they think, and how they operate. The question is, did the team he sent out find the Clines?"

Joe stood up, fighting a wave of nausea. He said, "And is Diane alive and well? Or did they get her, too?"

Nate stood as well. "I wouldn't be surprised, based on what Joe experienced, to find out that it's McKinty's team that's taking a dirt nap and not the brothers. But there's only one way we're going to find that out."

Joe stared out the window at the governor's plane and the tumbleweeds rolling down the runway. He said, "They called me a government man. Now I know why they went after me."

Coon said, "We're all government men, Joe."

"Not me," Nate said proudly.

*   *   *

"So," Joe said to the governor, "where do we stand?"

Rulon didn't hesitate. "Go up there and rescue that woman and bring those brothers out dead or alive."

Carson turned white. "Sir, you can't give an order like that."

"I just did."

Joe stood and clamped his hat on. Nate stood with him.

"Do you need more people?" Rulon asked Joe. "I could have a dozen DCI agents here by nightfall. I can send them back in Rulon One."

Joe shook his head, said, "I think the smaller the footprint the better. Those brothers own those mountains, and they know when a big contingent is after them, I think. A big group makes lots of noise and raises dust and quiets the wildlife. That's why I stumbled on Caleb on my own while Sheriff Baird and his men couldn't find them at all. I think the leaner the better."

"Meaning you and Mr. Romanowski here," Rulon said.

Joe nodded. "Plus, I have a pretty good idea where they hang out."

"Go get those bastards, then," Rulon said, narrowing his eyes. "Get them the hell out of my state. Send 'em back to Michigan, either vertical or horizontal—I don't have strong feelings either way."

Nate was out of the room before Joe could speak.

Rulon said, "Is he still with you?"

Joe shrugged. "I'm not sure."

"Would you go alone?"

"Probably not."

Rulon blew out a long breath and looked to Carson for solace. Carson looked away.

"Two questions," Joe said to Rulon. "One, what was the name of the developer in Michigan?"

Rulon shrugged and turned to Coon. "Do you know?"

Coon smiled wearily. "Brent Shober," he said.

Joe said, "Thought so. Second question. How will the state cope with the loss of money from the feds if Senator McKinty finds out you sent me up there?"

Rulon said, "That's a good question, Joe. Very politically astute. You're learning, aren't you?"

"Not that I'm proud of it," Joe said.

Rulon put his beefy hands on Joe's shoulders and leaned his face close. Joe could feel the heat from the governor's forehead. "If you bring those brothers down the mountain, we have a news story on our hands," Rulon said. "The story can be spun however we want it to be spun. Meaning McKinty might just find himself in the news again for the wrong reason. It'll be up to him how he plays it."

"But if we don't find the Cline Brothers and Diane Shober?" Joe asked.

Rulon said, "I'm screwed. You're screwed. We're all screwed."

26

THE STOPOVER IN RAWLINS WITH THE GOVERNOR
had cost Joe two hours and a big chunk of his sense of
purpose, he thought. Still, he was worried about getting
to the trailhead in the Sierra Madre before dark. As he
and Nate traveled west via I-80, Joe called Marybeth on
his cell phone and filled her in on the meeting that had
taken place with the governor. He was keenly aware of
Nate's presence in the passenger seat. Nate sat sullen and
still, his eyes fixed on something in the middle distance
out the side window. He was no doubt thinking whether
or not he even wanted to be on this adventure anymore.

"So do you think the Shobers were withholding information from you?" Marybeth asked.

Joe said, "I'm not sure yet. Each of them might be
withholding different things. If they don't know it was
the Cline Brothers up there in the first place, there wasn't
anything for them to come clean about. It's possible Mr.
Shober knows something, but I'm not sure. I think he's
focused solely on finding Diane."

"But still," Marybeth said, "the Michigan connection
is just too . . . convenient. There has to be something
there."

"I agree, but what?"

"I'm not sure. I'm not sure at all. But I could do a little research."

Joe grinned. "I was hoping you would say that."

Marybeth had assisted in a number of cases over the years. Joe found her a clear-eyed and determined researcher, a bulldog with a laptop. And she wasn't shy about making calls, either, and at times posing as someone else so she could get answers to questions. Joe was equally proud and a little frightened of her ruthlessness. She got information no one else seemed to be able to find, and she got it quickly. He hoped he never gave her a reason for her to turn her guns on *him*.

"Will you be able to stay in range?" she asked. "I'll call you back as soon as I have something."

"I'll try," he said. "There are dead spots ahead, as you know."

He could hear computer keys clicking in the background.

"Wow—this looks like a target-rich environment," she said, already distracted.

"What have you found?"

"I'll call later," she said, hanging up.

As he slowed down to take Exit 187 off I-80 south toward Baggs, Joe checked to make sure he still had a strong phone signal. He didn't want to miss Marybeth's return call.

"OKAY," NATE SAID after an hour of silence since they'd left Rawlins and the governor, "this new development about the Clines puts a whole new angle on the situation."

Joe grunted, noncommittal.

Nate said, "From the standpoint of the Cline Brothers,

they hunt, they fish, they go back to subsistence level. No doubt they even maintain some contacts with some of their kind around the country. And believe me, there's more of them than you'd think and the numbers are growing by the week. Have you been into a sporting goods store the last two years? It's impossible to find ammunition—it's sold out. Folks are hoarding, getting ready for something bad to happen."

Joe chose not to respond. He knew it was true. If he didn't have channels through the department to buy bullets, he wasn't sure where he would get them. Shelves in retail stores had been picked clean.

Said Nate, "Things are going on out here in the flyover states nobody wants to talk about."

Joe shook his head. "You've been thinking about this for a while."

Nate said, "Yes, I have. Hanging out in Hole in the Wall gives me plenty of time to think."

"Maybe you should get out more," Joe said.

"I don't even think it was the lack of a license so much," Nate said, ignoring Joe. "It was your threat about seeing them in court. You were telling them, in effect, that the jig was up. You just didn't realize what buttons you were pushing."

"No," Joe said, "how could I know that?"

Said Nate, "You couldn't. But you *are* stubborn."

"Yup, when it comes to doing my job. Besides, they stole that guy's elk, too."

Nate shrugged. "From their point of view, those hunters were in their territory and they didn't bother to ask permission. It's all a matter of how you look at it."

"This is going nowhere," Joe said. "We can't have the rule of law if people can choose which laws they want to obey based on their philosophy and point of view."

"Agreed," Nate said. "Which is why the big laws ought to be reasonable and fair and neither the people nor the government should breach their trust. But when the government decides to confiscate private property simply because they have the guns and judges on their side, the whole system starts to break down and all bets are off."

"Do we really want to have this discussion?"

Said Nate, "It might lead us into dark places."

"Yup."

"Speaking of dark places, where are you going to spread the ashes?"

"I have no idea," Joe said. "I hardly knew him. I don't know of any special places he liked except for barstools."

"You can't just drive around with him back there," Nate said.

"I'll think of something."

Nate nodded and changed the subject back.

"One thing, though," he said, pushing his seat as far back as it would go so he could cock a boot heel on the dashboard, "These boys may be losers, but *damn*. This is what happens when the government gets too big for its britches. Some folks get pushed out and they get angry."

"You sound sympathetic to them," Joe said.

Nate said, "Damned straight."

"Great," Joe said.

"I'm sympathetic to outliers among us," Nate said. "I'm kind of one myself." Then he paused and looked over at Joe, and said, *"Government man."*

Joe said, "Quit calling me that."

THEY WERE ROLLING DOWN the hard-packed gravel road into the forest, racing a plume of dust that threatened to overtake the cab, when Marybeth called back.

Joe snatched his phone from the seat between them and opened it. Nate looked on, interested.

"It wasn't hard to find a connection between Caryl Cline and Diane Shober," Marybeth said. "In fact, it was so easy I'm amazed others haven't been there before us."

Joe said, "We don't know they haven't been."

"Agreed. But it might also be an instance where no one has thought to look."

"Go on," Joe said. "Are you saying the two of them were associated with each other?"

"I can't confirm it," Marybeth said, "but it looks like they had the opportunity to meet each other at least once."

"When and where?" Joe asked.

She said, "I just did a simple Google search with both of their names. I came up with a bunch of hits, but in most cases the names are used in the same essays or news roundups during that year. Except for one instance."

"Fire away," Joe said.

"Caryl and Diane appeared on the same local cable news show years ago. They were both in Detroit the same day. It wasn't as if they were interviewed together. According to the schedule, Diane was on at the top of the hour to talk about her chances to make the Olympic team and Ma Cline was on at the bottom of the hour to talk about what it felt like to lose her appeal to the court. Like I said, they weren't on together and I found the YouTube clips to confirm that, but they very likely could have met in the green room before the show. Maybe they struck up a relationship there that continued."

"Goodness," Joe said, his mind swirling, marveling how simple it been for Marybeth to investigate and come up with positive results.

She said, "So we've got a Michigan connection now

between the Cline Family, Diane Shober, and Brent Shober. This is getting interesting, Joe."

"Yup," he said. Then: "This thing between Diane and Brent. It smells bad. I can see the basis of real animosity there."

Marybeth said, "Me, too. The guy is more than a creep. He's obsessed with her."

"And the Clines somehow connect with both of them," Joe said.

"Maybe Diane and the Clines figure they've got a common enemy," Marybeth said.

"Can you keep looking into it?" Joe asked. "See if you can find anything that links them up further?"

"I doubt we're going to find anything as public, but I'll do some advance searches and get creative. I'll also start adding in the Cline Brothers and see what we get."

JOE BRIEFED NATE on what Marybeth had found.

Nate nodded his head, said, "The dispossessed."

Joe said, "Talk about pure speculation, Nate."

"Trust me on this. These are my people," Nate said, only smiling a little.

THE SIERRA MADRE defined the muscular horizon of the west and south, and they appeared to flex slightly into the blue as Joe and Nate approached them. Joe used his service radio to call ahead to contact Sheriff Baird's office. The county dispatcher put him through directly to Baird's vehicle. Joe expected an immediate rebuke for being back in his county. Instead, the sheriff sounded relieved. "Are you close?" he asked.

"Yup," Joe said. "I wanted to let you know we're plan-

ning to take horses into the mountains this afternoon to
go after those brothers."

"I figured you'd come back," Baird said. "How far are
you from the trailhead now?"

Joe looked at the dashboard clock. "Twenty minutes."

Baird said, "Can you divert for now and take the road
straight up into the mountains? I'm up here now on the
eastern side of the mountains about an hour and a half
from you. I may need some help."

Joe frowned. "What's going on?"

"I'm not real sure," Baird said, his voice low. "I got a
call earlier today from a citizen about some vehicles sitting empty way up on the side of the mountain. A couple
of pickups and a big stock trailer with out-of-state plates.
That struck me as unusual since it's a little early for hunting season, as you know. I had a meeting in Saratoga this
morning so I thought I'd check them out on the way
back. Looks like I'm not the only one."

"Meaning what?" Joe asked.

"I'm parked up on a pullout where I can see into the
trees below me where the vehicles and horse trailer are
located. But as I started looking over the campsite, I saw
two men dressed exactly alike in the same clothes come
down out of the trees on the other side of the mountain
and walk toward the camp."

Joe felt the hair rise on his forearms and on the back
of his neck. He reached down while he drove and turned
up the volume on the radio so Nate could hear clearly.

"What's their description?" Joe asked.

"Taller than hell, skinnier than poles," Baird said. "Red
flannel shirts with big checks on them. Dirty denims.
Goofy-assed hats. Kind of zombie Elmer Fudds."

"It's them," Joe said. "The brothers. I wonder why
they're on the wrong side of the mountain?"

"Beats me," Baird said. "The last I saw 'em, they was crossing a little meadow up above headed toward the camp with the vehicles in it. They're out of view in the trees, but I wouldn't be surprised if they've reached those trucks by now. Maybe they plan to take the trucks and hightail it out of here once and for all. That would be okay with me," the sheriff said with a chuckle.

"One thing, though," he said. "I see a pickup truck down there I recognize that doesn't belong here. It belongs to Dave Farkus. You know him, don't you?"

Joe said, "Yup. He's on my watch list for poaching."

"Good place for him," Baird said. "Anyway, his county supervisor called our office yesterday and said he was AWOL. They haven't filed a report or anything, but I said I'd keep a lookout for him. I have no idea why he'd be over here on this side of the mountain with some out-of-staters, but that sure looks like his wheels."

"The brothers," Joe said. "Do you still see them?"

"Naw. Once they went down into the trees, I lost 'em."

Joe said, "Maybe you ought to pull back."

"I don't think they saw me."

Joe and Nate exchanged a quick look. "Don't be too sure of that," Joe said. "Those boys don't miss much, I don't think. In fact, you may want to back on out of there."

"I don't back off," Baird said, his voice hard.

"Where are your men?"

Baird sighed. "The timing of this couldn't be worse. Two of my deputies are in Douglas taking classes at the Law Enforcement Academy—one of 'em is in Rawlins for court today, and the other is on vacation," Baird said. "It's just me and I could use some help. I tried to raise a state trooper or two earlier, but they were too far away to respond."

"They're probably fetching Rulon's dinner," Nate grumbled. "Maybe giving him a nice foot massage."

"What was that?" Baird asked Joe.

"Nothing important," Joe said, glaring at his friend.

"Sheriff, can you see the license plates on the pickup and horse trailer at all?"

"Not real well," Baird said. "I can barely make one of them out through the trees. I can't see the numbers clearly, though."

Joe asked, "Is the plate blue?"

"Yes."

"I'd bet you a dollar it's a Michigan plate."

"That sounds right."

"We'll be there as soon as we can," Joe said.

"Who is we?" Baird asked.

"Yeah, who is *we*?" Nate asked as well.

"Keep in radio contact," Joe told Baird. "And back out of there if you see those guys again. Seriously. You don't want to take them on without help."

Joe was under no illusion the sheriff would believe him and retreat.

A HALF HOUR LATER, Joe's radio crackled to life.

"Joe, you there?" Baird asked. Joe noted the urgency of Baird's tone and his complete absence of radio protocol.

"Yes, sheriff, what is it?" He felt icy fingers pull back on his scalp.

"Jesus!" Baird said, and the transmission went to static.

Joe's pickup was in a steady climb into the mountains, struggling with the weight of the horse trailer full of horses behind it. When the animals shifted their weight around, Joe could feel the trailer shift and pull back at his truck. His motor was strained and the tachometer edged into the red. He floored it. While he did so, he tried to raise the dispatcher who'd originally connected them.

When she came on she was weeping. "Did you hear the sheriff?" she asked. "I think those bastards got him."

"I heard," Joe said. "But let's not speculate on what we don't know. Time to sit up and be a professional. Are you dispatching EMTs? Anybody?"

The dispatcher sniffed. "Everybody," she said. "But you're the closest to him by far. I hope you can help him. I hope they didn't . . ."

"Yes," Joe said. "Hey—you don't need to talk about him that way yet. He may be okay."

"Okay," she said, to placate Joe.

A few minutes later, Nate said, "Wonder what'll be left of him."

27

THE LACK OF WIND WAS RARE AND REMARKABLE, Joe thought, and the single thin plume of black smoke miles away deep in the timber rose straight up as if on a line until it finally dissipated at around 15,000 feet.

Joe and Nate had just summited the mountains, and the eastern slope was laid out before them in a sea of green between the ranges. The vista was stunning: a massive, undulating carpet veined with tendrils of gold and red. The thread of black smoke seemed to tenuously connect the mountains with the sky.

"It's like whoever set the fire said, *Look at me*," Nate said as they plunged down the other side of the mountain in the pickup. "I'm wondering if they wish they hadn't set a fire now. Or if they're trying to draw us in."

"Black smoke like that isn't from a forest fire," Joe said.

"Nope."

"Smoke that black usually means rubber is burning," Joe said.

"Do you know how to get there?" Nate asked.

Joe nodded. "There are quite a few old logging roads ahead. I've been on a few of them. It's been so dry, though, we should be able to find Baird's tire tracks and follow him in."

Nate surveyed the vista in front of him as Joe eased forward. "Rough country," he said.

"In every way," Joe said.

THERE WAS ONLY ONE open road that went to the southeast toward the smoke, and there were fresh tire tracks imprinted over a coating of dust. Joe made the turn and drove down the two-track as swiftly as he could over the washboarded surface without shaking the pickup apart. Nate hung out the passenger window like a Labrador, Joe thought, with his hand clamped on his hat.

"This looks like the right road," Nate said, pulling himself back in. "We need to be ready."

Joe nodded. Afternoon sun fanned through the lodgepole pines as he shot along the dirt road. In his peripheral vision, he saw Nate dig his weapon and holster out from under the bench seat and strap it back on.

"You loaded?" Nate asked, pulling Joe's new shotgun out from behind the seat and zipping off the gun cover.

"Shells in the glove box," Joe said.

Nate, who was *never* unloaded, sighed and found the shells and fitted them into the receiver.

"I have mixed feelings about this thing we are about to do," Nate said.

"I know."

"You do, too."

Joe grunted. "If it weren't for Diane, I might be tempted to turn around."

"But we can't let feelings get in the way," Nate said, putting the shotgun muzzle-down on the floor and shoving the stock between the bench seats so it wouldn't rattle around on the dirt road. "We've set our course. It doesn't matter what we think about politics or the law or anything else. It's not *Speed kills*, it's *Hesitation kills*. If we find those brothers and you've got a shot, take it. These boys aren't going to let us lead them back to jail. They've left all that behind, I'm afraid. Don't start talking or reading them their rights or trying to figure out where the hell they went off the rails. Just shoot."

When Joe started to object, Nate said, "It isn't about who is the fastest or the toughest hombre in the state. It's never about those things. It's about who can look up without any mist in their eyes or doubts in their heart, aim, and pull the trigger without thinking twice. It's about killing. It's always been that way."

SHERIFF RON BAIRD'S county Ford Excursion was parked twenty feet off the two-track in a grove of aspen trees that overlooked the campground below in the distance. It wasn't burning, but it had been worked over.

Joe pulled up beside it and jumped out of his pickup with his shotgun. He circled the Excursion. The hood was open and all visible wires had been sliced in half or pulled out and thrown to the ground like angel-hair packing from a shipping crate. The front windshield was smashed inward and cubes of safety glass sparkled like sheets of jewelry on the front bench seat, with errant cubes of it on the hood. The tires were flat and air had stopped seeping out from the open wounds in the sidewalls.

Baird was nowhere to be found.

Nate had opened the passenger door and stood outside the truck on the running board. Using both hands, he tracked through the air how he guessed the brothers had come up from down below on each side in a pincer movement converging on Baird's vehicle.

Joe said, "I wonder where they took him."

"They marched him down the hill," Nate said, binoculars at his eyes. "I see him."

Joe felt a spasm of fear shoot through him. "Is he alive?"

"I think so. But he doesn't look real good."

"How so?" Joe asked.

"Looks like he's got an arrow sticking out of his ass."

THE STENCH FROM BURNING FUEL, tires, and plastic was nearly overwhelming on the valley floor. The pickup that towed the horse trailer, the trailer itself, and Dave Farkus's pickup was on fire. Baird was fifty yards off to the side of the camp, and he appeared to be hugging the trunk of a tree.

"Do you see any sign of the brothers?" Joe asked as they drove down the hill toward the scene. He'd shifted to four-wheel drive because of the incline, and he let the compression of the motor hold back his truck and trailer.

Nate lowered the binoculars. "Nope."

"Think they're gone or using the sheriff to draw us in and ambush us?" Joe had used the same tactic two years before when he'd bound a wanted man to lure in his would-be assassin. It had been one of the most shameful decisions he'd ever made, even though he wasn't sure he wouldn't do it again, given the circumstances.

"If we get sucked in and ambushed using the same trap," Joe said, "it's not poetic justice, but it's something like it."

Nate shook his head. "My guess is those boys are running back into the mountains. They probably came down to disable the vehicles and didn't expect to get surprised by the sheriff."

"Or us," Joe said.

Nate said, "And I bet they're wondering why they

picked the only day in Wyoming history without wind to start a couple of cars on fire. Normally, we might not even see the smoke."

Joe drove to Baird and hit the brakes and leaped out. He could feel the heat from the burning pickup on his back.

Baird was conscious, his eyes wide open, his mustache twitching. He was hugging the tree because they'd cinched Flex-Cuffs around his wrists on the other side of the trunk. And, as Nate had mentioned, there was an arrow shaft sticking out of his left buttock. Joe recognized the craftsmanship of the arrow and knew it had been made by the Grim Brothers. He could see the rawhide where the shaft was bound to the point next to the Wrangler label on Baird's jeans. The arrow wasn't deep at all, although Joe guessed it probably hurt.

"Sheriff," Joe said, "you've got an arrow sticking out of your butt."

"Why, thanks, Joe. I was wondering what it was bothering me back there."

"You want me to pull it out or cut you down first?"

"Cut me down, please."

As Joe removed his Leatherman tool and opened the blade, he said, "How far are the brothers ahead of us?"

Baird nodded toward the forested slope on the other side of the burning pickups. "Maybe thirty minutes," he said.

"They on foot?"

Baird nodded. "They are, but they cover ground like demons. I saw them coming out of the trees at me on both sides, but they were so fast I didn't get a chance to fight them off."

"I understand," Joe said, cutting the plastic cuffs free. "I've tangled with them and lost, just like you."

Baird stepped away from the tree and rubbed hard on his wrists. His Stetson had fallen off, and strands of his wispy black hair reached down from his brow to his upper lip. As he rubbed his wrists, the arrow shaft danced up and down.

"So," Joe said, "do you believe me now?"

Baird reached up and pushed his stringy hair back. "I was waiting to see how long it took you to ask me that question."

As the two men looked at each other, Nate strode behind Baird toward the burning vehicles in the camp. As deft as a swallow plucking a gnat from the air, Nate reached out and pulled the arrow from Baird.

"Ouch, goddammit!" Baird said, spinning around. "Who said you could do that?"

Nate smirked, handed Baird the arrow, and continued on his way.

"THEY HAD NO INTENTION of killing you," Joe said to Baird a few minutes later, as he helped the sheriff limp to a downed log to rest on. "Or you'd be dead."

"I know," Baird agreed. He straddled the log and leaned over it so his chest rested against the bark. His wound was open to the sky.

"Same with me," Joe said to the sheriff. "For whatever reason, they did some real damage, but they didn't feel compelled to finish the job."

"It would have been easy," Baird said, then gestured over his shoulder toward his wound. "This thing hurts. How bad is it?"

Joe said, "This is when you find out who your friends are," looking at the trickle of fresh blood coming out of the wound.

"Just don't let that friend of *yours* near me again," Baird said.

Joe grimaced and turned for his pickup truck to get his first-aid kit.

JOE RIPPED ANOTHER STRIP of tape to bind the compress to the wound while doing his best to avoid looking at Sheriff Baird's bare butt, which was stunningly white. As Joe applied the tape, Nate came down out of the trees.

"Did those boys say anything?" Nate asked Baird.

"Like what?"

Nate shrugged. "Anything at all? Like, *Stay off our mountain, sheriff*, or *Damn, where'd you come from?*"

Baird shook his head. "Nothing at first. It's like they could communicate through hand signals or something. They never said a word the whole time. Until the end, I mean."

Joe paused, said, "What did they say at the end?"

Baird cleared his throat, coughed up a ball of phlegm, and spat it away. "After they cuffed me to that tree, I expected them to just cut my throat and leave me there. One of 'em got right behind me and kind of whispered into my ear. He said, 'The only reason we're letting you live is so you can tell anybody who will listen to leave us the hell alone.'"

"That's all?" Joe said.

"Pretty much. He repeated himself, though. *'Just leave us the hell alone.'* Then he stepped back and said, 'This is to show you how serious we are,' and shot me in the butt with that arrow. I could tell he took it easy on me, though. He barely shot that at me with much force. I mean, he could have done all kind of damage.

"I don't know which one it was who shot me," Baird

said. "It's not like they introduced themselves. And you know they look and dress exactly alike. The only difference between them was one of them had a bandage taped on his face, on his chin."

"That would be Caleb," Joe said. "Meaning Camish was the one who talked to you and shot you with the arrow."

Baird said, "Well, Caleb didn't talk. I got the impression maybe he couldn't anymore."

"Did he look wounded any other way?" Joe asked. "Did he appear to move stiffly or hang back, anything like that?"

"Not that I noticed," the sheriff said.

Joe shook his head. How could he shoot the man square in the chest and cause no harm?

Baird turned his head around toward Joe. "You know, I gotta tell you, I was scared at first. But when he said, *'Just leave us the hell alone,'* I felt sorry for them in a weird way. Even though they did this to me. Ain't that strange? Maybe it's because I think that way myself a lot these days."

Nate was close enough to hear Baird's question, but he didn't respond. To Joe, he said, "I saddled the horses. They've got an hour on us at best and they aren't on horseback. This may be the closest we'll ever get to them."

Joe nodded and felt his scalp twitch again from fear. He tried to hide his face from Nate.

"We'd best get going," Nate said.

"I heard you," Joe said. He told Baird to pull up his pants.

AS THEY RODE UP out of the camp where the vehicles still burned, they could hear the distant thumping of a helicopter to the east. The chopper was coming to get Baird and whisk him away to Rawlins, Laramie, or Cheyenne. Various state troopers and DCI agents were on their way as well, but hours behind them.

Baird's handheld had been propped against the log he was resting on and the volume was up. As Joe saddled the packhorse and packed gear into the panniers, he heard the chatter pick up as word spread of the ambush of Baird. Sheriff's departments from four Wyoming counties and two Colorado counties were mobilizing. DCI, FBI, and ATF were being contacted. There was even speculation about contacting the governor's office to request the National Guard.

Joe said to Nate, "By this time tomorrow, this camp will be a small city."

Nate said, "I'm not a city-type guy."

THEY RODE THEIR HORSES UP into the mountains. Joe led, followed by Nate and the packhorse.

The feeling of dread seemed to increase in direct proportion to the altitude, Joe thought. The sharp smell of pine and sweating horses, the gritty taste of dust from the trail, the beating of his heart as the air got thinner—it was as if he'd never been away. For the third time in an hour, Joe reached out and touched the butt plate of his shotgun with the tips of his fingers, as if assuring himself it was there.

Apparently, Nate saw him do it, said, "Remember what I said."

Joe said, "Yup."

"So we're agreed that the best way to do this is to drive hard on our own, right?" Nate said. "We're going to try to catch up with those boys while they're within striking distance? And we aren't going to give a good goddamn about all of the drummers on their way here right now?"

"Yup."

Nate said, "Okay, then."

Joe said, "I feel like we owe it to those brothers to find them before they're cornered by the cavalry that'll be coming."

"Even though the result may be the same," Nate said.

28

THEY FOLLOWED THE TRACKS OF THE HORSES
that had been there before them into the mountains. Joe
determined that the men from Michigan had six horses.
What he couldn't tell was if that meant there were six men
total or if at least a couple of the animals were packhorses.
The horses they were following had been recently shod,
based on the sharp edges of the imprints in the dust and
mud.

But who were they, these men? And how did Dave
Farkus get hooked up with them? Joe's best guess was
Farkus stumbled on the men and was taken along—or
disposed of along the way. The purpose of the riders was
unclear as well, although Joe was pummeled with the
many connections to Michigan and the Upper Peninsula
that kept cropping up. Were these riders after the brothers? Or allies with them?

Joe and Nate quickly fell into a procedure where if
they wanted or needed to talk, they would sidle next to
each other on horseback so they could lean into each
other and keep their voices down. Joe sidestepped his
horse off the trail and let Nate catch up and rein to stop.

Joe said, "What do you think happened to the boys
from Michigan?"

Nate narrowed his eyes while looking ahead of them up the mountain. "All I know is that they haven't come back down the trail to their vehicles. That says they're still up here. Or that they aren't ever coming down."

"I'd opt for the latter," Joe said, leaning on the pommel and looking ahead.

"I'm trying to figure out why the brothers went after their vehicles," Nate said. "It seems kind of pointless to expose themselves that way."

Joe nodded. "Unless the purpose was more general."

Nate caught Joe's meaning. He said, "Like a warning to everybody out there that if you try to go after the brothers, they'll come around behind you and destroy your property. They're saying, *Stay the hell out of these mountains.*"

"Just like the message they gave Sheriff Baird," Joe said.

Nate started to say something but didn't. He swallowed and made a face as if he'd tasted something bitter.

As HE RODE, Joe continually scanned the trail up ahead of him and shot hard looks into the trees lining both sides. His shotgun was within quick reach. If the brothers didn't know they were being pursued, it was possible he and Nate could simply ride up on them. He wanted to be ready.

The afternoon sun lengthened the shadows across the trail and enhanced the fall colors of the aspen into almost blinding acrylic hues. It would be effortless for the brothers to simply meld into the throbbing colors of the trees and for Joe not to see them, he thought.

A doe mule deer and her fawn stayed ahead of them on the trail and Joe kept seeing her at each turn. She'd graze with the fawn until the horses came into sight, then startle with a white flap of her tail and bound ahead again and again. Joe wished she'd move off the trail for good, because each time she saw him and jumped, his heart did, too.

AN HOUR LATER, as dusk muffled the eastside slopes and the acrylic colors muted into pastels, Joe again spooked the doe and fawn. But rather than running ahead along the trail where it narrowed and squeezed through the trunks of two massive spruce trees, the deer cut into the timber to the right. Joe was pleased the deer had finally got out of the way, but then he saw them reappear yet again on the trail farther up the mountain slope like before.

Instinctively, he leaned back in the saddle and pulled back on the reins. He said, "Hold it, Nate," quietly over his shoulder.

Nate rode up alongside. "Are you wondering if the packhorse and panniers are going to fit through that narrow chute?"

"No," Joe said. "I'm wondering why those deer went around in the trees instead of staying on the game trail."

JOE AND NATE APPROACHED the trap from behind after tying off their horses in the trees. The design of the trap was a brutal work of art, Joe thought. And if it weren't for the deer, he would have ridden right into it.

The brothers had cut down and trimmed a green lodgepole pine tree about as thick as Joe's fist near the base. The base was wedged into the gap between two branches on the large spruce, then bowed back almost to the point of breaking before being tied off with wire. The wire was fed through a smooth groove around the tree trunk and stretched ankle-high across the trail. It was tied off to a set of ten-inch lengths of wood that were notched back and fitted into one another. A thick foot-long sharpened stake was lashed to the tip of the lodgepole. If the wire was tripped, the notched lengths would pull apart sideways and release the tension that held the cocked arm and stake back.

"Chest high for a rider," Joe said, absently rubbing a spot just below his clavicle.

Nate found a stump in the timber and carried it toward the trap from behind. "Stand back," he said, and threw the stump with a grunt. It landed on the wire, which yanked the notched sticks apart and sent the lodgepole and stake slicing through the air with surprising speed and velocity.

While the pole and stake rocked back and forth, Joe said, "This was more than a warning to stay away."

"That it is," Nate said, inspecting the cuts on the lodgepole where branches had been trimmed away. With his fingertip, he touched an amber bead of sap that oozed from one of the cuts. "Fresh," he said. "The boys probably put this up within the last couple of days. Maybe they're expecting us."

At that moment, far up the mountainside, was the harsh crackle of snapping branches. Joe and Nate locked eyes for a moment, then dived for the ground. They lay helplessly while a dislodged boulder the size of a small car smashed down the slope leveling small trees and splintering big ones along its path. The boulder rolled end-over-end, coming within ten yards of where they were on the trail. Remarkably, the horses didn't snap their tethers and run away.

When the boulder finally stopped rolling and settled noisily below them, Joe stood up. The sharp smell of broken pine trees was in the air, along with the damp odor of churned-up soil.

"*Man . . .*" Joe whispered.

"They're real close," Nate said. "And they *know* we're right behind them."

WHEN THEY RODE to the edge of the tree line, Joe and Nate paused on their horses before continuing up. The sun had sunk behind the western mountains an hour before. The moon was narrow and white, a toenail clipping, and the wash of stars was so bright and close as to be almost creamy. Ahead of them was a long expanse of treeless scree. The trail they were on switchbacked up through the scree, but dissolved into darkness near the top of the summit.

"I can't see what's up there," Joe whispered. "But we'll be in the open. This would be a great place to get ambushed."

Nate said, "If we can't see them, they can't see us, right?"

"I wish there was a way to get over the top some other way," Joe said, trying not to ascribe powers to the Grim Brothers that they didn't realistically possess.

"There isn't," Nate said, nudging his horse on.

JOE HAD RARELY EVER FELT as vulnerable, as much of a target, as he did riding up through the talus. He urged his horse to keep him walking fast, hoping the herky-jerky gait would make him less easy to hit if someone was aiming. There was nothing quiet about his ascent; his horse's lungs billowed as it climbed, the gelding nickered from time to time to call to Nate's horse and the packhorse, and the gelding's steel shoes struck some of the shale rocks with discordant notes and tossed off sparks from time to time. By the time he made it to the summit and the ocean of mountaintops sprawled out before him to the west, his horse was worn out from the forced march and Joe had a slick of sweat between his skin and his clothing.

But no one fired, and nothing more happened.

He pushed the gelding on, over the top, so they'd no longer be in silhouette against the sky if the brothers were somewhere in the timber below them looking back. Nate was soon with him, his own horse breathing hard as well. They tucked away to rest the animals in a stand of aspen.

In the shadows of the trees, Joe's boot heels thumped the hard ground as he dismounted to let his horse get his breath back. Nate did the same. They stood in silence, holding the reins of their horses, eyeing the dark timber and meadows out in front of them, wondering where the Grim Brothers were.

IT WAS APPROACHING midnight when Joe's gelding stopped short. He recognized the horse's familiar signals of fear or agitation: the low rumbling *whoof*, the whites of his eyes, the ears stiffly cocked forward. Joe's horse took several steps back, nearly colliding with Nate's mount.

Nate whispered, "What's wrong?"

Joe shook his head. "Don't know. Something's spooked him." He managed to get control of his horse after spinning him back around.

When Joe looked up, he could see Nate grimacing, his face illuminated by a splash of starlight.

"Jesus," Nate said. "Look."

Joe leaned forward and peered ahead on the trail, willing his eyes to see better in the dark. Something hung across the trail, reminding him of gathered curtains hanging from a rod. He slipped his Maglite out of its holster and adjusted the beam on a moon-shaped human face—eyes open but without the gleam of life, a dried purple tongue hanging out of its mouth like a fat cigar.

Joe twisted the lens of this flashlight to increase the scope of the light. While he did, he forgot to breathe.

Three male bodies, two in black tactical clothing and one in camouflage, hung from ropes tied to a beam that crossed the trail. The bodies were hung by their necks, but it was obvious they hadn't died from hanging because of the wounds on them. One of the men in black had a hole in his chest, one's skull was crushed in on the side like a dropped egg, and the third had an arrow shaft sticking out of his throat.

Joe recognized the make of the arrow.

He squelched the light of his flashlight and reached out for the saddle horn to steady himself because he felt suddenly light-headed.

"Oh, God," he said, fighting nausea.

Nate said, "I think we found the boys from Michigan."

SATURDAY, SEPTEMBER 5

29

ONE BY ONE, THE GLASSY SURFACES OF THE AL-
pine cirques Joe and Nate rode past mirrored the stars
and slice of moon. When a trout rose and nosed the water
at the second cirque, Joe found himself unexpectedly
heartened as he watched lazy ringlets alter the reflection.

They'd cut down the bodies and stacked them on the
side of the trail. Joe rooted through their pockets and
found no personal items or identification of any kind. He
and Nate covered the bodies with dead logs and sheets of
bark to try to prevent predators from feeding on them,
and Joe bookmarked the location in his GPS so he could
later direct search teams to the exact place to recover and
identify the bodies. Dave Farkus had not been among the
dead.

It was two in the morning when they rode by the last
cirque and Joe clucked and pulled his horse off the trail
to parallel the meandering outlet stream.

Nate said, "Is this the creek you followed out of the
mountains last time?"

"Yup."

"What's the name of it?"

"No Name Creek," Joe said. "Really."

"Seems fitting," Nate said, clucking his horse forward.

"Stay alert," Joe said to Nate, although he was really talking to himself. "Those brothers could be anywhere."

DEEP IN THE TIMBER and far down the mountain on its western slope, Joe almost rode by the dark opening where the cabin had been. He didn't so much see it as feel it—a creeping shiver that rolled from his stomach to his throat that made him rein to a stop and turn to his right in the saddle.

"Here," he said. He nosed the gelding over, and the horse splashed through the shallow stream and to the other side. As he rode through the opening, the familiarity of it in the starlight made him relive his escape from the cabin. When he reached the clearing where the cabin had been, he rode around it, puzzled. Ghostly columns of pale starlight lit the opening. But there was no sign of the burned cabin, just a tangled pile of deadfall.

Nate asked, "Are you sure this is the right place?"

"It's got to be," Joe said. He probed the deadfall with the beam of his flashlight.

Sweeping the pool of light across the dead branches, he noted a small square of orange.

"Ah," he said with relief, and dismounted. With the flashlight in his mouth shining down, Joe tugged at branches and threw them away from the pile. He kicked away the last tangle to reveal a square foundation of bricks, which was where the woodstove had been.

"The Grim Brothers hid the scene," he said to Nate. "They carted away whatever was still here and covered the footprint of the cabin in downed timber. No wonder Sheriff Baird and his men never found this."

"I was starting to wonder myself," Nate said with a grin. "I was thinking maybe you made it all up."

"Ha ha," Joe said sourly.

JOE AND NATE SAT on opposite ends of a downed tree trunk at four in the morning, facing the slash pile that covered up the remains of the cabin, each with his own thoughts. Joe tried to eat some deer jerky he'd brought along, but every time he started to chew he thought of the faces of the three bodies hanging from the cross pole, and he lost his appetite. He could hear Nate slowly crunching gorp from a Ziploc bag on the other end of the log, and their horses munching mountain grass. There was no more reassuring sound, Joe thought, than horses eating grass. Their *grum-grum* chewing sound was restful.

If only everything else were, he thought.

That's when he clearly heard a branch snap deep in the timber. The sound came from the north, from somewhere up a wooded slope.

THERE WERE DISTINCTIVE sounds in the mountains, Joe knew. He was never a believer of trees' falling silently in the forest if there was no one there to hear it, because he didn't believe it was all about him, or any other human. Nature did what nature did. To philosophize that acts occurred in the wild in the presence of people and for their benefit was to acknowledge that humans were gods. Joe *knew* that not to be the case, and always thought anyone who bought that line of thought to be arrogant or new to the outdoors. In fact, from his experience, the forest could get downright loud. Trees, especially pines, had wide and shallow root systems. Hard winds knocked them over, where they'd fall with a crash and expose the upturned root pan. Dead branches blew off and fell down. One tree fell into another. Sometimes a bear or cat tried to climb one of the inferior high-altitude trees and the weight of the animal toppled it over. A herd of elk moving through dry and down timber sometimes sounded like a freight train that had jumped the tracks.

But there was a unique sound to a dry branch snapping under the foot of a man. It was a deep and muffled crack, like a silenced gunshot. It was a different sound from that of a twig breaking under the hard cloven hoof of an ungulate—an elk or moose—that produced a sharp snap like a pretzel stick being halved. At the sound, Joe rolled to his right and he sensed Nate roll to his left. Joe had no doubt Nate was on his knees with the .454 Casull drawn by now. For his own part, he had the shotgun ready. He slowly jacked a shell into the chamber to keep the metal-on-metal action as quiet as possible, and when the live shell was loaded into the chamber he fed another double-aught round into the receiver. He held his shotgun at the ready and felt his senses straining to determine if whoever had made the sound was closer, farther, or standing still.

Joe turned to his left to ask Nate if he could hear any more sounds, but Nate was gone. Joe squinted into the darkness, trying to find his friend.

When he couldn't, Joe settled back on his haunches behind the downed log, his shotgun muzzle pointed vaguely uphill.

There was another muffled snap, this one closer than the first. He estimated the sound coming from fifty feet away.

He raised the shotgun and lay the doused Maglite along the forward stock. His heart pounded in his chest, and he thought if it beat any harder, everybody would be able to hear it.

As he stared into the shadowed darkness of the trees, he saw a single small red dot for a moment six feet off the ground. It blinked out. Then he saw it again. Joe was sure that he was close enough that if he fired he'd probably hit the source of the light. He remembered Nate's admonition to shoot first, but he couldn't simply pull the trigger. Not without knowing who it was.

The roaring of blood in his ears nearly drowned out the voice of the man who said, "Joe, is that you?"

Then, "For Christ sake, Joe, don't fucking shoot me!"

Joe said, "Farkus?" And he heard the hollow sound of the heavy steel barrel of Nate's .454 smack hard into the side of Farkus's head, toppling him over.

"Don't kill him, Nate," Joe said, sighing and getting to his feet. "I know this guy. He's the local who owned one of the burned-up trucks back in the campground. The one who didn't seem to fit into all of this."

"NIGHT VISION GOGGLES," Nate said with contempt, nudging Farkus with the toe of his boot, "and unless I'm wrong, he's wearing body armor, too. I'm thinking this Farkus guy isn't quite what you and Baird thought he was."

Farkus moaned and reached up to put his hand over the new gash and bump on the side of his head.

Joe stepped over the downed log and fixed his Maglite on Farkus. The bright light through the lenses of the goggles must have burned his retinas as if he were look-ing into the sun itself, the way Farkus winced and pulled the goggles off. He threw the equipment away from him, saying, "It's like you blinded me."

"You didn't shoot," Joe said to Nate, ignoring Farkus.

"No reason to," Nate said. "I watched him come down through the trees focused totally on you. He was watching you every second. I was behind a trunk and he never even turned my way."

Farkus croaked, "Why'd you smack me?"

Nate squatted down next to Farkus. "Because we've nearly been killed twice tonight by people who more than likely had night vision gear. And because you were lurking around in the dark, you idiot. You're lucky I didn't blow your head off. Where did you get those goggles?"

Joe kept his flashlight on Farkus's face, trying to read it. Farkus said, "I stole them. The vest, too."

"Who'd you steal them *from*?" Nate asked.

"I took them off a dead guy," Farkus said, sitting up. "He didn't need them anymore. Being he was dead and all."

Said Nate, "Who was the dead guy?"

"His name was Capellen. He was with the other guys from Michigan up here to find the Cline Brothers. Capellen was killed first, and I took his stuff."

Joe said, "Start from the beginning, Dave. How did you get from the other side of the mountain to here?"

"They kidnapped me," Farkus said. "The men from Michigan, I mean. I drove up on them at my elk camp, and they took me along with them because I know the mountains. They were tracking those damned brothers, but everything went bad for them. The brothers ambushed us and I was the only one left alive. Them brothers, they ain't human, I tell you. They ain't. You guys should turn around and get the hell out of here while you have the chance."

Joe said, "What are they if they aren't human?"

"Wendigos. Monsters. They can move through the trees like phantoms or something, and they can just appear wherever they want. I told you back at the trailhead, remember?"

"I remember," Joe said.

"So how did you get away from them?" Nate asked with a smirk. "Did you hold a cross up and just walk away?"

"I waited until they were gone," Farkus said, "and I managed to get untied. They've completely left the mountains for somewhere else. They ain't around no more. They had me tied up in a cave, I mean a cabin."

Nate drew his arm back as if he were going to backhand Farkus, and the man flinched and grimaced, raising his arms to cover his face, ready for a blow.

"Nate," Joe said.

When Farkus lowered his arms, Nate slapped him hard across his face.

"Why'd you do that?" Farkus protested. "I haven't done nothing."

Nate said, "You scared us, that's what. And now you're speaking gibberish. I *hate* gibberish. Nobody confuses a cabin with a cave. So you'd better start telling us the truth about what's really going on up here, or you won't see morning come."

Joe nodded. "Your story doesn't jibe, Dave. Like maybe you're making it up as you go along." He kept his flashlight on Farkus's face and noted how the man averted his eyes and blinked rapidly as he spoke—two signs of a lying witness. "Somebody set a trap that could have killed either one of us and later rolled a boulder down the mountain that could have taken us out. The brothers were seen clearly this afternoon by a sheriff at the trailhead where they were in the process of burning your truck. No one else would match *that* description.

"Plus," Joe said, lowering the beam of the flashlight to Farkus's hands in his lap, "I don't see any marks on your wrists from rope or wire. Which says to me you weren't tied up at all. Now, I'm going to ask you some questions and you're going to answer them. If I think you're lying again, I'm going to get up and walk away and leave you with Mr. Romanowski."

He nodded toward Nate. "And whatever happens, happens. Got that?"

Farkus said, "Yes."

"Good. Let's start with the men from Michigan. We found three of them back on the trail. Who were they?"

"I told you. They were here to find the brothers and kill them."

"Why?"

"They wouldn't explain it all to me outright," Farkus said. "Every time I asked what they were doing up here, they basically told me to shut up. But from what I could get from what they said to each other, it had to do with something that happened back in Michigan, where all of them were from. They were taking orders from this guy named McCue. He was at my elk camp with them, but he didn't come along with us—"

"McCue?" Joe broke in. "Did I hear you right? Bobby McCue? Skinny guy? Older, kind of weary-looking?"

"That's him," Farkus said.

Joe took a deep breath.

Farkus continued, "The guys I was with knew the brothers, or knew enough about them, anyway. I got the feeling they might have clashed at one time or other."

"It was personal, then?" Nate said.

"Not really. I think they knew of the brothers, like I said. But I'm sure it wasn't personal. They were hired and outfitted by someone with plenty of money."

"Did you hear any names besides McCue?"

"None that meant anything."

"Try to remember," Joe said, his head spinning.

Farkus scrunched up his eyes and mouth. He said, "McGinty. I think that was it. And Sugar."

Joe felt a jolt. He said, "Senator McKinty and Brent Shober?"

"Could be right," Farkus said.

Nate's upper lip curled into a snarl.

Joe said to Nate: "What's going on?"

Nate said, "It's worse than we thought."

Then Joe said to Farkus, "And all of you rode into a trap of some kind?"

"At the last cirque," Farkus said, nodding. "We rode down the trail to the water and the lead guy, Parnell, rode through some rocks. He tripped a wire and a spike mounted on a green tree took him out."

"We're familiar with the trap," Joe said. "Go on."

"The brothers were on us like ugly on an ape," Farkus said. "The horses blew up and started rearing and everybody got bucked off. The brothers finished off the wounded except for me."

"Why'd they spare you?"

Farkus shook his head. "I don't know, Joe. I just don't know."

"So they took you to their cabin. Or was it a cave?"

"It was a cabin."

"Why did you say cave earlier?"

"You might have noticed there's a big guy with a big gun right next to me. I was nervous and probably misspoke."

"Ah," Joe said, as if he was happy with the explanation. "And then the brothers just left?"

"Yes. They packed up and left me to die. They are completely out of this county by now. Maybe even out of the state."

"Interesting you're sticking with that," Joe said. "So the rock that was rolled at us a while back was just a natural occurrence?"

"I don't know anything about a rock," Farkus said, his eyes blinking as if he'd got dust blown into them. "All I know is there's no point in you guys going after them anymore. They're gone."

"Were the brothers alone?"

"What do you mean?" When he asked, Farkus looked away and blinked his eyes.

"Was there a woman with them?" Joe asked softly.

"A woman?" Farkus said. "Up here?"

"Terri Wade or Diane Shober. I'm sure you've heard of at least one of them."

Farkus shook his head.

Joe said to Nate, "We're done here," and stood up. "Should we dig a hole for the body, or let the wolves scatter his bones?"

Nate said, "I say we put his head on a pike. That kind of thing spooks Wendigos, I believe. Sends 'em running back to Canada, where they belong."

Farkus looked from Nate to Joe, his eyes huge and his mouth hanging open.

"I've got no use for liars," Nate said.

Joe turned to say something to Nate, but his friend was gone. He was about to call after him, but didn't. Nate's stride as he walked away contained purpose. And when Joe listened, he realized how utterly silent it had become in the forest surrounding them. No sounds of night insects or squirrels or wildlife.

He quickly closed the gap with Farkus and shoved the muzzle of his shotgun into the man's chest. He whispered, "They're here, aren't they?"

Farkus gave an unwitting tell by shooting a glance into the trees to his left.

Joe said, "They sent you down here to distract us and pin us to one place while they moved in," Joe said, his voice as low as he could make it.

Farkus didn't deny the accusation, but looked at the shotgun barrel just below his chin.

"Hold it," Farkus stammered, his voice cracking. "Hold it. You're law enforcement. You can't do this."

Joe eased the safety off with a solid click.

"Really, please, oh, Jesus," Farkus whispered. Then he raised his voice, "Don't do this to me, please. You can't do this. . . ."

"Keep your voice down," Joe hissed, shoving the muzzle hard into Farkus's neck.

From the shadows of the forest, Camish said, "I'm real surprised you came back, game warden."

And fifty feet to the right of Camish, Nate said, "Guess what? I've got your brother."

30

THE STANDOFF THAT OCCURRED AT 4:35 A.M. ON
the western slope of the Sierra Madre transpired so
quickly and with such epic and final weight, and such a
simple but lethal potential conclusion, that Joe Pickett
found himself surprisingly calm. So calm, he calculated
his odds. They weren't good. He knew the likelihood of
his sudden death was high and he wished like hell he had
called his wife on the satellite phone and said good-bye
to her and his precious girls. He also knew he would have
apologized for dying for such a cause, and at the hands of
the dispossessed. As if a man could choose his killer.

In this moment of clarity, Joe thought, sharp points
elbowed their way to the fore:

- His shotgun was on Farkus and it would take
  one or two seconds to wheel and aim it at Camish;
- Camish had Joe's heart in the sights of his rifle;
  knew Joe and Nate could cut him in half, so he
  must have a trump card, likely . . .
- Caleb had a .454 muzzle pressed against his
  temple and was unable to speak anyway;
- Farkus was clueless—he'd obviously been co-

erced by the brothers but hadn't firmed up his storyline and he'd therefore stumbled into lies that piqued Joe's interest;

- If one man pulled a trigger, a cacophony of exploding shots would throw lead through the void like a buzz saw and cut down all of them for eternity, and;
- Nobody wanted *that*.

At least Joe didn't.

Joe said, "We all know the situation we've got here. It can go one way or the other. Things can get western in a hurry. If they do, I'm betting on my man Nate here to tip the scales, Camish. But I think a better idea may be sitting down and starting a fire and hashing this out."

After a beat, Camish said, "You're one of these folks thinks everything can be solved by talking?"

Said Joe, "No, I don't believe that. No one has ever accused me of excess talking. But I think something really bad will happen any second if we don't. I'm willing to sit down and discuss the possibility of more than two of us walking away from here."

Camish said, "Caleb, you okay?"

The response was a muffled groan.

Nate said, "He's about to lose the rest of his head."

Camish's voice was high and tight: "Don't you hurt my brother."

Joe realized his initial shocked calm had slipped away and he was sweating freely from fear. He struggled to keep his words even, hoping Camish would give in. It was easier to sound serious because he was.

"Tell you what," he said. "Let's meet at that downed log a few feet from me. Camish can keep aiming at me. Nate can keep his gun at Caleb's head. I'll keep my shotgun on Farkus here. But when we get to the log we'll sit down. How does that sound?"

From the dark, Joe heard Farkus say, "I'm kind of wondering where I fit into this deal."

And Nate growl, "You don't, idiot."

Camish said, "Deal."

CAMISH LOOKED EVEN THINNER than Joe remembered him. It had been a rough few days. The man's eyes seemed to have sunk deeper into hollows above his cheekbones and resembled marbles on a mantel. He hadn't shaved in weeks, and all the silver hairs in his beard made him look gaunt and wizened. Like a Wendigo, Joe thought.

Joe and Nate sat on one log, the Grim Brothers on another. They faced each other.

Caleb sat in utter, pained silence. If anything, he looked more skeletal than his brother. His dark eyes flicked like insects between his brother and Joe and Nate as if hoping for a place to land. A dirt-filthy bandage was taped to his lower jaw. Caleb had an AR-15 with a scope across his lap, with the muzzle loosely pointed a foot to the right of Joe. Joe was sure the weapon was locked and ready to fire, and that Caleb was capable of spraying full automatic fire at him and Nate in a heartbeat. The weapon must have come from the Michigan boys, Joe thought.

In between them, they'd started a small fire. Farkus sat on a stump near the fire, positioned carefully equidistant from both logs. Farkus fed the fire with pencil-sized twigs. The fire shot lizard tongues at the darkness and occasionally flared due to a particularly dry piece of wood or because of time-concentrated pitch within the stick.

The effect made Camish and Caleb's faces fade in and out of the darkness in various stages of orange.

Nate sat silently on the log to Joe's left. His friend didn't even attempt to hide his proclivities, and he kept his .454 lying across the top of his thighs with his hand on the grip and his finger on the trigger. Joe knew Nate was capable of raising the weapon and firing at both of them in less than a second.

Whether Nate could take out both brothers before Caleb could fire his weapon at Joe and Nate was the question.

Joe said to Caleb, "I see your tactical vest now. I guess you were wearing it when I shot you with my Glock. Now I know why you didn't go down."

Caleb glared back at him, his eyes dark and piercing but his expression inscrutable.

"You know he can't talk," Camish said. "That shot to his lower jaw splintered his chinbone and somehow drove slivers of it into his talk box. The point-blank shot to his chest later probably didn't help much, either. Anyways, he hasn't spoken a word since that night."

He said it matter-of-factly, and Joe let it sink in. Joe said, "I fired blindly when I hit him in the face. Not that I wasn't trying to do damage—I was."

Caleb almost imperceptibly nodded his head.

Joe said to Caleb, "I would have been happy to have killed you given the circumstances."

Camish nodded, and he and Nate shared a look, which Joe found disconcerting.

"The circumstances are different depending on where you stand, I guess," Camish said. "You have one version, we have a different version."

Joe nodded. "Maybe so. But what I know is you boys came after me and killed my horses."

Camish made his eyes big, and there was a slight smile on his face. "My version, game warden, is me and my brother were minding our own damned business and not bothering a soul when you rode up and wanted to collect a tax on behalf of the government, the tax being a license to fish so we could eat. And when we didn't produce the license, you threatened our liberty. We, as freeborn Americans, resisted you."

Joe held his tongue, but he shared a look with Nate. This confirmed his friend's earlier theory.

Nate tipped his head toward Joe, but never took his eyes off Caleb. He said, "Joe's kind of like that. It's his worst fault. He's damned stubborn."

"My horses," Joe said, glaring at Camish. "They belonged to my wife. She loved them like only a woman can love horses. You two killed them and butchered them."

"Better than letting them go to waste, eh, Caleb?" Camish said, as if it made all the sense in the world, Joe thought. "Anyway," Camish said, "we didn't target your horses. They were collateral damage. We came after you so hard because there was something in your eyes when we met you. We knew you'd follow this goddamned stupid fishing license deal to the gates of hell. Otherwise, we'd just have let you ride away. We practically begged you to just ride out of here. But you wouldn't let it go. You said you'd march us into court. All for a stupid twenty-four-dollar license."

Joe said, "You boys are out of state. It's ninety-four dollars for Michigan residents."

Camish leaned back on his log and tipped his head back and laughed. Caleb snorted, sounding like the angry pneumatic staccato spitting of a pressure cooker on a stovetop.

Nate moaned.

Joe felt his neck get hot. He said, "It's my job. I do my job."

Camish finished his run of laughter, then cut it off. He leaned forward on the log and thrust his face at Joe. "That may be. But the things you set in motion . . ."

Joe stood up. He let the muzzle of the shotgun swing lazily past Camish, past Caleb, past Nate. He said, "Tomorrow by this time, these mountains are going to be overrun. There will be hundreds of law enforcement personnel. Some of them will even know what they're doing. You boys assaulted a sheriff and humiliated him. You assaulted *me* and humiliated *me*. The people who'll be coming after you don't even know about those three men you killed yet, which makes you cold-blooded murderers."

From the far end of the downed log, Farkus said, "They killed four, not three."

Camish said, "I wish you'd shut up, Dave."

Joe broke in. "Four, three, it doesn't matter at this point. You boys are done. Even if you figure out a way to hole up and not get caught tomorrow, this is only the beginning. You can't really think you can stay here, do you? That you can set traps and hang dead men from cross poles and the world will just stay away? What are you thinking?"

With the last sentence, Joe stood and leaned into them and his voice rose. And he realized, by looking at Nate's face, and the Grim Brothers, and Farkus in the light of the fire, how utterly alone he was.

"YOU PEOPLE," CAMISH SAID, his eyes sliding off Nate and settling on Joe, "you government people just keep coming. It's like you won't stop coming until you've got us all and you own everything we've got. Until we all *submit* to you. It ain't right. It ain't American. All we want to do is be left alone. That's all.

"Hell, we know we make people nervous, me and Caleb. We know we look funny and we act funny to some people. We know they judge us. They made my mom out into some kind of stupid hillbilly when they went after her."

Joe studied Camish's face in the flickering firelight. Unlike Caleb's terrifying, almost manic glare, Camish's attitude had softened from its initial ferocity. Into what? Joe thought. Victory? Resignation?

"That's all," Camish echoed. "We thought you'd leave us alone back in Michigan if we just paid our taxes and kept our mouths shut. Didn't we, Caleb?"

Caleb nodded and grunted.

Said Camish, "When they tried to take our property the first time, we fought 'em off pretty good. We thought it was over, that there was just no damned chance in the United States of America that the government could take a man's land and give it to somebody just because they'd pay *more* taxes. They backed off at first, and we thought we won. But they was like you, like all governments, I guess. They just kept coming. Those three things that are supposed to be our rights—life, liberty, and the pursuit of happiness? Hell, the government's supposed to protect those things. Instead, they took the last two of them away from us, just like that. Finally, they took our place from us and we lost our dad, our mom, and our brother in the process. They took all three of those rights away from them, didn't they?"

He spoke in a flat, unsentimental way. Joe nodded for him to go on.

"When a thief comes into your home in the night and tries to take your property, it's okay to shoot him. But when the government comes and wants the same thing, you go to jail if you resist. At least the thief puts his *own* ass on the line."

Camish said, "We just wanted to find somewhere we could be left alone. Is that so damned much to ask?"

Nate said, "No, it isn't."

Joe sighed. "Problem is, no one can just walk away. Everyone has obligations."

Camish said, "You mean like paying taxes?"

"Yeah, I guess," Joe said, grateful it was dark so no one could see him flush. "Folks can't expect services and programs without paying for them somehow."

Camish said, "Why the hell should we pay for things we don't want and don't get? Why should the government take our money and our property and give it to other people? What the hell kind of place has this become?"

Joe said, "It's not that bad or that simple. This whole mountain range, for example. It's managed by the U.S. Forest Service, a government agency. Taxes pay for that."

"We do our part," Camish said. "We keep the riffraff out."

Caleb snorted a laugh.

Joe said, "You boys vandalized some vehicles and scared the hell out of some campers. Not to mention that elk you took."

Joe saw a flash of anger in Camish's eyes. He didn't even look at Caleb, hoping Nate had him covered. Camish said, "We did that to keep people away. To *spook* 'em. We didn't want to have to hurt somebody or take things too far, so we laid down a marker: *Leave us alone*. It's our way of managing the place. We didn't disturb or hurt anything that was perfect. Fish, deer, elk—whatever. If anything, we helped cull the herd. That's management, too. It just ain't done by bureaucrats sitting on their asses. Like the Forest Service, you know? Or you guys."

Joe could feel Nate's eyes on the side of his face, but he didn't look over.

Instead, Joe said, "Diane Shober. Tell me about her."

"Yeah," Camish said. "I was expecting you might have recognized her that night. She thought so, too."

Joe waited. He looked up and realized Caleb was trying to tell Camish something with his eyes. Caleb looked distressed.

Camish said, "I won't get too far into it, but Diane felt like she needed a refuge, too. So we offered her one."

Joe said, "I find that hard to believe."

Camish said, "Believe whatever the hell you want. But sometimes it's hard to see how much pressure is being put on a person. And how it's pretty damned nice to find a place where no one expects you to live up to a certain standard."

"Her fiancé?" Joe said.

"Yeah, him. But especially Daddy," Camish said. "That man expected one whole hell of a lot. He lived his life through her, but she can't stand him. He's one of those parasites. He got rich taking other people's property and money. We'd tangled before. She knew we didn't like or respect the man. She knew we'd help her out."

Joe nodded his head. "You had a common enemy," he said, echoing Marybeth's words.

" 'Course we did," Camish said. "He's the developer who got our family property. Friend of a damned crooked Senator McKinty from Michigan and his no-good son."

Joe sighed. He had no reason to disbelieve Camish, though he looked hard for one.

Camish turned to Farkus. "He's the one sent them Michigan boys after us, right Dave?"

Farkus nodded, his eyes moving from Joe to Camish as if watching a tennis match.

Joe said, "You mean the senator? Are you saying a U.S. senator sent a private hit squad after you?"

"Naw," Camish said. "Diane's old man did that. They were supposed to take us out and take her back. And the way things work, I'd bet the senator and his son knew all about it, but nobody would ever be able to prove that. That's how those folks are. We don't want no part of those politicians anymore. That's why we're here."

Joe thought: And when Shober heard about me, he tried to put me on the hunt for Diane, too, just for insurance.

"She stayed with you to rub her father's nose in it?" Joe said.

Caleb shrugged as if to say, *Why not?*

And Camish said, "Why not?"

"Shober's mother is worried about her. I don't think she knows anything about what you're accusing her father of."

"Wouldn't surprise me," Camish said, shrugging.

"So was it you who sent the postcard to Mrs. Shober?"

Camish sighed. "That was a dumb idea. But Diane insisted. Like she made us agree to call her Terri Wade. Half the time we forgot. But when a woman gets something in her head . . ."

"Is she okay now?" Joe asked. "Diane Shober?"

Said Camish, as a slow smile built on his face, "If you want to—if you figure out how to get out of here alive, I mean—you can ask her yourself. I don't mind. She won't mind, I don't think, as long as you don't try to take her back with you. See, we got some caves up in the rimrocks. Indians used to live there, then outlaws. They're sweet caves. Dave knows the way."

Joe didn't know what to say. He finally looked over at Nate. His friend mouthed, *We have to talk*. But because Joe knew what Nate wanted to talk about, he turned away.

Camish said, "We used to have a pretty good country. At least I think we did. Then something happened. It's our fault 'cause we let it. We used to be a people who had a government," he said, looking up, his eyes fierce again. "Now it's the other way around."

Joe didn't respond.

"And we ain't going back until things change. We want our property back and we want an apology. We want to see that senator go to prison. We want to see Brent Shober tarred and feathered. And most of all, we want to be left alone. Simple as that. And we ain't going to argue about it, game warden. If you can promise us those things, we'll put down our guns and come down with you. Can you promise them?"

Joe said, "I promise I'll try."

Camish snorted. "That's the way it is with you people. Good intentions are supposed to be the same as good works."

Joe had no reply.

Camish said, "Then it is what it is."

31

OUT OF EARSHOT OF THE BROTHERS, NATE SAID, "This isn't what I signed up for, Joe."

Joe said, "I know it isn't."

"We have a couple of options."

Joe said, "I'm not sure we do."

Nate had stood and backed slowly away from where the brothers and Dave Farkus sat by the fire. As he did, Caleb never took his eyes off him, and conspicuously tightened his fingers around the handgrip of the automatic rifle on his lap. Likewise, Nate didn't turn his back on Caleb and he held the .454, muzzle down, near his side. Joe knew how fast Nate was with the revolver, and he guessed Caleb knew it, too. Joe had stood and joined his friend. The eastern sky was rose-colored, and the trees within the dark forest began to define themselves. It was less than an hour before sunrise.

Nate said, "We could get on our horses and ride away. Let the locals and the state boys and the feds finish this. We're sort of signing the death warrants on these guys, but they know that and we won't have blood on our hands. Of course, there's the possibility these boys will make a stand. And who knows, they *could* win. Or maybe they'll just fade into the timber if we leave. They've done a pretty good job at surviving up here so far. Maybe they'll head north along the Continental Divide."

Joe's insides were on fire. He clamped his shotgun to his side with his arm and thrust his hands into his pockets to keep them from shaking.

Joe said, "I can't ride away. As long as they're up here, they'll keep breaking laws. You know that. We rode by three dead bodies earlier tonight. Maybe you can say they deserved it, but that's not for us to decide. More people will get hurt and die, and some of them will be innocent. Think of the traps these guys set. If we leave, they won't stop."

Nate said, "Nope, they won't. But that doesn't have to be our problem. This isn't right, Joe. Let me put this as clearly as I can: *We're on the wrong side.*"

Joe winced.

"Maybe we can make a deal with them," Nate said. "If they agree to dismantle the traps and promise to lay low, we'll ride away. I think they'd let us go under those conditions."

"Maybe," Joe said, "but I am what I am, Nate. I took an oath. I can't just ride away."

"That's how you got tangled up with them in the first place," Nate said. "They all but begged you to just leave them be. But you didn't."

"I couldn't."

Nate didn't turn his head. He kept his eyes on Caleb and Camish. But to Joe, it felt like his friend was glaring at him with puzzled contempt.

Joe said, "Maybe you should go, Nate. I know how you feel and I understand. Believe me, I do. You don't need to be any part of this. There'd be no hard feelings on my part if you rode away."

Nate said, "They'll kill you, Joe."

"Maybe."

"I'm sorry."

JOE STEPPED FORWARD toward the fire, narrowing the distance between them but not really feeling his boots walk across the grass. Caleb, Camish, and Farkus watched him.

Joe said, "Put down your weapons, get Diane Shober, and come with me. We can get to the trailhead before they get organized enough to come up after you. There will be dozens of law enforcement personnel—maybe hundreds. If we all get down there before they get assembled and get their blood up, I promise you I'll do all I can to get you secured away so you've got a chance."

Caleb and Camish looked at him without a change in their expressions. Farkus narrowed his eyes, again glancing between Joe and the brothers, obviously trying to read in advance what was going to happen, and which side he would choose to support.

Joe said, "I'll tell the locals, the state, and the feds how you cooperated. I'll ask Governor Rulon to get involved—we're pretty close. Look, you've got a story to tell. There are a lot of folks out there who will support you.

"I know of a lawyer," Joe continued, trying to keep his voice even. "His name is Marcus Hand. You may have heard of him. Big guy, long white hair, wears buckskins in the courtroom. He specializes in getting guilty people off. Believe me, I know. I have a feeling he'd find you guys sympathetic. Who knows—he might be able to get you what you want."

He waited.

The brothers didn't ask for a moment to discuss the

option. Camish said, "The only way we're going off this mountain is feetfirst. And I don't think that's likely to happen."

Even without turning around and seeing for himself, Joe knew Nate was gone.

Then, deep in the trees to the east, he heard Nate's horse whinny.

"TELL YOU WHAT," CAMISH SAID, standing almost casually. "Unlike your government, we believe in freedom and opportunity. We'll give you the opportunity to ride away. Just don't ever come back on our mountain."

Joe stood silent.

"We'll give you ten minutes to pack up and ride away," Camish said. "We won't interfere and we won't put you down. And if you ride on out of here, we won't follow you. I just hope we don't ever see you up here again."

He turned toward the fire. "Dave, you can go with him. No offense, but you're kind of useless. And if the game warden is correct, there will be a battle coming. You might get caught in the crossfire."

Farkus hopped to his feet, nodding. "Okay," he said. "Thank you, Camish."

Camish smirked and looked back to Joe. "You're still here," he said.

Joe felt himself nod once.

"You shouldn't still be here."

Farkus started to walk toward Joe but hesitated.

"Look," Camish said. "My brother and I are going to walk away and give you some space. Maybe then you'll think about what you're doing and take old Dave here and be gone. But if for some damned reason you want to force the issue, we'll meet you in that clearing over there," he gestured toward a small meadow to the west. The morning sun was building behind the trees, ready to launch and flood the meadow with light.

"We'll finish it there, I guess," Camish said, shaking his head. He seemed almost sad, Joe thought.

As they backed away from the fire, Camish said, "I think on some level you know we're right, game warden. But you sure are stubborn."

"It doesn't have to be this way," Joe said. "It's your government, too. You can work to change it."

"Too late for that," Camish said. "This is Rampart Mountain. This is where we turn you people back or we quit trying."

Joe said, "This is the wrong fight at the wrong time."

"Got to start somewhere," Camish said, turning away. And they were gone.

Farkus looked from Joe, toward where the brothers had melded into the trees, and back. He said, "Let's get out of here, Joe."

Joe said, "Go ahead."

THE TEMPERATURE DROPPED fifteen degrees as the cold morning air started to move through the timber in anticipation of the sun. Joe felt a long shiver start in his boots and roll through his body until his teeth chattered.

He stood on the side of his gelding, keeping the horse between himself and the meadow. The brothers couldn't be seen. Neither could Farkus, who'd dumped the panniers from the packhorse, mounted the animal bareback, and headed east in a hurry. He hadn't looked back.

Joe found the satellite phone, powered it up, and punched in the numbers. He woke her up, and sleep clogged her voice for a moment.

Joe said, "We found them."

"Are you okay? Are you hurt?"

"Not yet."

"What does that mean, Joe?"

"I'm going to try to bring them in," he said. "They don't want to come."

"Oh, no. Oh, my. Please be careful."

"I will."

"Did you find Diane?"

"No, but I know where she is. She's okay, they say."

"Thank God. Her mother will be so happy."

"Yup. I'm not so sure about her dad, though." Thinking: *How do we know the Michigan boys were going to bring her down? How do we know they weren't going to silence her, too?*

"Joe, are you okay? There's something in your voice. Are you all right?"

"Sure," he said.

"Is there anything I can do? Anyone I can call?"

"No."

Joe looked across the meadow as two yellow spear bars of sun shot through a break in the trees. Instantly, the clearing lightened up. In the shadows of the pine tree wall on the far side of the clearing, he could see Camish and Caleb. They were about fifty yards apart, still in the shadows of the trees but about to enter the meadow. Caleb held his rifle across his chest. Camish worked the pump on Joe's old shotgun.

"I've got to go," Joe said.

"Call me when you can," Marybeth said.

"I want you to know how much I love you," he said. "I want you to know I think I'm doing the right thing for you and the girls."

She was silent for a moment. Then he heard a sob.

"I'll call," he said, and punched off. It felt like a lie.

*   *   *

HE COULDN'T FEEL HIS FEET or his legs, and his heartbeat whumped in his ears as he walked out into the clearing with his shotgun. Camish and Caleb emerged from the trees. Joe guessed they were seventy-five yards away. Out of range for his shotgun or .40 Glock. He wondered when Caleb would simply raise the rifle and start firing.

Joe thought: They look silly, the Grim Brothers, dressed in the same clothes, identical except for the bandage on Caleb's jaw. They're such losers. From another place and another era, and their ideas of the way things ought to be are old and out of date. They know, he thought, if they come down from this mountain they'll be eaten alive. The poor bastards.

He thought: This is their mountain. It's where they feel safe. It's the only place they feel free.

He thought: He might give up his life for an argument he didn't think he agreed with.

Camish said something, but Joe didn't catch it due to the roaring in his head.

"What's that?" Joe called out.

"I said it's still not too late to leave," Camish said. "I admire your courage, but I question your judgment."

Joe thought, *Me too.*

The brothers were within fifty yards.

JOE THOUGHT, *Camish first.* Shoot Camish first. He was the leader, the spokesman. Taking out Camish might stun Caleb for a split second—in time for Joe to jack in another shell and fire.

Shoot, then run to the side, he thought. Make himself

a moving target. Duck and roll. Come up firing. Run right at Caleb, confuse him. Caleb wouldn't expect Joe to come right at him.

Forty yards.

WHEN JOE WAS GROWING UP, he'd read everything he could find about Old West outlaws and gunfights. He'd found himself disappointed. In real life, showdowns like the ones portrayed in movies and myths were almost nonexistent. Men rarely faced off against each other on a dusty cow town street at high noon, with the fastest gun winning. Much more likely was an ambush, with one man firing a rifle or a shotgun at his enemy before the victim could draw his weapon, or a gunman sneaking up on someone and putting a bullet in the back of his head from a foot away. Men didn't face off if they could help it.

He remembered what Nate had told him: *It's about who can look up without any mist in their eyes or doubts in their heart, aim, and pull the trigger without thinking twice. It's about killing. It's always worked that way.*

Thirty yards.

Not optimum for his shotgun, but close enough.

Without warning, he dropped to one knee, raised his weapon, and shot at Camish.

Camish was hit with a spray of double-aught pellets, but he didn't fall. Joe caught a glimpse of Camish's puzzled face, dotted with fresh new holes. He was hurt but the wounds weren't lethal. He seemed as surprised at what Joe had done as Joe did.

From the trees to Joe's left, there was a deep-throated boom and Caleb's throat exploded. A second shot blew his hat off and it dropped heavily to the grass because it was weighted by the top of Caleb's skull. Caleb spun on his heel and fell, dead before he hit the ground. The AR-15 caught the sun as it flew through the air.

Camish opened his mouth to call something out but a third .454 round punctured the body armor over his heart like a missile through tissue paper and dropped him like a bag of rocks.

JOE ROSE UNSTEADILY, his ears ringing from the gunshots. He was stunned by what had just happened and amazed by the fact that he wasn't hurt, that the brothers hadn't fired back.

From the trees, Nate walked out into the clearing and the morning sun lit him up. He ejected three smoking spent cartridges from the cylinder and replaced them with fresh rounds. He said, "That may have been the worst thing we've ever done, Joe."

Joe dropped his shotgun, turned away, bent over with his hands on his knees, and threw up in the dew-sparkled grass.

THE SHARP SMELL OF GUNPOWDER held in place a few feet above the meadow, the result of a morning low pressure. Gradually, it dissipated. The odor of spilled blood, however, got stronger as it flowed from the bodies of Caleb and Camish until the soil around them was muddy with it.

Nate found a downed log at the edge of the timber and sat down on it, his .454 held loosely in his fist, his head down as if studying the grass between his boots. Joe walked aimlessly toward the timber from where the brothers had emerged. He doubted the woman had been hiding there, but he wanted to check. His shotgun was still in the grass.

He stopped near to where Caleb had come out, noting a dull, unnatural glint on the edge of a shadow pool in the trees. Stepping closer, he took a deep breath. The glint came from a substantial pile of loose rifle cartridges in the pine needles, and something dark and square. He was puzzled.

Joe dropped and counted thirty .223 cartridges on the ground. A lot, he thought. More than Caleb would have dropped casually. In fact, Joe thought with a growing sense of dark unease, it was the entire quantity of a combat AR-15 magazine.

Short of breath, Joe lurched from tree to tree clutching a rifle bullet and the journal he recognized from the first time he'd encountered Caleb in the lake. It didn't take long to find the place a few yards away where Camish had unloaded his shotgun shells. Four of them, bright with their red plastic sleeves and high brass, lay in a single pile as if dropped from beneath the weapon like metal scat.

He opened the journal and thumbed through it as his eyes swam. The first three-quarters of the book were devoted to daily journal entries. The last quarter appeared to be an antigovernment screed. Joe thought, *Their manifesto.* Hundreds of words that could be summed up as *Don't Tread on Me.*

The last of Caleb's entries was a spidery scrawl that read, "*Please take good care of Diane. It ain't her fault. She done nothing wrong. She just wanted to be free of you people.*"

Nate had entered the trees with his gun drawn. Joe watched Nate as his eyes moved from the .223 bullets to the shotgun shells. His friend's upper lip curled into a frightening grimace.

Joe said, "No wonder they didn't shoot. They unloaded before they walked out there."

"Oh, man," Nate whispered. "It was bad before. It just got worse."

JOE CALLED MARYBETH. She picked it up on the first ring. He said, "I'm not hurt. Nate's not hurt. We're done here."

She said, "Joe, what's wrong?"

He took in a long breath of cool mountain air that tasted like pine, and he looked out on the meadow as the sun lit up the grass so green it hurt his eyes. "I don't even know where to start."

32

AT MIDMORNING, JOE COULD SMELL FOOD COOK-
ing from above in the rimrocks. The aroma wafted down
through the sparse lodgepole copse. He clucked at his
gelding and led the animal up toward the source of the
aroma and thought about how long it had been since
he'd eaten. Not that it mattered, since there was nothing
left in his stomach at all.

THEY'D LIFTED THE BODIES of Caleb and Camish
facedown over the saddles of their riding horses and
lashed them to the saddles as if they were packing out
game animals. Joe and Nate wordlessly tied lifeless hands
and feet together under the bellies of their mounts to
keep the bodies from sliding off. Before they guided the
horses and the bodies out of the meadow up toward the
rimrocks, Joe had called dispatch on his satellite phone.
The dispatcher offered to route him through to Sheriff
Baird or Special Agent Chuck Coon of the FBI, who were
both in place and in charge at the command center that
had been established at the trailhead.

Joe said, "No need. I don't want to talk to either of
them right now. Just pass on the word that the Grim

Brothers—or the Clines, or whatever the hell their real names are—are dead. There is no more threat. Tell them they can stand down. We'll be bringing the bodies out by nightfall."

The dispatcher said, "My God. They're going to want to talk directly with you."

Said Joe, "I'm not in the mood," and powered down the phone so they couldn't call him back.

WHEN THEY CLEARED THE TREES, Joe spotted Diane Shober. She was a hundred yards above them, peering down out of a vertical crack in the rimrock wall. When she saw them—and what they had strapped to their horses—her hand went to her mouth and he heard her cry out. Then she was gone back into the cave.

Joe thought that unless he'd been told specifically by Farkus and Camish where the cave was located, he never would have found it. He thought it unlikely that the search-and-rescue team would have found it, either. And certainly not the strike team building at the trailhead who, for the most part, weren't familiar with the terrain to begin with. There was a shelf of rock on the side of the mountain, and it was striated with sharp-edged columns over ten feet high, stretching for several miles in each direction. It was as if the mountain had been shoved down by a giant hand with tremendous pressure until the top fifth of it broke and slipped to the side, exposing the wound. The striation was deceptive in its uniform geology, and its columns made stripes of dark shadows on the granite. The opening Diane looked out of could have been one of the vertical-striped shadows.

"See her?" Joe said over his shoulder to Nate.

"Yes."

She slowly shook her head from side to side. The sun gleamed off the tears streaming down her face.

Joe called, "We're here to take you home."

The woman drew back a few feet into the shadow of the opening.

After a few moments, she said, "I *am* home."

He said, "Diane, the reason we're here is because your mom asked me to come. She misses you."

Joe wanted to persuade, to cajole, and not to threaten in any way. He couldn't bear the thought of forcing another result like what had happened with the brothers.

"We didn't want to hurt them," he said. "We did everything we could to talk them into coming down with us. Caleb and Camish forced the issue. In a way, they committed suicide."

Shober nodded. It wasn't news to her. Obviously, Joe thought, the brothers had indicated to her how things were likely to end if the first wave—Joe and Nate—wasn't turned back by the traps.

Behind Joe, the packhorse nickered. Up on top of the wall but out of sight, a horse called back, then another. The brothers had kept the horses ridden by the Michigan men and had picketed them up in the trees.

"If it's okay with you," Joe said, "we'll come on up there and get those horses and saddle them up for you. You can ride down with us."

Diane Shober stepped out of the cave opening. Her dark hair was tied into a ponytail. Her clothing was more formfitting than it had been before, and she looked younger than she had as Terri Wade, he thought.

She said, "What if I don't come with you?"

Said Joe, "Let's not find out. The truth is, this mountain will be crawling with law enforcement within the hour, I'd guess. We know where you are, and they'll find you. They might not be as sympathetic as us."

"Sympathetic?" Diane said, laughing bitterly. "Like you were sympathetic with Camish and Caleb there?"

Joe's voice held when he said, "They gave us no choice. You'll have to believe me when I tell you that. They must have decided they'd rather die up here than take their chances in court."

Diane nodded. "Yes," she said, "that's what they told me they might have to do."

"Then come with us," Nate said. "We'll do our best to protect you."

Again, Diane laughed. It was a high, plaintive laugh. "You think you can protect me, do you? From the government? From the press? From my father and the kind of people he works with?"

Joe said nothing.

Diane said, "Have things changed, then? Can we be free people again? Is that what you're saying?"

Nate said, "I know people who could help you. You aren't the only one who's gone underground."

Diane studied Nate for a long time, as if trying to make up her mind about something. Finally, she withdrew back into the cave. Joe waited without moving for five minutes, then turned to look at Nate. Nate looked back at him as if he were thinking the same thing.

"Damn," Joe said, and quickly tied his horse to a stump. Nate did the same. They ran up the slope, breathing hard.

Joe threw himself through the opening. The sudden darkness made him blink. It took a moment for his eyes to begin to adjust. He and Nate stood in the entrance of a surprisingly large cavern. There were beds, a stove, handmade tables and chairs, fabric and hides on the interior walls. It smelled damp, but the food odors made it surprisingly comfortable. It reminded Joe of where Nate hid out, and he wondered how many others there were in the country in hiding. How many people had gone underground, as Nate said?

On the table was a knife.

Diane Shober looked up from where she was packing items into a large duffel bag. "What, did you think—I wasn't coming out?"

Joe said, "I'm sorry. I couldn't live with the prospect of more blood on my hands."

As THEY RODE DOWN the mountain, Joe said to Diane, "I'm glad you're coming down. I'll be eternally grateful you saved my life, but this isn't any way to live."

Her mouth was tight, and she stared straight ahead. When she talked, her lips hardly moved. "It's crude and lonely, I agree. Growing up, this is the last thing I would have wanted. But when I was running, I went a lot to Europe. I got to experience socialism firsthand. At first, it's seductive. Free health care, free college, all that. But nothing is free. And anything that's free has no value. Zero means zero. I saw it close-up. So yes, you're right. This is crude and dirty. But it's my choice. There's no one here to tell me what to do or how to think. The trade-off is worth it."

Joe had no response.

"Will my mom be down there?" Diane asked.

"I'm not sure."

She hesitated, asked, "My dad?"

"It's possible," Joe said. "But we're in a pretty remote location. It would be hard for them to get here so fast."

"If he tries to talk to me, I might have to kill him," she said, tears welling in her eyes.

JOE LISTENED AS DIANE SHOBER talked to Nate.

"I'm an Objectivist," she said. "You know, Ayn Rand. It's the only good thing I got from Justin." She laughed. "I'm a freak, I know. Most of my friends drank the Kool-Aid. But you know how you used to see those RVs on the road with bumper stickers that read, WE'RE SPENDING OUR CHILDREN'S INHERITANCE? That always used to piss me off, just because of the attitude. I mean, ha-fucking-ha."

Joe watched her lean toward Nate on her horse and reach out and touch his arm. "Now every car in America should have that bumper sticker," she said. "Thieves like my father are stealing from me and my children, if I ever have any. He's politically connected, and the money flows to him downhill.

"You know," she said, "we're the first American gener-ation to expect less than our parents. I'm talking smaller houses, smaller cars, smaller families. It makes my blood boil. I want no part of it."

Nate nodded, said, "Did you know the brothers were up here before you went on your run?"

She took a minute, then said, "Yeah. We'd been in touch. I felt really awful for all the people who donated their time to come looking for me. I really did. But yes, I was in communication with the brothers. After all, we had a common enemy."

"Your father?" Nate said.

"Yeah, him too," she said.

*   *   *

As they rode down the switchback trail toward the trailhead, Joe got glimpses of what was below. As he'd predicted, it was a small city. Dozens of vehicles, tents, trailers, a makeshift corral, curls of smoke from lunchtime cooking fires. Satellite trucks from cable television news outlets. And the ashes of his father, still in his pickup. He had no more idea what to do with the old man in death than he had in life.

Nate walked up abreast and handed the reins of his gelding to Joe. "Time for me to go," he said.

Joe nodded.

"I'm taking her with me," Nate said, gesturing toward Diane Shober. "I know of people who are with us. They'll put her up. They'll treat her well."

Joe opened his mouth to object, but Nate reached down and touched the butt of his .454 with the tip of his fingers. He didn't grasp, draw, or cock the weapon. But the fact that he did it told Joe things had changed between them.

"I know what you're thinking," Nate said. "You're thinking there's no way I can take the victim with me before she's interviewed. That it wouldn't be procedure. And you're right, it wouldn't. But Joe, I shoved everything I believed in to the side to help you out up there. Now it's your turn to help me."

Joe studied his saddle horn. He said, "You promise me she'll be okay? I have these visions of the underground that aren't so good."

Nate smiled. "The underground isn't underground at all. It's not about people in caves, really. They're all around us. Everywhere you look, Joe. Real people, good people, are the underground. Believe me, Diane will be fine."

"I understand."

Nate reached out and touched Joe on the back of his hand. Then he gave Joe the reins to Caleb's horse, so Joe now had both brothers behind him.

Nate said, "You know where to find me."

Joe nodded but didn't say anything.

The last glance he got of Diane as she followed Nate into the timber was when she turned in her saddle and waved. There was something sad in the gesture. Thanking him for letting them go. He waved back.

Joe tied the ropes for Caleb's horse and Camish's horse together into a loose knot and wrapped them around his saddle horn with a tight dally and a pointless flourish. He smiled to himself in a bitter way and clucked his tongue. All the animals responded, and started stepping down the mountain trail. No doubt, Joe thought, they sensed some kind of conclusion when they reached the trailhead. If only he felt the same, he thought . . .

DAVE FARKUS had been astonished by the number of cars, pickups, SUVs, and equipment trucks that overflowed the campground below at the trailhead. He'd never seen so many vehicles—or so many people—in one place up in the mountains before. And when they'd seen him, as he broke over the timbered ridgeline and rode his horse for ten minutes through a treeless meadow, he saw them scramble like fighter pilots getting the nod to mount up to go out there and bomb something.

The high whine of all-terrain vehicles split open the morning quiet. He watched with interest as two, three, four ATVs shot across the stream below and started up the mountain to meet up with him. There were multiple people on each vehicle, as well as electronic equipment.

Not just electronic equipment: cameras.

He pulled the reins on his horse and jumped off. He wished he could see his face in a mirror, but he couldn't. But he did his best. He spat on his hands and scrubbed his face, then dried and cleaned himself with his shirttails. Judging by the gray smudges on the fabric he tucked back into his jeans, it was a good idea. He wanted to look rugged, but not dirty.

The ATVs were getting close. He found an extra horse bit in his saddlebag and shined it under his arm. Farkus leaned into the bend of the metal and the reflection, and he patted down his hair and made himself look weary and sympathetic.

And before the ATVs cleared the timber, he remounted, clicked his tongue, and got the animal moving again. The first ATV stopped just outside the trees, and a disheveled man jumped out and set up a tripod and put a camera on top of it under the arm-waving direction of a blonde who—no kidding—was the best-looking woman Farkus had ever seen in real life. She was tall, slim, coiffed, with large breasts and wore cool boots that she'd tucked her tight jeans into.

He thought, *Whoa.*

Although she was a long way down the mountain and other TV crews were making their way up, she took a second to look up and meet his eyes. He felt a jolt of electricity shoot through him.

He thought, *I'm from Baggs, but I've watched television. Hundreds of fucking hours of television. I've seen hundreds like you. You're stuck in Wyoming, trying to claw your way up. You need something spectacular for your audition tape. I can give that to you, darling. I can give that to you.*

So when she reached him on her ATV, he began to smile. He thought, *I know a hell of a lot more about you than you will ever know about me. . . .*

And the first thing he said was, "I've been in the heart of the right-wing crazies. I was there for everything and I saw everything. Remember the Cline Family? Diane Shober?"

Her eyes lit up. He pressed on. "But before we talk, I want to negotiate a deal with you. I want to be on TV. I want to be an expert on right-wing fringe groups and the anger in small-town America. I want to get paid and stay in nice hotels. And if we can work it out, you get the exclusive."

She smiled at the word "exclusive." She said, "I need a sign-off from the suits, but I can pretty much promise you a deal. Now, let's get out of here before anyone else can talk to you."

Farkus thought, *I may have just found my calling.*

BEFORE THE MOUNTED RIDERS from the trailhead could reach them—dozens streamed up the trail—Joe reached back and got his satellite phone and called the governor's direct line.

Rulon's chief of staff, Carson, came to the phone.

"The governor's in an emergency meeting," Carson said. "He asked me to talk with you. We understand you killed those brothers and rescued Diane Shober. That's outstanding."

Joe grunted.

"And we've got good news of our own," Carson said. "Senator McKinty of Michigan announced this morning he's not running for reelection. We don't have a reason. He's been our biggest impediment for years now. The governor's ecstatic."

"Interesting," Joe said.

"Look, you need to be available this evening. The governor's planning a press conference about the rescue and he wants you here. He's going to make you a hero, Joe."

"Nope," Joe said.

Carson coughed. "But you *are* a hero. We want the state to know. We want the *country* to know."

As Carson talked, Joe glanced over to make sure there was no sign of Nate. They were gone. He didn't know if he'd ever see Diane again, and wondered where Nate would take her. And how would he and Nate go on?

Finally, he said, "They aren't with me."

After a long pause, Carson said, "Who isn't with you?"

"Diane Shober. I let her go."

Carson stammered, "I'm not sure what to say. The governor is going to be very disappointed in you, Joe. Very disappointed."

He shrugged, even though Carson had no idea what he was doing. Joe said, "He's not the only one."

He rode down the trail to meet the throng of law enforcement personnel, media, and hangers-on who waited for him. At the side of the crowd he saw Brent and Jenna Shober. They looked anxious.

Something flashed in his peripheral vision as he rode, and he cocked his head. The lone wolf again, bidding him good-bye. He wondered how long they'd been tracked.

He turned in the saddle to make sure the bodies of the brothers were still tightly bound to the packhorses.

He thought: They were under control, at last. McKinty, Brent Shober, and Bobby McCue would be pleased.

The sun doused as massive black thunderheads rolled across the sky. Storm coming.

ACKNOWLEDGMENTS

The author would like to acknowledge the people who contributed to this book, most of all Wyoming game warden Mark Nelson, who first encountered a set of twin brothers in the Wind River Mountains and lived to tell the tale. Also Sherry Merryman, Brian Kalt, Brian Lally, Becky Box, Laurie Box, Molly Box, Don Hajicek of cjbox.net, and my stellar agent, Ann Rittenberg.

As always, a tip of the black hat to the team of pros at Putnam, including Ivan Held, Michael Barson, Summer Smith, Tom Colgan, and the legendary Neil Nyren.

TURN THE PAGE FOR AN EXCERPT

When Earl Alden is found dead, his wife Missy is arrested.
Unfortunately for Joe Pickett, Missy is his much-disliked
mother-in-law and all signs point to her being guilty as sin.
But Joe wonders if everything is as it seems. Whichever way
this case goes, it's not going to be good.

AUGUST 21

When you hear hoofbeats, think horses, not zebras.

—Age-old medical school admonition

1

HE SET OUT AFTER BREAKFAST ON WHAT WOULD be his last day on earth.

He was an old man, but like many men of his generation with his wealth and station, he refused to think of himself that way. Deep in his heart, he honestly entertained the possibility he would never break down and would perhaps live forever, while those less driven and less successful around him dropped away.

In fact, he'd recently taken to riding a horse over vast stretches of his landholdings when the weather was good. He rode a leggy black Tennessee walker, sixteen and a half hands in height—tall enough that he called for a mounting block in order to climb into the saddle. The horse seemed to glide over the sagebrush flats and wooded Rocky Mountain juniper-dotted foothills like a ghost, as if the gelding strode on a cushion of air. The gait spared the man's knees and lower back and allowed him to appreciate the ranch itself without constantly being interrupted by the stabs of pain that came from six and a half decades of not sitting a horse.

Riding got him closer to the land, which, like the horse, was *his*. He owned the sandy and chalky soil itself and the thousands of Black Angus that ate the same grass herds of buffalo had once grazed. He owned the water that flowed through it and the minerals beneath it and the air that coursed over it. The very air.

Although he was a man who'd always owned big things—homes, boats, aircraft, cars, buildings, large and small corporations, race horses, oil wells, and for a while a small island off the coast of North Carolina—he loved this land most of all because unlike everything else in his life, it would not submit to him (well, it and his woman, but that was a different story). Therefore, he didn't hold it in contempt.

So he rode over his ranch and beheld it and talked to it out loud, saying, "*How about if we compromise and agree that, for the time being, we own each other?*"

As the old man rode, he wore a 40X beaver silver belly short-brimmed Stetson, a long-sleeved yoked shirt with snap buttons, relaxed-fit Wranglers, and cowboy boots. He wasn't stupid and he always packed a cell phone and a satellite phone for those locations on his ranch where there was no signal. Just in case.

He'd asked one of his employees, an Ecuadoran named José Maria, to go to town and buy him an iPod and load it up with a playlist he'd entitled "Ranch Music." It consisted largely of film scores. Cuts from Ennio Morricone like "The Good, The Bad, and The Ugly," "Theme from *A Fistful of Dollars*," "*L'estasi dell'oro* (The Ecstasy of Gold)," "*La resa dei conti* (For a Few Dollars More)"; Elmer Bernstein's "*The Magnificent Seven* Theme," "The Journey," and "Calvera's Return"; and Jerome Moross's "Theme from *The Big Country*." Big, wonderful, rousing, swelling, sweeping, *triumphalist* music from another era. It was music that simply wasn't made anymore. The pieces were about tough (but fair) men under big skies on horseback, their women waiting for them at home, and bad guys—usually Mexicans—to be vanquished.

In fact, they'd vanquished some Mexicans of their own from the ranch in the last two months, the result of a surreptitious phone call to ICE placed by his wife. Although the Mexican ranch hands worked hard and were great stockmen, she could document how many times they'd refused to show her respect. She blamed their ingrained macho culture. So the immigration folks rounded them up and shipped them away. Their jobs had recently been filled by Ecuadorans like José Maria who were not as accomplished with cattle but were more deferential to his wife.

He threaded his horse up through gnarled, bell-shaped stands of juniper. The trees were heavy with clusters of green buds and the scent within the stand was sweet and heavy and reminded him of a gin martini. His horse spooked rabbits that shot out from bunches of tall grass like squeezed grapefruit seeds, and he pushed a small herd of mule deer out ahead of him. It had warmed to the mid-seventies and as the temperature rose so did the insect hum from the ankle-high grass. He hummed, too, along with "Theme from *The Big Country*." He tried to remember the movie itself—Gregory Peck or William Holden?—but that was beyond his recollection. He made a note to himself to ask José Maria to order it from Netflix.

He paused the iPod and stuffed the earbuds and cord into his breast pocket as he urged his horse up the gentle slope. The thrumming of insects gave way to the watery sound of wind in the tops of the trees. The transition from an earth sound to the sounds of the sky thrilled him every time, but not nearly as much as what he knew he'd see when he crested the hill.

Clamping his Stetson tight on his head with his free right hand as he cleared the timber, the old man urged his horse to step lively to the top. Now the only sound was the full-throated Class Five wind, but there was something folded inside it, almost on another auditory level that was high-pitched, rhythmic, and purposeful. He had once heard José Maria describe the sound as similar to a mallard drake in flight along the surface of a river: a furious beating of wings punctuated by a high-pitched but breathy *squeak-squeak-squeak* that meant the bird was getting closer.

From the crown of the hill, he looked down at the sagebrush prairie that stretched out as far as his eyes could see until it bumped up against the Bighorn Mountains of Wyoming. And it was all his.

From the gray and gold of the prairie floor, across five thousand acres, on a high ridge, sprung a hundred wind turbines in various stages of construction where just a year ago there had been nothing but wind-sculpted rock poking out of the surface like dry land coral. A fresh network of straight-line dirt roads connected them all. The finished turbines—and there were only ten of them operational—climbed 250 feet into the sky. He loved the fact that each tower was a hundred feet higher than the Statue of Liberty! And they were lined up tall and white and perfect in a straight line along the humpbacked spine of a ridge in the basin. All ten working turbines had blades attached. The blades spun, slicing through the Wyoming sky, making that unique whistling sound that was . . . the sound of money.

And he thought: *Ninety more to go.*

Behind the row of turbines were another row of towers only, and another, then seven more rows of ten each in different stages of construction. The rows were miles apart from each other, but he was far enough away on the top of the hill to see the whole of it, from the gaping drill holes at the rear where the hundreds of tons of concrete would be poured into the ground to the bolted foundations of the towers, and finally, to the turbines and blades that would be built on top. They reminded him of perfectly white shoots of grass in various stages of growth, sprouting from the dirt straight into the sky.

The blades on the completed turbines had a diameter of forty-four meters or one hundred forty-four feet each. They would spin at close to one hundred miles per hour. Semi trucks had delivered huge stacks of the blades, and they lay on the sagebrush surface like long white whale bones left by ships.

He was so far away from his wind farm that the construction equipment, the pickups and cranes and earthmoving equipment, looked like miniatures.

That first line of almost-completed turbines stood like soldiers, *his* soldiers, facing straight into the teeth of the wind. They spun with defiance and strength, transforming the wind that had denuded the basin of humans and homesteads more than a hundred years ago into power and wealth.

And he waved his hat and whooped at the sheer massive scale of it.

Meeting the supplier-slash-general-contractor for the project the year before had been a spectacular stroke of luck, one of many in his life. Here was a man, a desperate man, with a dream and connections and, most of all, a line on a supply of turbines at a time when the manufacturers couldn't turn out enough of them. This desperate man appeared at the right place and right time and had been literally days away from ruin. And the old man stumbled upon him and seized the opportunity, as he'd seized opportunities before, while those around him dithered and stuttered and consulted their attorneys, chief financial officers, and legislators. That chance meeting and the opportunity that came because of it had saved the old man millions of dollars a turbine, or $100 million total. The old man had gone with his gut and made the deal and here in front of him was the result of his unerring instinct.

Funny thing was, the old man thought, it wasn't the wind farm that would really make him the big money. For that, he would look eastward toward Washington, D.C. That was the epicenter of the breached dam that was sending cash flooding west across the country like waves from a tsunami.

When he heard a rumble of a vehicle motor, he instinctively swept his eyes over the wind farm for the source of the noise, but he quickly decided he was too far away to discern individual sounds.

Since there weren't any cows to move or fences to fix behind him, he doubted it was José Maria or his fellow Ecuadorans coming out his way. He turned in the saddle and squinted back down the hill he had come, but could see nothing.

The old man clicked his tongue and turned his horse back down the hill. As he rode down through the junipers, the harsh winds from on top began to mute, although they didn't quell into silence. They never would.

Again, he heard a motor coming and he rode right toward it.

When he emerged from the heavily scented timber, he smiled when he recognized the vehicle and the driver. The four-wheel drive was on an ancient two-track coming in his direction. He could hear the grinding of the motor as well as the spiny high-pitched scraping of sagebrush from beneath the undercarriage. Twin plumes of dust from the tires were snatched away by the wind.

He waved when he was a hundred feet from the vehicle, and was still waving when the driver braked and got
out holding a rifle.

"Oh, come on," the old man said, but suddenly he
could see everything in absolute gut-wrenching clarity.

The first bullet hit him square in the chest with the
impact of a hitter swinging for the upper deck. Shattered
his iPod.

AUGUST 22

If a man does not know what port he is steering for, no wind is favorable to him.

—Seneca

AN HOUR BEFORE DAWN BROKE ON MONDAY, Wyoming game warden Joe Pickett backed his green Ford pickup down his driveway and called dispatch in Cheyenne.

"This is G-53 heading out," he said. The pickup was less than a year old, but the new-car feel of the suspension had long been pounded out of it on rugged two-track roads, through grille-high sagebrush, and another hard winter's worth of snowdrifts. As always, he was crowded inside the cab by clothing, maps, gear, weapons, and electronics. The department refused to buy or provide standard crew-cab trucks for the fifty-four wardens in Wyoming for fear taxpayers would object to the showy extravagance, even though new single-cab pickups were so rare they needed to be special-ordered. Inside the cab it smelled of fresh coffee from his travel mug and an unusually flatulent Tube, his male corgi/Labrador mix, who was already curling up on the passenger seat. The newest addition to his standard arsenal was the .204 Ruger rifle mounted to the top of his cab for dispatching wounded or maimed game animals with a minimum of sound or impact. Since Joe's record with departmental vehicles was by far the worst in the agency, he'd vowed to baby this pickup until it hit maximum mileage, something that had not yet happened in his career.

"Good morning, Joe," the dispatcher said, with a lilt. The dispatchers found that phrase amusing and never got tired of saying it.

"Morning," he said. "I'll be in the east break lands in areas twenty-one and twenty-two this morning, checking antelope hunters."

"Ten-four." She paused, no doubt checking her manual. Then: "That would be the Middle Fork and Crazy Woman areas?"

"Affirmative."

As he began to sign off, she asked, "How are you doing? You had to take your daughter to college yesterday, right? How did it go?"

"Don't ask. G-53 out."

The day before, Sunday, Joe had been out of uniform, out of sorts, and nearly out of gas as he approached Laramie from the north in his wife Marybeth's aging minivan. It was the last week of August, but a front had moved in from the northwest, and thin waves of snow buffeted the van and shoved it toward the shoulder of the two-lane highway.

"Oh my *God*, is that *snow*?" Joe's sixteen-year-old foster daughter, April, said with contemptuous incredulity in a speech pattern she'd mastered that emphasized every third or fourth word. "It can't *snow* in friggin' *August*!" April was slight but tough and she had a hard edge to her look and style that seemed provocative even when it likely wasn't intended to be. As she matured, she looked frighteningly like her mother, Jeannie, who had never made it to forty. Same light-blonde hair. Same accusing narrow eyes.

Joe and Marybeth exchanged glances. They'd had a

discussion with no conclusion about whether *frigging* was an acceptable word in their family.

April said, "When I go to *college*, I want someplace *warm*. Someplace *way* far away from *here*."

"What makes you think you'll go to college?" Lucy, their fourteen-year-old, said just softly enough that perhaps her parents in the front seat wouldn't hear. Joe thought Lucy's mutter had been below the belt, even if possibly true. Lucy was usually more diplomatic and non-confrontational, so when she did unleash a zinger, it hit twice as hard as if one of the other girls had said it. Lucy was small herself, but not angular like April. Lucy was rounded in perfect proportion, and had blonde hair and striking features and the grace of a cat. Strangers were beginning to stare, Joe had noticed. He didn't like that.

Marybeth heard everything going on in the backseat, and turned to try to head off what could come next. Joe checked his review mirror for April's reaction and saw she was coiled and close to violence. Her face was drawn and red, her nostrils flared, and she was focused completely on Lucy sitting next to her.

"Girls, please," Marybeth said.

"Did you *hear* what she friggin' *said*?" April hissed.

"Yes, and it was inappropriate," Marybeth said. "Wasn't it, Lucy?"

A beat, then Lucy said, "Yes."

"So apologize already," April said. "I always have to friggin' *apologize* when I say something *stupid*."

"Sorry," Lucy whispered.

"This is an emotional day," Marybeth said, turning back around in her seat.

Joe shifted his gaze in the mirror and caught Lucy silently mouthing, "*But it's true.*"

And April leaned into Lucy and ran a finger across her

throat as if it were a knife. Lucy shrugged it away, but Joe felt a chill go up his back from the gesture.

"I hope we can get through this day without fireworks," Marybeth said, missing what was going on in the backseat. "Waterworks is another thing."

Her phone rang in her purse and she retrieved it and looked at the display and put it back. "My mother," she said. "She has a knack for calling me at just the wrong time."

"We need to get some gas," Joe said. "We're running on empty."

A gas station, announced by a green sign that read:

ROCK RIVER
POPULATION 235
ELEVATION 6892

. . . was just ahead.

Sheridan, their nineteen-year-old daughter, was going to college. The University of Wyoming in Laramie was forty-five minutes to the south on the hump of the high plains. She followed them on the exit ramp in their newly acquired fifteen-year-old Ford Ranger pickup with the bed filled with cardboard boxes of everything she owned. Joe had lashed a tarp over the load before they left Saddlestring four hours before, but the wind had ripped long rents into it. Luckily, the rope held the shards down. He'd spent most of the trip worrying about it.

Marybeth either didn't notice the ruined tarp or more likely didn't think about it while staring out the window and dabbing her eyes with dozens of tissues that were now crumpled near her shoes on the floorboards like a bird's nest.

Joe wished he'd brought his winter coat against the

wind and cold. This was a place where the wind always blew. The trees, as sparse as they were on top, were gnarled and twisted like high country gargoyles. Both sides of the highway were bordered with a long, ten-foot-high snow fence. It howled from the north, rocking both the van and Sheridan's pickup as he filled the tanks with gasoline.

He tightened the ropes across the bed of her pickup and checked to make sure none of her boxes had opened. Joe imagined her clothes blowing out and rocketing across the terrain until they snagged on bits of sagebrush.

Joe Pickett was in his mid-forties, slim, of medium height and build, with brown eyes and a perpetual squint, as if he was always assessing even the simplest things. He wore old Cinch jeans, worn Ariat cowboy boots, a long-sleeved yoked collar shirt with snap buttons, and a tooled belt that read JOE. Under the seat of the van was his holstered .40 Glock 23 semiautomatic service weapon, bear spray, cuffs, and a citation book. There had been a time when mixing his family and his weapons had struck him as discordant. But over the years, he'd made some enemies and he'd come to accept, if not embrace, his innate ability to so often find himself in the wrong place at the wrong time. He'd learned to accept suspicion and not feel guilty about checking over his shoulder. Even on freshman move-in day at the University of Wyoming in Laramie.

Sheridan watched him fill her tank and secure the load and gave him a little wave of thanks from inside the cab. He tried to grin back. Sheridan had blonde hair and green eyes like Marybeth and Lucy. She was mature beyond her years, but to Joe she looked vulnerable and frail, like a little girl. She wore a gray SADDLESTRING LADY WRANGLERS hoodie and had her hair tied back. When he looked at her behind the steering wheel, he saw her at seven years old, trying again and again with skinned knees and epic determination to ride her bike more than ten feet down the road without crashing. Until that moment, that very moment when they exchanged glances, it hadn't hit him she was leaving them.

Sheridan, after all, was his buddy. Apprentice falconer, struggling athlete, first child, big sister. She was the one who would come out into the garage and hand him tools while he tried to repair his pickup or snow machine. She was the one who really wanted to ride along with him on patrol, and she made valiant, if vain, attempts to try and get him interested in new music and social media. She wouldn't go far away, he hoped. She'd be back for summer and the holidays.

Joe swung into the van and struggled to close the door against the wind. When it latched, there was a charged silence inside. Marybeth took him in and said, "Are you all right?"

He wiped his eyes dry with his sleeve. "The wind," he said.

Four hours later, having gotten Sheridan settled in at her dorm room in Laramie, met her roommate, had a final meal together at Washakie Center, shed more tears, and dodged two more phone calls from Marybeth's mother, they were on their way back to Saddlestring. No words were spoken in the van. Everyone was consumed with their own thoughts, and the situation reminded Joe of the ride home from a memorial service. Well, maybe not that bad . . .

Marybeth's phone burred again in her purse and she grabbed it. Joe could tell from her expression she was both hopeful and fearful that it would be Sheridan calling.

Marybeth sighed deeply. "Mom again," she sighed. "Maybe I ought to take it."

After a moment, Marybeth said, "What do you mean, he's gone?"

Marybeth's mother Missy was back on the ranch near Saddlestring she shared with her new husband, the multibillionaire developer and media mogul Earl Alden. He was known as "The Earl of Lexington," because that's where he'd originally come from when he was a mere millionaire. Between them, Marybeth's mother—*Missy Vankueren Longbrake Alden*—and The Earl were the largest landholders in northern Wyoming now that they'd married and combined ranches. Missy had acquired her spread by divorcing a third-generation landowner named Bud Longbrake, who'd discovered during the divorce proceedings what the pre-nup she had him sign actually said.

The Earl was Missy's fifth husband. She'd traded up with each one after her first (and Marybeth's realtor father) died young in a car wreck. After a five-month mourning period, Missy married a doctor the day his divorce papers were finalized, then an Arizona developer and U.S. Congressman who was later convicted of fraud, then rancher Bud Longbrake. The Earl was her greatest triumph. Joe couldn't imagine a sixth wedding. Missy was in her mid-sixties. Although she still a stunner—given the right light and enough time to prepare—she'd met The Earl as her string was running out. Luckily for Missy, she took—and made—her last desperate shot just as her biological buzzer went off. Joe and Missy had a complicated relationship, as she put it. Joe couldn't stand her, and she still wondered out loud why her favorite daughter—the one with pluck and promise—had stuck with that game warden all these years.

Marybeth said to her mother, "I'll ask Joe what he thinks and call you back, okay?" Then, after a pause, she said irritably, "Well, *I* care. Goodbye."

Joe snorted, but kept his eyes on the road.

"Mom says Earl went out riding this morning and hasn't come back. He was supposed to be home for lunch. She's worried something happened to him—an accident or something."

He glanced at his wristwatch. "So he's three hours late."

"Yes."

"Has she done anything about it besides call you over and over?"

Marybeth sighed. "She asked José Maria to take a truck out and look for him."

Joe nodded.

"She says Earl isn't a very good rider, even though he thinks he is. She's worried the horse took off on him or bucked him off somewhere."

"As you know, that can happen with horses," Joe said.

"She's getting really worked up. He's supposed to have his phone with him, but he hasn't called, and when she tries him he doesn't pick up. I can tell from her voice she's starting to panic."

Joe said, "Maybe he got clear of her and just kept riding to freedom. I could understand that."

"I don't find that's very funny."

The small house was on two levels, with three bedrooms and a detached garage and a loafing shed barn in the back. Joe sighed with relief when they pulled up in front of it, but if he thought he was done with drama for the day, he was mistaken. The House of Feelings, as Joe called it, had been percolating at a rolling boil ever since. First, April moved into Sheridan's old bedroom—she'd been sharing a room with Lucy the same way rival armies "shared" a battlefield. Lucy, giddy with pent-up gratitude, helped move April out, and Marybeth showed up just in time to spot the corner of a bag of marijuana in April's near-empty dresser drawer. Marybeth was stunned and angry at the revelation, April defensive and even more angry she'd been found out, and Lucy managed to slip away and vanish somewhere in the small house to avoid the fight.

Joe was disappointed by the discovery, but not surprised. April's return from the dead two years before had rocked them all, and the situation since then had been far from storybook. For the years she'd been away, April had bounced from foster family to foster family, and she'd had seen and done things that were just now dribbling out in her two-times-a-week therapy sessions. April had been damaged by both neglect and untoward attention depending on the family she was with, but neither Joe nor Marybeth were convinced she was beyond repair. Marybeth had made it a life goal to save the girl. But April's moods and rages made it tough on Sheridan and Lucy, who had expected a smoother—and more grateful—reconciliation.

After the discovery of the marijuana, there was yelling, crying, and recriminations late into the night. Whether April would be grounded for two months or three was a major point of contention. They settled on two and a half months. Joe did his best to support Marybeth, but as always he felt out of his depth.

Then, at two-thirty in the morning, shortly after Marybeth and April retired to their separate bedrooms, the telephone rang. It was Missy again, and she was beside herself, and asked Marybeth to implore Joe to put out an all-points alert for her husband. She wanted him to contact the governor's people immediately—apparently Governor Spencer Rulon had taken his phone off the hook after three calls from Missy, and her insistence that he call out the National Guard to look for The Earl.

Joe was slightly impressed Missy seemed to finally grasp what he did for a living. He took the phone long enough to confirm that she'd already reported her husband's absence to County Sheriff Kyle McLanahan, the police chief in Saddlestring, and had left messages with the FBI office in Cheyenne and Wyoming's two U.S. Senators and lone congresswoman. She had all her ranch hands out searching for him, despite the hour.

Joe assured her he would follow up in the morning, all the time thinking The Earl had probably tied his horse to a fence at the airport and escaped to one of his other homes in Lexington, Aspen, New York, or Chamonix.

3

NOW IT WAS MONDAY, AND IT FELT GOOD TO BE heading out. The front had passed through, and the morning was warm and sultry, which brought out the sweet smell of sage as Joe rolled down the gravel of Bighorn Road. He sipped his coffee and was grateful he was going to work. Bighorn Road was the primary access into the mountains, and it passed by the front of his house. The Bighorns loomed like slump-shouldered giants, dominating the skyline. The view from his front porch and picture window was of a vast angled landscape that dipped into a willow-choked draw where the Twelve Sleep River formed from six different creek fingers and gained strength and volume before its muscular rush through and past the Town of Saddlestring eight miles away. Beyond the nascent river to the south, the terrain rose sharply into several saddle slopes that bowed around a precipitous mountain known as Wolf Mountain. He had never tired of seeing the colors of the sun at dawn and at dusk on the naked granite face of the mountain, and doubted he ever would. But it was too early for sun.

* * *

IT HAD BEEN a tough and eventful summer, and it was continuing into the fall.

Marybeth's small business consulting firm, MBP, had all but dissolved. A larger firm had been in the long process of purchasing the assets when the recession finally came to Wyoming and three of four of MBP's largest clients ceased operations. Within months, MBP's assets were nothing like what they'd been when negotiations began, and both parties agreed to call off the sale. While Marybeth still worked for several small local firms on her own, the protracted deal had taken the steam out of her. She'd recently resumed her part-time job in the Twelve Sleep County Library while she looked for new business opportunities. It had been an unexpected and unusual defeat because Marybeth was the toughest and most pragmatic woman Joe'd ever met. Joe had no doubt she—and they—would be back.

The lack of MBP income had caused them to cancel their plans to purchase a new home outside of town. The development was disappointing to Joe, who desperately wanted to live without neighbors several feet away—especially his next-door neighbor, lawn and maintenance nemesis Ed Nedny.

In July, however, the other game warden in the district, Phil Kiner, had retired unexpectedly due to poor health, and the department in Cheyenne had given Joe the opportunity to move his family back to the state-owned house they'd once occupied on Bighorn Road, eight miles outside of Saddlestring. Kiner's departure meant Joe's numerical designation climbed a notch from 54 to 53. At one time, before he'd been fired, he'd reached 24, and he wondered if he'd ever get back there. Their former house in town was on the market, and until it sold, things would continue to be tight. Joe reveled in being back in the shadow of Wolf Mountain where his children had grown up. But there was no denying the fact that after all they'd been through, they were essentially back where they'd started ten years before: in the original House of Feelings. Without Sheridan.

"Don't fret," Marybeth had said, "backwards is the new normal."

HE PASSED THROUGH the town of Saddlestring as it woke up and the single traffic light switched over from flashing amber, and he drove five miles to the interstate highway. As he merged onto the westbound two-lane, he paused for a convoy of tractor-trailers laden with the long, sleek, twenty-one-and-a-half-meter white blades for wind turbines. They came from manufacturing facilities to the south and east, and were no longer a curiosity on the highway. Massive parts for turbines and wind farms coursed down the highway bound for construction sites throughout Wyoming and the mountain west. Joe remembered seeing the first ones two years before, and he'd been intrigued and followed the convoy for a while to behold the sheer size and grace of the equipment, which reminded him of buffoonishly large parts for a massive toy. But now the frequency of the convoys was routine, as turbines sprouted in perfect white rows throughout the state and the region.

The sudden emergence of wind farms had added another dimension to his day-to-day responsibilities as well. He sighed and eased out onto the highway for areas twenty-one and twenty-two.

He turned from the highway onto the ranch owned by Bob and Dode Lee, a checkerboard of public and private land that contained a vast herd of pronghorn antelope.

*   *   *

HE GROUND HIS TRUCK up the side of a flat-topped bench that overlooked the vast sagebrush flats of the Lee Ranch. The top sliver of sun winked over the eastern horizon as he positioned his pickup on the top so he could look out over dozens of square miles. The sunlight was orange and intense and lit up the side of the bench, and it was at the perfect angle and intensity to reveal hundreds of tiny American Indian arrowhead and tool chips that still clung to the surface of the rise. Like so many off-road locations he'd found over the years, Joe was struck by the fact that he wasn't the first to use this dramatic geography for the purpose of work. In his mind's eye, he envisioned a small band of Cheyenne or Pawnee on the same bench hundreds of years before, making weapons and tools, looking out at the landscape for friends and enemies.

But as the sun rose, it also lit up row after row of wind turbines to the south. They looked like spindly white toothpicks. Shafts of sunlight bounced and sparked on the slowly turning blades. He knew they signified the border of the Lee Ranch where it butted up against the massive holdings of The Earl and, of course, Missy.

Joe slid down the driver's-side window and fitted his Redfield spotting scope to the frame of the door. As the dawn melded into morning, the vista below him came into view. Hundreds of brown-and-white pronghorn antelope grazed amidst knee-high sagebrush. Mule deer descended from windswept grassy flats back into shadowed draws. Eagles and hawks soared above it all in morning thermals, making long-distance loops at his eye level.

He focused on a single blue pickup that was crawling along a two-track, a thin plume of dust giving chase. There was a flash of orange through the windows of the vehicle, as he identified the occupants—a driver and passenger—as hunters. As far as he could tell, they didn't know he was up on the bench watching them.

The blue pickup was too far away to hear, but he slowly swiveled his spotting scope as it passed beneath him traveling left to right. They were headed south, and because of the contours of the land, they had no idea that the huge herd was to their east on the other side of a ridge. Joe wondered if they'd catch a glimpse of the antelope as they drove along, but the vehicle continued on slowly, apparently looking for all the game out their front windshield.

"Road hunters," Joe whispered to himself. If the hunters fired at game from the vehicle, they'd be in violation and Joe would cite them. He hoped they were ethical and law-abiding, and would leave the truck on foot to stalk the antelope—if they even saw them.

He followed the progress of the pickup. He caught a glimpse of a license plate—Wyoming—but was too far away to read the numbers, so he focused in and narrowed his field of vision until the vehicle filled his scope. It was a shaky view at that distance, but he could see the passenger lower his window and extend his arm out of it, pointing toward something ahead of them.

Joe leaned back from the scope and surveyed the basin with his naked eye. He followed the road the hunters were on until it became a thin tan thread in the distance. And where the two-track crested a hill and vanished, he saw the dark form of a big animal. It was too large to be an antelope, and too dark to be a deer. Puzzled, he swung the spotting scope far to the right.

It was a riderless horse. The animal was big and sleek, well groomed, with a saddle hanging upside down under its belly. Joe knew from experience that when the saddle was inverted, it meant the horse had run hard and usually at great distance. The exertion loosened the cinch and the top-heavy configuration of the saddle caused it to slide. The horse was grazing on a strip of grass between the tracks of the road, but it had obviously noted the oncoming pickup by the way it periodically raised its head and noted the approach.

Joe looked back at the truck, expecting it to be closer to the horse by now. But the pickup had stopped in the road, and the occupants—two older men bundled in Carhartt jackets and fluorescent orange headgear—were out of their vehicle and gesturing to each other. The passenger was again pointing ahead, but it wasn't at the horse, but higher. Much higher.

"What?" Joe asked, as he opened up the field of vision on his spotting scope and swung it back to the right.

He scoped the horizon behind the horse and saw nothing worth noting, nothing unusual enough to prompt two lazy road hunters to jump from their vehicle. Then he looked beyond the crest at the long straight line of wind turbines in the distance. They were now bathed in full morning light and framed against the deep clear blue of the cloudless sky.

The blades all spun in the lazy rotation that Joe had come to learn in reality wasn't lazy at all at the blade-tip. At least nine of the ten were spinning swiftly. He concentrated on the one that wasn't. He'd observed enough wind turbines before to know there could sometimes be a marked disparity of wind speed from unit to unit. And he knew that sometimes turbines were damaged or disabled and the blades turned roughly in comparison with the other machines. But there was no doubt there was something strange about this one, because it turned at less than half the speed of the others in the row.

Joe climbed the tower with his scope until he could see the nacelle, a structure on top where the hub held the turning blades. And he could see what was wrong and he whispered, "Jesus."

A form was suspended from a chain or cable that was looped around the shaft of one of the three spinning blades. The form was close to the hub. It hadn't slid down the length of the blade because the tether held fast where the blade widened. Even with the weight, the rotor turned fast enough that the object flew through the air between the blades, circling up and around the hub like a spider held by a web on a rotating fan.

Although the distance was great and Joe's trembling fingers shook the view within the scope as he adjusted it, he caught glimpses of the form as it flashed through his field of vision. Portly, solid, arms cocked out to both sides, legs spread in a V—it certainly *looked* like a body.

Was it a real body? Joe could imagine workers hanging a dummy or mannequin in some kind of prank. How was it possible for someone even to get up there, much less get caught up in a chain attached to the shaft of a blade? How long had it been up there?

Then he linked the area, the horse without a rider, the location of the wind turbines, and Missy's frantic phone calls the day and night before.

"Oh, no," he said aloud, while he plucked the mike from his dashboard and called dispatch in Cheyenne. He'd hold off calling Marybeth, he decided, until he could confirm the flying body belonged to the former Earl of Lexington.

C. J. BOX

"One of today's solid-gold, A-list, must-read writers."

—Lee Child

For a complete list of titles and to sign up for our newsletter, please visit prh.com/CJBox